PRINCE DARLING TRANSFORMED INTO THE MONSTER. *See p.* 284.

The
BLUE FAIRY BOOK

Edited by Andrew Lang

*With Numerous Illustrations
by H. J. Ford and G. P. Jacomb Hood*

DOVER PUBLICATIONS, INC., NEW YORK

Published in Canada by General Publishing Company, Ltd., 30 Lesmill Road, Don Mills, Toronto, Ontario.

Published in the United Kingdom by Constable and Company, Ltd., 10 Orange Street, London W. C. 2.

This Dover edition, first published in 1965, is an unabridged and unaltered republication of the work first published by Longmans, Green, and Co. circa 1889.

Standard Book Number: 486-21437-0
Library of Congress Catalog Card Number 65-25707

Manufactured in the United States of America

Dover Publications, Inc.
180 Varick Street
New York, N. Y. 10014

TO

ELSPETH ANGELA CAMPBELL

PREFACE

THE TALES in this volume are intended for children, who will like, it is hoped, the old stories that have pleased so many generations.

The tales of Perrault are printed from the old English version of the eighteenth century.

The stories from the *Cabinet des Fées* and from Madame d'Aulnoy are translated, or rather adapted, by Miss Minnie Wright, who has also, by M. Henri Carnoy's kind permission, rendered ' The Bronze Ring ' from his *Traditions Populaires de l'Asie Mineure* (Maisonneuve, Paris, 1889).

The stories from Grimm are translated by Miss May Sellar ; another from the German by Miss Sylvia Hunt ; the Norse tales are a version by Mrs. Alfred Hunt ; 'The Terrible Head ' is adapted from Apollodorus, Simonides, and Pindar by the Editor ; Miss Violet Hunt condensed ' Aladdin ' ; Miss May Kendall did the same for *Gulliver's Travels* ; ' The Fairy Paribanou ' is abridged from the old English translation of Galland.

Messrs. Chambers have kindly allowed us to reprint 'The Red Etin ' and ' The Black Bull of Norroway ' from Mr. Robert Chambers' *Popular Traditions of Scotland.*

' Dick Whittington ' is from the chap book edited by Mr. Gomme and Mr. Wheatley for the Villon Society ; ' Jack the Giant-Killer ' is from a chap book, but a good version of this old favourite is hard to procure.

ANDREW LANG.

CONTENTS

PLATES

THE BRONZE RING

ONCE upon a time in a certain country there lived a king whose palace was surrounded by a spacious garden. But, though the gardeners were many and the soil was good, this garden yielded neither flowers nor fruits, not even grass or shady trees.

The King was in despair about it when a wise old man said to him:

'Your gardeners do not understand their business: but what can you expect of men whose fathers were cobblers and carpenters? How should they have learnt to cultivate your garden?'

'You are quite right,' cried the King.

'Therefore,' continued the old man, 'you should send for a gardener whose father and grandfather have been gardeners before him, and very soon your garden will be full of green grass and gay flowers, and you will enjoy its delicious fruit.'

So the King sent messengers to every town, village, and hamlet in his dominions, to look for a gardener whose forefathers had been gardeners also, and after forty days one was found.

'Come with us and be gardener to the King,' they said to him.

'How can I go to the King,' said the gardener, 'a poor wretch like me?'

'That is of no consequence,' they answered. 'Here are new clothes for you and your family.'

'But I owe money to several people.'

'We will pay your debts,' they said.

So the gardener allowed himself to be persuaded, and went away with the messengers, taking his wife and his son with him; and the King, delighted to have found a real gardener, entrusted him with the care of his garden. The man found no difficulty in making the royal garden produce flowers and fruit, and at the end of a year the park was not like the same place, and the King showered gifts upon his new servant.

The gardener, as you have heard already, had a son, who was a very handsome young man, with most agreeable manners, and every day he carried the best fruit of the garden to the King, and all the prettiest flowers to his daughter. Now this princess was wonderfully pretty and was just sixteen years old, and the King was beginning to think it was time that she should be married.

'My dear child,' said he, 'you are of an age to take a husband, therefore I am thinking of marrying you to the son of my prime minister.'

'Father,' replied the Princess, 'I will never marry the son of the minister.'

'Why not?' asked the King.

'Because I love the gardener's son,' answered the Princess.

On hearing this the King was at first very angry, and then he wept and sighed, and declared that such a husband was not worthy of his daughter; but the young Princess was not to be turned from her resolution to marry the gardener's son.

Then the King consulted his ministers. 'This is what you must do,' they said. 'To get rid of the gardener you must send both suitors to a very distant country, and the one who returns first shall marry your daughter.'

The King followed this advice, and the minister's son was presented with a splendid horse and a purse full of gold pieces, while the gardener's son had only an old lame horse and a purse full of copper money, and every one thought he would never come back from his journey.

The day before they started the Princess met her lover and said to him:

'Be brave, and remember always that I love you. Take this purse full of jewels and make the best use you can of them for love of me, and come back quickly and demand my hand.'

The two suitors left the town together, but the minister's son went off at a gallop on his good horse, and very soon was lost to sight behind the most distant hills. He travelled on for some days, and presently reached a fountain beside which an old woman all in rags sat upon a stone.

'Good-day to you, young traveller,' said she.

But the minister's son made no reply.

'Have pity upon me, traveller,' she said again. 'I am dying of hunger, as you see, and three days have I been here and no one has given me anything.'

'Let me alone, old witch,' cried the young man; 'I can do nothing for you,' and so saying he went on his way.

That same evening the gardener's son rode up to the fountain upon his lame grey horse.

'Good-day to you, young traveller,' said the beggar-woman.

'Good-day, good woman,' answered he.

'Young traveller, have pity upon me.'

'Take my purse, good woman,' said he, 'and mount behind me, for your legs can't be very strong.'

The old woman didn't wait to be asked twice, but mounted

behind him, and in this style they reached the chief city of a power-ful kingdom. The minister's son was lodged in a grand inn, the gardener's son and the old woman dismounted at the inn for beggars.

The next day the gardener's son heard a great noise in the street, and the King's heralds passed, blowing all kinds of instru-ments, and crying:

'The King, our master, is old and infirm. He will give a great reward to whoever will cure him and give him back the strength of his youth.'

Then the old beggar-woman said to her benefactor:

'This is what you must do to obtain the reward which the King promises. Go out of the town by the south gate, and there you will find three little dogs of different colours; the first will be white, the second black, the third red. You must kill them and then burn them separately, and gather up the ashes. Put the ashes of each dog into a bag of its own colour, then go before the door of the palace and cry out, " A celebrated physician has come from Janina in Albania. He alone can cure the King and give him back the strength of his youth." The King's physicians will say, " This is an impostor, and not a learned man," and they will make all sorts of difficulties, but you will overcome them all at last, and will present yourself before the sick King. You must then demand as much wood as three mules can carry, and a great cauldron, and must shut yourself up in a room with the Sultan, and when the cauldron boils you must throw him into it, and there leave him until his flesh is completely separated from his bones. Then arrange the bones in their proper places, and throw over them the ashes out of the three bags. The King will come back to life, and will be just as he was when he was twenty years old. For your reward you must demand the bronze ring which has the power to grant you everything you desire. Go, my son, and do not forget any of my instructions.'

The young man followed the old beggar-woman's directions. On going out of the town he found the white, red, and black dogs, and killed and burnt them, gathering the ashes into three bags. Then he ran to the palace and cried:

'A celebrated physician has just come from Janina in Albania. He alone can cure the King and give him back the strength of his youth.'

The King's physicians at first laughed at the unknown wayfarer, but the Sultan ordered that the stranger should be admitted. They brought the cauldron and the loads of wood, and very soon the King was boiling away. Towards mid-day the gardener's son arranged the bones in their places, and he had hardly scattered the ashes over them before the old King revived, to find himself once more young and hearty.

'How can I reward you, my benefactor?' he cried. 'Will you take half my treasures?'

'No,' said the gardener's son.

'My daughter's hand?'

'No.'

'Take half my kingdom.'

' No. Give me only the bronze ring which can instantly grant me anything I wish for.'

' Alas!' said the King, ' I set great store by that marvellous ring; nevertheless, you shall have it.' And he gave it to him.

The gardener's son went back to say good-bye to the old beggar-woman; then he said to the bronze ring :

' Prepare a splendid ship in which I may continue my journey. Let the hull be of fine gold, the masts of silver, the sails of brocade; let the crew consist of twelve young men of noble appearance, dressed like kings. St. Nicholas will be at the helm. As to the cargo, let it be diamonds, rubies, emeralds, and carbuncles.'

And immediately a ship appeared upon the sea which resembled in every particular the description given by the gardener's son, and, stepping on board, he continued his journey. Presently he arrived at a great town and established himself in a wonderful palace. After several days he met his rival, the minister's son, who had spent all his money and was reduced to the disagreeable employ-ment of a carrier of dust and rubbish. The gardener's son said to him :

' What is your name, what is your family, and from what country do you come?'

' I am the son of the prime minister of a great nation, and yet see what a degrading occupation I am reduced to.'

' Listen to me; though I don't know anything more about you, I am willing to help you. I will give you a ship to take you back to your own country upon one condition.'

' Whatever it may be, I accept it willingly.'

' Follow me to my palace.'

The minister's son followed the rich stranger, whom he had not recognised. When they reached the palace the gardener's son made a sign to his slaves, who completely undressed the new-comer.

' Make this ring red hot,' commanded the master, ' and mark the man with it upon his back.'

The slaves obeyed him.

' Now, young man,' said the rich stranger, ' I am going to give you a vessel which will take you back to your own country.'

And, going out, he took the bronze ring and said :

' Bronze ring, obey thy master. Prepare me a ship of which the half-rotten timbers shall be painted black, let the sails be in rags, and the sailors infirm and sickly. One shall have lost a leg, another an arm, the third shall be a hunchback, another lame or club-footed or blind, and most of them shall be ugly and covered with scars. Go, and let my orders be executed.'

The minister's son embarked in this old vessel, and, thanks to favourable winds, at length reached his own country. In spite of the pitiable condition in which he returned they received him joyfully.

' I am the first to come back,' said he to the King; 'now fulfil your promise, and give me the princess in marriage.'

So they at once began to prepare for the wedding festivities. As to the poor princess, she was sorrowful and angry enough about it.

The next morning, at daybreak, a wonderful ship with every sail set came to anchor before the town. The King happened at that moment to be at the palace window.

' What strange ship is this,' he cried, ' that has a golden hull, silver masts, and silken sails, and who are the young men like princes who man it ? And do I not see St. Nicholas at the helm ? Go at once and invite the captain of the ship to come to the palace.'

His servants obeyed him, and very soon in came an enchantingly handsome young prince, dressed in rich silk, ornamented with pearls and diamonds.

' Young man,' said the King, 'you are welcome, whoever you may be. Do me the favour to be my guest as long as you remain in my capital.'

' Many thanks, sire,' replied the captain, ' I accept your offer.'

' My daughter is about to be married,' said the King; 'will you give her away ? '

' I shall be charmed, sire.'

Soon after came the Princess and her betrothed.

' Why, how is this ? ' cried the young captain; 'would you marry this charming princess to such a man as that ? '

' But he is my prime minister's son ! '

' What does that matter ? I cannot give your daughter away. The man she is betrothed to is one of my servants.'

' Your servant ? '

' Without doubt. I met him in a distant town reduced to carrying away dust and rubbish from the houses. I had pity on him and engaged him as one of my servants.'

' It is impossible ! ' cried the King.

' Do you wish me to prove what I say ? This young man returned in a vessel which I fitted out for him, an unseaworthy ship with a black battered hull, and the sailors were infirm and crippled.'

'It is quite true,' said the King.

'It is false,' cried the minister's son. 'I do not know this man!'

'Sire,' said the young captain, 'order your daughter's betrothed to be stripped, and see if the mark of my ring is not branded upon his back.'

The King was about to give this order, when the minister's son, to save himself from such an indignity, admitted that the story was true.

'And now, sire,' said the young captain, 'do not you recognise me?'

'I recognise you,' said the Princess; 'you are the gardener's son whom I have always loved, and it is you I wish to marry.'

'Young man, you shall be my son-in-law,' cried the King. 'The marriage festivities are already begun, so you shall marry my daughter this very day.'

And so that very day the gardener's son married the beautiful Princess.

Several months passed. The young couple were as happy as the day was long, and the King was more and more pleased with himself for having secured such a son-in-law.

But, presently, the captain of the golden ship found it necessary to take a long voyage, and after embracing his wife tenderly he embarked.

Now in the outskirts of the capital there lived a man who had spent his life in studying black arts—alchemy, astrology, magic, and enchantment. This man found out that the gardener's son had only succeeded in marrying the Princess by the help of the genii who obeyed the bronze ring.

'I will have that ring,' said he to himself. So he went down to the sea-shore and caught some little red fishes. Really, they were quite wonderfully pretty. Then he came back, and, passing before the Princess's window, he began to cry out:

'Who wants some pretty little red fishes?'

The Princess heard him, and sent out one of her slaves, who said to the magician:

'What will you take for your fish?'

'A bronze ring.'

'A bronze ring, old simpleton! And where shall I find one?'

'Under the cushion in the Princess's room.'

The slave went back to her mistress.

'The old madman will take neither gold nor silver,' said she.

'What does he want then?'

'A bronze ring that is hidden under a cushion.'

'Find the ring and give it to him,' said the Princess.

And at last the slave found the bronze ring, which the captain of the golden ship had accidentally left behind, and carried it to the magician, who made off with it instantly.

Hardly had he reached his own house when, taking the ring, he said, 'Bronze ring, obey thy master. I desire that the golden ship shall turn to black wood, and the crew to hideous ogres ; that St. Nicholas shall leave the helm, and that the only cargo shall be black cats.'

And the genii of the bronze ring obeyed him.

Finding himself upon the sea in this miserable condition, the young captain understood that some one must have stolen the bronze ring from him, and he lamented his misfortune loudly; but that did him no good.

'Alas!' he said to himself, 'whoever has taken my ring has probably taken my dear wife also. What good will it do me to go back to my own country?' And he sailed about from island to island, and from shore to shore, believing that wherever he went everybody was laughing at him, and very soon his poverty was so great that he and his crew and the poor black cats had nothing to eat but herbs and roots. After wandering about a long time he reached an island inhabited by mice. The captain landed upon the shore and began to explore the country. There were mice everywhere, and nothing but mice. Some of the black cats had followed him, and, not having been fed for several days, they were fearfully hungry, and made terrible havoc among the mice.

Then the queen of the mice held a council.

'These cats will eat every one of us,' she said, 'if the captain of the ship does not shut the ferocious animals up. Let us send a deputation to him of the bravest among us.'

Several mice offered themselves for this mission and set out to find the young captain.

'Captain,' said they, 'go away quickly from our island, or we shall perish, every mouse of us.'

'Willingly,' replied the young captain, 'upon one condition. That is that you shall first bring me back a bronze ring which

THE OLD MAN SHOWS THE FISHES TO THE PRINCESS.

some clever magician has stolen from me. If you do not do this I will land all my cats upon your island, and you shall be exterminated.'

The mice withdrew in great dismay. 'What is to be done?' said the queen. 'How can we find this bronze ring?' She held a new council, calling in mice from every quarter of the globe, but nobody knew where the bronze ring was. Suddenly three mice arrived from a very distant country. One was blind, the second lame, and the third had her ears cropped.

'Ho, ho, ho!' said the new-comers. 'We come from a far distant country.'

'Do you know where the bronze ring is which the genii obey?'

'Ho, ho, ho! we know; a wicked man has taken possession of it, and now he keeps it in his pocket by day and in his mouth by night.'

'Go and take it from him, and come back as soon as possible.'

So the three mice made themselves a boat and set sail for the magician's country. When they reached the capital they landed and ran to the palace, leaving only the blind mouse on the shore to take care of the boat. Then they waited till it was night. The magician lay down in bed and put the bronze ring into his mouth, and very soon he was asleep.

'Now, what shall we do?' said the two little animals to each other.

The mouse with the cropped ears found a lamp full of oil, and a bottle full of pepper. So she dipped her tail first in the oil and then in the pepper, and held it to the man's nose.

'Atisha! atisha!' he sneezed, but he did not wake, and the shock made the bronze ring jump out of his mouth. Quick as thought the lame mouse snatched up the precious talisman and carried it off to the boat.

Imagine the despair of the magician when he awoke and the bronze ring was nowhere to be found!

But by that time our three mice had set sail with their prize. A favouring breeze was carrying them towards the island where the queen of the mice was awaiting them. Naturally they began to talk about the bronze ring.

'Which of us deserves the most credit?' they cried all at once.

'I do,' said the blind mouse, 'for without my watchfulness our boat would have drifted away to the open sea.'

'No, indeed,' cried the mouse with the cropped ears; 'the credit is mine. Did I not cause the ring to jump out of the man's mouth?'

'No, it is mine,' cried the lame one, 'for I ran off with the ring.'

And from high words they soon came to blows, and, alas! when the quarrel was fiercest the bronze ring fell into the sea.

'How are we to face our queen,' said the three mice, 'when by our folly we have lost the talisman and condemned our people to be utterly exterminated? We cannot go back to our country; let us land on this desert island and there end our miserable lives.' No sooner said than done. The boat reached the island, and the mice landed.

The blind mouse was speedily deserted by her two sisters, who went off to hunt flies, but as she wandered sadly along the shore she

found a dead fish, and was eating it, when she felt something very hard. At her cries the other two mice ran up.

'It is the bronze ring! It is the talisman!' they cried joyfully, and, getting into their boat again, they soon reached the mouse island. It was time they did, for the captain was just going to land his cargo of cats, when a deputation of mice brought him the precious bronze ring.

'Bronze ring,' commanded the young man, 'obey thy master. Let my ship appear as it was before.'

Immediately the genii of the ring set to work, and the old black vessel became once more the wonderful golden ship with sails of brocade; the handsome sailors ran to the silver masts and the silken ropes, and very soon they set sail for the capital.

Ah! how merrily the sailors sang as they flew over the glassy sea!

At last the port was reached.

The captain landed and ran to the palace, where he found the magician asleep. The Princess clasped her husband in a long embrace. The magician tried to escape, but he was seized and bound with strong cords.

The next day the magician, tied to the tail of a savage mule loaded with nuts, was broken into as many pieces as there were nuts upon the mule's back.[1]

---

[1] *Traditions Populaires de l'Asie Mineure.* Carnoy et Nicolaides. Paris: Maisonneuve, 1889.

PRINCE HYACINTH
AND THE DEAR LITTLE PRINCESS

ONCE upon a time there lived a king who was deeply in love with a princess, but she could not marry anyone, because she was under an enchantment. So the King set out to seek a fairy, and asked what he could do to win the Princess's love. The Fairy said to him :

' You know that the Princess has a great cat which she is very fond of. Whoever is clever enough to tread on that cat's tail is the man she is destined to marry.'

The King said to himself that this would not be very difficult, and he left the Fairy, determined to grind the cat's tail to powder rather than not tread on it at all.

You may imagine that it was not long before he went to see the Princess, and puss, as usual, marched in before him, arching his back. The King took a long step, and quite thought he had the tail under his foot, but the cat turned round so sharply that he only trod on air. And so it went on for eight days, till the King began to think that this fatal tail must be full of quicksilver—it was never still for a moment.

At last, however, he was lucky enough to come upon puss fast asleep and with his tail conveniently spread out. So the King, without losing a moment, set his foot upon it heavily.

With one terrific yell the cat sprang up and instantly changed into a tall man, who, fixing his angry eyes upon the King, said:

'You shall marry the Princess because you have been able to break the enchantment, but I will have my revenge. You shall have a son, who will never be happy until he finds out that his nose is too long, and if you ever tell anyone what I have just said to you, you shall vanish away instantly, and no one shall ever see you or hear of you again.'

Though the King was horribly afraid of the enchanter, he could not help laughing at this threat.

'If my son has such a long nose as that,' he said to himself, 'he must always see it or feel it; at least, if he is not blind or without hands.'

But, as the enchanter had vanished, he did not waste any more time in thinking, but went to seek the Princess, who very soon consented to marry him. But after all, they had not been married very long when the King died, and the Queen had nothing left to care for but her little son, who was called Hyacinth. The little Prince had large blue eyes, the prettiest eyes in the world, and a sweet little mouth, but, alas! his nose was so enormous that it covered half his face. The Queen was inconsolable when she saw this great nose, but her ladies assured her that it was not really as large as it looked; that it was a Roman nose, and you had only to open any history to see that every hero has a large nose. The Queen, who was devoted to her baby, was pleased with what they told her, and when she looked at Hyacinth again, his nose certainly did not seem to her *quite* so large.

The Prince was brought up with great care; and, as soon as he could speak, they told him all sorts of dreadful stories about people who had short noses. No one was allowed to come near him whose nose did not more or less resemble his own, and the courtiers, to get into favour with the Queen, took to pulling their babies' noses several times every day to make them grow long. But, do what they would, they were nothing by comparison with the Prince's.

When he grew sensible he learnt history; and whenever any great prince or beautiful princess was spoken of, his teachers took care to tell him that they had long noses.

His room was hung with pictures, all of people with very large noses; and the Prince grew up so convinced that a long nose was a great beauty, that he would not on any account have had his own a single inch shorter!

When his twentieth birthday was past, the Queen thought it was time that he should be married, so she commanded that the portraits of several princesses should be brought for him to see, and among the others was a picture of the Dear Little Princess!

Now, she was the daughter of a great king, and would some day possess several kingdoms herself; but Prince Hyacinth had not a thought to spare for anything of that sort, he was so much struck with her beauty. The Princess, whom he thought quite charming, had, however, a little saucy nose, which, in her face, was the prettiest thing possible, but it was a cause of great embarrassment to the courtiers, who had got into such a habit of laughing at little noses that they sometimes found themselves laughing at hers before they had time to think; but this did not do at all before the Prince, who quite failed to see the joke, and actually banished two of his courtiers who had dared to mention disrespectfully the Dear Little Princess's tiny nose!

The others, taking warning from this, learnt to think twice before they spoke, and one even went so far as to tell the Prince that, though it was quite true that no man could be worth anything unless he had a long nose, still, a woman's beauty was a different thing; and he knew a learned man who understood Greek and had read in some old manuscripts that the beautiful Cleopatra herself had a 'tip-tilted' nose!

The Prince made him a splendid present as a reward for this good news, and at once sent ambassadors to ask the Dear Little Princess in marriage. The King, her father, gave his consent; and Prince Hyacinth, who, in his anxiety to see the Princess, had gone three leagues to meet her, was just advancing to kiss her hand when, to the horror of all who stood by, the enchanter appeared as suddenly as a flash of lightning, and, snatching up the Dear Little Princess, whirled her away out of their sight!

The Prince was left quite inconsolable, and declared that nothing should induce him to go back to his kingdom until he had found her again, and refusing to allow any of his courtiers to follow

him, he mounted his horse and rode sadly away, letting the animal
choose his own path.

So it happened that he came presently to a great plain, across
which he rode all day long without seeing a single house, and
horse and rider were quite
terribly hungry, when, as
the night fell, the Prince
caught sight of a light,
which seemed to shine
from a cavern.

He rode up to it, and
saw a little old woman,
who appeared to be at
least a hundred years old.

She put on her spec-
tacles to look at Prince
Hyacinth, but it was quite
a long time before she
could fix them securely
because her nose was so
very short.

The Prince and the
Fairy (for that was who
she was) had no sooner
looked at one another
than they went into fits
of laughter, and cried at
the same moment, 'Oh,
what a funny nose!'

'Not so funny as your own,' said Prince Hyacinth to the Fairy;
'but, madam, I beg you to leave the consideration of our noses—
such as they are—and to be good enough to give me something to
eat, for I am starving, and so is my poor horse.'

'With all my heart,' said the Fairy. 'Though your nose is
so ridiculous you are, nevertheless, the son of my best friend. I
loved your father as if he had been my brother. Now *he* had a
very handsome nose!'

'And pray what does mine lack?' said the Prince.

'Oh! it doesn't *lack* anything,' replied the Fairy. 'On the contrary quite, there is only too much of it. But never mind, one may
be a very worthy man though his nose is too long. I was telling

you that I was your father's friend; he often came to see me in the old times, and you must know that I was very pretty in those days; at least, he used to say so. I should like to tell you of a conversation we had the last time I ever saw him.'

'Indeed,' said the Prince, 'when I have supped it will give me the greatest pleasure to hear it; but consider, madam, I beg of you, that I have had nothing to eat to-day.'

'The poor boy is right,' said the Fairy; 'I was forgetting. Come in, then, and I will give you some supper, and while you are eating I can tell you my story in a very few words—for I don't like endless tales myself. Too long a tongue is worse than too long a nose, and I remember when I was young that I was so much admired for not being a great chatterer. They used to tell the Queen, my mother, that it was so. For though you see what I am now, I was the daughter of a great king. My father——'

'Your father, I dare say, got something to eat when he was hungry!' interrupted the Prince.

'Oh! certainly,' answered the Fairy, 'and you also shall have supper directly. I only just wanted to tell you——'

'But I really cannot listen to anything until I have had something to eat,' cried the Prince, who was getting quite angry; but then, remembering that he had better be polite as he much needed the Fairy's help, he added:

'I know that in the pleasure of listening to you I should quite forget my own hunger; but my horse, who cannot hear you, must really be fed!'

The Fairy was very much flattered by this compliment, and said, calling to her servants:

'You shall not wait another minute, you are so polite, and in spite of the enormous size of your nose you are really very agreeable.'

'Plague take the old lady! How she does go on about my nose!' said the Prince to himself. 'One would almost think that mine had taken all the extra length that hers lacks! If I were not so hungry I would soon have done with this chatterpie who thinks she talks very little! How stupid people are not to see their own faults! that comes of being a princess: she has been spoilt by flatterers, who have made her believe that she is quite a moderate talker!'

Meanwhile the servants were putting the supper on the table, and the Prince was much amused to hear the Fairy, who asked them a thousand questions simply for the pleasure of hearing herself speak; especially he noticed one maid who, no matter what was being said, always contrived to praise her mistress's wisdom.

'Well!' he thought, as he ate his supper, 'I'm very glad I came here. This just shows me how sensible I have been in never listening to flatterers. People of that sort praise us to our faces without shame, and hide our faults or change them into virtues. For my part I never will be taken in by them. I know my own defects, I hope.'

Poor Prince Hyacinth! He really believed what he said, and hadn't an idea that the people who had praised his nose were laughing at him, just as the Fairy's maid was laughing at her; for the Prince had seen her laugh slyly when she could do so without the Fairy's noticing her.

However, he said nothing, and presently, when his hunger began to be appeased, the Fairy said:

'My dear Prince, might I beg you to move a little more that way, for your nose casts such a shadow that I really cannot see what I have on my plate. Ah! thanks. Now let us speak of your father. When I went to his Court he was only a little boy, but that is forty years ago, and I have been in this desolate place ever since. Tell me what goes on nowadays; are the ladies as fond of amusement as ever? In my time one saw them at parties, theatres, balls, and promenades every day. Dear me! *What* a long nose you have! I cannot get used to it!'

'Really, madam,' said the Prince, 'I wish you would leave off mentioning my nose. It cannot matter to you what it is like. I am quite satisfied with it, and have no wish to have it shorter. One must take what is given one.'

'Now you are angry with me, my poor Hyacinth,' said the Fairy, 'and I assure you that I didn't mean to vex you; on the contrary, I wished to do you a service. However, though I really cannot help your nose being a shock to me, I will try not to say

anything about it. I will even try to think that you have an
ordinary nose. To tell the truth, it would make three reasonable
ones.'

The Prince, who was no longer hungry, grew so impatient at the
Fairy's continual remarks about his nose that at last he threw himself upon his horse and rode hastily away. But wherever he came
in his journeyings he thought the people were mad, for they all
talked of his nose, and yet he could not bring himself to admit that
it was too long, he had been so used all his life to hear it called
handsome.

The old Fairy, who wished to make him happy, at last hit upon
a plan. She shut the Dear Little Princess up in a palace of
crystal, and put this palace down where the Prince could not fail to
find it. His joy at seeing the Princess again was extreme, and he
set to work with all his might to try to break her prison; but in
spite of all his efforts he failed utterly. In despair he thought at
least that he would try to get near enough to speak to the Dear
Little Princess, who, on her part, stretched out her hand that he
might kiss it; but turn which way he might, he never could raise
it to his lips, for his long nose always prevented it. For the first
time he realised how long it really was, and exclaimed:

' Well, it must be admitted that my nose *is* too long!'

In an instant the crystal prison flew into a thousand splinters,
and the old Fairy, taking the Dear Little Princess by the hand,
said to the Prince:

' Now, say if you are not very much obliged to me. Much
good it was for me to talk to you about your nose! You would
never have found out how extraordinary it was if it hadn't hindered
you from doing what you wanted to. You see how self-love keeps
us from knowing our own defects of mind and body. Our reason
tries in vain to show them to us; we refuse to see them till we find
them in the way of our interests.'

Prince Hyacinth, whose nose was now just like anyone else's,
did not fail to profit by the lesson he had received. He married
the Dear Little Princess, and they lived happily ever after.[1]

---

[1] *Le Prince Désir et la Princesse Mignonne.* Par Madame Leprince de Beaumont.

EAST OF THE SUN & WEST OF THE MOON

ONCE upon a time there was a poor husbandman who had many children and little to give them in the way either of food or clothing. They were all pretty, but the prettiest of all was the youngest daughter, who was so beautiful that there were no bounds to her beauty.

So once—it was late on a Thursday evening in autumn, and wild weather outside, terribly dark, and raining so heavily and blowing so hard that the walls of the cottage shook again—they were all sitting together by the fireside, each of them busy with something or other, when suddenly some one rapped three times against the window-pane. The man went out to see what could be the matter, and when he got out there stood a great big white bear.

'Good-evening to you,' said the White Bear.

'Good-evening,' said the man.

'Will you give me your youngest daughter?' said the White Bear; 'if you will, you shall be as rich as you are now poor.'

Truly the man would have had no objection to be rich, but he thought to himself: 'I must first ask my daughter about this,' so he went in and told them that there was a great white bear outside who had faithful'y promised to make them all rich if he might but have the youngest daughter.

She said no, and would not hear of it; so the man went out again, and settled with the White Bear that he should come again next Thursday evening, and get her answer. Then the man persuaded her, and talked so much to her about the wealth that they would have, and what a good thing it would be for herself, that at last she made up her mind to go, and washed and mended all her rags, made herself as smart as she could, and held herself in readiness to set out. Little enough had she to take away with her.

Next Thursday evening the White Bear came to fetch her. She seated herself on his back with her bundle, and thus they departed.

When they had gone a great part of the way, the White Bear said:
'Are you afraid?'

'No, that I am not,' said she.

'Keep tight hold of my fur, and then there is no danger,' said
he.

And thus she rode far, far away, until they came to a great
mountain. Then the White Bear knocked on it, and a door opened,
and they went into a castle where there were many brilliantly
lighted rooms which shone with gold and silver, likewise a large

hall in which there was a well-spread table, and it was so magnificent that it would be hard to make anyone understand how
splendid it was. The White Bear gave her a silver bell, and told
her that when she needed anything she had but to ring this bell,
and what she wanted would appear. So after she had eaten, and
night was drawing near, she grew sleepy after her journey, and
thought she would like to go to bed. She rang the bell, and
scarcely had she touched it before she found herself in a chamber
where a bed stood ready made for her, which was as pretty as anyone could wish to sleep in. It had pillows of silk, and curtains of

silk fringed with gold, and everything that was in the room was of gold or silver; but when she had lain down and put out the light a man came and lay down beside her, and behold it was the White Bear, who cast off the form of a beast during the night. She never saw him, however, for he always came after she had put out her light, and went away before daylight appeared.

So all went well and happily for a time, but then she began to be very sad and sorrowful, for all day long she had to go about alone ; and she did so wish to go home to her father and mother and brothers and sisters. Then the White Bear asked what it was that she wanted, and she told him that it was so dull there in the mountain, and that she had to go about all alone, and that in her parents' house at home there were all her brothers and sisters, and it was because she could not go to them that she was so sorrowful.

'There might be a cure for that,' said the White Bear, 'if you would but promise me never to talk with your mother alone, but only when the others are there too; for she will take hold of your hand,' he said, 'and will want to lead you into a room to talk with you alone; but that you must by no means do, or you will bring great misery on both of us.'

So one Sunday the White Bear came and said that they could now set out to see her father and mother, and they journeyed thither, she sitting on his back, and they went a long, long way, and it took a long, long time ; but at last they came to a large white farmhouse, and her brothers and sisters were running about outside it, playing, and it was so pretty that it was a pleasure to look at it.

'Your parents dwell here now,' said the White Bear; 'but do not forget what I said to you, or you will do much harm both to yourself and me.'

'No, indeed,' said she, 'I shall never forget;' and as soon as she was at home the White Bear turned round and went back again.

There were such rejoicings when she went in to her parents that it seemed as if they would never come to an end. Everyone thought that he could never be sufficiently grateful to her for all she had done for them all. Now they had everything that they wanted, and everything was as good as it could be. They all asked her how she was getting on where she was. All was well with her too, she said; and she had everything that she could want. What other answers she gave I cannot say, but I am pretty sure that they did not learn much from her. But in the afternoon, after they had dined at mid-day, all happened just as the White Bear had said. Her mother wanted to talk with her alone in her own chamber. But she remembered what the White Bear had said, and would on no account go. 'What we have to say can be said at any time,' she answered. But somehow or other her mother at last persuaded her, and she was forced to tell the whole story. So she told how every night a man came and lay down beside her when the lights were all put out, and how she never saw him, because he always went away before it grew light in the morning, and how she continually went about in sadness, thinking how happy she would be if she could but see him, and how all day long she had to go about alone, and it was so dull and solitary. 'Oh!' cried the mother, in horror, 'you are very likely sleeping with a troll! But I will teach you a way to see him. You shall have a bit of one of my candles, which you can take away with you hidden in your breast. Look at him with that when he is asleep, but take care not to let any tallow drop upon him.'

So she took the candle, and hid it in her breast, and when evening drew near the White Bear came to fetch her away. When they had gone some distance on their way, the White Bear asked her if everything had not happened just as he had foretold, and she could not but own that it had. 'Then, if you have done what your mother wished,' said he, 'you have brought great misery on both of us.' 'No,' she said, 'I have not done anything at all.' So when she had reached home and had gone to bed it was just the same as it had been before, and a man came and lay down beside her, and late at night, when she could hear that he was sleeping, she got up and kindled a light, lit her candle, let her light shine on him, and saw him, and he was the handsomest prince that eyes had ever beheld, and she loved him so much that it seemed to her that she must die if she did not kiss him that very moment. So she did kiss him; but while she was doing it she let three drops of hot tallow fall upon his shirt, and he awoke. 'What have you done now?' said he; 'you have brought misery on both of us. If you had but held out for the space of one year I should have been free. I have a stepmother who has bewitched me so that I am a white bear by day and a man by night; but now all is at an end between you and me, and I must leave you, and go to her. She lives in a castle which lies east of the sun and west of the moon, and there too is a princess with a nose which is three ells long, and she now is the one whom I must marry.'

She wept and lamented, but all in vain, for go he must.   Then
she asked him if she could not go with him.   But no, that could
not be.   ' Can you tell me the way then, and I will seek you—that
I may surely be allowed to do ! '

' Yes, you may do that,' said he ; ' but there is no way thither.
It lies east of the sun and west of the moon, and never would you
find your way there.'

When she awoke in the morning both the Prince and the castle

were gone, and she was lying on a small green patch in the midst of
a dark, thick wood.   By her side lay the self-same bundle of rags
which she had brought with her from her own home.   So when
she had rubbed the sleep out of her eyes, and wept till she was
weary, she set out on her way, and thus she walked for many and
many a long day, until at last she came to a great mountain.   Outside it an aged woman was sitting, playing with a golden apple.
The girl asked her if she knew the way to the Prince who lived
with his stepmother in the castle which lay east of the sun and

west of the moon, and who was to marry a princess with a nose which was three ells long. 'How do you happen to know about him?' enquired the old woman; 'maybe you are she who ought to have had him.' 'Yes, indeed, I .am,' she said. 'So it is you, then?' said the old woman; 'I know nothing about him but that he dwells in a castle which is east of the sun and west of the moon. You will be a long time in getting to it, if ever you get to it at all; but you shall have the loan of my horse, and then you can ride on it to an old woman who is a neighbour of mine: perhaps she can tell you about him. When you have got there you must just strike the horse beneath the left ear and bid it go home again; but you may take the golden apple with you.'

So the girl seated herself on the horse, and rode for a long, long way, and at last she came to the mountain, where an aged woman was sitting outside with a gold carding-comb. The girl asked her if she knew the way to the castle which lay east of the sun and west of the moon; but she said what the first old woman had said: 'I know nothing about it, but that it is east of the sun and west of the moon, and that you will be a long time in getting to it, if ever you get there at all; but you shall have the loan of my horse to an old woman who lives the nearest to me: perhaps she may know where the castle is, and when you have got to her you may just strike the horse beneath the left ear and bid it go home again.' Then she gave her the gold carding-comb, for it might, perhaps, be of use to her, she said.

So the girl seated herself on the horse, and rode a wearisome long way onwards again, and after a very long time she came to a great mountain, where an aged woman was sitting, spinning at a golden spinning-wheel. Of this woman, too, she enquired if she knew the way to the Prince, and where to find the castle which lay east of the sun and west of the moon. But it was only the same thing once again. 'Maybe it was you who should have had the Prince,' said the old woman. 'Yes, indeed, I should have been the one,' said the girl. But this old crone knew the way no better than the others—it was east of the sun and west of the moon, she knew that, 'and you will be a long time in getting to it, if ever you get to it at all,' she said; 'but you may have the loan of my horse, and I think you had better ride to the East Wind, and ask him: perhaps he may know where the castle is, and will blow you thither. But when you have got to him you must just strike the horse beneath the left ear, and he will come home again.' And then she gave her the golden spinning-wheel, saying: 'Perhaps you may find that you have a use for it.'

The girl had to ride for a great many days, and for a long and wearisome time, before she got there; but at last she did arrive, and then she asked the East Wind if he could tell her the way to the Prince who dwelt east of the sun and west of the moon. 'Well,' said the East Wind, 'I have heard tell of the Prince, and of his castle, but I do not know the way to it, for I have never blown so far; but, if you like, I will go with you to my brother the West Wind: he may know that, for he is much stronger than I am. You may sit on my back, and then I can carry you there.' So she seated herself on his back, and they did go so swiftly! When they got there, the East Wind went in and said that the girl whom he had brought was the one who ought to have had the Prince up at the castle which lay east of the sun and west of the moon, and that now she was travelling about to find him again, so he had come there with her, and would like to hear if the West Wind knew whereabouts the castle was. 'No,' said the West Wind; 'so far as that have I never blown: but if you like I will go with you to the South Wind, for he is much stronger than either of us, and he has roamed far and wide, and perhaps he can tell you what you want to know. You may seat yourself on my back, and then I will carry you to him.'

So she did this, and journeyed to the South Wind, neither was she very long on the way. When they had got there, the West Wind asked him if he could tell her the way to the castle that lay east of the sun and west of the moon, for she was the girl who ought to marry the Prince who lived there. 'Oh, indeed!' said the South Wind, 'is that she? Well,' said he, 'I have wandered about a great deal in my time, and in all kinds of places, but I have never blown so far as that. If you like, however, I will go with you to my brother the North Wind; he is the oldest and strongest of all of us, and if he does not know where it is no one in the whole world will be able to tell you. You may sit upon my back, and then I will carry you there.' So she seated herself on his back, and off he went from his house in great haste, and they were not long on the way. When they came near the North Wind's dwelling, he was so wild and frantic that they felt cold gusts a long while before they got there. 'What do you want?' he roared out from afar, and they froze as they heard. Said the South Wind: 'It is I, and this is she who should have had the Prince who lives in the castle which lies east of the sun and west of the moon. And now she wishes to ask you if you have ever been there, and can tell her the way, for she would gladly find him again.'

'Yes,' said the North Wind, 'I know where it is. I once blew an aspen leaf there, but I was so tired that for many days afterwards I was not able to blow at all. However, if you really are anxious to go there, and are not afraid to go with me, I will take you on my back, and try if I can blow you there.'

'Get there I must,' said she; 'and if there is any way of going I will; and I have no fear, no matter how fast you go.'

'Very well then,' said the North Wind; 'but you must sleep here to-night, for if we are ever to get there we must have the day before us.'

The North Wind woke her betimes next morning, and puffed

himself up, and made himself so big and so strong that it was frightful to see him, and away they went, high up through the air, as if they would not stop until they had reached the very end of the world. Down below there was such a storm! It blew down woods and houses, and when they were above the sea the ships were wrecked by hundreds. And thus they tore on and on, and a long time went by, and then yet more time passed, and still they were above the sea, and the North Wind grew tired, and more tired, and at last so utterly weary that he was scarcely able to blow any longer, and he sank and sank, lower and lower, until at last he went so low that the crests of the waves dashed against the heels of the poor girl he was carrying. 'Art thou afraid?' said the North Wind. 'I have no fear,' said she; and it was true. But they were not very, very far from land, and there was just enough strength left in the North Wind to enable him to throw her on to the shore, immediately under the windows of a castle which lay east of the sun and west of the moon ; but then he was so weary and worn out that he was forced to rest for several days before he could go to his own home again.

Next morning she sat down beneath the walls of the castle to play with the golden apple, and the first person she saw was the maiden with the long nose, who was to have the Prince. ' How much do you want for that gold apple of yours, girl ? ' said she, opening the window. 'It can't be bought either for gold or money,' answered the girl. ' If it cannot be bought either for gold or money, what will buy it ? You may say what you please,' said the Princess.

' Well, if I may go to the Prince who is here, and be with him to-night, you shall have it,' said the girl who had come with the North Wind. ' You may do that,' said the Princess, for she had made up her mind what she would do. So the Princess got the golden apple, but when the girl went up to the Prince's apartment that night he was asleep, for the Princess had so contrived it. The poor girl called to him, and shook him, and between whiles she wept ; but she could not wake him. In the morning, as soon as day dawned, in came the Princess with the long nose, and drove her out again. In the daytime she sat down once more beneath the windows of the castle, and began to card with her golden carding-comb ; and then all happened as it had happened before. The princess asked her what she wanted for it, and she replied that it was not for sale, either for gold or money, but that if she could get leave to go to the Prince, and be with him during the night, she should have it. But when she went up to the Prince's room he was again asleep, and, let her call him, or shake him, or weep as she would, he still slept on, and she could not put any life in him. When daylight came in the morning, the Princess with the long nose came too, and once more drove her away. When day had quite come, the girl seated herself under the castle windows, to spin with her golden spinning-wheel, and the Princess with the long nose wanted to have that also. So she opened the window, and asked what she would take for it. The girl said what she had said on each of the former occasions—that it was not for sale either for gold or for money, but if she could get leave to go to the Prince who lived there, and be with him during the night, she should have it.

' Yes,' said the Princess, ' I will gladly consent to that.

But in that place there were some Christian folk who had been carried off, and they had been sitting in the chamber which was next to that of the Prince, and had heard how a woman had been in there who had wept and called on him two nights running, and they told the Prince of this. So that evening, when the Princess came once more with her sleeping-drink, he pretended to drink, but threw it away behind him, for he suspected that it was a sleeping-drink. So, when the girl went into the Prince's room this time he was awake, and she had to tell him how she had come there. 'You have come just in time,' said the Prince, 'for I should have been married to-morrow; but I will not have the long-nosed Princess, and you alone can save me. I will say that I want to see what my bride can do, and bid her wash the shirt which has the three drops of tallow on it. This she will consent to do, for she

does not know that it is you who let them fall on it; but no one can wash them out but one born of Christian folk: it cannot be done by one of a pack of trolls; and then I will say that no one shall ever be my bride but the woman who can do this, and I know that you can.' There was great joy and gladness between them all that night, but the next day, when the wedding was to take place, the Prince said, 'I must see what my bride can do.' 'That you may do,' said the stepmother.

'I have a fine shirt which I want to wear as my wedding shirt, but three drops of tallow have got upon it which I want to have washed off, and I have vowed to marry no one but the woman who is able to do it. If she cannot do that, she is not worth having.'

Well, that was a very small matter, they thought, and agreed to do it. The Princess with the long nose began to wash as well as she could, but, the more she washed and rubbed, the larger the spots grew. 'Ah! you can't wash at all,' said the old troll-hag, who was her mother. 'Give it to me.' But she too had not had the shirt very long in her hands before it looked worse still, and, the more she washed it and rubbed it, the larger and blacker grew the spots.

So the other trolls had to come and wash, but, the more they did, the blacker and uglier grew the shirt, until at length it was as black as if it had been up the chimney. 'Oh,' cried the Prince, 'not one of you is good for anything at all! There is a beggar-girl sitting outside the window, and I'll be bound that she can wash better than any of you! Come in, you girl there!' he cried. So she came in. 'Can you wash this shirt clean?' he cried. 'Oh! I don't know,' she said; 'but I will try.' And no sooner had she taken the shirt and dipped it in the water than it was white as driven snow, and even whiter than that. 'I will marry you,' said the Prince.

Then the old troll-hag flew into such a rage that she burst, and the Princess with the long nose and all the little trolls must have burst too, for they have never been heard of since. The Prince and his bride set free all the Christian folk who were imprisoned there, and took away with them all the gold and silver that they could carry, and moved far away from the castle which lay east of the sun and west of the moon.[1]

[1] Asbjornsen and Moe.

THE YELLOW DWARF

ONCE upon a time there lived a queen who had been the mother of a great many children, and of them all only one daughter was left. But then *she* was worth at least a thousand.

Her mother, who, since the death of the King, her father, had nothing in the world she cared for so much as this little princess, was so terribly afraid of losing her that she quite spoiled her, and never tried to correct any of her faults. The consequence was that this little person, who was as pretty as possible, and was one day to wear a crown, grew up so proud and so much in love with her own beauty that she despised everyone else in the world.

The Queen, her mother, by her caresses and flatteries, helped to make her believe that there was nothing too good for her. She was dressed almost always in the prettiest frocks, as a fairy, or as a queen going out to hunt, and the ladies of the Court followed her dressed as forest-fairies.

And to make her more vain than ever the Queen caused her portrait to be taken by the cleverest painters and sent it to several neighbouring kings with whom she was very friendly.

When they saw this portrait they fell in love with the Princess— every one of them, but upon each it had a different effect. One fell ill, one went quite crazy, and a few of the luckiest set off to see her as soon as possible ; but these poor princes became her slaves the moment they set eyes on her.

Never has there been a gayer Court. Twenty delightful kings did everything they could think of to make themselves agreeable, and after having spent ever so much money in giving a single entertainment thought themselves very lucky if the Princess said 'That's pretty.'

All this admiration vastly pleased the Queen. Not a day passed but she received seven or eight thousand sonnets, and as many elegies, madrigals, and songs, which were sent her by all the poets in the world. All the prose and the poetry that was written just then was about Bellissima—for that was the Princess's name—and all the bonfires that they had were made of these verses, which crackled and sparkled better than any other sort of wood.

Bellissima was already fifteen years old, and every one of the Princes wished to marry her, but not one dared to say so. How could they when they knew that any of them might have cut off his head five or six times a day just to please her, and she would have thought it a mere trifle, so little did she care? You may imagine how hard-hearted her lovers thought her; and the Queen, who wished to see her married, did not know how to persuade her to think of it seriously.

'Bellissima,' she said, 'I do wish you would not be so proud. What makes you despise all these nice kings? I wish you to marry one of them, and you do not try to please me.'

'I am so happy,' Bellissima answered: 'do leave me in peace, madam. I don't want to care for anyone.'

'But you would be very happy with any of these princes,' said the Queen, 'and I shall be very angry if you fall in love with any-one who is not worthy of you.'

But the Princess thought so much of herself that she did not consider any one of her lovers clever or handsome enough for her; and her mother, who was getting really angry at her determination not to be married, began to wish that she had not allowed her to have her own way so much.

At last, not knowing what else to do, she resolved to consult a certain witch who was called 'The Fairy of the Desert.' Now this was very difficult to do, as she was guarded by some terrible lions; but happily the Queen had heard a long time before that whoever wanted to pass these lions safely must throw to them a cake made of millet flour, sugar-candy, and crocodile's eggs. This cake she prepared with her own hands, and putting it in a little basket, she set out to seek the Fairy. But as she was not used to walking far, she soon felt very tired and sat down at the foot of a tree to rest, and presently fell fast asleep. When she awoke she was dismayed to find her basket empty. The cake was all gone! and, to make matters worse, at that moment she heard the roaring of the great lions, who had found out that she was near and were coming to look for her.

'What shall I do?' she cried; 'I shall be eaten up,' and being too much frightened to run a single step, she began to cry, and leant against the tree under which she had been asleep.

Just then she heard some one say: 'H'm, h'm!'

She looked all round her, and then up at the tree, and there she saw a little tiny man, who was eating oranges.

'Oh! Queen,' said he, 'I know you very well, and I know how much afraid you are of the lions; and you are quite right too, for they have eaten many other people : and what can you expect, as you have not any cake to give them ? '

' I must make up my mind to die,' said the poor Queen. 'Alas ! I should not care so much if only my dear daughter were married.'

' Oh ! you have a daughter,' cried the Yellow Dwarf (who was so called because he *was* a dwarf and had such a yellow face, and lived in the orange tree). ' I'm really glad to hear that, for I've been looking for a wife all over the world. Now, if you will promise that she shall marry me, not one of the lions, tigers, or bears shall touch you.'

The Queen looked at him and was almost as much afraid of his ugly little face as she had been of the lions before, so that she could not speak a word.

' What ! you hesitate, madam,' cried the Dwarf. ' You must be very fond of being eaten up alive.'

And, as he spoke, the Queen saw the lions, which were running down a hill towards them.

Each one had two heads, eight feet, and four rows of teeth, and their skins were as hard as turtle shells, and were bright red.

At this dreadful sight, the poor Queen, who was trembling like a dove when it sees a hawk, cried out as loud as she could, ' Oh ! dear Mr. Dwarf, Bellissima shall marry you.'

' Oh, indeed ! ' said he disdainfully. ' Bellissima is pretty enough, but I don't particularly want to marry her—you can keep her.'

' Oh ! noble sir,' said the Queen in great distress, ' do not refuse her. She is the most charming Princess in the world.'

' Oh ! well,' he replied, ' out of charity I will take her ; but be sure you don't forget that she is mine.'

As he spoke a little door opened in the trunk of the orange tree, in rushed the Queen, only just in time, and the door shut with a bang in the faces of the lions.

The Queen was so confused that at first she did not notice another little door in the orange tree, but presently it opened and she found herself in a field of thistles and nettles. It was encircled by a muddy ditch, and a little further on was a tiny thatched cottage, out of which came the Yellow Dwarf with a very jaunty air. He wore wooden shoes and a little yellow coat, and as he had no hair and very long ears he looked altogether a shocking little object.

' I am delighted,' said he to the Queen, ' that, as you are to be my mother-in-law, you should see the little house in which your

Bellissima will live with me. With these thistles and nettles she can feed a donkey which she can ride whenever she likes; under this humble roof no weather can hurt her; she will drink the water of this brook, and eat frogs—which grow very fat about here; and then she will have me always with her, handsome, agreeable, and gay as you see me now. For if her shadow stays by her more closely than I do I shall be surprised.'

The unhappy Queen, seeing all at once what a miserable life her daughter would have with this Dwarf, could not bear the idea, and fell down insensible without saying a word.

When she revived she found to her great surprise that she was lying in her own bed at home, and, what was more, that she had on the loveliest lace nightcap that she had ever seen in her life. At first she thought that all her adventures, the terrible lions, and her promise to the Yellow Dwarf that he should marry Bellissima must have been a dream, but there was the new cap with its beautiful ribbon and lace to remind her that it was all true, which

made her so unhappy that she could neither eat, drink, nor sleep for thinking of it.

The Princess, who, in spite of her wilfulness, really loved her mother with all her heart, was much grieved when she saw her looking so sad, and often asked her what was the matter; but the Queen, who didn't want her to find out the truth, only said that she was ill, or that one of her neighbours was threatening to make war against her. Bellissima knew quite well that something was being hidden from her—and that neither of these was the real reason of the Queen's uneasiness. So she made up her mind that she would go and consult the Fairy of the Desert about it, especially as she had often heard how wise she was, and she thought that at the same time she might ask her advice as to whether it would be as well to be married, or not.

So, with great care, she made some of the proper cake to pacify the lions, and one night went up to her room very early, pretending that she was going to bed; but, instead of that, she wrapped herself up in a long white veil, and went down a secret staircase, and set off, all by herself, to find the Witch.

But when she got as far as the same fatal orange tree, and saw it covered with flowers and fruit, she stopped and began to gather some of the oranges—and then, putting down her basket, she sat down to eat them. But when it was time to go on again the basket had disappeared, and, though she looked everywhere, not a trace of it could she find. The more she hunted for it the more frightened she got, and at last she began to cry. Then all at once she saw before her the Yellow Dwarf.

'What's the matter with you, my pretty one?' said he. 'What are *you* crying about?'

'Alas!' she answered; 'no wonder that I am crying, seeing that I have lost the basket of cake that was to help me to get safely to the cave of the Fairy of the Desert.'

'And what do you want with her, pretty one?' said the little monster, 'for I am a friend of hers, and, for the matter of that, I am quite as clever as she is.'

'The Queen, my mother,' replied the Princess, 'has lately fallen into such deep sadness that I fear that she will die; and I am afraid that perhaps I am the cause of it, for she very much wishes me to be married, and I must tell you truly that as yet I have not found anyone I consider worthy to be my husband. So for all these reasons I wished to talk to the Fairy.'

'Do not give yourself any further trouble, Princess,' answered the Dwarf. 'I can tell you all you want to know better than she could. The Queen, your mother, has promised you in marriage——'

'Has promised *me*!' interrupted the Princess. 'Oh! no. I'm sure she has not. She would have told me if she had. I am too much interested in the matter for her to promise anything without my consent—you must be mistaken.'

'Beautiful Princess,' cried the Dwarf suddenly, throwing himself on his knees before her, 'I flatter myself that you will not be displeased at her choice when I tell you that it is to *me* she has promised the happiness of marrying you.'

'You!' cried Bellissima, starting back. 'My mother wishes me to marry you! How can you be so silly as to think of such a thing?'

'Oh! it isn't that I care much to have that honour,' cried the Dwarf angrily; 'but here are the lions coming; they'll eat you up in three mouthfuls, and there will be an end of you and your pride.'

And, indeed, at that moment the poor Princess heard their dreadful howls coming nearer and nearer.

'What shall I do?' she cried. 'Must all my happy days come to an end like this?'

The malicious Dwarf looked at her and began to laugh spitefully. 'At least,' said he, 'you have the satisfaction of dying unmarried. A lovely princess like you must surely prefer to die rather than be the wife of a poor little dwarf like myself.'

'Oh! don't be angry with me,' cried the Princess, clasping her hands. 'I'd rather marry all the dwarfs in the world than die in this horrible way.'

'Look at me well, Princess, before you give me your word,' said he. 'I don't want you to promise me in a hurry.'

'Oh!' cried she, 'the lions are coming. I have looked at you enough. I am so frightened. Save me this minute, or I shall die of terror.'

Indeed, as she spoke she fell down insensible, and when she recovered she found herself in her own little bed at home; how she got there she could not tell, but she was dressed in the most beautiful lace and ribbons, and on her finger was a little ring, made of a single red hair, which fitted so tightly that, try as she might, she could not get it off.

When the Princess saw all these things, and remembered what had happened, she, too, fell into the deepest sadness, which surprised and alarmed the whole Court, and the Queen more than anyone else. A hundred times she asked Bellissima if anything was the matter with her; but she always said that there was nothing.

At last the chief men of the kingdom, anxious to see their Princess married, sent to the Queen to beg her to choose a husband for her as soon as possible. She replied that nothing would please her better, but that her daughter seemed so unwilling to marry, and she recommended them to go and talk to the Princess about it themselves; so this they at once did. Now Bellissima was much less proud since her adventure with the Yellow Dwarf, and she could not think of a better way of getting rid of the little monster than to marry some powerful king, therefore she replied to their request much more favourably than they had hoped, saying that, though she was very happy as she was, still, to please them, she would consent to marry the King of the Gold Mines. Now he was a very handsome and powerful Prince, who had been in love with the Princess for years, but had not thought that she would ever care about him at all. You can easily imagine how delighted he was when he heard the news, and how angry it made all the other kings to lose for ever the hope of marrying the Princess; but after all Bellissima could not have married twenty kings—indeed, she had found it quite difficult enough to choose one, for her vanity made her believe that there was nobody in the world who was worthy of her.

Preparations were begun at once for the grandest wedding that

had ever been held at the palace. The King of the Gold Mines sent such immense sums of money that the whole sea was covered with the ships that brought it. Messengers were sent to all the gayest and most refined Courts, particularly to the Court of France, to seek out everything rare and precious to adorn the Princess, although her beauty was so perfect that nothing she wore could make her look prettier. At least that is what the King of the Gold Mines thought, and he was never happy unless he was with her.

As for the Princess, the more she saw of the King the more she liked him; he was so generous, so handsome and clever, that at last she was almost as much in love with him as he was

with her. How happy they were as they wandered about in the beautiful gardens together, sometimes listening to sweet music! and the King used to write songs for Bellissima. This is one that she liked very much:

> In the forest all is gay
> When my Princess walks that way.
> All the blossoms then are found
> Downward fluttering to the ground,

Hoping she may tread on them.
And bright flowers on slender stem
Gaze up at her as she passes,
Brushing lightly through the grasses.
Oh! my Princess, birds above
Echo back our songs of love,
As through this enchanted land
Blithe we wander, hand in hand.

They really were as happy as the day was long. All the King's unsuccessful rivals had gone home in despair. They said good-bye to the Princess so sadly that she could not help being sorry for them.

' Ah! madam,' the King of the Gold Mines said to her, ' how is this? Why do you waste your pity on these princes, who love you so much that all their trouble would be well repaid by a single smile from you? '

' I should be sorry,' answered Bellissima, ' if you had not noticed how much I pitied these princes who were leaving me for ever; but for you, sire, it is very different: you have every reason to be pleased with me, but they are going sorrowfully away, so you must not grudge them my compassion.'

The King of the Gold Mines was quite overcome by the Princess's good-natured way of taking his interference, and, throwing himself at her feet, he kissed her hand a thousand times and begged her to forgive him.

At last the happy day came. Everything was ready for Bellissima's wedding. The trumpets sounded, all the streets of the town were hung with flags and strewn with flowers, and the people ran in crowds to the great square before the palace. The Queen was so over-joyed that she had hardly been able to sleep at all, and she got up before it was light to give the necessary orders and to choose the jewels that the Princess was to wear. These were nothing less than diamonds, even to her shoes, which were covered with them, and her dress of silver brocade was embroidered with a dozen of the sun's rays. You may imagine how much these had cost; but then nothing could have been more brilliant, except the beauty of the Princess! Upon her head she wore a splendid crown, her lovely hair waved nearly to her feet, and her stately figure could easily be distinguished among all the ladies who attended her.

The King of the Gold Mines was not less noble and splendid;

it was easy to see by his face how happy he was, a who went near him returned loaded with presents, for a great banqueting hall had been arranged a thousand _____ of gold, and numberless bags made of velvet embroidered with pearls and filled with money, each one containing at least a hundred thousand gold pieces, which were given away to everyone who liked to hold out his hand, which numbers of people hastened to do, you may be sure—indeed, some found this by far the most amusing part of the wedding festivities.

The Queen and the Princess were just ready to set out with the King when they saw, advancing towards them from the end of the long gallery, two great basilisks, dragging after them a very badly made box; behind them came a tall old woman, whose ugliness was even more surprising than her extreme old age. She wore a ruff of black taffeta, a red velvet hood, and a farthingale all in rags, and she leaned heavily upon a crutch. This strange old woman, without saying a single word, hobbled three times round the gallery, followed by the basilisks, then stopping in the middle, and brandishing her crutch threateningly, she cried:

' Ho, ho, Queen ! Ho, ho, Princess ! Do you think you are going to break with impunity the promise that you made to my friend the Yellow Dwarf? I am the Fairy of the Desert; without the Yellow Dwarf and his orange tree my great lions would soon have eaten you up, I can tell you, and in Fairyland we do not suffer ourselves to be insulted like this. Make up your minds at once what you will do, for I vow that you shall marry the Yellow Dwarf. If you don't, may I burn my crutch ! '

' Ah ! Princess,' said the Queen, weeping, ' what is this that I hear? What have you promised ? '

' Ah ! my mother,' replied Bellissima sadly, ' what did *you* promise, yourself ? '

The King of the Gold Mines, indignant at being kept from his happiness by this wicked old woman, went up to her, and threatening her with his sword, said :

' Get away out of my country at once, and for ever, miserable creature, lest I take your life, and so rid myself of your malice.'

He had hardly spoken these words when the lid of the box fell back on the floor with a terrible noise, and to their horror out sprang the Yellow Dwarf, mounted upon a great Spanish cat. ' Rash youth ! ' he cried, rushing between the Fairy of the Desert and the King. ' Dare to lay a finger upon this illustrious Fairy !

Your quarrel is with me only. I am your enemy and your rival.
That faithless Princess who would have married you is promised
to me. See if she has not upon her finger a ring made of one of

my hairs. Just try to
take it off, and you will
soon find out that I am
more powerful than you
are!'

'Wretched little mon-
ster!' said the King; 'do
you dare to call yourself
the Princess's lover, and
to lay claim to such a
treasure? Do you know
that you are a dwarf—
that you are so ugly
that one cannot bear to
look at you—and that I
should have killed you
myself long before this
if you had been worthy
of such a glorious death?'

The Yellow Dwarf,
deeply enraged at these
words, set spurs to his
cat, which yelled hor-
ribly, and leapt hither and thither—terrifying everybody except the
brave King, who pursued the Dwarf closely, till he, drawing a
great knife with which he was armed, challenged the King to
meet him in single combat, and rushed down into the courtyard
of the palace with a terrible clatter. The King, quite provoked,
followed him hastily, but they had hardly taken their places
facing one another, and the whole Court had only just had time
to rush out upon the balconies to watch what was going on, when
suddenly the sun became as red as blood, and it was so dark
that they could scarcely see at all. The thunder crashed, and
the lightning seemed as if it must burn up everything; the two
basilisks appeared, one on each side of the bad Dwarf, like giants,
mountains high, and fire flew from their mouths and ears, until
they looked like flaming furnaces. None of these things could terrify
the noble young King, and the boldness of his looks and actions

reassured those who were looking on, and perhaps even embarrassed the Yellow Dwarf himself; but even *his* courage gave way when he saw what was happening to his beloved Princess. For the Fairy of the Desert, looking more terrible than before, mounted upon a winged griffin, and with long snakes coiled round her neck, had given her such a blow with the lance she carried that Bellissima fell into the Queen's arms bleeding and senseless. Her fond mother, feeling as much hurt by the blow as the Princess herself, uttered such piercing cries and lamentations that the King, hearing them, entirely lost his courage and presence of mind. Giving up the combat, he flew towards the Princess, to rescue or to die with her ; but the Yellow Dwarf was too quick for him. Leaping with his Spanish cat upon the balcony, he snatched Bellissima from the Queen's arms, and before any of the ladies of the Court could stop him he had sprung upon the roof of the palace and disappeared with his prize.

The King, motionless with horror, looked on despairingly at this dreadful occurrence, which he was quite powerless to prevent, and to make matters worse his sight failed him, everything became dark, and he felt himself carried along through the air by a strong hand.

This new misfortune was the work of the wicked Fairy of the Desert, who had come with the Yellow Dwarf to help him carry off the Princess, and had fallen in love with the handsome young King of the Gold Mines directly she saw him. She thought that if she carried him off to some frightful cavern and chained him to a rock, then the fear of death would make him forget Bellissima and become her slave. So, as soon as they reached the place, she gave him back his sight, but without releasing him from his chains, and by her magic power she appeared before him as a young and beautiful fairy, and pretended to have come there quite by chance.

' What do I see ? ' she cried. ' Is it *you*, dear Prince ? What misfortune has brought you to this dismal place ? '

The King, who was quite deceived by her altered appearance, replied :

' Alas ! beautiful Fairy, the fairy who brought me here first took away my sight, but by her voice I recognised her as the Fairy of the Desert, though what she should have carried me off for I cannot tell you.'

' Ah ! ' cried the pretended Fairy, ' if you have fallen into *her* hands, you won't get away until you have married her. She has carried off more than one Prince like this, and she will certainly

have anything she takes a fancy to.' While she was thus pretending to be sorry for the King, he suddenly noticed her feet, which
were like those of a griffin, and knew in a moment that this must
be the Fairy of the Desert, for her feet were the one thing she
could not change, however pretty she might make her face.

Without seeming to have noticed anything, he said, in a con-
fidential way:

'Not that I have any dislike to the Fairy of the Desert, but I
really cannot endure the way in which she protects the Yellow
Dwarf and keeps me chained here like a criminal. It is true that
I love a charming princess, but if the Fairy should set me free my
gratitude would oblige me to love her only.'

'Do you really mean what you say, Prince?' said the Fairy,
quite deceived.

'Surely,' replied the Prince; 'how could I deceive you? You
see it is so much more flattering to my vanity to be loved by a
fairy than by a simple princess. But, even if I am dying of love
for her, I shall pretend to hate her until I am set free.'

The Fairy of the Desert, quite taken in by these words, resolved
at once to transport the Prince to a pleasanter place. So, making
him mount her chariot, to which she had harnessed swans instead
of the bats which generally drew it, away she flew with him. But
imagine the distress of the Prince when, from the giddy height at
which they were rushing through the air, he saw his beloved
Princess in a castle built of polished steel, the walls of which
reflected the sun's rays so hotly that no one could approach it
without being burnt to a cinder! Bellissima was sitting in a
little thicket by a brook, leaning her head upon her hand and
weeping bitterly, but just as they passed she looked up and saw
the King and the Fairy of the Desert. Now, the Fairy was so
clever that she could not only seem beautiful to the King, but
even the poor Princess thought her the most lovely being she had
ever seen.

'What!' she cried; 'was I not unhappy enough in this lonely
castle to which that frightful Yellow Dwarf brought me? Must I
also be made to know that the King of the Gold Mines ceased to
love me as soon as he lost sight of me? But who can my rival
be, whose fatal beauty is greater than mine?'

While she was saying this, the King, who really loved her as
much as ever, was feeling terribly sad at being so rapidly torn away
from his beloved Princess, but he knew too well how powerful the

Fairy was to have any hope of escaping from her except by great patience and cunning.

The Fairy of the Desert had also seen Bellissima, and she tried to read in the King's eyes the effect that this unexpected sight had had upon him.

'No one can tell you what you wish to know better than I can,' said he. 'This chance meeting with an unhappy princess for whom I once had a passing fancy, before I was lucky enough to meet *you*, has affected me a little, I admit, but you are so much more to me than she is that I would rather die than leave you.'

'Ah! Prince,' she said, 'can I believe that you really love me so much?'

'Time will show, madam,' replied the King; 'but if you wish to convince me that you have some regard for me, do not, I beg of you, refuse to aid Bellissima.'

'Do you know what you are asking?' said the Fairy of the Desert, frowning, and looking at him suspiciously. 'Do you want me to employ my art against the Yellow Dwarf, who is my best friend, and take away from him a proud princess whom I can but look upon as my rival?'

The King sighed, but made no answer—indeed, what was there to be said to such a clear-sighted person? At last they reached a vast meadow, gay with all sorts of flowers; a deep river surrounded it, and many little brooks murmured softly under the shady trees, where it was always cool and fresh. A little way off stood a splendid palace, the walls of which were of transparent emeralds. As soon as the swans which drew the Fairy's chariot had alighted under a porch, which was paved with diamonds and had arches of rubies, they were greeted on all sides by thousands of beautiful beings, who came to meet them joyfully, singing these words:

> When Love within a heart would reign,
>   Useless to strive against him 'tis.
> The proud but feel a sharper pain,
>   And make a greater triumph his.

The Fairy of the Desert was delighted to hear them sing of her triumphs; she led the King into the most splendid room that can be imagined, and left him alone for a little while, just that he might not feel that he was a prisoner; but he felt sure that she had not really gone quite away, but was watching him from some hiding-place. So walking up to a great mirror, he said to it, 'Trusty counsellor, let me see what I can do to make myself agreeable to the charming Fairy of the Desert; for I can think of nothing but how to please her.'

And he at once set to work to curl his hair, and, seeing upon a table a grander coat than his own, he put it on carefully. The Fairy came back so delighted that she could not conceal her joy.

'I am quite aware of the trouble you have taken to please me,' said she, 'and I must tell you that you have succeeded perfectly already. You see it is not difficult to do if you really care for me.'

The King, who had his own reasons for wishing to keep the old Fairy in a good humour, did not spare pretty speeches, and after a time he was allowed to walk by himself upon the sea-shore. The Fairy of the Desert had by her enchantments raised such a terrible storm that the boldest pilot would not venture out in it, so she was not afraid of her prisoner's being able to escape; and he found it some relief to think sadly over his terrible situation without being interrupted by his cruel captor.

Presently, after walking wildly up and down, he wrote these verses upon the sand with his stick:

> At last may I upon this shore
>   Lighten my sorrow with soft tears.
> Alas! alas! I see no more
>   My Love, who yet my sadness cheers.
>
> And thou, O raging, stormy Sea,
>   Stirred by wild winds, from depth to height,
> Thou hold'st my loved one far from me,
>   And I am captive to thy might.
>
> My heart is still more wild than thine,
>   For Fate is cruel unto me.
> Why must I thus in exile pine?
>   Why is my Princess snatched from me?
>
> O! lovely Nymphs, from ocean caves,
>   Who know how sweet true love may be,
> Come up and calm the furious waves
>   And set a desperate lover free!

While he was still writing he heard a voice which attracted his attention in spite of himself. Seeing that the waves were rolling in higher than ever, he looked all round him, and presently saw a lovely lady floating gently towards him upon the crest of a huge

billow, her long hair spread all about her; in one hand she held
a mirror, and in the other a comb, and instead of feet she had
a beautiful tail like a fish, with which she swam.

The King was struck dumb with astonishment at this unexpected sight; but as soon as she came within speaking distance,
she said to him, 'I know how sad you are at losing your Princess
and being kept a prisoner by the Fairy of the Desert; if you like
I will help you to escape from this fatal place, where you may
otherwise have to drag on a weary existence for thirty years or
more.'

The King of the Gold Mines hardly knew what answer to make
to this proposal. Not because he did not wish very much to escape,

but he was afraid that this might be only another device by which
the Fairy of the Desert was trying to deceive him. As he hesitated
the Mermaid, who guessed his thoughts, said to him:

'You may trust me: I am not trying to entrap you. I am so
angry with the Yellow Dwarf and the Fairy of the Desert that I
am not likely to wish to help them, especially since I constantly
see your poor Princess, whose beauty and goodness make me pity
her so much: and I tell you that if you will have confidence in me
I will help you to escape.'

'I trust you absolutely,' cried the King, 'and I will do whatever
you tell me; but if you have seen my Princess I beg of you to tell
me how she is and what is happening to her.'

'We must not waste time in talking,' said she. 'Come with

me and I will carry you to the Castle of Steel, and we will leave upon this shore a figure so like you that even the Fairy herself will be deceived by it.'

So saying she quickly collected a bundle of sea-weed, and, blowing it three times, she said :

' My friendly sea-weeds, I order you to stay here stretched upon the sand until the Fairy of the Desert comes to take you away.' And at once the sea-weeds became like the King, who stood looking at them in great astonishment, for they were even dressed in a coat like his, but they lay there pale and still as the King himself might have lain if one of the great waves had overtaken him and thrown him senseless upon the shore. And then the Mermaid caught up the King, and away they swam joyfully together.

' Now,' said she, ' I have time to tell you about the Princess. In spite of the blow which the Fairy of the Desert gave her, the Yellow Dwarf compelled her to mount behind him upon his terrible Spanish cat ; but she soon fainted away with pain and terror, and did not recover till they were within the walls of his frightful Castle of Steel. Here she was received by the prettiest girls it was possible to find, who had been carried there by the Yellow Dwarf, who hastened to wait upon her and showed her every possible attention. She was laid upon a couch covered with cloth of gold, embroidered with pearls as big as nuts.'

' Ah ! ' interrupted the King of the Gold Mines, ' if Bellissima forgets me, and consents to marry him, I shall break my heart.'

' You need not be afraid of that,' answered the Mermaid ; ' the Princess thinks of no one but you, and the frightful Dwarf cannot persuade her to look at him.'

' Pray go on with your story,' said the King.

' What more is there to tell you ? ' replied the Mermaid. ' Bellissima was sitting in the wood when you passed, and saw you with the Fairy of the Desert, who was so cleverly disguised that the Princess took her to be prettier than herself ; you may imagine her despair, for she thought that you had fallen in love with her.'

' She believes that I love her ! ' cried the King. ' What a fatal mistake ! What is to be done to undeceive her ? '

' You know best,' answered the Mermaid, smiling kindly at him. ' When people are as much in love with one another as you two are, they don't need advice from anyone else.'

As she spoke they reached the Castle of Steel, the side next the sea being the only one which the Yellow Dwarf had left unprotected by the dreadful burning walls.

'I know quite well,' said the Mermaid, 'that the Princess is sitting by the brook-side, just where you saw her as you passed, but as you will have many enemies to fight with before you can reach her, take this sword ; armed with it you may dare any danger, and overcome the greatest difficulties, only beware of one thing— that is, never to let it fall from your hand. Farewell ; now I will wait by that rock, and if you need my help in carrying off your beloved Princess I will not fail you, for the Queen, her mother, is my best friend, and it was for her sake that I went to rescue you.'

So saying, she gave to the King a sword made from a single diamond, which was more brilliant than the sun. He could not find words to express his gratitude, but he begged her to believe that he fully appreciated the importance of her gift, and would never forget her help and kindness.

We must now go back to the Fairy of the Desert. When she found that the King did not return, she hastened out to look for him, and reached the shore, with a hundred of the ladies of her train, loaded with splendid presents for him. Some carried baskets full of diamonds, others golden cups of wonderful workmanship, and amber, coral, and pearls, others, again, balanced upon their heads bales of the richest and most beautiful stuffs, while the rest brought fruit and flowers, and even birds. But what was the horror of the Fairy, who followed this gay troop, when she saw, stretched upon the sands, the image of the King which the Mermaid had made with the sea-weeds. Struck with astonishment and sorrow, she uttered a terrible cry, and threw herself down beside the pretended King, weeping, and howling, and calling upon her eleven sisters, who were also fairies, and who came to her assistance. But they were all taken in by the image of the King, for, clever as they were, the Mermaid was still cleverer, and all they could do was to help the Fairy of the Desert to make a wonderful monument over what they thought was the grave of the King of the Gold Mines. But while they were collecting jasper and porphyry, agate and marble, gold and bronze, statues and devices, to immortalise the King's memory, he was thanking the good Mermaid and begging her still to help him, which she graciously promised to do as she disappeared ; and then he set out for the Castle of Steel. He walked fast, looking anxiously round him, and longing once more to see his darling Bellissima, but he had not gone far before he was surrounded by four terrible sphinxes who would very soon have torn him to pieces with their sharp talons if it had not been for the Mermaid's diamond sword. For, no sooner had he flashed it before their eyes than down they fell at his feet quite helpless, and he killed them with one blow. But he had hardly turned to continue his search when he met six dragons covered with scales that were harder than iron. Frightful as this encounter was the King's courage was unshaken, and by the aid of his wonderful sword he cut them in pieces one after the other. Now he hoped his difficulties were over, but at the next turning he was met by one which he did not know how to overcome. Four-and-twenty pretty and graceful nymphs advanced towards him, holding garlands of flowers, with which they barred the way.

'Where are you going, Prince?' they said; 'it is our duty to guard this place, and if we let you pass great misfortunes will happen to you and to us. We beg you not to insist upon going on. Do you want to kill four-and-twenty girls who have never displeased you in any way?'

The King did not know what to do or to say. It went against all his ideas as a knight to do anything a lady begged him not to do; but, as he hesitated, a voice in his ear said:

'Strike! strike! and do not spare, or your Princess is lost for ever!'

So, without replying to the nymphs, he rushed forward instantly, breaking their garlands, and scattering them in all directions; and then went on without further hindrance to the little wood where he had seen Bellissima. She was seated by the brook looking pale and weary when he reached her, and he would have thrown himself down at her feet, but she drew herself away from him with as much indignation as if he had been the Yellow Dwarf.

'Ah! Princess,' he cried, 'do not be angry with me. Let me explain everything. I am not faithless or to blame for what has happened. I am a miserable wretch who has displeased you without being able to help himself.'

'Ah!' cried Bellissima, 'did I not see you flying through the air with the loveliest being imaginable? Was that against your will?'

'Indeed it was, Princess,' he answered; 'the wicked Fairy of the Desert, not content with chaining me to a rock, carried me off in her chariot to the other end of the earth, where I should even now be a captive but for the unexpected help of a friendly mer-

THE KING OF THE GOLD MINES ENCOUNTERS THE FOUR-AND-TWENTY
MAIDENS.

maid, who brought me here to rescue you, my Princess, from the unworthy hands that hold you. Do not refuse the aid of your most faithful lover.' So saying, he threw himself at her feet and held her by her robe. But, alas! in so doing he let fall the magic sword, and the Yellow Dwarf, who was crouching behind a lettuce, no sooner saw it than he sprang out and seized it, well knowing its wonderful power.

The Princess gave a cry of terror on seeing the Dwarf, but this only irritated the little monster; muttering a few magical words he summoned two giants, who bound the King with great chains of iron.

'Now,' said the Dwarf, 'I am master of my rival's fate, but I will give him his life and permission to depart unharmed if you, Princess, will consent to marry me.'

'Let me die a thousand times rather,' cried the unhappy King.

'Alas!' cried the Princess, 'must you die? Could anything be more terrible?'

'That you should marry that little wretch would be far more terrible,' answered the King.

'At least,' continued she, 'let us die together.'

'Let me have the satisfaction of dying for you, my Princess,' said he.

'Oh, no, no!' she cried, turning to the Dwarf; 'rather than that I will do as you wish.'

'Cruel Princess!' said the King, 'would you make my life horrible to me by marrying another before my eyes?'

'Not so,' replied the Yellow Dwarf; 'you are a rival of whom I am too much afraid: you shall not see our marriage.' So saying, in spite of Bellissima's tears and cries, he stabbed the King to the heart with the diamond sword.

The poor Princess, seeing her lover lying dead at her feet, could no longer live without him; she sank down by him and died of a broken heart.

So ended these unfortunate lovers, whom not even the Mermaid could help, because all the magic power had been lost with the diamond sword.

As to the wicked Dwarf, he preferred to see the Princess dead rather than married to the King of the Gold Mines; and the Fairy of the Desert, when she heard of the King's adventures, pulled down the grand monument which she had built, and was so angry at the trick that had been played her that she hated him as much as she had loved him before.

The kind Mermaid, grieved at the sad fate of the lovers, caused them to be changed into two tall palm trees, which stand always side by side, whispering together of their faithful love and caressing one another with their interlacing branches.[1]

[1] Madame d'Aulnoy.

LITTLE RED RIDING-HOOD

ONCE upon a time there lived in a certain village a little country girl, the prettiest creature was ever seen. Her mother was excessively fond of her; and her grandmother doted on her still more. This good woman got made for her a little red riding-hood; which became the girl so extremely well that everybody called her Little Red Riding-Hood.

One day her mother, having made some custards, said to her:

'Go, my dear, and see how thy grandmamma does, for I hear she has been very ill; carry her a custard, and this little pot of butter.'

Little Red Riding-Hood set out immediately to go to her grandmother, who lived in another village.

As she was going through the wood, she met with Gaffer Wolf, who had a very great mind to eat her up, but he durst not, because of some faggot-makers hard by in the forest. He asked her whither she was going. The poor child, who did not know that it was dangerous to stay and hear a wolf talk, said to him:

'I am going to see my grandmamma and carry her a custard and a little pot of butter from my mamma.'

'Does she live far off?' said the Wolf.

'Oh! ay,' answered Little Red Riding-Hood; 'it is beyond that mill you see there, at the first house in the village.'

'Well,' said the Wolf, 'and I'll go and see her too. I'll go this way and go you that, and we shall see who will be there soonest.'

The Wolf began to run as fast as he could, taking the nearest way, and the little girl went by that farthest about, diverting herself in gathering nuts, running after butterflies, and making nosegays of such little flowers as she met with. The Wolf was not long before he got to the old woman's house. He knocked at the door— tap, tap.

'Who's there?'

'Your grandchild, Little Red Riding-Hood,' replied the Wolf, counterfeiting her voice; 'who has brought you a custard and a little pot of butter sent you by mamma.'

The good grandmother, who was in bed, because she was somewhat ill, cried out:

'Pull the bobbin, and the latch will go up.'

The Wolf pulled the bobbin, and the door opened, and then presently he fell upon the good woman and ate her up in a moment, for it was above three days that he had not touched a bit. He

then shut the door and went into the grandmother's bed, expecting Little Red Riding-Hood, who came some time afterwards and knocked at the door—tap, tap.

'Who's there?'

Little Red Riding-Hood, hearing the big voice of the Wolf, was at first afraid; but believing her grandmother had got a cold and was hoarse, answered:

''Tis your grandchild, Little Red Riding-Hood, who has brought you a custard and a little pot of butter mamma sends you.'

The Wolf cried out to her, softening his voice as much as he could:
' Pull the bobbin, and the latch will go up.'

Little Red Riding-Hood pulled the bobbin, and the door opened.

The Wolf, seeing her come in, said to her, hiding himself under
the bed-clothes :

' Put the custard and the little pot of butter upon the stool, and
come and lie down with me.'

Little Red Riding-Hood undressed herself and went into bed,
where, being greatly amazed to see how her grandmother looked
in her night-clothes, she said to her :

' Grandmamma, what great arms you have got ! '

' That is the better to hug thee, my dear.'
' Grandmamma, what great legs you have got ! '
' That is to run the better, my child.'
' Grandmamma, what great ears you have got ! '
' That is to hear the better, my child.'
' Grandmamma, what great eyes you have got ! '
' It is to see the better, my child.'
' Grandmamma, what great teeth you have got ! '
' That is to eat thee up.'

And, saying these words, this wicked wolf fell upon Little Red
Riding-Hood, and ate her all up.

THE SLEEPING BEAUTY IN THE WOOD

T HERE were formerly a king and a queen, who were so sorry that they had no children; so sorry that it cannot be expressed. They went to all the waters in the world; vows, pilgrimages, all ways were tried, and all to no purpose.

At last, however, the Queen had a daughter. There was a very fine christening; and the Princess had for her god-mothers all the fairies they could find in the whole kingdom (they found seven), that every one of them might give her a gift, as was the custom of fairies in those days. By this means the Princess had all the perfections imaginable.

After the ceremonies of the christening were over, all the company returned to the King's palace, where was prepared a great feast for the fairies. There was placed before every one of them a magnificent cover with a case of massive gold, wherein were a spoon, knife, and fork, all of pure gold set with diamonds and rubies. But as they were all sitting down at table they saw come into the hall a very old fairy, whom they had not invited, because it was above fifty years since she had been out of a certain tower, and she was believed to be either dead or enchanted.

The King ordered her a cover, but could not furnish her with a case of gold as the others, because they had seven only made for the seven fairies. The old Fairy fancied she was slighted, and muttered some threats between her teeth. One of the young fairies who sat by her overheard how she grumbled; and, judging that she might give the little Princess some unlucky gift, went, as soon as they rose from table, and hid herself behind the hangings, that she might speak last, and repair, as much as she could, the evil which the old Fairy might intend.

In the meanwhile all the fairies began to give their gifts to the Princess. The youngest gave her for gift that she should be the most beautiful person in the world; the next, that she should have the wit of an angel; the third, that she should have a wonderful grace in everything she did; the fourth, that she should dance perfectly well; the fifth, that she should sing like a nightingale; and the sixth, that she should play all kinds of music to the utmost perfection.

The old Fairy's turn coming next, with a head shaking more with spite than age, she said that the Princess should have her hand pierced with a spindle and die of the wound. This terrible gift made the whole company tremble, and everybody fell a-crying.

At this very instant the young Fairy came out from behind the hangings, and spake these words aloud:

'Assure yourselves, O King and Queen, that your daughter shall not die of this disaster. It is true, I have no power to undo entirely what my elder has done. The Princess shall indeed pierce her hand with a spindle; but, instead of dying, she shall only fall into a profound sleep, which shall last a hundred years, at the expiration of which a king's son shall come and awake her.'

The King, to avoid the misfortune foretold by the old Fairy, caused immediately proclamation to be made, whereby everybody was forbidden, on pain of death, to spin with a distaff and spindle, or to have so much as any spindle in their houses. About fifteen or sixteen years after, the King and Queen being gone to one of their houses of pleasure, the young Princess happened one day to divert herself in running up and down the palace ; when going up from one apartment to another, she came into a little room on the top of the tower, where a good old woman, alone, was spinning with her spindle. This good woman had never heard of the King's procla-mation against spindles.

'What are you doing there, goody ? ' said the Princess.

' I am spinning, my pretty child,' said the old woman, who did not know who she was.

' Ha ! ' said the Princess, ' this is very pretty ; how do you do it ?   Give it to me, that I may see if I can do so.'

She had no sooner taken it into her hand than, whether being very hasty at it, somewhat unhandy, or that the decree of the Fairy had so ordained it, it ran into her hand, and she fell down in a swoon.

The good old woman, not knowing very well what to do in this affair, cried out for help. People came in from every quarter in great numbers; they threw water upon the Princess's face, unlaced her, struck her on the palms of her hands, and rubbed her temples with Hungary-water; but nothing would bring her to herself.

And now the King, who came up at the noise, bethought himself of the prediction of the fairies, and, judging very well that this must necessarily come to pass, since the fairies had said it, caused the Princess to be carried into the finest apartment in his palace, and to be laid upon a bed all embroidered with gold and silver.

One would have taken her for a little angel, she was so very beautiful; for her swooning away had not diminished one bit of her complexion : her cheeks were carnation, and her lips were coral; indeed her eyes were shut, but she was heard to breathe softly, which satisfied those about her that she was not dead. The King commanded that they should not disturb her, but let her sleep quietly till her hour of awaking was come.

The good Fairy who had saved her life by condemning her to sleep a hundred years was in the kingdom of Matakin, twelve thousand leagues off, when this accident befell the Princess; but she was instantly informed of it by a little dwarf, who had boots of seven leagues, that is, boots with which he could tread over seven leagues of ground in one stride. The Fairy came away immediately, and she arrived, about an hour after, in a fiery chariot drawn by dragons.

The King handed her out of the chariot, and she approved everything he had done; but as she had very great foresight, she thought when the Princess should awake she might not know what to do with herself, being all alone in this old palace; and this was what she did: she touched with her wand everything in the palace (except the King and the Queen)—governesses, maids of honour, ladies of the bedchamber, gentlemen, officers, stewards, cooks, undercooks, scullions, guards, with their beefeaters, pages, footmen; she likewise touched all the horses which were in the stables, as well pads as others, the great dogs in the outward court and pretty little Mopsey too, the Princess's little spaniel, which lay by her on the bed.

Immediately upon her touching them they all fell asleep, that they might not awake before their mistress, and that they might be ready to wait upon her when she wanted them. The very spits at the fire, as full as they could hold of partridges and pheasants, did fall asleep also. All this was done in a moment. Fairies are not long in doing their business.

And now the King and the Queen, having kissed their dear child without waking her, went out of the palace and put forth a proclamation that nobody should dare to come near it.

This, however, was not necessary, for in a quarter of an hour's time there grew up all round about the park such a vast number of trees, great and small, bushes and brambles, twining one within another, that neither man nor beast could pass through; so that nothing could be seen but the very top of the towers of the palace; and that, too, not unless it was a good way off. Nobody doubted but the Fairy gave herein a very extraordinary sample of her art, that the Princess, while she continued sleeping, might have nothing to fear from any curious people.

When a hundred years were gone and passed the son of the King then reigning, and who was of another family from that of the sleeping Princess, being gone a-hunting on that side of the country, asked:

What those towers were which he saw in the middle of a great thick wood?

Everyone answered according as they had heard. Some said:

That it was a ruinous old castle, haunted by spirits;

Others, That all the sorcerers and witches of the country kept there their sabbath or night's meeting.

The common opinion was: That an ogre lived there, and that he carried thither all the little children he could catch, that he might eat them up at his leisure, without anybody being able to follow him, as having himself only the power to pass through the wood.

The Prince was at a stand, not knowing what to believe, when a very aged countryman spake to him thus:

' May it please your royal highness, it is now about fifty years since I heard from my father, who heard my grandfather say, that there was then in this castle a princess, the most beautiful was ever seen; that she must sleep there a hundred years, and should be waked by a king's son, for whom she was reserved.'

The young Prince was all on fire at these words, believing, without weighing the matter, that he could put an end to this rare adventure; and, pushed on by love and honour, resolved that moment to look into it.

Scarce had he advanced towards the wood when all the great

trees, the bushes, and brambles gave way of themselves to let him pass through; he walked up to the castle which he saw at the end of a large avenue which he went into; and what a little surprised him was that he saw none of his people could follow him, because the trees closed again as soon as he had passed through them. However, he did not cease from continuing his way; a young and amorous prince is always valiant.

He came into a spacious outward court, where everything he saw might have frozen up the most fearless person with horror. There reigned over all a most frightful silence; the image of death everywhere showed itself, and there was nothing to be seen but stretched-out bodies of men and animals, all seeming to be dead. He, however, very well knew, by the ruby faces and pimpled noses of the beefeaters, that they were only asleep; and their goblets, wherein still remained some drops of wine, showed plainly that they fell asleep in their cups.

He then crossed a court paved with marble, went up the stairs, and came into the guard chamber, where guards were standing in their ranks, with their muskets upon their shoulders, and snoring as loud as they could. After that he went through several rooms full of gentlemen and ladies, all asleep, some standing, others sitting. At last he came into a chamber all gilded with gold, where he saw upon a bed, the curtains of which were all open, the finest sight was ever beheld—a princess, who appeared to be about fifteen or sixteen years of age, and whose bright and, in a manner, resplendent beauty, had somewhat in it divine. He approached with trembling and admiration, and fell down before her upon his knees.

And now, as the enchantment was at an end, the Princess awaked, and looking on him with eyes more tender than the first view might seem to admit of:

'Is it you, my Prince?' said she to him. 'You have waited a long while.'

The Prince, charmed with these words, and much more with the manner in which they were spoken, knew not how to show his joy and gratitude; he assured her that he loved her better than he did himself; their discourse was not well connected, they did weep more than talk—little eloquence, a great deal of love. He was more at a loss than she, and we need not wonder at it: she had time to think on what to say to him; for it is very probable (though history mentions nothing of it) that the good Fairy, during so long a sleep, had given her very agreeable dreams. In short, they talked four hours together, and yet they said not half what they had to say.

In the meanwhile all the palace awaked; everyone thought upon their particular business, and as all of them were not in love they were ready to die for hunger. The chief lady of honour, being as sharp set as other folks, grew very impatient, and told the Princess aloud that supper was served up. The Prince helped the Princess to rise; she was entirely dressed, and very magnificently, but his royal highness took care not to tell her that she was dressed like his great-grandmother, and had a point band peeping over a high collar; she looked not a bit the less charming and beautiful for all that.

They went into the great hall of looking-glasses, where they supped, and were served by the Princess's officers; the violins and hautboys played old tunes, but very excellent, though it was now above a hundred years since they had played; and after supper, without losing any time, the lord almoner married them in the chapel of the castle, and the chief lady of honour drew the curtains. They had but very little sleep—the Princess had no occasion; and the Prince left her next morning to return into the city, where his father must needs have been in pain for him. The Prince told him:

That he lost his way in the forest as he was hunting, and that he had lain in the cottage of a charcoal-burner, who gave him cheese and brown bread.

The King, his father, who was a good man, believed him; but his mother could not be persuaded it was true; and seeing that he went almost every day a-hunting, and that he always had some excuse ready for so doing, though he had lain out three or four nights together, she began to suspect that he was married, for he lived with the Princess above two whole years, and had by her two children, the eldest of which, who was a daughter, was named *Morning*, and the youngest, who was a son, they called *Day*, because he was a great deal handsomer and more beautiful than his sister.

The Queen spoke several times to her son, to inform herself after what manner he did pass his time, and that in this he ought in duty to satisfy her. But he never dared to trust her with his secret; he feared her, though he loved her, for she was of the race of the Ogres, and the King would never have married her had it not been for her vast riches; it was even whispered about the Court that she had Ogreish inclinations, and that, whenever she saw little children passing by, she had all the difficulty in the world to avoid falling upon them. And so the Prince would never tell her one word.

But when the King was dead, which happened about two years afterwards, and he saw himself lord and master, he openly declared his marriage; and he went in great ceremony to conduct his Queen to the palace. They made a magnificent entry into the capital city, she riding between her two children.

Soon after the King went to make war with the Emperor Contalabutte, his neighbour. He left the government of the kingdom to the Queen his mother, and earnestly recommended to her care his wife and children. He was obliged to continue his expedition all the summer, and as soon as he departed the Queen-mother sent her daughter-in-law to a country house among the woods, that she might with the more ease gratify her horrible longing.

Some few days afterwards she went thither herself, and said to her clerk of the kitchen:

' I have a mind to eat little Morning for my dinner to-morrow.'

' Ah ! madam,' cried the clerk of the kitchen.

' I will have it so,' replied the Queen (and this she spoke in the tone of an Ogress who had a strong desire to eat fresh meat), ' and will eat her with a *sauce Robert*.'

The poor man, knowing very well that he must not play tricks with Ogresses, took his great knife and went up into little Morning's chamber. She was then four years old, and came up to him jumping and laughing, to take him about the neck, and ask him for some sugar-candy. Upon which he began to weep, the great knife fell out of his hand, and he went into the back yard, and killed a little lamb, and dressed it with such good sauce that his mistress assured

him she had never eaten anything so good in her life. He had at the same time taken up little Morning, and carried her to his wife, to conceal her in the lodging he had at the bottom of the court-yard.

About eight days afterwards the wicked Queen said to the clerk of the kitchen, ' I will sup upon little Day.'

He answered not a word, being resolved to cheat her as he had done before. He went to find out little Day, and saw him with a little foil in his hand, with which he was fencing with a great monkey, the child being then only three years of age. He took him up in his arms and carried him to his wife, that she might conceal him in her chamber along with his sister, and in the room of little Day cooked up a young kid, very tender, which the Ogress found to be wonderfully good.

This was hitherto all mighty well; but one evening this wicked Queen said to her clerk of the kitchen:

'I will eat the Queen with the same sauce I had with her children.'

It was now that the poor clerk of the kitchen despaired of being able to deceive her. The young Queen was turned of twenty, not reckoning the hundred years she had been asleep; and how to find in the yard a beast so firm was what puzzled him. He took then a resolution, that he might save his own life, to cut the Queen's throat; and going up into her chamber, with intent to do it at once, he put himself into as great fury as he could possibly, and came into the young Queen's room with his dagger in his hand. He would not, however, surprise her, but told her, with a great deal of respect, the orders he had received from the Queen-mother.

'Do it; do it' (said she, stretching out her neck). 'Execute your orders, and then I shall go and see my children, my poor children, whom I so much and so tenderly loved.'

For she thought them dead ever since they had been taken away without her knowledge.

'No, no, madam' (cried the poor clerk of the kitchen, all in tears); 'you shall not die, and yet you shall see your children again; but then you must go home with me to my lodgings, where I have concealed them, and I shall deceive the Queen once more, by giving her in your stead a young hind.'

Upon this he forthwith conducted her to his chamber, where, leaving her to embrace her children, and cry along with them, he went and dressed a young hind, which the Queen had for her supper, and devoured it with the same appetite as if it had been the young Queen. Exceedingly was she delighted with her cruelty, and she had invented a story to tell the King, at his return, how the mad wolves had eaten up the Queen his wife and her two children.

One evening, as she was, according to her custom, rambling round about the courts and yards of the palace to see if she could smell any fresh meat, she heard, in a ground room, little Day crying, for his mamma was going to whip him, because he had been naughty; and she heard, at the same time, little Morning begging pardon for her brother.

The Ogress presently knew the voice of the Queen and her children, and being quite mad that she had been thus deceived, she commanded next morning, by break of day (with a most horrible voice, which made everybody tremble), that they should bring into the middle of the great court a large tub, which she caused to be filled with toads, vipers, snakes, and all sorts of serpents, in order to have thrown into it the Queen and her children, the clerk of the kitchen, his wife and maid; all whom she had given orders should be brought thither with their hands tied behind them.

They were brought out accordingly, and the executioners were just going to throw them into the tub, when the King (who was not so soon expected) entered the court on horseback (for he came post) and asked, with the utmost astonishment, what was the meaning of that horrible spectacle.

No one dared to tell him, when the Ogress, all enraged to see what had happened, threw herself head foremost into the tub, and was instantly devoured by the ugly creatures she had ordered to be thrown into it for others. The King could not but be very sorry, for she was his mother; but he soon comforted himself with his beautiful wife and his pretty children.

CINDERELLA

OR THE LITTLE GLASS SLIPPER

ONCE there was a gentleman who married, for his second wife, the proudest and most haughty woman that was ever seen. She had, by a former husband, two daughters of her own humour, who were, indeed, exactly like her in all things. He had likewise, by another wife, a young daughter, but of unparalleled goodness and sweetness of temper, which she took from her mother, who was the best creature in the world.

No sooner were the ceremonies of the wedding over but the mother-in-law began to show herself in her true c'olours. She could not bear the good qualities of this pretty girl, and the less because they made her own daughters appear the more odious. She employed her in the meanest work of the house : she scoured the dishes, tables, etc., and rubbed madam's chamber, and those of misses, her daughters; she lay up in a sorry garret, upon a wretched straw bed, while her sisters lay in fine rooms, with floors all inlaid, upon beds of the very newest fashion, and where they had looking-glasses so large that they might see themselves at their full length from head to foot.

The poor girl bore all patiently, and dared not tell her father, who would have rattled her off; for his wife governed him entirely. When she had done her work, she used to go into the chimney-corner, and sit down among cinders and ashes, which made her commonly be called *Cinderwench*; but the youngest, who was not so rude and uncivil as the eldest, called her Cinderella. However, Cinderella, notwithstanding her mean apparel, was a hundred times handsomer than her sisters, though they were always dressed very richly.

It happened that the King's son gave a ball, and invited all persons of fashion to it. Our young misses were also invited, for they cut a very grand figure among the quality. They were mightily delighted at this invitation, and wonderfully busy in choosing out such gowns, petticoats, and head-clothes as might become them. This was a new trouble to Cinderella; for it was she who ironed her sister's linen, and plaited their ruffles; they talked all day long of nothing but how they should be dressed.

G.P.J.H

'For my part,' said the eldest, 'I will wear my red velvet suit with French trimming.'

'And I,' said the youngest, 'shall have my usual petticoat; but then, to make amends for that, I will put on my gold-flowered manteau, and my diamond stomacher, which is far from being the most ordinary one in the world.'

They sent for the best tire-woman they could get to make up their head-dresses and adjust their double pinners, and they had their red brushes and patches from Mademoiselle de la Poche.

Cinderella was likewise called up to them to be consulted in all these matters, for she had excellent notions, and advised them always for the best, nay, and offered her services to dress their heads, which they were very willing she should do. As she was doing this, they said to her:

'Cinderella, would you not be glad to go to the ball?'

'Alas!' said she, 'you only jeer me; it is not for such as I am to go thither.'

'Thou art in the right of it,' replied they; 'it would make the people laugh to see a Cinderwench at a ball.'

Anyone but Cinderella would have dressed their heads awry, but she was very good, and dressed them perfectly well. They were almost two days without eating, so much they were transported with joy. They broke above a dozen of laces in trying to be laced up close, that they might have a fine slender shape, and they were continually at their looking-glass. At last the happy day came; they went to Court, and Cinderella followed them with her eyes as long as she could, and when she had lost sight of them, she fell a-crying.

Her godmother, who saw her all in tears, asked her what was the matter.

'I wish I could—I wish I could—;' she was not able to speak the rest, being interrupted by her tears and sobbing.

This godmother of hers, who was a fairy, said to her, 'Thou wishest thou couldst go to the ball; is it not so?'

'Y—es,' cried Cinderella, with a great sigh.

'Well,' said her godmother, 'be but a good girl, and I will contrive that thou shalt go.' Then she took her into her chamber, and said to her, 'Run into the garden, and bring me a pumpkin.'

Cinderella went immediately to gather the finest she could get, and brought it to her godmother, not being able to imagine how this pumpkin could make her go to the ball. Her godmother scooped out all the inside of it, having left nothing but the rind; which done, she struck it with her wand, and the pumpkin was instantly turned into a fine coach, gilded all over with gold.

She then went to look into her mouse-trap, where she found six mice, all alive, and ordered Cinderella to lift up a little the trap-door, when, giving each mouse, as it went out, a little tap with her wand, the mouse was that moment turned into a fine horse, which altogether made a very fine set of six horses of a beautiful mouse-coloured dapple-grey.   Being at a loss for a coachman,

'I will go and see,' says Cinderella, 'if there is never a rat in the rat-trap—we may make a coachman of him.'

'Thou art in the right,' replied her godmother; 'go and look.'

Cinderella brought the trap to her, and in it there were three

huge rats.   The fairy made choice of one of the three which had the largest beard, and, having touched him with her wand, he was turned into a fat, jolly coachman, who had the smartest whiskers eyes ever beheld.   After that, she said to her:

'Go again into the garden, and you will find six lizards behind the watering-pot, bring them to me.'

She had no sooner done so but her godmother turned them into six footmen, who skipped up immediately behind the coach, with their liveries all bedaubed with gold and silver, and clung as close behind each other as if they had done nothing else their whole lives. The Fairy then said to Cinderella :

'Well, you see here an equipage fit to go to the ball with ; are you not pleased with it ? '

'Oh! yes,' cried she; 'but must I go thither as I am, in these nasty rags ? '

Her godmother only just touched her with her wand, and, at the same instant, her clothes were turned into cloth of gold and silver, all beset with jewels. This done, she gave her a pair of glass slippers, the prettiest in the whole world. Being thus decked out, she got up into her coach ; but her godmother, above all things, commanded her not to stay till after midnight, telling her, at the same time, that if she stayed one moment longer, the coach would be a pumpkin again, her horses mice, her coachman a rat, her footmen lizards, and her clothes become just as they were before.

She promised her godmother she would not fail of leaving the ball before midnight; and then away she drives, scarce able to contain herself for joy. The King's son, who was told that a great princess, whom nobody knew, was come, ran out to receive her ; he gave her his hand as she alighted out of the coach, and led her into the hall, among all the company. There was immediately a profound silence, they left off dancing, and the violins ceased to play, so attentive was everyone to contemplate the singular beauties of the unknown new-comer. Nothing was then heard but a confused noise of :

'Ha! how handsome she is! Ha! how handsome she is ! '

The King himself, old as he was, could not help watching her, and telling the Queen softly that it was a long time since he had seen so beautiful and lovely a creature.

All the ladies were busied in considering her clothes and headdress, that they might have some made next day after the same pattern, provided they could meet with such fine materials and as able hands to make them.

The King's son conducted her to the most honourable seat, and afterwards took her out to dance with him ; she danced so very gracefully that they all more and more admired her. A fine collation was served up, whereof the young prince ate not a morsel, so intently was he busied in gazing on her.

She went and sat down by her sisters, showing them a thousand civilities, giving them part of the oranges and citrons which the

Prince had presented her with, which very much surprised them, for they did not know her. While Cinderella was thus amusing her sisters, she heard the clock strike eleven and three-quarters, whereupon she immediately made a courtesy to the company and hasted away as fast as she could.

Being got home, she ran to seek out her godmother, and, after having thanked her, she said she could not but heartily wish she might go next day to the ball, because the King's son had desired her.

As she was eagerly telling her godmother whatever had passed at the ball, her two sisters knocked at the door, which Cinderella ran and opened.

'How long you have stayed!' cried she, gaping, rubbing her eyes and stretching herself as if she had been just waked out of her sleep; she had not, however, any manner of inclination to sleep since they went from home.

'If thou hadst been at the ball,' says one of her sisters, 'thou wouldst not have been tired with it. There came thither the finest princess, the most beautiful ever was seen with mortal eyes; she showed us a thousand civilities, and gave us oranges and citrons.'

Cinderella seemed very indifferent in the matter; indeed, she asked them the name of that princess; but they told her they did not know it, and that the King's son was very uneasy on her account and would give all the world to know who she was. At this Cinderella, smiling, replied:

'She must, then, be very beautiful indeed; how happy you have been! Could not I see her? Ah! dear Miss Charlotte, do lend me your yellow suit of clothes which you wear every day.'

'Ay, to be sure!' cried Miss Charlotte; 'lend my clothes to such a dirty Cinderwench as thou art! I should be a fool.'

Cinderella, indeed, expected well such answer, and was very glad of the refusal; for she would have been sadly put to it if her sister had lent her what she asked for jestingly.

The next day the two sisters were at the ball, and so was Cinderella, but dressed more magnificently than before. The King's son was always by her, and never ceased his compliments and kind speeches to her; to whom all this was so far from being tiresome that she quite forgot what her godmother had recommended to her; so that she, at last, counted the clock striking twelve when she took it to be no more than eleven; she then rose up and fled, as nimble as a deer. The Prince followed, but could not overtake her. She left behind one of her glass slippers, which the Prince took up most carefully. She got home, but quite out of breath, and in her nasty old clothes, having nothing left her of all her finery but one of the little slippers, fellow to that she dropped. The guards at the palace gate were asked:

If they had not seen a princess go out.

Who said: They had seen nobody go out but a young girl, very meanly dressed, and who had more the air of a poor country wench than a gentlewoman.

When the two sisters returned from the ball Cinderella asked them: If they had been well diverted, and if the fine lady had been there.

They told her: Yes, but that she hurried away immediately when it struck twelve, and with so much haste that she dropped one of her little glass slippers, the prettiest in the world, which the King's son had taken up; that he had done nothing but look at her all the time at the ball, and that most certainly he was very much in love with the beautiful person who owned the glass slipper.

What they said was very true; for a few days after the King's son caused it to be proclaimed, by sound of trumpet, that he would marry her whose foot this slipper would just fit. They whom he employed began to try it upon the princesses, then the duchesses and all the Court, but in vain; it was brought to the two sisters, who did all they possibly could to thrust their foot into the slipper, but they could not effect it. Cinderella, who saw all this, and knew her slipper, said to them, laughing:

' Let me see if it will not fit me.'

Her sisters burst out a-laughing, and began to banter her. The gentleman who was sent to try the slipper looked earnestly at Cinderella, and, finding her very handsome, said:

It was but just that she should try, and that he had orders to let everyone make trial.

He obliged Cinderella to sit down, and, putting the slipper to her foot, he found it went on very easily, and fitted her as if it had been made of wax. The astonishment her two sisters were in was excessively great, but still abundantly greater when Cinderella pulled out of her pocket the other slipper, and put it on her foot. Thereupon, in came her godmother, who, having touched with her wand Cinderella's clothes, made them richer and more magnificent than any of those she had before.

And now her two sisters found her to be that fine. beautiful lady

CINDERELLA'S FLIGHT.

whom they had seen at the ball.   They threw themselves at her feet to beg pardon for all the ill-treatment they had made her undergo.   Cinderella took them up, and, as she embraced them, cried :

That she forgave them with all her heart, and desired them always to love her.

She was conducted to the young Prince, dressed as she was ; he thought her more charming than ever, and, a few days after, married her.   Cinderella, who was no less good than beautiful, gave her two sisters lodgings in the palace, and that very same day matched them with two great lords of the Court.[1]

[1] Charles Perrault.

ALADDIN AND THE WONDERFUL LAMP

THERE once lived a poor tailor, who had a son called Aladdin, a careless, idle boy who would do nothing but play all day long in the streets with little idle boys like himself. This so grieved the father that he died; yet, in spite of his mother's tears and prayers, Aladdin did not mend his ways. One day, when he was playing in the streets as usual, a stranger asked him his age, and if he was not the son of Mustapha the tailor. 'I am, sir,' replied Aladdin; 'but he died a long while ago.' On this the stranger, who was a famous African magician, fell on his neck and kissed him, saying: 'I am your uncle, and knew you from your likeness to my brother. Go to your mother and tell her I am coming.' Aladdin ran home and told his mother of his newly found uncle. 'Indeed, child,' she said, 'your father had a brother, but I always thought he was dead.' However, she prepared supper, and bade Aladdin seek his uncle, who came laden with wine and fruit. He presently fell down and kissed the place where Mustapha used to sit, bidding Aladdin's mother not to be surprised at not having seen him before, as he had been forty years out of the country. He then turned to Aladdin, and asked him his trade, at which the boy hung his head, while his mother burst into tears. On learning that Aladdin was idle and would learn no trade, he offered to take a shop for him and stock it with merchandise. Next day he bought Aladdin a fine suit of clothes and took him all over the city, showing him the sights, and brought him home at nightfall to his mother, who was overjoyed to see her son so fine.

Next day the magician led Aladdin into some beautiful gardens a long way outside the city gates. They sat down by a fountain and the magician pulled a cake from his girdle, which he divided between them. They then journeyed onwards till they almost reached the mountains. Aladdin was so tired that he begged to go back, but the magician beguiled him with pleasant stories, and led him on in spite of himself. At last they came to two mountains divided by a narrow valley. 'We will go no farther,' said the false uncle. 'I will show you something wonderful; only do you gather up sticks while I kindle a fire.' When it was lit the magician threw

on it a powder he had about him, at the same time saying some magical words. The earth trembled a little and opened in front of them, disclosing a square flat stone with a brass ring in the middle to raise it by. Aladdin tried to run away, but the magician caught him and gave him a blow that knocked him down. 'What have I done, uncle?' he said piteously; whereupon the magician said more kindly: 'Fear nothing, but obey me. Beneath this stone lies a treasure which is to be yours, and no one else may touch it, so you must do exactly as I tell you.' At the word treasure Aladdin forgot his fears, and grasped the ring

as he was told, saying the names of his father and grandfather. The stone came up quite easily, and some steps appeared. 'Go down,' said the magician; 'at the foot of those steps you will find an open door leading into three large halls. Tuck up your gown and go through them without touching anything, or you will die instantly. These halls lead into a garden of fine fruit trees. Walk on till you come to a niche in a terrace where stands a lighted lamp. Pour out the oil it contains, and bring it me.' He drew a ring from his finger and gave it to Aladdin, bidding him prosper.

Aladdin found everything as the magician had said, gathered some fruit off the trees, and, having got the lamp, arrived at the mouth of the cave. The magician cried out in a great hurry: 'Make haste and give me the lamp.' This Aladdin refused to do until he was out of the cave. The magician flew into a terrible passion, and throwing some more powder on to the fire, he said something, and the stone rolled back into its place.

The magician left Persia for ever, which plainly showed that he was no uncle of Aladdin's, but a cunning magician, who had read in his magic books of a wonderful lamp, which would make him the most powerful man in the world. Though he alone knew where to find it, he could only receive it from the hand of another. He had picked out the foolish Aladdin for this purpose, intending to get the lamp and kill him afterwards.

For two days Aladdin remained in the dark, crying and lamenting. At last he clasped his hands in prayer, and in so doing rubbed the ring, which the magician had forgotten to take from him. Immediately an enormous and frightful genie rose out of the earth, saying : ' What wouldst thou with me ? I am the Slave of the Ring, and will obey thee in all things.' Aladdin fearlessly replied : ' Deliver me from this place ! ' whereupon the earth opened, and he found himself outside. As soon as his eyes could bear the light he went home, but fainted on the threshold. When he came to himself he told his mother what had passed, and showed her the lamp and the fruits he had gathered in the garden, which were in reality precious stones. He then asked for some food. ' Alas ! child,' she said, ' I have nothing in the house, but I have spun a little cotton and will go and sell it.' Aladdin bade her keep her cotton, for he would sell the lamp instead. As it was very dirty she began to rub it, that it might fetch a higher price. Instantly a hideous genie appeared, and asked what she would have. She fainted away, but Aladdin, snatching the lamp, said boldly : ' Fetch me something to eat ! ' The genie returned with a silver bowl, twelve silver plates containing rich meats, two silver cups, and two bottles of wine. Aladdin's mother, when she came to herself, said : ' Whence comes this splendid feast ? ' ' Ask not, but eat,' replied Aladdin. So they sat at breakfast till it was dinner-time, and Aladdin told his mother about the lamp. She begged him to sell it, and have nothing to do with devils. ' No,' said Aladdin, ' since chance hath made us aware of its virtues, we will use it, and the ring likewise, which I shall always wear on my finger.' When they had eaten all the genie had brought Aladdin sold one of the silver plates, and so on until none were left He then had recourse to the genie, who gave him another set of plates, and thus they lived for many years.

One day Aladdin heard an order from the Sultan proclaimed that everyone was to stay at home and close his shutters while the Princess, his daughter, went to and from the bath. Aladdin was seized by a desire to see her face, which was very difficult, as she always went veiled. He hid himself behind the door of the bath, and peeped through a chink. The Princess lifted her veil as she went in, and looked so beautiful that Aladdin fell in love with her at first sight. He went home so changed that his mother was frightened. He told her he loved the Princess so deeply that he

could not live without her, and meant to ask her in marriage of her father. His mother, on hearing this, burst out laughing, but Aladdin at last prevailed upon her to go before the Sultan and carry his request. She fetched a napkin and laid in it the magic fruits from the enchanted garden, which sparkled and shone like the most beautiful jewels. She took these with her to please the Sultan, and set out, trusting in the lamp. The Grand Vizier and the lords of council had just gone in as she entered the hall and placed herself in front of the Sultan. He, however, took no notice of her.

She went every day for a week, and stood in the same place. When the council broke up on the sixth day the Sultan said to his Vizier: 'I see a certain woman in the audience-chamber every day carrying something in a napkin. Call her next time, that I may find out what she wants.' Next day, at a sign from the Vizier, she went up to the foot of the throne and remained kneeling till the Sultan said to her: 'Rise, good woman, and tell me what you want.' She hesitated, so the Sultan sent away all but the Vizier, and bade her speak freely, promising to forgive her beforehand for anything she might say. She then told him of her son's violent love for the Princess. 'I prayed him to forget her,' she said, 'but in vain; he threatened to do some desperate deed if I refused to go and ask your Majesty for the hand of the Princess. Now I pray you to forgive not me alone, but my son Aladdin.' The Sultan asked her kindly what she had in the napkin, whereupon she unfolded the jewels and presented them. He was thunderstruck, and turning to the Vizier said: 'What sayest thou? Ought I not to bestow the Princess on one who values her at such a price?' The Vizier, who wanted her for his own son, begged the Sultan to withhold her for three months, in the course of which he hoped his son would contrive to make him a richer present. The Sultan granted this, and told Aladdin's mother that, though he consented to the marriage, she must not appear before him again for three months.

Aladdin waited patiently for nearly three months, but after two had elapsed his mother, going into the city to buy oil, found every one rejoicing, and asked what was going on. 'Do you not know,' was the answer, 'that the son of the Grand Vizier is to marry the Sultan's daughter to-night?' Breathless, she ran and told Aladdin, who was overwhelmed at first, but presently bethought him of the lamp. He rubbed it, and the genie appeared, saying: 'What is thy will?' Aladdin replied: 'The Sultan, as thou knowest, has broken his promise to me, and the Vizier's son is to have the Princess. My command is that to-night you bring hither the bride and bride-groom.' 'Master, I obey,' said the genie. Aladdin then went to his chamber, where, sure enough, at midnight the genie transported the bed containing the Vizier's son and the Princess. 'Take this new-married man,' he said, 'and put him outside in the cold, and return at daybreak.' Whereupon the genie took the Vizier's son out of bed, leaving Aladdin with the Princess. 'Fear nothing,' Aladdin said to her; 'you are my wife, promised to me by your unjust father, and no harm shall come to you.' The Princess was too frightened to speak, and passed the most miserable night of her life, while Aladdin lay down beside her and slept soundly. At the appointed hour the genie fetched in the shivering bridegroom, laid him in his place, and transported the bed back to the palace.

Presently the Sultan came to wish his daughter good-morning. The unhappy Vizier's son jumped up and hid himself, while the Princess would not say a word, and was very sorrowful. The Sultan sent her mother to her, who said: 'How comes it, child, that you will not speak to your father? What has happened?' The Princess sighed deeply, and at last told her mother how, during the night, the bed had been carried into some strange house, and what had passed there. Her mother did not believe her in the least, but bade her rise and consider it an idle dream.

The following night exactly the same thing happened, and next morning, on the Princess's refusing to speak, the Sultan threatened to cut off her head. She then confessed all, bidding him ask the Vizier's son if it were not so. The Sultan told the Vizier to ask his son, who owned the truth, adding that, dearly as he loved the Princess, he had rather die than go through another such fearful night, and wished to be separated from her. His wish was granted, and there was an end of feasting and rejoicing.

When the three months were over, Aladdin sent his mother to remind the Sultan of his promise. She stood in the same place as before, and the Sultan, who had forgotten Aladdin, at once remembered him, and sent for her. On seeing her poverty the Sultan felt less inclined than ever to keep his word, and asked his Vizier's advice, who counselled him to set so high a value on the Princess that no man living could come up to it. The Sultan then turned to Aladdin's mother, saying: 'Good woman, a sultan must remember his promises, and I will remember mine, but your son must first send me forty basins of gold brimful of jewels, carried by forty black slaves, led by as many white ones, splendidly dressed. Tell him that I await his answer.' The mother of Aladdin bowed low and went home, thinking all was lost. She gave Aladdin the message, adding: 'He may wait long enough for your answer!' 'Not so long, mother, as you think,' her son replied. 'I would do a great deal more than that for the Princess.' He summoned the genie, and in a few moments the eighty slaves arrived, and filled up the small house and garden. Aladdin made them set out to the palace, two and two, followed by his mother. They were so richly dressed, with such splendid jewels in their girdles, that everyone crowded to see them and the basins of gold they carried on their heads. They entered the palace, and, after kneeling before the Sultan, stood in a half-circle round the throne with their arms crossed, while Aladdin's mother presented them to the Sultan. He hesitated no longer, but said : 'Good woman, return and tell your son that I wait for him with open arms.' She lost no time in telling Aladdin, bidding him make haste. But Aladdin first called the genie. 'I want a scented bath,' he said, ' a richly embroidered habit, a horse surpassing the Sultan's, and twenty slaves to attend me. Besides this, six slaves, beautifully dressed, to wait on my mother ; and lastly, ten thousand pieces of

gold in ten purses.' No sooner said than done. Aladdin mounted his horse and passed through the streets, the slaves strewing gold as they went. Those who had played with him in his childhood knew him not, he had grown so handsome. When the Sultan saw him he came down from his throne, embraced him, and led him into a hall where a feast was spread, intending to marry him to the Princess that very day. But Aladdin refused, saying, 'I must build a palace fit for her,' and took his leave. Once home, he said to the genie : 'Build me a palace of the finest marble, set with jasper, agate, and other precious stones. In the middle you shall build me a large hall with a dome, its four walls of massy gold and silver, each side having six windows, whose lattices, all except one which is to be left unfinished, must be set with diamonds and rubies. There must be stables and horses and grooms and slaves ; go and see about it ! '

The palace was finished by next day, and the genie carried him there and showed him all his orders faithfully carried out, even to the laying of a velvet carpet from Aladdin's palace to the Sultan's. Aladdin's mother then dressed herself carefully, and walked to the palace with her slaves, while he followed her on horseback. The Sultan sent musicians with trumpets and cymbals to meet them, so that the air resounded with music and cheers. She was taken to the Princess, who saluted her and treated her with great honour. At night the Princess said good-bye to her father, and set out on the carpet for Aladdin's palace, with his mother at her side, and followed by the hundred slaves. She was charmed at the sight of Aladdin, who ran to receive her. ' Princess,' he said, ' blame your beauty for my boldness if I have displeased you.' She told him that, having seen him, she willingly obeyed her father in this matter. After the wedding had taken place Aladdin led her into the hall, where a feast was spread, and she supped with him, after which they danced till midnight.

Next day Aladdin invited the Sultan to see the palace. On entering the hall with the four-and-twenty windows, with their rubies, diamonds, and emeralds, he cried : ' It is a world's wonder ! There is only one thing that surprises me. Was it by accident that one window was left unfinished ? ' ' No, sir, by design,' returned Aladdin. ' I wished your Majesty to have the glory of finishing this palace.' The Sultan was pleased, and sent for the best jewellers in the city. He showed them the unfinished window, and bade them fit it up like the others. ' Sir,' replied their spokesman, ' we cannot find jewels enough.' The Sultan had his own fetched, which they soon used, but to no purpose, for in a month's time the work was not half done. Aladdin, knowing that their task was vain, bade them undo their work and carry the jewels back, and the genie finished the window at his command. The Sultan was surprised to receive his jewels again, and visited Aladdin, who showed him the window finished. The Sultan embraced him, the envious Vizier meanwhile hinting that it was the work of enchantment.

Aladdin had won the hearts of the people by his gentle bearing. He was made captain of the Sultan's armies, and won several battles for him, but remained modest and courteous as before, and lived thus in peace and content for several years.

But far away in Africa the magician remembered Aladdin, and by his magic arts discovered that Aladdin, instead of perishing miserably in the cave, had escaped, and had married a princess, with whom he was living in great honour and wealth. He knew that the poor tailor's son could only have accomplished this by means of the lamp, and travelled night and day till he reached the capital of China, bent on Aladdin's ruin. As he passed through the town he heard people talking everywhere about a marvellous palace. 'Forgive my ignorance,' he asked, 'what is this palace you speak of?' 'Have you not heard of Prince Aladdin's palace,' was the reply, 'the greatest wonder of the world? I will direct you if you have a mind to see it.' The magician thanked him who spoke, and having seen the palace knew that it had been raised by the Genie of the Lamp, and became half mad with rage. He determined to get hold of the lamp, and again plunge Aladdin into the deepest poverty.

Unluckily, Aladdin had gone a-hunting for eight days, which gave the magician plenty of time. He bought a dozen copper lamps, put them into a basket, and went to the palace, crying: 'New lamps for old!' followed by a jeering crowd. The Princess, sitting in the hall of four-and-twenty windows, sent a slave to find out what the noise was about, who came back laughing, so that the Princess scolded her. 'Madam,' replied the slave, 'who can help laughing to see an old fool offering to exchange fine new lamps for old ones?' Another slave, hearing this, said: 'There is an old one on the cornice there which he can have.' Now this was the magic lamp, which Aladdin had left there, as he could not take it out hunting with him. The Princess, not knowing its value, laughingly bade the slave take it and make the exchange. She went and said to the magician: 'Give me a new lamp for this.' He snatched it and bade the slave take her choice, amid the jeers of the crowd. Little he cared, but left off crying his lamps, and went out of the city gates to a lonely place, where he remained till nightfall, when he pulled out the lamp and rubbed it. The genie appeared, and at the magician's command carried him, together with the palace and the Princess in it, to a lonely place in Africa.

Next morning the Sultan looked out of the window towards Aladdin's palace and rubbed his eyes, for it was gone. He sent for the Vizier and asked what had become of the palace. The Vizier looked out too, and was lost in astonishment. He again put it down to enchantment, and this time the Sultan believed him, and sent thirty men on horseback to fetch Aladdin in chains. They met him riding home, bound him, and forced him to go with them on foot. The people, however, who loved him, followed, armed, to see that he came to no harm. He was carried before the Sultan, who ordered the executioner to cut off his head. The executioner made Aladdin kneel down, bandaged his eyes, and raised his scimitar to strike. At that instant the Vizier, who saw that the crowd had forced their way into the courtyard and were scaling the walls to rescue Aladdin, called to the executioner to stay his hand. The people, indeed, looked so threatening that the Sultan gave way and ordered Aladdin to be unbound, and pardoned him in the sight of the crowd. Aladdin now begged to know what he had done. 'False wretch!' said the Sultan, 'come hither,' and showed him from the window the place where his palace had stood. Aladdin was so amazed that he could not say a word. 'Where is my palace and my daughter?' demanded the Sultan. 'For the first I am not so deeply concerned, but my daughter I must have, and you must find her or lose your head.' Aladdin begged for forty days in which to find her, promising if he failed to return and suffer death at the Sultan's pleasure. His prayer was granted, and he went forth sadly from the Sultan's presence. For three days he wandered about like a madman, asking everyone what had become of his palace, but they only laughed and pitied him. He came to the banks of a river, and knelt down to say his prayers before throwing himself in. In so doing he rubbed the magic ring he still wore. The genie he had seen in the cave appeared, and asked his will. 'Save my life, genie,' said Aladdin, 'and bring my palace back.' 'That is not in my power,' said the genie; 'I am only the Slave of the Ring; you must ask him of the lamp.' 'Even so,' said Aladdin, 'but thou canst take me to the palace, and set me down under my dear wife's window.' He at once found himself in Africa, under the window of the Princess, and fell asleep out of sheer weariness.

He was awakened by the singing of the birds, and his heart was lighter. He saw plainly that all his misfortunes were owing to the loss of the lamp, and vainly wondered who had robbed him of it.

That morning the Princess rose earlier than she had done since she had been carried into Africa by the magician, whose company she was forced to endure once a day. She, however, treated him so harshly that he dared not live there altogether. As she was dress-

ing, one of her women looked out and saw Aladdin. The Princess
ran and opened the window, and at the noise she made Aladdin
looked up. She called to him to come to her, and great was the joy

of these lovers at seeing
each other again. After
he had kissed her Aladdin
said : ' I beg of you, Princess, in God's name, be-
fore we speak of anything
else, for your own sake
and mine, tell me what
has become of an old lamp
I left on the cornice in the
hall of four-and-twenty
windows, when I went
a-hunting.' ' Alas ! ' she
said, ' I am the innocent
cause of our sorrows,' and
told him of the exchange
of the lamp. ' Now I
know,' cried Aladdin, ' that
we have to thank the
African magician for this !
Where is the lamp ? ' ' He
carries it about with him,'
said the Princess. ' I know,
for he pulled it out of his
breast to show me.   He

wishes me to break my faith with you and marry him, saying
that you were beheaded by my father's command. He is for
ever speaking ill of you, but I only reply by my tears. If I
persist, I doubt not but he will use violence.' Aladdin comforted
her, and left her for a while. He changed clothes with the first
person he met in the town, and having bought a certain powder
returned to the Princess, who let him in by a little side door.
' Put on your most beautiful dress,' he said to her, ' and receive
the magician with smiles, leading him to believe that you have
forgotten me. Invite him to sup with you, and say you wish
to taste the wine of his country. He will go for some and
while he is gone I will tell you what to do.' She listened carefully to Aladdin and when he left her arrayed herself gaily

for the first time since she left China. She put on a girdle and head-dress of diamonds, and, seeing in a glass that she was more beautiful than ever, received the magician, saying, to his great amazement: ' I have made up my mind that Aladdin is dead, and that all my tears will not bring him back to me, so I am resolved to mourn no more, and have therefore invited you to sup with me ; but I am tired of the wines of China, and would fain taste those of Africa.' The magician flew to his cellar, and the Princess put the powder Aladdin had given her in her cup. When he returned she asked him to drink her health in the wine of Africa, handing him her cup in exchange for his, as a sign she was reconciled to him. Before drinking the magician made her a speech in praise of her beauty, but the Princess cut him short, saying : ' Let us drink first, and you shall say what you will afterwards.' She set her cup to her lips and kept it there, while the magician drained his to the dregs and fell back lifeless. The Princess then opened the door to Aladdin, and flung her arms round his neck ; but Aladdin put her away, bidding her leave him, as he had more to do. He then went to the dead magician, took the lamp out of his vest, and bade the genie carry the palace and all in it back to China. This was done, and the Princess in her chamber only felt two little shocks, and little thought she was at home again.

The Sultan, who was sitting in his closet, mourning for his lost daughter, happened to look up, and rubbed his eyes, for there stood the palace as before ! He hastened thither, and Aladdin received him in the hall of the four-and-twenty windows, with the Princess at his side. Aladdin told him what had happened, and showed him the dead body of the magician, that he might believe. A ten days' feast was proclaimed, and it seemed as if Aladdin might now live the rest of his life in peace ; but it was not to be.

The African magician had a younger brother, who was, if possible, more wicked and more cunning than himself. He travelled to China to avenge his brother's death, and went to visit a pious woman called Fatima, thinking she might be of use to him. He entered her cell and clapped a dagger to her breast, telling her to rise and do his bidding on pain of death. He changed clothes with her, coloured his face like hers, put on her veil, and murdered her, that she might tell no tales. Then he went towards the palace of Aladdin, and all the people, thinking he was the holy woman, gathered round him, kissing his hands and begging his blessing. When he got to the palace there was such a noise going on round him that the Princess bade her slave look out of the window and ask what was the matter. The slave said it was the holy woman, curing people by her touch of their ailments, whereupon the Princess, who had long desired to see Fatima, sent for her. On coming to the Princess the magician offered up a prayer for her health and prosperity. When he had done the Princess made him sit by her, and begged him to stay with her always. The false Fatima, who wished for nothing better, consented, but kept his veil

down for fear of discovery. The Princess showed him the hall, and asked him what he thought of it. 'It is truly beautiful,' said the false Fatima. 'In my mind it wants but one thing.' 'And what is that?' said the Princess. 'If only a roc's egg,' replied he, 'were hung up from the middle of this dome, it would be the wonder of the world.'

After this the Princess could think of nothing but the roc's egg, and when Aladdin returned from hunting he found her in a very ill humour. He begged to know what was amiss, and she told him that all her pleasure in the hall was spoilt for the want of a roc's egg hanging from the dome. 'If that is all,' replied Aladdin, 'you shall soon be happy.' He left her and rubbed the lamp, and when the genie appeared commanded him to bring a roc's egg. The genie gave such a loud and terrible shriek that the hall shook. 'Wretch!' he cried, 'is it not enough that I have done everything for you, but you must command me to bring my master and hang him up in the midst of this dome? You and your wife and your palace deserve to be burnt to ashes, but that this request does not come from you, but from the brother of the African magician, whom you destroyed. He is now in your palace disguised as the holy woman—whom he murdered. He it was who put that wish into your wife's head. Take care of yourself, for he means to kill you.' So saying, the genie disappeared.

Aladdin went back to the Princess, saying his head ached, and requesting that the holy Fatima should be fetched to lay her hands on it. But when the magician came near, Aladdin, seizing his dagger, pierced him to the heart. 'What have you done?' cried the Princess. 'You have killed the holy woman!' 'Not so,' replied Aladdin, 'but a wicked magician,' and told her of how she had been deceived.

After this Aladdin and his wife lived in peace. He succeeded the Sultan when he died, and reigned for many years, leaving behind him a long line of kings.[1]

[1] Arabian Nights.

THE TALE OF A YOUTH WHO SET OUT TO LEARN WHAT FEAR WAS

A FATHER had two sons, of whom the eldest was clever and bright, and always knew what he was about ; but the youngest was stupid, and couldn't learn or understand anything. So much so that those who saw him exclaimed : ' What a burden he'll be to his father ! ' Now when there was anything to be done, the eldest had always to do it ; but if something was required late or in the night-time, and the way led through the churchyard or some such ghostly place, he always replied : ' Oh ! no, father : nothing will induce me to go there, it makes me shudder ! ' for he was afraid. Or, when they sat of an evening round the fire telling stories which made one's flesh creep, the listeners sometimes said : ' Oh ! it makes one shudder,' the youngest sat in a corner, heard the exclamation, and could not understand what it meant. 'They are always saying it makes one shudder ! it makes one shudder ! Nothing makes me shudder. It's probably an art quite beyond me.'

Now it happened that his father said to him one day : ' Hearken, you there in the corner ; you are growing big and strong, and you must learn to earn your own bread. Look at your brother, what pains he takes ; but all the money I've spent on your education is thrown away.' ' My dear father,' he replied, ' I will gladly learn—in fact, if it were possible I should like to learn to shudder ; I don't understand that a bit y et.' The eldest laughed when he heard this, and thought to hims elf : ' Good heavens ! what a ninny my brother is ! he'll never come to any good ; as the twig is bent, so is the tree inclined.' The father sighed, and answered him : ' You'll soon learn to shudder ; but that won't help you to make a living.'

Shortly after this, when the sexton came to pay them a visit, the father broke out to him, and told him what a bad hand his young- est son was at everything : he knew nothing and learnt nothing. ' Only think ! when I asked him how he purposed gaining a livelihood, he actually asked to be taught to shudder.' 'If that's all he wants,' said the sexton, 'I can teach him that; just you send him to me, I'll soon polish him up.' The father was quite pleased with the proposal, because he thought: 'It will be a good discipline for the youth.' And so the sexton took him into his house, and his duty was to toll the bell. After a few days he woke him at midnight, and bade him rise up and climb into the tower and toll. 'Now, my

friend, I'll teach you to shudder,' thought he. He stole forth secretly in front, and when the youth was up above, and had turned round to grasp the bell-rope, he saw, standing opposite the hole of the belfry, a white figure. 'Who's there?' he called out, but the figure gave no answer, and neither stirred nor moved. 'Answer,' cried the youth, 'or begone; you have no business here at this hour of the night.' But the sexton remained motionless, so that the youth might think it was a ghost. The youth called out the second time : ' What do you want here ? Speak if you are an honest fellow, or I'll knock you down the stairs.' The sexton thought: 'He can't mean that in earnest,' so gave forth no sound, and stood as though he were made of stone. Then the youth shouted out to him the third time, and as that too had no effect he made a dash at the spectre and knocked it down the stairs, so that it fell about ten steps and remained lying in a corner. Thereupon he tolled the bell, went home to bed without saying a word, and fell asleep. The sexton's wife waited a long time for her husband, but he never appeared. At last she became anxious, and woke the youth, and asked : ' Don't you know where my husband is ? He went up to the tower in front of you.' ' No,' answered the youth ; ' but someone stood on the stairs up there just opposite the trap-door in the belfry, and because he wouldn't answer me, or go away, I took him for a rogue and knocked him down. You'd better go and see if it was he ; I should be much distressed if it were.' The wife ran and found her husband, who was lying groaning in a corner, with his leg broken.

She carried him down, and then hurried with loud protestations to the youth's father. ' Your son has been the cause of a pretty misfortune,' she cried ; ' he threw my husband downstairs so that he broke his leg. Take the good-for-nothing wretch out of our house.' The father was horrified, hurried to the youth, and gave him a scolding.

' What unholy pranks are these ? The evil one must have put them into your head.' ' Father,' he replied, ' only listen to me ; I am quite guiltless. He stood there in the night, like one who meant harm. I didn't know who it was, and warned him three times to speak or to begone.' ' Oh !' groaned the father, ' you'll bring me nothing but misfortune ; get out of my sight, I won't have anything more to do with you.' ' Yes, father, willingly ; only wait till daylight, then I'll set out and learn to shudder, and in that way I shall be master of an art which will gain me a living.' ' Learn what you will,' said the father, ' it's all one to me. Here are fifty dollars for you, set forth into the wide world with them ; but see and tell no one where you come from or who your father is, for I am ashamed of you.' ' Yes, father, whatever you wish ; and if that's all you ask, I can easily keep it in mind.'

When day broke the youth put the fifty dollars into his pocket, set out on the hard high road, and kept muttering to himself : ' If I could only shudder ! if I could only shudder ! ' Just at this moment a man came by who heard the youth speaking to himself, and when they had gone on a bit and were in sight of the gallows the man said to him: 'Look! there is the tree where seven people have been hanged, and are now learning to fly; sit down under it and wait till nightfall, and then you'll pretty soon learn to shudder.' 'If that's all I have to do,' answered the youth, ' it's easily done ; but if I learn to shudder so quickly, then you shall have my fifty dollars. Just come back to me to-morrow morning early.' Then the youth went to the gallows-tree and sat down underneath it, and waited for the evening; and because he felt cold he lit himself a fire. But at midnight it got so chill that in spite of the fire he couldn't keep warm. And as the wind blew the corpses one against the other, tossing them to and fro, he thought to himself : ' If you are perishing down here by the fire, how those poor things up there must be shaking and shivering ! ' And because he had a tender heart, he put up a ladder which he climbed, unhooked one body after the other, and took down all the seven. Then he stirred the fire, blew it up, and placed them all round in a circle, that they might warm themselves. But they sat there and did not move, and the fire caught their clothes. Then he spoke : 'Take care, or I'll hang you up again.' But the dead men did not hear, and let their rags go on burning. Then he got angry, and said : ' If you aren't careful yourselves, then I can't help you, and I don't mean to burn with you ; ' and he hung them up again in a row. Then he sat down at his fire and fell asleep. On the following morning the man came to him, and, wishing to get his fifty dollars, said : ' Now you know what it is to shudder.' No,' he answered, 'how should I ? Those fellows up there never opened their mouths, and were so stupid that they let those few old tatters they have on their bodies burn.' Then the man saw he wouldn't get his fifty dollars that day, and went off, saying : ' Well, I'm blessed if I ever met such a person in my life before.'

The youth too went on his way, and began to murmur to himself : ' Oh ! if I could only shudder ! if I could only shudder ! ' A carrier who was walking behind him heard these words, and asked him : ' Who are you ? ' ' I don't know,' said the youth. ' Where do you hail from ? ' ' I don't know.' ' Who's your father ? ' ' I mayn't say.' ' What are you constantly muttering to yourself? ' ' Oh ! ' said the youth, ' I would give worlds to shudder, but no one can teach me.' ' Stuff and nonsense ! ' spoke the carrier ; ' come along with me, and I'll soon put that right.' The youth went with the

carrier, and in the evening they reached an inn, where they were
to spend the night.   Then, just as he was entering the room, he
said again, quite aloud : ' Oh ! if I could only shudder ! if I could only
shudder ! '   The landlord, who heard this, laughed and said : ' If
that's what you're sighing for, you shall be given every opportunity
here.'   ' Oh ! hold your tongue ! ' said the landlord's wife ; ' so many
people have paid for their curiosity with their lives, it were a
thousand pities if those beautiful eyes were never again to behold
daylight.'   But the youth said : ' No matter how difficult, I insist
on learning it ; why, that's what I've set out to do.'   He left the
landlord no peace till he told him that in the neighbourhood stood
a haunted castle, where one could easily learn to shudder if one
only kept watch in it for three nights.   The King had promised the
man who dared to do this thing his daughter as wife, and she was
the most beautiful maiden under the sun.   There was also much
treasure hid in the castle, guarded by evil spirits, which would then
be free, and was sufficient to make a poor man more than rich.
Many had already gone in, but so far none had ever come out
again.   So the youth went to the King and spoke : ' If I were
allowed, I should much like to watch for three nights in the
castle.'   The King looked at him, and because he pleased him he
said : ' You can ask for three things, none of them living, and those
you may take with you into the castle.'   Then he answered : ' Well,
I shall beg for a fire, a turning lathe, and a carving bench with the
knife attached.'

On the following day the King had everything put into the castle ;
and when night drew on the youth took up his position there, lit
a bright fire in one of the rooms, placed the carving bench with the
knife close to it, and sat himself down on the turning lathe.   ' Oh !
if I could only shudder ! ' he said ; ' but I shan't learn it here either.'
Towards midnight he wanted to make up the fire, and as he was
blowing up a blaze he heard a shriek from a corner.   ' Ou, miou !
how cold we are ! ' ' You fools ! ' he cried ; ' why do you scream ?   If
you are cold, come and sit at the fire and warm yourselves.'   And as
he spoke two huge black cats sprang fiercely forwards and sat down.
one on each side of him, and gazed wildly at him with their fiery eyes.
After a time, when they had warmed themselves, they said : ' Friend,
shall we play a little game of cards ? '   ' Why not ? ' he replied ; ' but
first let me see your paws.'   Then they stretched out their claws.
' Ha ! ' said he ; ' what long nails you've got !   Wait a minute : I must
first cut them off.'   Thereupon he seized them by the scruff of their

necks, lifted them on to the carving bench, and screwed down their paws firmly. 'After watching you narrowly,' said he, 'I no longer feel any desire to play cards with you ;' and with these words he struck them dead and threw them out into the water. But when he had thus sent the two of them to their final rest, and was again about to sit down at the fire, out of every nook and corner came forth black cats and black dogs with fiery chains in such swarms that he couldn't possibly get away from them. They yelled in the most ghastly manner, jumped upon his fire, scattered it all, and

tried to put it out. He looked on quietly for a time, but when it got beyond a joke he seized his carving-knife and called out : 'Be off, you rabble rout !' and let fly at them. Some of them fled away, and the others he struck dead and threw them out into the pond below. When he returned he blew up the sparks of the fire once more, and warmed himself. And as he sat thus his eyes refused to keep open any longer, and a desire to sleep stole over him. Then he looked around him and beheld in the corner a large bed. 'The very thing,' he said, and laid himself down in it. But when he wished to close his eyes the bed began to move by itself, and ran all round the castle. 'Capital,' he said, 'only a little quicker.' Then the bed sped on as if drawn by six horses, over thresholds and stairs, up this way and down that. All of a sudden—crish, crash! with a bound it turned over, upside down, and lay like a mountain on the top of him. But he tossed the blankets and pillows in the air, emerged from underneath, and said: 'Now anyone who has the fancy for it may go a drive,' lay down at his fire, and slept till daylight. In the morning the King came, and when he beheld him lying on the ground he imagined the ghosts had been too much for him, and that he was dead. Then he said: 'What a pity! and such a fine fellow as he was.' The youth heard this, got up, and said: 'It's not come to that yet.' Then the King was astonished, but very glad, and asked how it had fared with him. 'First-rate,' he answered; 'and now I've survived the one night, I shall get through the other two also.' The landlord, when he went to him, opened his eyes wide, and said: 'Well, I never thought to see you alive again. Have you learnt now what shuddering is?' 'No,' he replied, 'it's quite hopeless; if someone could only tell me how to!'

The second night he went up again to the old castle, sat down at the fire, and began his old refrain: 'If I could only shudder!' As midnight approached, a noise and din broke out, at first gentle, but gradually increasing; then all was quiet for a minute, and at length, with a loud scream, half of a man dropped down the chimney and fell before him. 'Hi, up there!' shouted he; 'there's another half wanted down here, that's not enough;' then the din commenced once more, there was a shrieking and a yelling, and then the other half fell down. 'Wait a bit,' he said; 'I'll stir up the fire for you.' When he had done this and again looked round, the two pieces had united, and a horrible-looking man sat on his seat. 'Come,' said the youth, 'I didn't bargain for that, the seat is mine.' The man tried to shove him away, but the youth wouldn't allow it for a moment, and, pushing him off by force, sat down in his place again. Then more men dropped down, one after the other, who, fetching nine skeleton legs and two skulls, put them up and played ninepins with them. The youth thought he would like to play too, and said: 'Look here; do you mind my joining the game?' 'No, not if you have money.' 'I've money enough,' he replied, 'but your balls aren't very round.' Then he took the skulls, placed them on his lathe, and turned them till they were round. 'Now they'll roll along better,' said he, 'and houp-la! now the fun begins.' He played with them and lost some of his money, but when twelve struck everything vanished before his eyes. He lay down and slept peacefully. The next morning the King came, anxious for news. 'How have you got on this time?' he asked. 'I played ninepins,' he answered, 'and lost a few pence.' 'Didn't you shudder then?' 'No such luck,' said he; 'I made myself merry. Oh! if I only knew what it was to shudder!'

On the third night he sat down again on his bench, and said, in the most desponding way: 'If I could only shudder!' When it got late, six big men came in carrying a coffin. Then he cried: 'Ha! ha! that's most likely my little cousin who only died a few days ago;' and beckoning with his finger he called out: 'Come, my small cousin, come.' They placed the coffin on the ground, and he approached it and took off the cover. In it lay a dead man. He felt his face, and it was cold as ice. 'Wait,' he said, 'I'll heat you up a bit,' went to the fire, warmed his hand, and laid it on the man's face, but the dead remained cold. Then he lifted him out, sat down at the fire, laid him on his knee, and rubbed his arms that the blood should circulate again. When that too had no effect it occurred to him that if two people lay together in bed they warmed each other; so he put him into the bed, covered him up, and lay down beside him; after a time the corpse became warm and began to move. Then the youth said: 'Now, my little cousin, what would have happened if I hadn't warmed you?' But the dead man rose up and cried out: 'Now I will strangle you.' 'What!' said he, 'is that all the thanks I get? You shall be put straight back into your coffin,' lifted him up, threw him in, and closed the lid. Then the six men came and carried him out again. 'I simply can't shudder,' he said, 'and it's clear I shan't learn it in a lifetime here.'

Then a man entered, of more than ordinary size and of a very fearful appearance; but he was old and had a white beard. 'Oh! you miserable creature, now you will soon know what it is to shudder,' he cried, 'for you must die.' 'Not so quickly,' answered the youth. 'If I am to die, you must catch me first.' 'I shall soon lay hold of you,' spoke the monster. 'Gently, gently; don't boast too much, I'm as strong as you, and stronger too.' 'We'll soon see,' said the old man; 'if you are stronger than I, then I'll let you off; come, let's have a try.' Then he led him through some dark passages to a forge, and grasping an axe he drove one of the anvils with a blow into the earth. 'I can do better than that,' cried the

youth, and went to the other anvil.   The old man drew near him
in order to watch closely, and his white beard hung right down.
Then the youth seized the axe, cleft the anvil open, and jammed in
the old man's beard.   Now I have you,' said the youth; 'this time
it's your turn to die.'   Then he seized an iron rod and belaboured
the old man till he, whimpering, begged him to leave off, and he
would give him great riches.   The youth drew out the axe and let
him go.   The old man led him back to the castle and showed him
in a cellar three chests of gold.   'One of these,' he said, 'belongs

to the poor, one to the King, and the third is yours.'   At that moment twelve struck, and the spirit vanished, leaving the youth alone
in the dark.   'I'll surely be able to find a way out,' said he, and
groping about he at length found his way back to the room, and fell
asleep at his fire.   The next morning the King came, and said:
'Well, now you've surely learnt to shudder?'   'No,' he answered;
'what can it be?   My dead cousin was there, and an old bearded
man came, who showed me heaps of money down below there, but
what shuddering is no one has told me.'   Then the King spoke:

' You have freed the castle from its curse, and you shall marry my daughter.' ' That's all charming,' he said ; ' but I still don't know what it is to shudder.'

Then the gold was brought up, and the wedding was celebrated, but the young King, though he loved his wife dearly, and though he was very happy, still kept on saying : ' If I could only shudder ! if I could only shudder ! ' At last he reduced her to despair. Then her maid said : ' I'll help you ; we'll soon make him shudder.' So she went out to the stream that flowed through the garden, and had a pail full of little gudgeon brought to her. At night, when the young King was asleep, his wife had to pull the clothes off him, and pour the pail full of little gudgeon over him, so that the little fish swam all about him. Then he awoke and cried out : ' Oh ! how I shudder, how I shudder, dear wife ! Yes, now I know what shuddering is.' [1]

[1] Grimm.

RUMPELSTILTZKIN

THERE was once upon a time a poor miller who had a very beautiful daughter. Now it happened one day that he had an audience with the King, and in order to appear a person of some importance he told him that he had a daughter who could spin straw into gold. 'Now that's a talent worth having,' said the King to the miller; 'if your daughter is as clever as you say, bring her to my palace to-morrow, and I'll put her to the test.' When the girl was brought to him he led her into a room full of straw, gave her a spinning-wheel and spindle, and said: 'Now set to work and spin all night till early dawn, and if by that time you haven't spun the straw into gold you shall die.' Then he closed the door behind him and left her alone inside.

So the poor miller's daughter sat down, and didn't know what in the world she was to do. She hadn't the least idea of how to spin straw into gold, and became at last so miserable that she began to cry. Suddenly the door opened, and in stepped a tiny little man and said: 'Good-evening, Miss Miller-maid; why are you crying so bitterly?' 'Oh!' answered the girl, 'I have to spin straw into gold, and haven't a notion how it's done.' 'What will you give me if I spin it for you?' asked the manikin. 'My necklace,' replied the girl. The little man took the necklace, sat himself down at the wheel, and whir, whir, whir, the wheel went round three times, and the bobbin was full. Then he put on another, and whir, whir, whir, the wheel went round three times, and the second too was full; and so it went on till the morning, when all the straw was spun away, and all the bobbins were full of gold. As soon as the sun rose the King came, and when he perceived the gold he was astonished and delighted, but his heart only lusted more than ever after the precious metal. He had the miller's daughter put into another room full of straw, much bigger than the first, and bade her, if she valued her life, spin it all into gold before the following

morning. The girl didn't know what to do, and began to cry; then
the door opened as before, and the tiny little man appeared and
said: ' What'll you give me if I spin the straw into gold for you?'

' The ring from my finger,' answered the girl. The manikin took
the ring, and whir! round went the spinning-wheel again, and
when morning broke he had spun all the straw into glittering gold.
The King was pleased beyond measure at the sight, but his greed

for gold was still not satisfied, and he had the miller's daughter brought into a yet bigger room full of straw, and said : ' You must spin all this away in the night; but if you succeed this time you shall become my wife.' ' She's only a miller's daughter, it's true,' he thought; 'but I couldn't find a richer wife if I were to search the whole world over.' When the girl was alone the little man appeared for the third time, and said : 'What'll you give me if I spin the straw for you once again?' 'I've nothing more to give,' answered the girl. ' Then promise me when you are Queen to give me your first child.' 'Who knows what mayn't happen before that?' thought the miller's daughter; and besides, she saw no other way out of it, so she promised the manikin what he demanded, and he set to work once more and spun the straw into gold. When the King came in the morning, and found everything as he had desired, he straightway made her his wife, and the miller's daughter became a queen.

When a year had passed a beautiful son was born to her, and she thought no more of the little man, till all of a sudden one day he stepped into her room and said : ' Now give me what you promised.' The Queen was in a great state, and offered the little man all the riches in her kingdom if he would only leave her the child. But the manikin said : ' No, a living creature is dearer to me than all the treasures in the world.' Then the Queen began to cry and sob so bitterly that the little man was sorry for her, and said : ' I'll give you three days to guess my name, and if you find it out in that time you may keep your child.'

Then the Queen pondered the whole night over all the names she had ever heard, and sent a messenger to scour the land, and to pick up far and near any names he should come across. When the little man arrived on the following day she began with Kasper, Melchior, Belshazzar, and all the other names she knew, in a string, but at each one the manikin called out : 'That's not my name.' The next day she sent to inquire the names of all the people in the neighbourhood, and had a long list of the most uncommon and extraordinary for the little man when he made his appearance. ' Is your name, perhaps, Sheepshanks, Cruickshanks, Spindleshanks?' but he always replied : 'That's not my name.' On the third day the messenger returned and announced : ' I have not been able to find any new names, but as I came upon a high hill round the corner of the wood, where the foxes and hares bid each other good night, I saw a little house, and in front of the

house burned a fire, and round the fire sprang the most grotesque
little man, hopping on one leg and crying :

> To-morrow I brew, to-day I bake,
> And then the child away I'll take ;
> For little deems my royal dame
> That Rumpelstiltzkin is my name !

You may imagine the Queen's delight at hearing the name, and
when the little man stepped in shortly afterwards and asked : ' Now,
my lady Queen, what's my name ? ' she asked first : ' Is your
name Conrad ? ' ' No.' ' Is your name Harry ? ' ' No.' ' Is
your name, perhaps, Rumpelstiltzkin ? ' ' Some demon has told you
that, some demon has told you that,' screamed the little man, and in
his rage drove his right foot so far into the ground that it sank in up
to his waist ; then in a passion he seized the left foot with both hands
and tore himself in two.[1]

[1] Grimm.

BEAUTY AND THE BEAST

ONCE upon a time, in a very far-off country, there lived a mer-chant who had been so fortunate in all his undertakings that he was enormously rich. As he had, however, six sons and six daughters, he found that his money was not too much to let them all have everything they fancied, as they were accustomed to do.

But one day a most unexpected misfortune befell them. Their house caught fire and was speedily burnt to the ground, with all the splendid furniture, the books, pictures, gold, silver, and precious goods it contained; and this was only the beginning of their troubles. Their father, who had until this moment prospered in all ways, suddenly lost every ship he had upon the sea, either by dint of pirates, shipwreck, or fire. Then he heard that his clerks in dis-tant countries, whom he trusted entirely, had proved unfaithful; and at last from great wealth he fell into the direst poverty.

All that he had left was a little house in a desolate place at least a hundred leagues from the town in which he had lived, and to this he was forced to retreat with his children, who were in despair at the idea of leading such a different life. Indeed, the daughters at first hoped that their friends, who had been so numerous while they were rich, would insist on their staying in their houses now they no longer possessed one. But they soon found that they were left alone, and that their former friends even attributed their misfor-tunes to their own extravagance, and showed no intention of offer-ing them any help. So nothing was left for them but to take their departure to the cottage, which stood in the midst of a dark forest, and seemed to be the most dismal place upon the face of the earth. As they were too poor to have any servants, the girls had to work hard, like peasants, and the sons, for their part, cultivated the fields to earn their living. Roughly clothed, and living in the simplest way, the girls regretted unceasingly the luxuries and amusements of their former life; only the youngest tried to be brave and cheerful. She had been as sad as anyone when misfortune first overtook her father, but, soon recovering her natural gaiety, she set to work to make the best of things, to amuse her father and brothers as well as she could, and to try to persuade her sisters to join her in dancing and singing. But they would do nothing of the sort, and, because she was not as doleful as themselves, they declared that this miserable life was all she was fit for. But she was really far prettier and cleverer than they were; indeed, she was so lovely that she was always called Beauty. After two years, when they were all beginning to get used to their new life, something happened to disturb their tranquillity. Their father received the news that one of his ships, which he had believed to be lost, had come safely into port with a rich cargo. All the sons and daughters at once thought that their poverty was at an end, and wanted to set out directly for the town; but their father, who was more prudent, begged them to wait a little, and, though it was harvest-time, and he could ill be spared, determined to go himself first, to make inquiries. Only the youngest daughter had any doubt but that they would soon again be as rich as they were before, or at least rich enough to live comfortably in some town where they would find amusement and gay companions once more. So they all loaded their father with commissions for jewels and dresses which it would have taken a fortune to buy; only Beauty, feeling sure that it was of no use, did not ask for anything. Her father, noticing her silence, said: 'And what shall I bring for you, Beauty?'

'The only thing I wish for is to see you come home safely,' she answered.

But this reply vexed her sisters, who fancied she was blaming them for having asked for such costly things. Her father, however, was pleased, but as he thought that at her age she certainly ought to like pretty presents, he told her to choose something.

'Well, dear father,' she said, 'as you insist upon it, I beg that you will bring me a rose. I have not seen one since we came here, and I love them so much.'

So the merchant set out and reached the town as quickly as possible, but only to find that his former companions, believing him to be dead, had divided between them the goods which the ship had brought; and after six months of trouble and expense he found himself as poor as when he started, having been able to recover only just enough to pay the cost of his journey. To make matters worse, he was obliged to leave the town in the most terrible weather, so that by the time he was within a few leagues of his home he was almost exhausted with cold and fatigue. Though he knew it would take some hours to get through the forest, he was so anxious to be at his journey's end that he resolved to go on; but night overtook him, and the deep snow and bitter frost made it impossible for his horse to carry him any further. Not a house was to be seen; the only shelter he could get was the hollow trunk of a great tree, and

there he crouched all the night, which seemed to him the longest he had ever known. In spite of his weariness the howling of the wolves kept him awake, and even when at last the day broke he was not much better off, for the falling snow had covered up every path, and he did not know which way to turn.

At length he made out some sort of track, and though at the beginning it was so rough and slippery that he fell down more than once, it presently became easier, and led him into an avenue of trees which ended in a splendid castle. It seemed to the merchant very strange that no snow had fallen in the avenue, which was entirely composed of orange trees, covered with flowers and fruit. When he reached the first court of the castle he saw before him a flight of agate steps, and went up them, and passed through several splendidly furnished rooms. The pleasant warmth of the air revived him, and he felt very hungry ; but there seemed to be nobody in all this vast and splendid palace whom he could ask to give him something to eat. Deep silence reigned everywhere, and at last, tired of roaming through empty rooms and galleries, he stopped in a room smaller than the rest, where a clear fire was burning and a couch was drawn up cosily close to it. Thinking that this must be prepared for someone who was expected, he sat down to wait till he should come, and very soon fell into a sweet sleep.

When his extreme hunger wakened him after several hours, he was still alone ; but a little table, upon which was a good dinner, had been drawn up close to him, and, as he had eaten nothing for twenty-four hours, he lost no time in beginning his meal, hoping that he might soon have an opportunity of thanking his considerate entertainer, whoever it might be. But no one appeared, and even after another long sleep, from which he awoke completely refreshed, there was no sign of anybody, though a fresh meal of dainty cakes and fruit was prepared upon the little table at his elbow. Being naturally timid, the silence began to terrify him, and he resolved to search once more through all the rooms ; but it was of no use. Not even a servant was to be seen ; there was no sign of life in the palace ! He began to wonder what he should do, and to amuse himself by pretending that all the treasures he saw were his own, and considering how he would divide them among his children. Then he went down into the garden, and though it was winter everywhere else, here the sun shone, and the birds sang, and the flowers bloomed, and the air was soft and sweet. The merchant, in ecstacies with all he saw and heard, said to himself :

' All this must be meant for me. I will go this minute and bring my children to share all these delights.'

In spite of being so cold and weary when he reached the castle, he had taken his horse to the stable and fed it. Now he thought he would saddle it for his homeward journey, and he turned down the path which led to the stable. This path had a hedge of roses on each side of it, and the merchant thought he had never seen or smelt such exquisite flowers.　　They reminded him of his promise to Beauty, and he stopped and had just gathered one to take to her when he was startled by a strange noise behind him.　　Turning round, he saw a frightful Beast, which seemed to be very angry and said, in a terrible voice :

'Who told you that you might gather my roses?　　Was it not

enough that I allowed you to be in my palace and was kind to you?　This is the way you show your gratitude, by stealing my flowers !　　But your insolence shall not go unpunished.'　　The merchant, terrified by these furious words, dropped the fatal rose, and, throwing himself on his knees, cried : ' Pardon me, noble sir.　I am truly grateful to you for your hospitality, which was so magnificent that I could not imagine that you would be offended by my taking such a little thing as a rose.' But the Beast's anger was not lessened by this speech.

' You are very ready with excuses and flattery,' he cried ; ' but that will not save you from the death you deserve.'

' Alas ! ' thought the merchant, ' if my daughter Beauty could only know what danger her rose has brought me into ! '

And in despair he began to tell the Beast all his misfortunes, and the reason of his journey, not forgetting to mention Beauty's request.

' A king's ransom would hardly have procured all that my other daughters asked,' he said ; ' but I thought that I might at least take Beauty her rose. I beg you to forgive me, for you see I meant no harm.'

The Beast considered for a moment, and then he said, in a less furious tone :

' I will forgive you on one condition—that is, that you will give me one of your daughters.'

' Ah ! ' cried the merchant, ' if I were cruel enough to buy my own life at the expense of one of my children's, what excuse could I invent to bring her here ? '

' No excuse would be necessary,' answered the Beast. ' If she comes at all she must come willingly. On no other condition will I have her. See if any one of them is courageous enough, and loves you well enough to come and save your life. You seem to be an honest man, so I will trust you to go home. I give you a month to see if either of your daughters will come back with you and stay here, to let you go free. If neither of them is willing, you must come alone, after bidding them good-bye for ever, for then you will belong to me. And do not imagine that you can hide from me, for if you fail to keep your word I will come and fetch you ! ' added the Beast grimly.

The merchant accepted this proposal, though he did not really think any of his daughters would be persuaded to come. He promised to return at the time appointed, and then, anxious to escape from the presence of the Beast, he asked permission to set off at once. But the Beast answered that he could not go until the next day.

' Then you will find a horse ready for you,' he said. ' Now go and eat your supper, and await my orders.'

The poor merchant, more dead than alive, went back to his room, where the most delicious supper was already served on the little table which was drawn up before a blazing fire. But he was too terrified to eat, and only tasted a few of the dishes, for fear the Beast should be angry if he did not obey his orders. When he had finished he heard a great noise in the next room, which he knew meant that the Beast was coming. As he could do nothing to escape his visit, the only thing that remained was to seem as little afraid as possible; so when the Beast appeared and asked roughly if he had supped well, the merchant answered humbly that he had, thanks to his host's kindness. Then the Beast warned him to re-member their agreement, and to prepare his daughter exactly for what she had to expect.

' Do not get up to-morrow,' he added, ' until you see the sun and hear a golden bell ring. Then you will find your breakfast waiting for you here, and the horse you are to ride will be ready in the courtyard. He will also bring you back again when you come with your daughter a month hence. Farewell. Take a rose to Beauty, and remember your promise ! '

The merchant was only too glad when the Beast went away, and though he could not sleep for sadness, he lay down until the sun rose. Then, after a hasty breakfast, he went to gather Beauty's rose, and mounted his horse, which carried him off so swiftly that in an instant he had lost sight of the palace, and he was still wrapped in gloomy thoughts when it stopped before the door of the cottage.

His sons and daughters, who had been very uneasy at his long absence, rushed to meet him, eager to know the result of his jour-ney, which, seeing him mounted upon a splendid horse and wrapped in a rich mantle, they supposed to be favourable. But he hid the truth from them at first, only saying sadly to Beauty as he gave her the rose :

' Here is what you asked me to bring you; you little know what it has cost.'

But this excited their curiosity so greatly that presently he told them his adventures from beginning to end, and then they were all very unhappy. The girls lamented loudly over their lost hopes, and the sons declared that their father should not return to this terrible castle, and began to make plans for killing the Beast if it should come to fetch him. But he reminded them that he had promised to go back. Then the girls were very angry with Beauty, and said it was all her fault, and that if she had asked for something sensible this would never have happened, and complained bitterly that they should have to suffer for her folly.

Poor Beauty, much distressed, said to them :

' I have indeed caused this misfortune, but I assure you I did it innocently. Who could have guessed that to ask for a rose in the middle of summer would cause so much misery ? But as I did the mischief it is only just that I should suffer for it. I will therefore go back with my father to keep his promise.'

At first nobody would hear of this arrangement, and her father and brothers, who loved her dearly, declared that nothing should make them let her go ; but Beauty was firm. As the time drew near she divided all her little possessions between her sisters, and said good-bye to everything she loved, and when the fatal day came she encouraged and cheered her father as they mounted together the horse which had brought him back. It seemed to fly rather than gallop, but so smoothly that Beauty was not frightened ; indeed, she would have enjoyed the journey if she had not feared what might happen to her at the end of it. Her father still tried to persuade her to go back, but in vain. While they were talking the night fell, and then, to their great surprise, wonderful coloured lights began to shine in all directions, and splendid fireworks blazed out before them ; all the forest was illuminated by them, and even felt pleasantly warm, though it had been bitterly cold before. This lasted until they reached the avenue of orange trees, where were statues holding flaming torches, and when they got nearer to the palace they saw that it was illuminated from the roof to the ground, and music sounded softly from the courtyard. ' The Beast must be very hungry,' said Beauty, trying to laugh, ' if he makes all this rejoicing over the arrival of his prey.'

But, in spite of her anxiety, she could not help admiring all the wonderful things she saw.

The horse stopped at the foot of the flight of steps leading to the terrace, and when they had dismounted her father led her to the little room he had been in before, where they found a splendid fire burning, and the table daintily spread with a delicious supper.

The merchant knew that this was meant for them, and Beauty, who was rather less frightened now that she had passed through so many rooms and seen nothing of the Beast, was quite willing to begin, for her long ride had made her very hungry. But they had hardly finished their meal when the noise of the Beast's footsteps was heard approaching, and Beauty clung to her father in terror, which became all the greater when she saw how frightened he was. But when the Beast really appeared, though she trembled at the sight of him, she made a great effort to hide her horror, and saluted him respectfully.

This evidently pleased the Beast. After looking at her he said, in a tone that might have struck terror into the boldest heart, though he did not seem to be angry :

' Good-evening, old man. Good-evening, Beauty.'

The merchant was too terrified to reply, but Beauty answered sweetly :

' Good-evening, Beast.'

' Have you come willingly ? ' asked the Beast. ' Will you be content to stay here when your father goes away ? '

Beauty answered bravely that she was quite prepared to stay.

' I am pleased with you,' said the Beast. ' As you have come of your own accord, you may stay. As for you, old man,' he added, turning to the merchant, ' at sunrise to-morrow you will take your departure. When the bell rings get up quickly and eat your breakfast, and you will find the same horse waiting to take you home ; but remember that you must never expect to see my palace again.'

Then turning to Beauty, he said :

' Take your father into the next room, and help him to choose everything you think your brothers and sisters would like to have. You will find two travelling-trunks there ; fill them as full as you can. It is only just that you should send them something very precious as a remembrance of yourself.'

Then he went away, after saying, ' Good-bye, Beauty ; good-bye, old man ; ' and though Beauty was beginning to think with great dismay of her father's departure, she was afraid to disobey the Beast's orders; and they went into the next room, which had shelves and cupboards all round it. They were greatly surprised at the riches it contained. There were splendid dresses fit for a queen, with all the ornaments that were to be worn with them ; and when Beauty opened the cupboards she was quite dazzled by the gorgeous jewels that lay in heaps upon every shelf. After choosing a vast quantity, which she divided between her sisters --for she had made a heap of the wonderful dresses for each of them—she opened the last chest, which was full of gold.

' I think, father,' she said, ' that, as the gold will be more useful to you, we had better take out the other things again, and fill the trunks with it.' So they did this; but the more they put in, the more room there seemed to be, and at last they put back all the jewels and dresses they had taken out, and Beauty even added as many more of the jewels as she could carry at once ; and then the trunks were not too full, but they were so heavy that an elephant could not have carried them !

'The Beast was mocking us,' cried the merchant; 'he must have pretended to give us all these things, knowing that I could not carry them away.'

'Let us wait and see,' answered Beauty. 'I cannot believe that he meant to deceive us. All we can do is to fasten them up and leave them ready.'

So they did this and returned to the little room, where, to their astonishment, they found breakfast ready. The merchant ate his with a good appetite, as the Beast's generosity made him believe that he might perhaps venture to come back soon and see Beauty. But she felt sure that her father was leaving her for ever, so she was very sad when the bell rang sharply for the second time, and warned them that the time was come for them to part. They went down into the courtyard, where two horses were waiting, one loaded with the two trunks, the other for him to ride. They were pawing the ground in their impatience to start, and the merchant was forced to bid Beauty a hasty farewell; and as soon as he was mounted he went off at such a pace that she lost sight of him in an instant. Then Beauty began to cry, and wandered sadly back to her own room. But she soon found that she was very sleepy, and as she had nothing better to do she lay down and instantly fell asleep. And then she dreamed that she was walking by a brook bordered with trees, and lamenting her sad fate, when a young prince, handsomer than anyone she had ever seen, and with a voice that went straight to her heart, came and said to her, 'Ah, Beauty ! you are not so unfortunate as you suppose. Here you will be re-warded for all you have suffered elsewhere. Your every wish shall be gratified. Only try to find me out, no matter how I may be disguised, as I love you dearly, and in making me happy you will find your own happiness. Be as true-hearted as you are beautiful, and we shall have nothing left to wish for.'

'What can I do, Prince, to make you happy ? ' said Beauty.

'Only be grateful,' he answered, 'and do not trust too much to your eyes. And, above all, do not desert me until you have saved me from my cruel misery.'

After this she thought she found herself in a room with a stately and beautiful lady, who said to her :

' Dear Beauty, try not to regret all you have left behind you, for you are destined to a better fate. Only do not let yourself be deceived by appearances.'

Beauty found her dreams so interesting that she was in no hurry to awake, but presently the clock roused her by calling her name softly twelve times, and then she got up and found her dressing-table set out with everything she could possibly want ; and when her toilet was finished she found dinner was waiting in the room

next to hers. But dinner does not take very long when you are all by yourself, and very soon she sat down cosily in the corner of a sofa, and began to think about the charming Prince she had seen in her dream.

' He said I could make him happy,' said Beauty to herself.

' It seems, then, that this horrible Beast keeps him a prisoner. How can I set him free ? I wonder why they both told me not to trust to appearances ? I don't understand it. But, after all, it was only a dream, so why should I trouble myself about it ? I had better go and find something to do to amuse myself.'

So she got up and began to explore some of the many rooms of the palace.

The first she entered was lined with mirrors, and Beauty saw herself reflected on every side, and thought she had never seen such a charming room. Then a bracelet which was hanging from a chandelier caught her eye, and on taking it down she was greatly surprised to find that it held a portrait of her unknown admirer, just as she had seen him in her dream. With great delight she slipped the bracelet on her arm, and went on into a gallery of pictures, where she soon found a portrait of the same handsome Prince, as large as life, and so well painted that as she studied it he seemed to smile kindly at her. Tearing herself away from the portrait at last, she passed through into a room which contained every musical instrument under the sun, and here she amused herself for a long while in trying some of them, and singing until she was tired. The next room was a library, and she saw everything she had ever wanted to read, as well as everything she had read, and it seemed to her that a whole lifetime would not be enough even to read the names of the books, there were so many. By this time it was growing dusk, and wax candles in diamond and ruby candlesticks were beginning to light themselves in every room.

Beauty found her supper served just at the time she preferred to have it, but she did not see anyone or hear a sound, and, though her father had warned her that she would be alone, she began to find it rather dull.

But presently she heard the Beast coming, and wondered tremblingly if he meant to eat her up now.

However, as he did not seem at all ferocious, and only said gruffly :

'Good-evening, Beauty,' she answered cheerfully and managed to conceal her terror. Then the Beast asked her how she had been amusing herself, and she told him all the rooms she had seen.

Then he asked if she thought she could be happy in his palace ; and Beauty answered that everything was so beautiful that she would be very hard to please if she could not be happy. And after about an hour's talk Beauty began to think that the Beast was not nearly so terrible as she had supposed at first. Then he got up to leave her, and said in his gruff voice :

'Do you love me, Beauty ? Will you marry me ?'

'Oh ! what shall I say ?' cried Beauty, for she was afraid to make the Beast angry by refusing.

' Say " yes " or " no " without fear,' he replied.

' Oh ! no, Beast,' said Beauty hastily.

' Since you will not, good-night, Beauty,' he said. And she answered :

' Good-night, Beast,' very glad to find that her refusal had not provoked him. And after he was gone she was very soon in bed and asleep, and dreaming of her unknown Prince. She thought he came and said to her :

' Ah, Beauty ! why are you so unkind to me ? I fear I am fated to be unhappy for many a long day still.'

And then her dreams changed, but the charming Prince figured in them all ; and when morning came her first thought was to look at the portrait and see if it was really like him, and she found that it certainly was.

This morning she decided to amuse herself in the garden, for the sun shone, and all the fountains were playing; but she was astonished to find that every place was familiar to her, and presently she came to the brook where the myrtle trees were growing where she had first met the Prince in her dream, and that made her think more than ever that he must be kept a prisoner by the Beast. When she was tired she went back to the palace, and found a new room full of materials for every kind of work—ribbons to make into bows, and silks to work into flowers. Then there was an aviary full of rare birds, which were so tame that they flew to Beauty as soon as they saw her, and perched upon her shoulders and her head.

' Pretty little creatures,' she said, ' how I wish that your cage was nearer to my room, that I might often hear you sing ! '

So saying she opened a door, and found to her delight that it led into her own room, though she had thought it was quite the other side of the palace.

There were more birds in a room farther on, parrots and cockatoos that could talk, and they greeted Beauty by name ; indeed, she found them so entertaining that she took one or two back to her room, and they talked to her while she was at supper ; after which the Beast paid her his usual visit, and asked the same questions as before, and then with a gruff ' good-night ' he took his departure, and Beauty went to bed to dream of her mysterious Prince. The days passed swiftly in different amusements, and after a while Beauty found out another strange thing in the palace, which often pleased her when she was tired of being alone. There

was one room which she had not noticed particularly ; it was
empty, except that under each of the windows stood a very comfortable chair ; and the first time she had looked out of the window it

had seemed to her that a black curtain prevented her from seeing
anything outside. But the second time she went into the room,
happening to be tired, she sat down in one of the chairs, when

instantly the curtain was rolled aside, and a most amusing panto-
mime was acted before her ; there were dances, and coloured lights,
and music, and pretty dresses, and it was all so gay that Beauty was
in ecstacies. After that she tried the other seven windows in turn,
and there was some new and surprising entertainment to be seen
from each of them, so that Beauty never could feel lonely any
more. Every evening after supper the Beast came to see her, and
always before saying good-night asked her in his terrible voice :

' Beauty, will you marry me ? '

And it seemed to Beauty, now she understood him better, that
when she said, ' No, Beast,' he went away quite sad. But her
happy dreams of the handsome young Prince soon made her forget
the poor Beast, and the only thing that at all disturbed her was to
be constantly told to distrust appearances, to let her heart guide her,
and not her eyes, and many other equally perplexing things, which,
consider as she would, she could not understand.

So everything went on for a long time, until at last, happy as
she was, Beauty began to long for the sight of her father and her
brothers and sisters; and one night, seeing her look very sad, the
Beast asked her what was the matter. Beauty had quite ceased to be
afraid of him. Now she knew that he was really gentle in spite of
his ferocious looks and his dreadful voice. So she answered that
she was longing to see her home once more. Upon hearing this
the Beast seemed sadly distressed, and cried miserably.

' Ah ! Beauty, have you the heart to desert an unhappy Beast
like this ? What more do you want to make you happy ? Is it
because you hate me that you want to escape ? '

' No, dear Beast,' answered Beauty softly, ' I do not hate you,
and I should be very sorry never to see you any more, but I long
to see my father again. Only let me go for two months, and I
promise to come back to you and stay for the rest of my life.'

The Beast, who had been sighing dolefully while she spoke, now
replied :

' I cannot refuse you anything you ask, even though it should
cost me my life. Take the four boxes you will find in the room
next to your own, and fill them with everything you wish to take
with you. But remember your promise and come back when the
two months are over, or you may have cause to repent it, for if you
do not come in good time you will find your faithful Beast dead.
You will not need any chariot to bring you back. Only say good-
bye to all your brothers and sisters the night before you come away,

and when you have gone to bed turn this ring round upon your finger and say firmly : " I wish to go back to my palace and see my Beast again." Good-night, Beauty. Fear nothing, sleep peacefully, and before long you shall see your father once more.'

As soon as Beauty was alone she hastened to fill the boxes with all the rare and precious things she saw about her, and only when she was tired of heaping things into them did they seem to be full.

Then she went to bed, but could hardly sleep for joy. And when at last she did begin to dream of her beloved Prince she was grieved to see him stretched upon a grassy bank sad and weary, and hardly like himself.

' What is the matter ? ' she cried.

But he looked at her reproachfully, and said :

How can you ask me, cruel one ? Are you not leaving me to my death perhaps ? '

' Ah ! don't be so sorrowful,' cried Beauty ; ' I am only going to assure my father that I am safe and happy. I have promised the Beast faithfully that I will come back, and he would die of grief if I did not keep my word ! '

' What would that matter to you ? ' said the Prince. ' Surely you would not care ? '

' Indeed I should be ungrateful if I did not care for such a kind Beast,' cried Beauty indignantly. ' I would die to save him from pain. I assure you it is not his fault that he is so ugly.'

Just then a strange sound woke her—someone was speaking not very far away ; and opening her eyes she found herself in a room she had never seen before, which was certainly not nearly so splendid as those she was used to in the Beast's palace. Where could she be ? She got up and dressed hastily, and then saw that the boxes she had packed the night before were all in the room. While she was wondering by what magic the Beast had transported them and herself to this strange place she suddenly heard her father's voice, and rushed out and greeted him joyfully. Her brothers and sisters were all astonished at her appearance, as they had never expected to see her again, and there was no end to the questions they asked her. She had also much to hear about what had happened to them while she was away, and of her father's journey home. But when they heard that she had only come to be with them for a short time, and then must go back to the Beast's palace for ever, they lamented loudly. Then Beauty asked her father what he thought could be the meaning of her strange dreams, and why the Prince constantly begged her not to trust to appearances. After much consideration he answered: 'You tell me yourself that the Beast, frightful as he is, loves you dearly, and deserves your love and gratitude for his gentleness and kindness; I think the Prince must mean you to understand that you ought to reward him by doing as he wishes you to, in spite of his ugliness.'

Beauty could not help seeing that this seemed very probable; still, when she thought of her dear Prince who was so handsome, she did not feel at all inclined to marry the Beast. At any rate, for two months she need not decide, but could enjoy herself with her sisters. But though they were rich now, and lived in a town again, and had plenty of acquaintances, Beauty found that nothing amused her very much; and she often thought of the palace, where she was so happy, especially as at home she never once dreamed of her dear Prince, and she felt quite sad without him.

Then her sisters seemed to have got quite used to being without her, and even found her rather in the way, so she would not have been sorry when the two months were over but for her father and brothers, who begged her to stay, and seemed so grieved at the thought of her departure that she had not the courage to say good-bye to them. Every day when she got up she meant to say it at night, and when night came she put it off again, until at last she had a dismal dream which helped her to make up her mind. She thought she was wandering in a lonely path in the palace gardens, when she heard groans which seemed to come from some bushes hiding the entrance of a cave, and running quickly to see what could be the matter, she found the Beast stretched out upon his side, apparently dying. He reproached her faintly with being the cause of his distress, and at the same moment a stately lady appeared, and said very gravely:

'Ah! Beauty, you are only just in time to save his life. See what happens when people do not keep their promises! If you had delayed one day more, you would have found him dead.'

Beauty was so terrified by this dream that the next morning she announced her intention of going back at once, and that very night she said good-bye to her father and all her brothers and sisters, and as soon as she was in bed she turned her ring round upon her finger, and said firmly:

'I wish to go back to my palace and see my Beast again,' as she had been told to do.

Then she fell asleep instantly, and only woke up to hear the clock saying, 'Beauty, Beauty,' twelve times in its musical voice, which told her at once that she was really in the palace once more. Everything was just as before, and her birds were so glad to see her! but Beauty thought she had never known such a long day, for she was so anxious to see the Beast again that she felt as if supper-time would never come.

But when it did come and no Beast appeared she was really frightened; so, after listening and waiting for a long time, she ran down into the garden to search for him. Up and down the paths and avenues ran poor Beauty, calling him in vain, for no one

answered, and not a trace of him could she find; until at last, quite tired, she stopped for a minute's rest, and saw that she was standing opposite the shady path she had seen in her dream. She rushed down it, and, sure enough, there was the cave, and in it lay the Beast—asleep, as Beauty thought. Quite glad to have found him, she ran up and stroked his head, but to her horror he did not move or open his eyes.

'Oh! he is dead; and it is all my fault,' said Beauty, crying bitterly.

But then, looking at him again, she fancied he still breathed, and, hastily fetching some water from the nearest fountain, she sprinkled it over his face, and to her great delight he began to revive.

'Oh! Beast, how you frightened me!' she cried. 'I never knew how much I loved you until just now, when I feared I was too late to save your life.'

'Can you really love such an ugly creature as I am?' said the Beast faintly. 'Ah! Beauty, you only came just in time. I was dying because I thought you had forgotten your promise. But go back now and rest, I shall see you again by-and-by.'

Beauty, who had half expected that he would be angry with her, was reassured by his gentle voice, and went back to the palace, where supper was awaiting her; and afterwards the Beast came in as usual, and talked about the time she had spent with her father, asking if she had enjoyed herself, and if they had all been very glad to see her.

Beauty answered politely, and quite enjoyed telling him all that had happened to her. And when at last the time came for him to go, and he asked, as he had so often asked before:

'Beauty, will you marry me?' she answered softly:

'Yes, dear Beast.'

As she spoke a blaze of light sprang up before the windows of the palace; fireworks crackled and guns banged, and across the avenue of orange trees, in letters all made of fire-flies, was written: 'Long live the Prince and his Bride.'

Turning to ask the Beast what it could all mean, Beauty found that he had disappeared, and in his place stood her long-loved Prince! At the same moment the wheels of a chariot were heard upon the terrace, and two ladies entered the room. One of them Beauty recognised as the stately lady she had seen in her dreams; the other was also so grand and queenly that Beauty hardly knew which to greet first.

But the one she already knew said to her companion:

'Well, Queen, this is Beauty, who has had the courage to rescue your son from the terrible enchantment. They love one another, and only your consent to their marriage is wanting to make them perfectly happy.'

'I consent with all my heart,' cried the Queen. 'How can I ever thank you enough, charming girl, for having restored my dear son to his natural form?'

And then she tenderly embraced Beauty and the Prince, who had meanwhile been greeting the Fairy and receiving her congratulations.

' Now,' said the Fairy to Beauty, ' I suppose you would like me to send for all your brothers and sisters to dance at your wedding ? '

And so she did, and the marriage was celebrated the very next day with the utmost splendour, and Beauty and the Prince lived happily ever after.[1]

---

[1] *La Belle et la Bête.* Par Madame de Villeneuve.

THE MASTER-MAID

ONCE upon a time there was a king who had many sons. I do not exactly know how many there were, but the youngest of them could not stay quietly at home, and was determined to go out into the world and try his luck, and after a long time the King was forced to give him leave to go. When he had travelled about for several days, he came to a giant's house, and hired himself to the giant as a servant. In the morning the giant had to go out to pasture his goats, and as he was leaving the house he told the King's son that he must clean out the stable. 'And after you have done that,' he said, ' you need not do any more work to-day, for you have come to a kind master, and that you shall find. But what I set you to do must be done both well and thoroughly, and you must on no account go into any of the rooms which lead out of the room in which you slept last night. If you do, I will take your life.'

' Well to be sure, he is an easy master ! ' said the Prince to himself as he walked up and down the room humming and singing, for he thought there would be plenty of time left to clean out the stable ; ' but it would be amusing to steal a glance into his other rooms as well,' thought the Prince, ' for there must be something that he is afraid of my seeing, as I am not allowed to enter them.' So he went into the first room. A cauldron was hanging from the walls ; it was boiling, but the Prince could see no fire under it. ' I wonder what is inside it,' he thought, and dipped a lock of his hair in, and the hair became just as if it were all made of copper. ' That's a nice kind of soup. If anyone were to taste that his throat would be gilded,' said the youth, and then he went into the next chamber. There, too, a cauldron was hanging from the wall, bubbling and boiling, but there was no fire under this either. ' I will just try what this is like too,' said the Prince, thrusting another lock of his hair into it, and it came out silvered over. ' Such costly soup is not to be had in my father's palace,' said the Prince ; ' but everything depends on how it tastes,' and then he went into the third room. There, too, a cauldron was hanging from the wall, boiling, exactly the same as in the two other rooms, and the Prince took pleasure in trying this also, so he dipped a lock of hair in, and it came out so brightly gilded that it shone again. 'Some talk about going from bad to worse,' said the Prince; 'but this is better and better. If he boils gold here, what can he boil in there?' He was determined to see, and went through the door into the fourth room. No cauldron was to be seen there, but on a bench someone was seated who was like a king s daughter, but, whosoever she was, she was so beautiful that never in the Prince's life had he seen her equal.

'Oh! in heaven's name what are you doing here?' said she who sat upon the bench.

'I took the place of servant here yesterday,' said the Prince.

'May you soon have a better place, if you have come to serve here!' said she.

'Oh! but I think I have got a kind master,' said the Prince. 'He has not given me hard work to do to-day. When I have cleaned out the stable I shall be done.'

'Yes, but how will you be able to do that?' she asked again. 'If you clean it out as other people do, ten pitchforksful will come in for every one you throw out. But I will teach you how to do it: you must turn your pitchfork upside down, and work with the handle, and then all will fly out of its own accord,'

' Yes, I will attend to that,' said the Prince, and stayed sitting where he was the whole day, for it was soon settled between them that they would marry each other, he and the King's daughter; so the first day of his service with the giant did not seem long to him. But when evening was ᴬrawing near she said that it would now be better for him to clean out the stable before the giant came home. When he got there he had a fancy to try if what she had said were true, so he began to work in the same way that he had seen the stable-boys doing in his father's stables, but he soon saw that he must give up that, for when he had worked a very short time he had scarcely room left to stand.　So he did what the Princess had taught him, turned the pitchfork round, and worked with the handle, and in the twinkling of an eye the stable was as clean as if it had been scoured.　When he had done that, he went back again into the room in which the giant had given him leave to stay, and there he walked backwards and forwards on the floor, and began to hum and to sing.

Then came the giant home with the goats.　' Have you cleaned the stable ? ' asked the giant.

' Yes, now it is clean and sweet, master,' said the King's son.

' I shall see about that,' said the giant, and went round to the stable, but it was just as the Prince had said.

' You have certainly been talking to my Master-maid, for you never got that out of your own head,' said the giant.

' Master-maid !　What kind of a thing is that, master ? ' said the Prince, making himself look as stupid as an ass ; ' I should like to see that.'

' Well, you will see her quite soon enough,' said the giant.

On the second morning the giant had again to go out with his goats, so he told the Prince that on that day he was to fetch home his horse, which was out on the mountain-side, and when he had done that he might rest himself for the remainder of the day, ' for you have come to a kind master, and that you shall find,' said the giant once more.　' But do not go into any of the rooms that I spoke of yesterday, or I will wring your head off,' said he, and then went away with his flock of goats.

' Yes, indeed, you are a kind master,' said the Prince ; ' but I will go in and talk to the Master-maid again ; perhaps before long she may like better to be mine than yours.'

So he went to her.　Then she asked him what he had to do that day.

' Oh! not very dangerous work, I fancy,' said the King's son. ' I have only to go up the mountain-side after his horse.'

' Well, how do you mean to set about it ? ' asked the Master-maid.

' Oh! there is no great art in riding a horse home,' said the King's son. ' I think I must have ridden friskier horses before now.'

' Yes, but it is not so easy a thing as you think to ride the horse home,' said the Master-maid; ' but I will teach you what to do. When you go near it, fire will burst out of its nostrils like flames from a pine torch : but be very careful, and take the bridle which is hanging by the door there, and fling the bit straight into its jaws, and then it will become so tame that you will be able to do what you like with it.' He said he would bear this in mind, and then he again sat in there the whole day by the Master-maid, and they chatted and talked of one thing and another, but the first thing and the last now was, how happy and delightful it would be if they could but marry each other, and get safely away from the giant ; and the Prince would have forgotten both the mountain-side and the horse if the Master-maid had not reminded him of them as evening drew near, and said that now it would be better if he went to fetch the horse before the giant came. So he did this, and took the bridle which was hanging on a crook, and strode up the mountain-side, and it was not long before he met with the horse, and fire and red flames streamed forth out of its nostrils. But the youth carefully watched his opportunity, and just as it was rushing at him with open jaws he threw the bit straight into its mouth, and the horse stood as quiet as a young lamb, and there was no difficulty at all in getting it home to the stable. Then the Prince went back into his room again, and began to hum and to sing.

Towards evening the giant came home. ' Have you fetched the horse back from the mountain-side ? ' he asked.

' That I have, master ; it was an amusing horse to ride, but I rode him straight home, and put him in the stable too,' said the Prince.

' I will see about that,' said the giant, and went out to the stable, but the horse was standing there just as the Prince had said. ' You have certainly been talking with my Master-maid, for you never got that out of your own head,' said the giant again.

' Yesterday, master, you talked about this Master-maid, and to-day you are talking about her ; ah! heaven bless you, master, why will you not show me the thing ? for it would be a real pleasure to me to see it,' said the Prince, who again pretended to be silly and stupid.

'Oh! you will see her quite soon enough,' said the giant.

On the morning of the third day the giant again had to go into the wood with the goats. 'To-day you must go underground and fetch my taxes,' he said to the Prince. 'When you have done this, you may rest for the remainder of the day, for you shall see what an easy master you have come to,' and then he went away.

'Well, however easy a master you may be, you set me very hard work to do,' thought the Prince; 'but I will see if I cannot find your Master-maid; you say she is yours, but for all that she may be able to tell me what to do now,' and he went to her. So, when the Master-maid asked him what the giant had set him to do that day, he told her that he was to go underground and get the taxes.

'And how will you set about that?' said the Master-maid.

'Oh! you must tell me how to do it,' said the Prince, 'for I have never yet been underground, and even if I knew the way I do not know how much I am to demand.'

'Oh! yes, I will soon tell you that; you must go to the rock there under the mountain-ridge, and take the club that is there, and knock on the rocky wall,' said the Master-maid. 'Then some-one will come out who will sparkle with fire: you shall tell him your errand, and when he asks you how much you want to have you are to say: "As much as I can carry."'

'Yes, I will keep that in mind,' said he, and then he sat there with the Master-maid the whole day, until night drew near, and he would gladly have stayed there till now if the Master-maid had not reminded him that it was time to be off to fetch the taxes before the giant came.

So he set out on his way, and did exactly what the Master-maid had told him. He went to the rocky wall, and took the club, and knocked on it. Then came one so full of sparks that they flew both out of his eyes and his nose. 'What do you want?' said he.

'I was to come here for the giant, and demand the tax for him,' said the King's son.

'How much are you to have then?' said the other.

'I ask for no more than I am able to carry with me,' said the Prince.

'It is well for you that you have not asked for a horse-load,' said he who had come out of the rock. 'But now come in with me.'

This the Prince did, and what a quantity of gold and silver he saw! It was lying inside the mountain like heaps of stones in a waste place, and he got a load that was as large as he was able to carry, and with that he went his way. So in the evening, when

the giant came home with the goats, the Prince went into the chamber and hummed and sang again as he had done on the other two evenings.

' Have you been for the tax ? ' said the giant.

' Yes, that I have, master,' said the Prince.

' Where have you put it then ? ' said the giant again.

' The bag of gold is standing there on the bench,' said the Prince.

' I will see about that,' said the giant, and went away to the bench, but the bag was standing there, and it was so full that gold and silver dropped out when the giant untied the string.

' You have certainly been talking with my Master-maid ! ' said the giant, ' and if you have I will wring your neck.'

' Master-maid ? ' said the Prince ; ' yesterday my master talked about this Master-maid, and to-day he is talking about her again, and the first day of all it was talk of the same kind. I do wish I could see the thing myself,' said he.

' Yes, yes, wait till to-morrow,' said the giant, ' and then I myself will take you to her.'

' Ah ! master, I thank you—but you are only mocking me,' said the King's son.

Next day the giant took him to the Master-maid. ' Now you shall kill him, and boil him in the great big cauldron you know of, and when you have got the broth ready give me a call,' said the giant ; then he lay down on the bench to sleep, and almost immediately began to snore so that it sounded like thunder among the hills.

So the Master-maid took a knife, and cut the Prince's little fingers, and dropped three drops of blood upon a wooden stool ; then she took all the old rags, and shoe-soles, and all the rubbish she could lay hands on, and put them in the cauldron; and then she filled a chest with gold dust, and a lump of salt, and a water-flask which was hanging by the door, and she also took with her a golden apple, and two gold chickens ; and then she and the Prince went away with all the speed they could, and when they had gone a little way they came to the sea, and then they sailed, but where they got the ship from I have never been able to learn.

Now, when the giant had slept a good long time, he began to stretch himself on the bench on which he was lying. ' Will it soon boil ? ' said he.

' It is just beginning,' said the first drop of blood on the stool.

So the giant lay down to sleep again, and slept for a long, long time. Then he began to move about a little again. ' Will it soon be ready now ? ' said he, but he did not look up this time any more than he had done the first time, for he was still half asleep.

' Half done ! ' said the second drop of blood, and the giant believed it was the Master-maid again, and turned himself on the bench, and lay down to sleep once more. When he had slept again for many hours, he began to move and stretch himself. ' Is it not done yet ? ' said he.

' It is quite ready,' said the third drop of blood. Then the giant began to sit up, and rub his eyes, but he could not see who it was who had spoken to him, so he asked for the Master-maid, and called her. But there was no one to give him an answer.

' Ah ! well, she has just stolen out for a little,' thought the giant, and he took a spoon, and went off to the cauldron to have a taste ; but there was nothing in it but shoe-soles, and rags, and such trumpery as that, and all was boiled up together, so that he could not tell whether it was porridge or milk pottage. When he saw this, he understood what had happened, and fell into such a rage that he hardly knew what he was doing. Away he went after the prince and the Master-maid, so fast that the wind whistled behind him, and it was not long before he came to the water, but he could not get over it. ' Well, well, I will soon find a cure for that : I have only to call my river-sucker,' said the giant, and he did call him. So his river-sucker came and lay down, and drank one, two, three draughts, and with that the water in the sea fell so low that the giant saw the Master-maid and the Prince out on the sea in their ship. ' Now you must throw out the lump of salt,' said the Master-maid, and the Prince did so, and it grew up into such a great high mountain right across the sea that the giant could not come over it, and the river-sucker could not drink any more water. ' Well, well, I will soon find a cure for that,' said the giant, so he called to his hill-borer to come and bore through the mountain so that the river-sucker might be able to drink up the water again. But just as the hole was made, and the river-sucker was beginning to drink, the Master-maid told the Prince to throw one or two drops out of the flask, and when he did this the sea instantly became full of water again, and before the river-sucker could take one drink they reached the land and were in safety. So they determined to go home to the Prince's father, but the Prince would on no account permit the Master-maid to walk there, for he thought that it was unbecoming either for her or for him to go on foot.

' Wait here the least little bit of time, while I go home for the seven horses which stand in my father's stable,' said he ; ' it is not far off, and I shall not be long away, but I will not let my betrothed bride go on foot to the palace.'

'Oh! no, do not go, for if you go home to the King's palace you will forget me, I foresee that.'

'How could I forget you? We have suffered so much evil together, and love each other so much,' said the Prince; and he insisted on going home for the coach with the seven horses, and she was to wait for him there, by the sea-shore. So at last the Master-maid had to yield, for he was so absolutely determined to do it. 'But when you get there you must not even give yourself time to greet anyone, but go straight into the stable, and take the

horses, and put them in the coach, and drive back as quickly as you can. For they will all come round about you; but you must behave just as if you did not see them, and on no account must you taste anything, for if you do it will cause great misery both to you and to me,' said she; and this he promised.

But when he got home to the King's palace one of his brothers was just going to be married, and the bride and all her kith and kin had come to the palace; so they all thronged round him, and questioned him about this and that, and wanted him to go in with them; but he behaved as if he did not see them, and went straight to the stable, and got out the horses and began to harness them. When they saw that they could not by any means prevail on him to go in with them, they came out to him with meat and drink, and the best of everything that they had prepared for the wedding ; but the Prince refused to touch anything, and would do nothing but put the horses in as quickly as he could. At last, however, the bride's sister rolled an apple across the yard to him, and said : ' As you won't eat anything else, you may like to take a bite of that, for you must be both hungry and thirsty after your long journey.' And he took up the apple and bit a piece out of it. But no sooner had he got the piece of apple in his mouth than he forgot the Master-maid and that he was to go back in the coach to fetch her.

' I think I must be mad ! what do I want with this coach and horses ? ' said he ; and then he put the horses back into the stable, and went into the King's palace, and there it was settled that he should marry the bride's sister, who had rolled the apple to him.

The Master-maid sat by the sea-shore for a long, long time, waiting for the Prince, but no Prince came. So she went away, and when she had walked a short distance she came to a little hut which stood all alone in a small wood, hard by the King's palace. She entered it and asked if she might be allowed to stay there. The hut belonged to an old crone, who was also an ill-tempered and malicious troll. At first she would not let the Master-maid remain with her ; but at last, after a long time, by means of good words and good payment, she obtained leave. But the hut was as dirty and black inside as a pigstye, so the Master-maid said that she would smarten it up a little, that it might look a little more like what other people's houses looked inside. The old crone did not like this either. She scowled, and was very cross, but the Master-maid did not trouble herself about that. She took out her chest of gold, and flung a handful of it or so into the fire, and the gold boiled up and poured out over the whole of the hut, until every part of it both inside and out was gilded. But when the gold began to bubble up the old hag grew so terrified that she fled away as if the Evil One himself were pursuing her, and she did not remember to stoop down as she went through the doorway, and so she split her head and died. Next morning the sheriff came travelling by there. He was greatly astonished when he saw the gold hut shining and glittering there in the copse, and he was still more astonished when he went in and caught sight of the beautiful young maiden who was sitting there; he fell in love with her at once, and straightway on the spot he begged her, both prettily and kindly, to marry him.

'Well, but have you a great deal of money?' said the Master-maid.

'Oh! yes; so far as that is concerned, I am not ill off,' said the sheriff. So now he had to go home to get the money, and in the evening he came back, bringing with him a bag with two bushels in it, which he set down on the bench. Well, as he had such a fine lot of money, the Master-maid said she would have him, so they sat down to talk.

But scarcely had they sat down together before the Master-maid wanted to jump up again. 'I have forgotten to see to the fire,' she said.

'Why should you jump up to do that?' said the sheriff; 'I will do that!' So he jumped up, and went to the chimney in one bound.

'Just tell me when you have got hold of the shovel,' said the Master-maid.

'Well, I have hold of it now,' said the sheriff.

'Then may you hold the shovel, and the shovel you, and pour red-hot coals over you, till day dawns,' said the Master-maid. So the sheriff had to stand there the whole night and pour red-hot coals over himself, and, no matter how much he cried and begged and entreated, the red-hot coals did not grow the colder for that. When the day began to dawn, and he had power to throw down the shovel, he did not stay long where he was, but ran away as fast as he possibly could; and everyone who met him stared and looked after him, for he was flying as if he were mad, and he could not have looked worse if he had been both flayed and tanned, and everyone wondered where he had been, but for very shame he would tell nothing.

The next day the attorney came riding by the place where the Master-maid dwelt. He saw how brightly the hut shone and gleamed through the wood, and he too went into it to see who lived there, and when he entered and saw the beautiful young maiden he fell even more in love with her than the sheriff had done, and began to woo her at once. So the Master-maid asked him, as she had asked the sheriff, if he had a great deal of money, and the attorney said he was not ill off for that, and would at once go home to get it; and at night he came with a great big sack of money—this time it was a four-bushel sack—and set it on the bench by the Master-maid. So she promised to have him, and he sat down on the bench by her to arrange about it, but suddenly she said that she had forgotten to lock the door of the porch that night, and must do it.

'Why should you do that?' said the attorney; 'sit still, I will do it.'

So he was on his feet in a moment, and out in the porch.

'Tell me when you have got hold of the door-latch,' said the Master-maid.

'I have hold of it now,' cried the attorney.

'Then may you hold the door, and the door you, and may you go between wall and wall till day dawns.'

What a dance the attorney had that night! He had never had such a waltz before, and he never wished to have such a dance again. Sometimes he was in front of the door, and sometimes the door was in front of him, and it went from one side of the porch to the other, till the attorney was well-nigh beaten to death. At first he began to abuse the Master-maid, and then to beg and pray, but the door did not care for anything but keeping him where he was till break of day.

As soon as the door let go its hold of him, off went the attorney. He forgot who ought to be paid off for what he had suffered, he forgot both his sack of money and his wooing, for he was so afraid lest the house-door should come dancing after him. Everyone who met him stared and looked after him, for he was flying like a madman, and he could not have looked worse if a herd of rams had been butting at him all night long.

On the third day the bailiff came by, and he too saw the gold house in the little wood, and he too felt that he must go and see who lived there; and when he caught sight of the Master-maid he became so much in love with her that he wooed her almost before he greeted her.

The Master-maid answered him as she had answered the other two, that if he had a great deal of money she would have him. 'So far as that is concerned, I am not ill off,' said the bailiff; so he was at once told to go home and fetch it, and this he did. At night he came back, and he had a still larger sack of money with him than the attorney had brought; it must have been at least six bushels, and he set it down on the bench. So it was settled that he was to have the Master-maid. But hardly had they sat down together before she said that she had forgotten to bring in the calf, and must go out to put it in the byre.

' No, indeed, you shall not do that,' said the bailiff; ' I am the one to do that.' And, big and fat as he was, he went out as briskly as a boy.

' Tell me when you have got hold of the calf's tail,' said the Master-maid.

' I have hold of it now,' cried the bailiff.

' Then may you hold the calf's tail, and the calf's tail hold you, and may you go round the world together till day dawns ! ' said the Master-maid. So the bailiff had to bestir himself, for the calf went over rough and smooth, over hill and dale, and, the more the bailiff cried and screamed, the faster the calf went. When daylight began to appear, the bailiff was half dead; and so glad was he to leave loose of the calf's tail that he forgot the sack of money and all else.

He walked now slowly—more slowly than the sheriff and the attorney had done, but, the slower he went, the more time had everyone to stare and look at him; and they used it too, and no one can imagine how tired out and ragged he looked after his dance with the calf.

On the following day the wedding was to take place in the King's palace, and the elder brother was to drive to church with his bride, and the brother who had been with the giant with her sister. But when they had seated themselves in the coach and were about to drive off from the palace one of the trace-pins broke, and, though they made one, two, and three to put in its place, that did not help them, for each broke in turn, no matter what kind of wood they used to make them of. This went on for a long time, and they could not get away from the palace, so they were all in great trouble. Then the sheriff said (for he too had been bidden to the wedding at Court) : ' Yonder away in the thicket dwells a maiden, and if you can but get her to lend you the handle of the shovel that she uses to make up her fire I know very well that it will hold fast.' So they sent off a messenger to the thicket, and begged so prettily that they might have the loan of her shovel-handle of which the sheriff had spoken that they were not refused ; so now they had a trace-pin which would not snap in two.

But all at once, just as they were starting, the bottom of the coach fell in pieces. They made a new bottom as fast as they could, but, no matter how they nailed it together, or what kind of wood they used, no sooner had they got the new bottom into the coach and were about to drive off than it broke again, so that they were still worse off than when they had broken the trace-pin. Then the attorney said, for he too was at the wedding in the palace : ' Away there in the thicket dwells a maiden, and if you could but get her to lend you one-half of her porch-door I am certain that it will hold together.' So they again sent a messenger to the thicket, and begged so prettily for the loan of the gilded porch-door of which the attorney had told them that they got it at once. They were just setting out again, but now the horses were not able to draw the coach. They had six horses already, and now they put in eight, and then ten, and then twelve, but the more they put in, and the more the coachman whipped them, the less good it did ; and the coach never stirred from the spot. It was already beginning to be late in the day, and to church they must and would go, so everyone who was in the palace was in a state of great distress. Then the bailiff spoke up and said : ' Out there in the gilded cottage in the thicket dwells a girl, and if you could but get her to lend you her calf I know it could draw the coach, even if it were as heavy as a mountain.' They all thought that it was ridiculous to be drawn to church by a calf, but there was nothing else for it but to send a messenger once more, and beg as prettily as they could, on behalf of the King, that she would let them have the loan of the calf that the bailiff had told them about. The Master-maid let them have it immediately—this time also she would not say ' no.'

Then they harnessed the calf to see if the coach would move ; and away it went, over rough and smooth, over stock and stone, so that they could scarcely breathe, and sometimes they were on the ground, and sometimes up in the air; and when they came to the church the coach began to go round and round like a spinning-wheel, and it was with the utmost difficulty and danger that they were able to get out of the coach and into the church. And when they went back again the coach went quicker still, so that most of them did not know how they got back to the palace at all.

When they had seated themselves at the table the Prince who had been in service with the giant said that he thought they ought to have invited the maiden who had lent them the shovel-handle, and the porch-door, and the calf up to the palace, 'for,' said he, 'if we had not got these three things, we should never have got away from the palace.'

The King also thought that this was both just and proper, so he sent five of his best men down to the gilded hut, to greet the maiden courteously from the King, and to beg her to be so good as to come up to the palace to dinner at mid-day.

'Greet the King, and tell him that, if he is too good to come to me, I am too good to come to him,' replied the Master-maid.

So the King had to go himself, and the Master-maid went with him immediately, and, as the King believed that she was more than she appeared to be, he seated her in the place of honour by the youngest bridegroom. When they had sat at table for a short time, the Master-maid took out the cock, and the hen, and the golden apple which she had brought away with her from the giant's house, and set them on the table in front of her, and instantly the cock and the hen began to fight with each other for the golden apple.

' Oh ! look how those two there are fighting for the golden apple,' said the King's son.

' Yes, and so did we two fight to get out that time when we were in the mountain,' said the Master-maid.

So the Prince knew her again, and you may imagine how delighted he was. He ordered the troll-witch who had rolled the apple to him to be torn in pieces between four-and-twenty horses, so that not a bit of her was left, and then for the first time they began really to keep the wedding, and, weary as they were, the sheriff, the attorney, and the bailiff kept it up too.[1]

[1] Asbjornsen and Möe.

WHY THE SEA IS SALT

ONCE upon a time, long, long ago, there were two brothers, the one rich and the other poor. When Christmas Eve came, the poor one had not a bite in the house, either of meat or bread; so he went to his brother, and begged him, in God's name, to give him something for Christmas Day. It was by no means the first time that the brother had been forced to give something to him, and he was not better pleased at being asked now than he generally was.

'If you will do what I ask you, you shall have a whole ham,' said he. The poor one immediately thanked him, and promised this.

'Well, here is the ham, and now you must go straight to Dead Man's Hall,' said the rich brother, throwing the ham to him.

'Well, I will do what I have promised,' said the other, and he took the ham and set off. He went on and on for the livelong day, and at nightfall he came to a place where there was a bright light.

'I have no doubt this is the place,' thought the man with the ham.

An old man with a long white beard was standing in the out-house, chopping Yule logs.

'Good-evening,' said the man with the ham.

'Good-evening to you. Where are you going at this late hour?' said the man.

'I am going to Dead Man's Hall, if only I am in the right track,' answered the poor man.

'Oh! yes, you are right enough, for it is here,' said the old man. 'When you get inside they will all want to buy your ham, for they don't get much meat to eat there: but you must not sell it unless you can get the hand-mill which stands behind the door for it. When you come out again I will teach you how to stop the hand-mill, which is useful for almost everything.

So the man with the ham thanked the other for his good advice, and rapped at the door.

When he got in, everything happened just as the old man had
said it would : all the people, great and small, came round him like
ants on an ant-hill, and each tried to outbid the other for the ham.

'By rights my old woman and I ought to have it for our
Christmas dinner, but, since you have set your hearts upon it, I
must just give it up to you,' said the man.   'But, if I sell it, I will
have the hand-mill which is standing there behind the door.'

At first they would not hear of this, and haggled and bargained with the man, but he stuck to what he had said, and the
people were forced to give him the hand-mill.   When the man came
out again into the yard, he asked the old wood-cutter how he was

to stop the hand-mill, and when he had learnt that he thanked
him and set off home with all the speed he could, but did not get
there until after the clock had struck twelve on Christmas Eve.

'But where in the world have you been ? ' said the old woman.
'Here I have sat waiting hour after hour, and have not even
two sticks to lay across each other under the Christmas porridge-
pot.'

'Oh ! I could not come before ; I had something of importance
to see about, and a long way to go, too ; but now you shall just see ! '
said the man, and then he set the hand-mill on the table, and bade
it first grind light, then a table-cloth, and then meat, and beer, and

everything else that was good for a Christmas Eve's supper; and the mill ground all that he ordered. 'Bless me!' said the old woman as one thing after another appeared; and she wanted to know where her husband had got the mill from, but he would not tell her that.

'Never mind where I got it; you can see that it is a good one, and the water that turns it will never freeze,' said the man. So he ground meat and drink, and all kinds of good things, to last all Christmas-tide, and on the third day he invited all his friends to come to a feast.

Now when the rich brother saw all that there was at the banquet and in the house, he was both vexed and angry, for he grudged everything his brother had. 'On Christmas Eve he was so poor that he came to me and begged for a trifle, for God's sake, and now he gives a feast as if he were both a count and a king!' thought he. 'But, for heaven's sake, tell me where you got your riches from,' said he to his brother.

'From behind the door,' said he who owned the mill, for he did not choose to satisfy his brother on that point; but later in the evening, when he had taken a drop too much, he could not refrain from telling how he had come by the hand-mill. 'There you see what has brought me all my wealth!' said he, and brought out the mill, and made it grind first one thing and then another. When the brother saw that he insisted on having the mill, and after a great deal of persuasion got it; but he had to give three hundred dollars for it, and the poor brother was to keep it till the haymaking was over, for he thought: 'If I keep it as long as that, I can make it grind meat and drink that will last many a long year.' During that time you may imagine that the mill did not grow rusty, and when hay-harvest came the rich brother got it, but the other had taken good care not to teach him how to stop it. It was evening when the rich man got the mill home, and in the morning he bade the old woman go out and spread the hay after the mowers, and he would attend to the house himself that day, he said.

So, when dinner-time drew near, he set the mill on the kitchen-table, and said: 'Grind herrings and milk pottage, and do it both quickly and well.'

So the mill began to grind herrings and milk pottage, and first all the dishes and tubs were filled, and then it came out all over the kitchen-floor. The man twisted and turned it, and did all he could to make the mill stop, but, howsoever he turned it and screwed it, the mill went on grinding, and in a short time the pottage rose so high that the man was like to be drowned. So he threw open the parlour-door, but it was not long before the mill had ground the parlour full too, and it was with difficulty and danger that the man could go through the stream of pottage and get hold of the door-latch. When he got the door open, he did not stay long in the room, but ran out, and the herrings and pottage came after him, and it streamed out over both farm and field. Now the old woman, who was out spreading the hay, began to think dinner was long in coming, and said to the women and the mowers : ' Though the master does not call us home, we may as well go. It may be that he finds he is not good at making pottage, and I should do well to help him.' So they began to straggle homewards, but when they had got a little way up the hill they met the herrings and pottage and bread, all pouring forth and winding about one over the other, and the man himself in front of the flood. ' Would to heaven that each of you had a hundred stomachs ! Take care that you are not drowned in the pottage ! ' he cried as he went by them as if Mischief were at his heels, down to where his brother dwelt. Then he begged him, for God's sake, to take the mill back again, and that in an instant, for, said he : ' If it grind one hour more the whole district will be destroyed by herrings and pottage.' But the brother would not take it until the other paid him three hundred dollars, and that he was obliged to do. Now the poor brother had both the money and the mill again. So it was not long before he had a farmhouse much finer than that in which his brother lived, but the mill ground him so much money that he covered it with plates of gold ; and the farmhouse lay close by the sea-shore, so it shone and glittered far out to sea. Everyone who sailed by there now had to put in to visit the rich man in the gold farmhouse, and everyone wanted to see the wonderful mill, for the report of it spread far and wide, and there was no one who had not heard tell of it.

After a long, long time came also a skipper who wished to see the mill. He asked if it could make salt. ' Yes, it could make salt,' said he who owned it, and when the skipper heard that he wished with all his might and main to have the mill, let it cost what it might, for, he thought, if he had it, he would get off having to sail far away over the perilous sea for freights of salt. At first the man would not hear of parting with it, but the skipper begged and prayed, and at last the man sold it to him, and got many, many thousand dollars for it. When the skipper had got the mill on his back he did not long stay there, for he was so afraid that the man should change his mind, and he had no time to ask how he was to stop it grinding, but got on board his ship as fast as he could.

When he had gone a little way out to sea he took the mill on deck. ' Grind salt, and grind both quickly and well,' said the skipper. So the mill began to grind salt, till it spouted out like water, and when the skipper had got the ship filled he wanted to stop the mill, but, whichsoever way he turned it, and how much soever he tried, it went on grinding, and the heap of salt grew higher and higher, until at last the ship sank.   There lies the mill at the bottom of the sea, and still, day by day, it grinds on : and that is why the sea is salt.[1]

[1] Asbjornsen and Möe.

THE MASTER CAT; OR, PUSS IN BOOTS

THERE was a miller who left no more estate to the three sons he had than his mill, his ass, and his cat. The partition was soon made. Neither the scrivener nor attorney was sent for. They would soon have eaten up all the poor patrimony. The eldest had the mill, the second the ass, and the youngest nothing but the cat.

The poor young fellow was quite comfortless at having so poor a lot.

'My brothers,' said he, 'may get their living handsomely enough by joining their stocks together; but, for my part, when I have eaten up my cat, and made me a muff of his skin, I must die of hunger.'

The Cat, who heard all this, but made as if he did not, said to him with a grave and serious air:

'Do not thus afflict yourself, my good master; you have nothing else to do but to give me a bag, and get a pair of boots made for me, that I may scamper through the dirt and the brambles, and you shall see that you have not so bad a portion of me as you imagine.'

The Cat's master did not build very much upon what he said; he had, however, often seen him play a great many cunning tricks to catch rats and mice; as when he used to hang by the heels, or hide himself in the meal, and make as if he were dead; so that he did not altogether despair of his affording him some help in his miserable condition. When the Cat had what he asked for, he booted himself very gallantly, and, putting his bag about his neck, he held the strings of it in his two fore paws, and went into a warren where was great abundance of rabbits. He put bran and sow-thistle into his bag, and, stretching out at length, as if he had been dead, he waited for some young rabbits, not yet acquainted with the deceits of the world, to come and rummage his bag for what he had put into it.

Scarce was he lain down but he had what he wanted: a rash
and foolish young rabbit jumped into his bag, and Monsieur Puss,
immediately drawing close the strings, took and killed him without
pity.   Proud of his prey, he went with it to the palace, and asked
to speak with his Majesty.   He was shown upstairs into the King's
apartment, and, making a low reverence, said to him:

'I have brought you, sir, a rabbit of the warren, which my noble
Lord, the Master of Carabas' (for that was the title which Puss was

pleased to give his master) 'has commanded me to present to your
Majesty from him.'

'Tell thy master,' said the King, 'that I thank him, and that he
does me a great deal of pleasure.'

Another time he went and hid himself among some standing
corn, holding still his bag open; and, when a brace of partridges
ran into it, he drew the strings, and so caught them both.   He went
and made a present of these to the King, as he had done before of
the rabbit which he took in the warren.   The King, in like manner,

received the partridges with great pleasure, and ordered him some money, to drink.

The Cat continued for two or three months thus to carry his Majesty, from time to time, game of his master's taking. One day in particular, when he knew for certain that he was to take the air along the river-side, with his daughter, the most beautiful princess in the world, he said to his master:

'If you will follow my advice your fortune is made. You have nothing else to do but go and wash yourself in the river, in that part I shall show you, and leave the rest to me.'

The Marquis of Carabas did what the Cat advised him to, without knowing why or wherefore. While he was washing the King passed by, and the Cat began to cry out:

'Help! help! My Lord Marquis of Carabas is going to be drowned.'

At this noise the King put his head out of the coach-window, and, finding it was the Cat who had so often brought him such good game, he commanded his guards to run immediately to the assistance of his Lordship the Marquis of Carabas. While they were drawing the poor Marquis out of the river, the Cat came up to the coach and told the King that, while his master was washing, there came by some rogues, who went off with his clothes, though he had cried out: 'Thieves! thieves!' several times, as loud as he could.

This cunning Cat had hidden them under a great stone. The King immediately commanded the officers of his wardrobe to run and fetch one of his best suits for the Lord Marquis of Carabas.

The King caressed him after a very extraordinary manner, and as the fine clothes he had given him extremely set off his good mien (for he was well made and very handsome in his person), the King's daughter took a secret inclination to him, and the Marquis of Carabas had no sooner cast two or three respectful and somewhat tender glances but she fell in love with him to distraction. The King would needs have him come into the coach and take part of the airing. The Cat, quite over-joyed to see his project begin to succeed, marched on before, and, meeting with some countrymen, who were mowing a meadow, he said to them:

'Good people, you who are mowing, if you do not tell the King that the meadow you mow belongs to my Lord Marquis of Carabas, you shall be chopped as small as herbs for the pot.'

The King did not fail asking of the mowers to whom the meadow they were mowing belonged.

'To my Lord Marquis of Carabas,' answered they altogether, for the Cat's threats had made them terribly afraid.

'You see, sir,' said the Marquis, 'this is a meadow which never fails to yield a plentiful harvest every year.'

The Master Cat, who went still on before, met with some reapers, and said to them:

'Good people, you who are reaping, if you do not tell the King that all this corn belongs to the Marquis of Carabas, you shall be chopped as small as herbs for the pot.'

The King, who passed by a moment after, would needs know to whom all that corn, which he then saw, did belong.

'To my Lord Marquis of Carabas,' replied the reapers, and the

King was very well pleased with it, as well as the Marquis, whom he congratulated thereupon. The Master Cat, who went always before, said the same words to all he met, and the King was astonished at the vast estates of my Lord Marquis of Carabas.

Monsieur Puss came at last to a stately castle, the master of which was an ogre, the richest had ever been known; for all the lands which the King had then gone over belonged to this castle. The Cat, who had taken care to inform himself who this ogre was and what he could do, asked to speak with him, saying he could not pass so near his castle without having the honour of paying his respects to him.

The ogre received him as civilly as an ogre could do, and made him sit down.

'I have been assured,' said the Cat, 'that you have the gift of being able to change yourself into all sorts of creatures you have a mind to; you can, for example, transform yourself into a lion, or elephant, and the like.'

'That is true,' answered the ogre very briskly; 'and to convince you, you shall see me now become a lion.'

Puss was so sadly terrified at the sight of a lion so near him

that he immediately got into the gutter, not without abundance of trouble and danger, because of his boots, which were of no use at all to him in walking upon the tiles. A little while after, when Puss saw that the ogre had resumed his natural form, he came down, and owned he had been very much frightened.

'I have been moreover informed,' said the Cat, 'but I know not how to believe it, that you have also the power to take on you the shape of the smallest animals; for example, to change

yourself into a rat or a mouse ; but I must own to you I take this
to be impossible.'

' Impossible ! ' cried the ogre ; ' you shall see that presently.'

And at the same time he changed himself into a mouse, and
began to run about the floor. Puss no sooner perceived this but
he fell upon him and ate him up.

Meanwhile the King, who saw, as he passed, this fine castle of
the ogre's, had a mind to go into it. Puss, who heard the noise
of his Majesty's coach running over the draw-bridge, ran out, and
said to the King :

' Your Majesty is welcome to this castle of my Lord Marquis of
Carabas.'

' What ! my Lord Marquis,' cried the King, ' and does this castle
also belong to you ? There can be nothing finer than this court
and all the stately buildings which surround it ; let us go into it, if
you please.'

The Marquis gave his hand to the Princess, and followed the
King, who went first. They passed into a spacious hall, where they
found a magnificent collation, which the ogre had prepared for
his friends, who were that very day to visit him, but dared not to
enter, knowing the King was there. His Majesty was perfectly

charmed with the good qualities of my Lord Marquis of Carabas, as was his daughter, who had fallen violently in love with him, and, seeing the vast estate he possessed, said to him, after having drunk five or six glasses:

'It will be owing to yourself only, my Lord Marquis, if you are not my son-in-law.'

The Marquis, making several low bows, accepted the honour which his Majesty conferred upon him, and forthwith, that very same day, married the Princess.

Puss became a great lord, and never ran after mice any more but only for his diversion.[1]

[1] Charles Perrault.

FELICIA AND THE POT OF PINKS

ONCE upon a time there was a poor labourer who, feeling that he had not much longer to live, wished to divide his possessions between his son and daughter, whom he loved dearly.

So he called them to him, and said : ' Your mother brought me as her dowry two stools and a straw bed ; I have, besides, a hen, a pot of pinks, and a silver ring, which were given me by a noble lady who once lodged in my poor cottage. When she went away she said to me :

'" Be careful of my gifts, good man ; see that you do not lose the ring or forget to water the pinks. As for your daughter, I promise you that she shall be more beautiful than anyone you ever saw in your life ; call her Felicia, and when she grows up give her the ring and the pot of pinks to console her for her poverty." Take them both then, my dear child,' he added, ' and your brother shall have everything else.'

The two children seemed quite contented, and when their father died they wept for him, and divided his possessions as he had told them. Felicia believed that her brother loved her, but when she sat down upon one of the stools he said angrily :

' Keep your pot of pinks and your ring, but let my things alone. I like order in my house.'

Felicia, who was very gentle, said nothing, but stood up crying quietly ; while Bruno, for that was her brother's name, sat comfortably by the fire. Presently, when supper-time came, Bruno had a delicious egg, and he threw the shell to Felicia, saying :

' There, that is all I can give you ; if you don't like it, go out and catch frogs ; there are plenty of them in the marsh close by.' Felicia did not answer, but she cried more bitterly than ever, and went away to her own little room. She found it filled with the sweet scent of the pinks, and, going up to them, she said sadly :

' Beautiful pinks, you are so sweet and so pretty, you are the only comfort I have left.   Be very sure that I will take care of you, and water you well, and never allow any cruel hand to tear you from your stems.'

As she leant over them she noticed that they were very dry. So taking her pitcher, she ran off in the clear moonlight to the fountain, which was at some distance.   When she reached it she sat down upon the brink to rest, but she had hardly done so when she saw a stately lady coming towards her, surrounded by numbers of attendants.   Six maids of honour carried her train, and she leaned upon the arm of another.

When they came near the fountain a canopy was spread for her, under which was placed a sofa of cloth-of-gold, and presently a dainty supper was served, upon a table covered with dishes of gold and crystal, while the wind in the trees and the falling water of the fountain murmured the softest music.

Felicia was hidden in the shade, too much astonished by all she saw to venture to move; but in a few moments the Queen said :

' I fancy I see a shepherdess near that tree; bid her come hither.'

So Felicia came forward and saluted the Queen timidly, but with so much grace that all were surprised.

' What are you doing here, my pretty child ? ' asked the Queen. ' Are you not afraid of robbers ? '

' Ah ! madam,' said Felicia, ' a poor shepherdess who has nothing to lose does not fear robbers.'

' You are not very rich, then ? ' said the Queen, smiling.

' I am so poor,' answered Felicia, ' that a pot of pinks and a silver ring are my only possessions in the world.'

'But you have a heart,' said the Queen. 'What should you say if anybody wanted to steal that?'

'I do not know what it is like to lose one's heart, madam,' she replied; 'but I have always heard that without a heart one cannot live, and if it is broken one must die; and in spite of my poverty I should be sorry not to live.'

'You are quite right to take care of your heart, pretty one,' said the Queen. 'But tell me, have you supped?'

'No, madam,' answered Felicia; 'my brother ate all the supper there was.'

Then the Queen ordered that a place should be made for her at the table, and herself loaded Felicia's plate with good things; but she was too much astonished to be hungry.

'I want to know what you were doing at the fountain so late?' said the Queen presently.

'I came to fetch a pitcher of water for my pinks, madam,' she answered, stooping to pick up the pitcher which stood beside her; but when she showed it to the Queen she was amazed to see that it had turned to gold, all sparkling with great diamonds, and the water, of which it was full, was more fragrant than the sweetest roses.   She was afraid to take it until the Queen said:

'It is yours, Felicia; go and water your pinks with it, and let it remind you that the Queen of the Woods is your friend.'

The shepherdess threw herself at the Queen's feet, and thanked her humbly for her gracious words.

'Ah! madam,' she cried, 'if I might beg you to stay here a moment I would run and fetch my pot of pinks for you—they could not fall into better hands.'

'Go, Felicia,' said the Queen, stroking her cheek softly; 'I will wait here until you come back.'

So Felicia took up her pitcher and ran to her little room, but while she had been away Bruno had gone in and taken the pot of pinks, leaving a great cabbage in its place. When she saw the unlucky cabbage Felicia was much distressed, and did not know what to do; but at last she ran back to the fountain, and, kneeling before the Queen, said:

'Madam, Bruno has stolen my pot of pinks, so I have nothing but my silver ring; but I beg you to accept it as a proof of my gratitude.'

'But if I take your ring, my pretty shepherdess,' said the Queen, 'you will have nothing left; and what will you do then?'

'Ah! madam,' she answered simply, 'if I have your friendship I shall do very well.'

So the Queen took the ring and put it on her finger, and mounted her chariot, which was made of coral studded with emeralds, and drawn by six milk-white horses. And Felicia looked after her until the winding of the forest path hid her from her sight, and then she went back to the cottage, thinking over all the wonderful things that had happened.

The first thing she did when she reached her room was to throw the cabbage out of the window.

But she was very much surprised to hear an odd little voice cry out: 'Oh! I am half killed!' and could not tell where it came from, because cabbages do not generally speak.

As soon as it was light, Felicia, who was very unhappy about her pot of pinks, went out to look for it, and the first thing she found was the unfortunate cabbage. She gave it a push with her foot, saying: 'What are you doing here, and how dared you put yourself in the place of my pot of pinks?'

'If I hadn't been carried,' replied the cabbage, 'you may be very sure that I shouldn't have thought of going there.'

It made her shiver with fright to hear the cabbage talk, but he went on:

'If you will be good enough to plant me by my comrades again, I can tell you where your pinks are at this moment—hidden in Bruno's bed!'

Felicia was in despair when she heard this, not knowing how she was to get them back. But she replanted the cabbage very kindly in his old place, and, as she finished doing it, she saw Bruno's hen, and said, catching hold of it:

'Come here, horrid little creature! you shall suffer for all the unkind things my brother has done to me.'

'Ah! shepherdess,' said the hen, 'don't kill me; I am rather a gossip, and I can tell you some surprising things that you will like to hear. Don't imagine that you are the daughter of the poor labourer who brought you up; your mother was a queen who had six girls already, and the King threatened that unless she had a son who could inherit his kingdom she should have her head cut off.

'So when the Queen had another little daughter she was quite frightened, and agreed with her sister (who was a fairy) to exchange her for the fairy's little son. Now the Queen had been shut up in a great tower by the King's orders, and when a great many days went by and still she heard nothing from the Fairy she made her escape from the window by means of a rope ladder, taking her little baby with her. After wandering about until she was half

dead with cold and fatigue she reached this cottage. I was the labourer's wife, and was a good nurse, and the Queen gave you into my charge, and told me all her misfortunes, and then died before she had time to say what was to become of you.

'As I never in all my life could keep a secret, I could not help telling this strange tale to my neighbours, and one day a beautiful lady came here, and I told it to her also. When I had finished she touched me with a wand she held in her hand, and instantly I became a hen, and there was an end of my talking! I was very sad, and my husband, who was out when it happened, never knew what had become of me. After seeking me everywhere he believed that I must have been drowned, or eaten up by wild beasts in the forest. That same lady came here once more, and commanded that you should be called Felicia, and left the ring and the pot of pinks to be given to you; and while she was in the house twenty-five of the King's guards came to search for you, doubtless meaning to kill you; but she muttered a few words, and immediately they all turned into cabbages. It was one of them whom you threw out of your window yesterday.

'I don't know how it was that he could speak—I have never heard either of them say a word before, nor have I been able to do it myself until now.'

The Princess was greatly astonished at the hen's story, and said kindly: 'I am truly sorry for you, my poor nurse, and wish it was in my power to restore you to your real form. But we must not despair; it seems to me, after what you have told me, that something must be going to happen soon. Just now, however, I must go and look for my pinks, which I love better than anything in the world.'

Bruno had gone out into the forest, never thinking that Felicia would search in his room for the pinks, and she was delighted by his unexpected absence, and thought to get them back without further trouble. But as soon as she entered the room she saw a terrible army of rats, who were guarding the straw bed; and when she attempted to approach it they sprang at her, biting and scratching furiously. Quite terrified, she drew back, crying out: ' Oh! my dear pinks, how can you stay here in such bad company ? '

Then she suddenly bethought herself of the pitcher of water, and, hoping that it might have some magic power, she ran to fetch it, and sprinkled a few drops over the fierce-looking swarm of rats. In a moment not a tail or a whisker was to be seen. Each one had made for his hole as fast as his legs could carry him, so that the Princess could safely take her pot of pinks. She found them nearly dying for want of water, and hastily poured all that was left in the pitcher upon them. As she bent over them, enjoying their delicious scent, a soft voice, that seemed to rustle among the leaves, said :

' Lovely Felicia, the day has come at last when I may have the happiness of telling you how even the flowers love you and rejoice in your beauty.'

The Princess, quite overcome by the strangeness of hearing a cabbage, a hen, and a pink speak, and by the terrible sight of an army of rats, suddenly became very pale, and fainted away.

At this moment in came Bruno. Working hard in the heat had not improved his temper, and when he saw that Felicia had succeeded in finding her pinks he was so angry that he dragged her out into the garden and shut the door upon her. The fresh air soon made her open her pretty eyes, and there before her stood the Queen of the Woods, looking as charming as ever.

' You have a bad brother,' she said ; `` I saw how cruelly he turned you out. Shall I punish him for it ? '

' Ah! no, madam,' she said ; ' I am not angry with him.

' But supposing he was not your brother, after all, what would you say then ? ' asked the Queen.

' Oh! but I think he must be,' said Felicia.

'What!' said the Queen, 'have you not heard that you are a princess?'

'I was told so a little while ago, madam, but how could I believe it without a single proof?'

'Ah! dear child,' said the Queen, 'the way you speak assures me that, in spite of your humble upbringing, you are indeed a real princess, and I can save you from being treated in such a way again.'

She was interrupted at this moment by the arrival of a very handsome young man. He wore a coat of green velvet fastened with emerald clasps, and had a crown of pinks on his head. He knelt upon one knee and kissed the Queen's hand.

'Ah!' she cried, 'my pink, my dear son, what a happiness to see you restored to your natural shape by Felicia's aid!' And she embraced him joyfully. Then turning to Felicia she said:

'Charming Princess, I know all the hen told you, but you cannot have heard that the zephyrs, to whom was entrusted the task of carrying my son to the tower where the Queen, your mother, so anxiously waited for him, left him instead in a garden of flowers, while they flew off to tell your mother. Whereupon a fairy with whom I had quarrelled changed him into a pink, and I could do nothing to prevent it.

'You may imagine how angry I was, and how I tried to find some means of undoing the mischief she had done; but there was no help for it. I could only bring Prince Pink to the place where you were being brought up, hoping that when you grew up he might love you, and by your care be restored to his natural form. And you see everything has come right, as I hoped it would. Your giving me the silver ring was the sign that the power of the charm was nearly over, and my enemy's last chance was to frighten you with her army of rats. That she did not succeed in doing; so now, my dear Felicia, if you will be married to my son with this silver ring your future happiness is certain. Do you think him handsome and amiable enough to be willing to marry him?'

'Madam,' replied Felicia, blushing, 'you overwhelm me with your kindness. I know that you are my mother's sister, and that by your art you turned the soldiers who were sent to kill me into cabbages, and my nurse into a hen, and that you do me only too much honour in proposing that I shall marry your son. How can I explain to you the cause of my hesitation? I feel, for the first time in my life, how happy it would make me to be beloved. Can you indeed give me the Prince's heart?'

'It is yours already, lovely Princess!' he cried, taking her hand in his; 'but for the horrible enchantment which kept me silent I should have told you long ago how dearly I love you.'

This made the Princess very happy, and the Queen, who could not bear to see her dressed like a poor shepherdess, touched her with her wand, saying:

'I wish you to be attired as befits your rank and beauty.' And immediately the Princess's cotton dress became a magnificent robe of silver brocade embroidered with carbuncles, and her soft dark hair was encircled by a crown of diamonds, from which floated a clear white veil. With her bright eyes, and the charming colour in her cheeks, she was altogether such a dazzling sight that the Prince could hardly bear it.

'How pretty you are, Felicia!' he cried. 'Don't keep me in suspense, I entreat you; say that you will marry me.'

'Ah!' said the Queen, smiling, 'I think she will not refuse now.'

Just then Bruno, who was going back to his work, came out of the cottage, and thought he must be dreaming when he saw Felicia; but she called him very kindly, and begged the Queen to take pity on him.

'What!' she said, 'when he was so unkind to you?'

'Ah! madam,' said the Princess, 'I am so happy that I should like everybody else to be happy too.'

The Queen kissed her, and said: 'Well, to please you, let me see what I can do for this cross Bruno.' And with a wave of her wand she turned the poor little cottage into a splendid palace, full of treasures; only the two stools and the straw bed remained just as they were, to remind him of his former poverty. Then the Queen touched Bruno himself, and made him gentle and polite and grateful, and he thanked her and the Princess a thousand times. Lastly, the Queen restored the hen and the cabbages to their natural forms, and left them all very contented. The Prince and Princess were married as soon as possible with great splendour, and lived happily ever after.[1]

[1] *Fortunée.* Par Madame la Comtesse d'Aulnoy.

THE WHITE CAT

ONCE upon a time there was a king who had three sons, who were all so clever and brave that he began to be afraid that they would want to reign over the kingdom before he was dead. Now the King, though he felt that he was growing old, did not at all wish to give up the government of his kingdom while he could still manage it very well, so he thought the best way to live in peace would be to divert the minds of his sons by promises which he could always get out of when the time came for keeping them.

So he sent for them all, and, after speaking to them kindly, he added :

' You will quite agree with me, my dear children, that my great age makes it impossible for me to look after my affairs of state as carefully as I once did. I begin to fear that this may affect the welfare of my subjects, therefore I wish that one of you should succeed to my crown ; but in return for such a gift as this it is only right that you should do something for me. Now, as I think of retiring into the country, it seems to me that a pretty, lively, faithful little dog would be very good company for me ; so, without any regard for your ages, I promise that the one who brings me the most beautiful little dog shall succeed me at once.'

The three Princes were greatly surprised by their father's sudden fancy for a little dog, but as it gave the two younger ones a chance they would not otherwise have had of being king, and as the eldest was too polite to make any objection, they accepted the commission with pleasure. They bade farewell to the King, who gave them presents of silver and precious stones, and appointed to meet them at the same hour, in the same place, after a year had passed, to see the little dogs they had brought for him.

Then they went together to a castle which was about a league from the city, accompanied by all their particular friends, to whom they gave a grand banquet, and the three brothers promised to be

friends always, to share whatever good fortune befell them, and not
to be parted by any envy or jealousy; and so they set out, agreeing
to meet at the same castle at the appointed time, to present themselves before the King together. Each one took a different road,
and the two eldest met with many adventures; but it is about the
youngest that you are going to hear. He was young, and gay, and
handsome, and knew everything that a prince ought to know; and
as for his courage, there was simply no end to it.

Hardly a day passed without his buying several dogs—big and

little, greyhounds, mastiffs, spaniels, and lapdogs. As soon as he
had bought a pretty one he was sure to see a still prettier, and then
he had to get rid of all the others and buy that one, as, being alone, he
found it impossible to take thirty or forty thousand dogs about with
him. He journeyed from day to day, not knowing where he was
going, until at last, just at nightfall, he reached a great, gloomy forest.
He did not know his way, and, to make matters worse, it began to
thunder, and the rain poured down. He took the first path he could
find, and after walking for a long time he fancied he saw a faint light,

and began to hope that he was coming to some cottage where he might find shelter for the night. At length, guided by the light, he reached the door of the most splendid castle he could have imagined. This door was of gold covered with carbuncles, and it was the pure red light which shone from them that had shown him the way through the forest. The walls were of the finest porcelain in all the most delicate colours, and the Prince saw that all the stories he had ever read were pictured upon them; but as he was quite terribly wet, and the rain still fell in torrents, he could not stay to look about any more, but came back to the golden door. There he saw a deer's foot hanging by a chain of diamonds, and he began to wonder who could live in this magnificent castle.

They must feel very secure against robbers,' he said to himself. ' What is to hinder anyone from cutting off that chain and digging out those carbuncles, and making himself rich for life ? '

He pulled the deer's foot, and immediately a silver bell sounded and the door flew open, but the Prince could see nothing but numbers of hands in the air, each holding a torch. He was so much surprised that he stood quite still, until he felt himself pushed forward by other hands, so that, though he was somewhat uneasy, he could not help going on. With his hand on his sword, to be prepared for whatever might happen, he entered a hall paved with lapis-lazuli, while two lovely voices sang :

> The hands you see floating above
> Will swiftly your bidding obey ;
> If your heart dreads not conquering Love,
> In this place you may fearlessly stay.

The Prince could not believe that any danger threatened him when he was welcomed in this way, so, guided by the mysterious hands, he went towards a door of coral, which opened of its own accord, and he found himself in a vast hall of mother-of-pearl, out of which opened a number of other rooms, glittering with thou-sands of lights, and full of such beautiful pictures and precious things that the Prince felt quite bewildered. After passing through sixty rooms the hands that conducted him stopped, and the Prince saw a most comfortable-looking arm-chair drawn up close to the chimney-corner; at the same moment the fire lighted itself, and the pretty, soft, clever hands took off the Prince's wet, muddy clothes, and presented him with fresh ones made of the richest stuffs, all embroidered with gold and emeralds. He could not help admiring everything he saw, and the deft way in which the hands waited on him, though they sometimes appeared so suddenly that they made him jump.

When he was quite ready—and I can assure you that he looked very different from the wet and weary Prince who had stood outside in the rain, and pulled the deer's foot—the hands led him to a splendid room, upon the walls of which were painted the histories of Puss in Boots and a number of other famous cats. The table was laid for supper with two golden plates, and golden spoons and forks, and the sideboard was covered with dishes and glasses of crystal set with precious stones. The Prince was wondering who the second place could be for, when suddenly in came about a dozen cats carrying guitars and rolls of music, who took their places at one end of the room, and under the direction of a cat who beat time with a roll of paper began to mew in every imaginable key, and to draw their claws across the strings of the guitars, making the strangest kind of music that could be heard. The Prince hastily stopped up his ears, but even then the sight of these comical musicians sent him into fits of laughter.

'What funny thing shall I see next?' he said to himself, and instantly the door opened, and in came a tiny figure covered by a long black veil. It was conducted by two cats wearing black mantles and carrying swords, and a large party of cats followed, who brought in cages full of rats and mice.

The Prince was so much astonished that he thought he must be dreaming, but the little figure came up to him and threw back its veil, and he saw that it was the loveliest little white cat it is possible to imagine. She looked very young and very sad, and in a sweet little voice that went straight to his heart she said to the Prince:

'King's son, you are welcome; the Queen of the Cats is glad to see you.'

'Lady Cat,' replied the Prince, 'I thank you for receiving me so kindly, but surely you are no ordinary pussy-cat? Indeed, the way you speak and the magnificence of your castle prove it plainly.'

'King's son,' said the White Cat, 'I beg you to spare me these compliments, for I am not used to them. But now,' she added, 'let supper be served, and let the musicians be silent, as the Prince does not understand what they are saying.'

So the mysterious hands began to bring in the supper, and

first they put on the table two dishes, one containing stewed pigeons and the other a fricassée of fat mice. The sight of the latter made the Prince feel as if he could not enjoy his supper at all; but the White Cat seeing this assured him that the dishes intended for him were prepared in a separate kitchen, and he might be quite certain that they contained neither rats nor mice; and the Prince felt so sure that she would not deceive him that he had no more hesitation in beginning. Presently he noticed that on the little paw that was next him the White Cat wore a bracelet con-

taining a portrait, and he begged to be allowed to look at it. To his great surprise he found it represented an extremely handsome young man, who was so like himself that it might have been his own portrait! The White Cat sighed as he looked at it, and seemed sadder than ever, and the Prince dared not ask any questions for fear of displeasing her; so he began to talk about other things, and found that she was interested in all the subjects he cared for himself, and seemed to know quite well what was going on in the world. After supper they went into another room, which was fitted up as a theatre, and the cats acted and danced for their amusement, and then the White Cat said good-night to him, and the hands conducted him into a room he had not seen before, hung with tapestry worked with butterflies' wings of every colour; there were mirrors that reached from the ceiling to the floor, and a little white bed with curtains of gauze tied up with ribbons. The Prince went to bed in silence, as he did not quite know how to begin a conversation with the hands that waited on him, and in the morning he was awakened by a noise and confusion outside his window, and the hands came and quickly dressed him in hunting costume. When he looked out all the cats were assembled in the courtyard, some leading greyhounds, some blowing horns, for the White Cat was going out hunting. The hands led a wooden horse up to the Prince, and seemed to expect him to mount it, at which he was very indignant; but it was no use for him to object, for he speedily found himself upon its back, and it pranced gaily off with him.

The White Cat herself was riding a monkey, which climbed even up to the eagles' nests when she had a fancy for the young eaglets. Never was there a pleasanter hunting party, and when they returned to the castle the Prince and the White Cat supped together as before, but when they had finished she offered him a crystal goblet, which must have contained a magic draught, for, as soon as he had swallowed its contents, he forgot everything, even the little dog that he was seeking for the King, and only thought how happy he was to be with the White Cat! And so the days passed, in every kind of amusement, until the year was nearly gone. The Prince had forgotten all about meeting his brothers: he did not even know what country he belonged to; but the White Cat knew when he ought to go back, and one day she said to him:

'Do you know that you have only three days left to look for the little dog for your father, and your brothers have found lovely ones?'

Then the Prince suddenly recovered his memory, and cried:

'What can have made me forget such an important thing? my whole fortune depends upon it; and even if I could in such a short time find a dog pretty enough to gain me a kingdom, where should I find a horse who could carry me all that way in three days?' And he began to be very vexed. But the White Cat said to him: 'King's son, do not trouble yourself; I am your friend, and will make everything easy for you. You can still stay here for a day, as the good wooden horse can take you to your country in twelve hours.'

'I thank you, beautiful Cat,' said the Prince; 'but what good will it do me to get back if I have not a dog to take to my father ? '

' See here,' answered the White Cat, holding up an acorn ; ' there is a prettier one in this than in the Dog-star ! '

' Oh ! White Cat dear,' said the Prince, 'how unkind you are to laugh at me now ! '

' Only listen,' she said, holding the acorn to his ear.

And inside it he distinctly heard a tiny voice say : ' Bow-wow ! '

The Prince was delighted, for a dog that can be shut up in an acorn must be very small indeed. He wanted to take it out and look at it, but the White Cat said it would be better not to open the acorn till he was before the King, in case the tiny dog should be cold on the journey. He thanked her a thousand times, and said good-bye quite sadly when the time came for him to set out.

' The days have passed so quickly with you,' he said, ' I only wish I could take you with me now.'

But the White Cat shook her head and sighed deeply in answer.

After all the Prince was the first to arrive at the castle where he had agreed to meet his brothers, but they came soon after, and stared in amazement when they saw the wooden horse in the court-yard jumping like a hunter.

The Prince met them joyfully, and they began to tell him all their adventures ; but he managed to hide from them what he had been doing, and even led them to think that a turnspit dog which he had with him was the one he was bringing for the King. Fond as they all were of one another, the two eldest could not help being glad to think that their dogs certainly had a better chance. The next morning they started in the same chariot. The elder brothers carried in baskets two such tiny, fragile dogs that they hardly dared to touch them. As for the turnspit, he ran after the chariot, and got so covered with mud that one could hardly see what he was like at all. When they reached the palace everyone crowded round to welcome them as they went into the King's great hall ; and when the two brothers presented their little dogs nobody could decide which was the prettier. They were already arranging between them-selves to share the kingdom equally, when the youngest stepped for-ward, drawing from his pocket the acorn the White Cat had given him. He opened it quickly, and there upon a white cushion they saw a dog so small that it could easily have been put through a ring. The Prince laid it upon the ground, and it got up at once and began to dance. The King did not know what to say, for it was impossible

that anything could be prettier than this little creature.   Nevertheless, as he was in no hurry to part with his crown, he told his sons
that, as they had been so successful the first time, he would ask them
to go once again, and seek by land and sea for a piece of muslin so fine
that it could be drawn through the eye of a needle.   The brothers
were not very willing to set out again, but the two eldest consented
because it gave them another chance, and they started as before.
The youngest again mounted the wooden horse, and rode back at
full speed to his beloved White Cat.   Every door of the castle

C.P.J.H.

stood wide open, and every window and turret was illuminated, so
it looked more wonderful than before. The hands hastened to meet
him, and led the wooden horse off to the stable, while he hurried
in to find the White Cat.   She was asleep in a little basket on a
white satin cushion, but she very soon started up when she heard
the Prince, and was over-joyed at seeing him once more.

' How could I hope that you would come back to me, King's son ? '
she said.   And then he stroked and petted her, and told her of his
successful journey, and how he had come back to ask her help, as

he believed that it was impossible to find what the King demanded. The White Cat looked serious, and said she must think what was to be done, but that, luckily, there were some cats in the castle who could spin very well, and if anybody could manage it they could, and she would set them the task herself.

And then the hands appeared carrying torches, and conducted the Prince and the White Cat to a long gallery which overlooked the river, from the windows of which they saw a magnificent display of fireworks of all sorts; after which they had supper, which the Prince liked even better than the fireworks, for it was very late, and he was hungry after his long ride. And so the days passed quickly as before; it was impossible to feel dull with the White Cat, and she had quite a talent for inventing new amusements—indeed, she was cleverer than a cat has any right to be. But when the Prince asked her how it was that she was so wise, she only said :

'King's son, do not ask me ; guess what you please. I may not tell you anything.'

The Prince was so happy that he did not trouble himself at all about the time, but presently the White Cat told him that the year was gone, and that he need not be at all anxious about the piece of muslin, as they had made it very well.

'This time,' she added, 'I can give you a suitable escort;' and on looking out into the courtyard the Prince saw a superb chariot of burnished gold, enamelled in flame colour with a thousand different devices. It was drawn by twelve snow-white horses, harnessed four abreast; their trappings were of flame-coloured velvet, embroidered with diamonds. A hundred chariots followed, each drawn by eight horses, and filled with officers in splendid uniforms, and a thousand guards surrounded the procession. 'Go !' said the White Cat, 'and when you appear before the King in such state he surely will not refuse you the crown which you deserve. Take this walnut, but do not open it until you are before him, then you will find in it the piece of stuff you asked me for.'

'Lovely Blanchette,' said the Prince, 'how can I thank you properly for all your kindness to me ? Only tell me that you wish it, and I will give up for ever all thought of being king, and will stay here with you always.'

'King's son,' she replied, 'it shows the goodness of your heart that you should care so much for a little white cat, who is good for nothing but to catch mice; but you must not stay.'

So the Prince kissed her little paw and set out. You can imagine how fast he travelled when I tell you that they reached the King's palace in just half the time it had taken the wooden horse to get there. This time the Prince was so late that he did not try to meet his brothers at their castle, so they thought he could not be coming, and were rather glad of it, and displayed their pieces of muslin to the King proudly, feeling sure of success. And indeed the stuff was very fine, and would go through the eye of a very large needle; but the King, who was only too glad to make a difficulty, sent for a particular needle, which was kept among the Crown jewels, and had such a small eye that everybody

saw at once that it was impossible that the muslin should pass through it. The Princes were angry, and were beginning to complain that it was a trick, when suddenly the trumpets sounded and the youngest Prince came in. His father and brothers were quite astonished at his magnificence, and after he had greeted them he took the walnut from his pocket and opened it, fully expecting to find the piece of muslin, but instead there was only a hazel-nut. He cracked it, and there lay a cherry-stone. Everybody was looking on, and the King was chuckling to himself at the idea of finding the piece of muslin in a nutshell.

However, the Prince cracked the cherry-stone, but everyone

laughed when he saw it contained only its own kernel. He opened that and found a grain of wheat, and in that was a millet seed. Then he himself began to wonder, and muttered softly :

' White Cat, White Cat, are you making fun of me ? '

In an instant he felt a cat's claw give his hand quite a sharp scratch, and hoping that it was meant as an encouragement he opened the millet seed, and drew out of it a piece of muslin four hundred ells long, woven with the loveliest colours and most wonderful patterns ; and when the needle was brought it went through the eye six times with the greatest ease ! The King turned pale, and the other Princes stood silent and sorrowful, for nobody could deny that this was the most marvellous piece of muslin that was to be found in the world.

Presently the King turned to his sons, and said, with a deep sigh :

' Nothing could console me more in my old age than to realise your willingness to gratify my wishes. Go then once more, and whoever at the end of a year can bring back the loveliest princess shall be married to her, and shall, without further delay, receive the crown, for my successor must certainly be married.' The Prince considered that he had earned the kingdom fairly twice over, but still he was too well bred to argue about it, so he just went back to his gorgeous chariot, and, surrounded by his escort, returned to the White Cat faster than he had come. This time she was expecting him, the path was strewn with flowers, and a thousand braziers were burning scented woods which perfumed the air. Seated in a gallery from which she could see his arrival, the White Cat waited for him. ' Well, King's son,' she said, ' here you are once more, without a crown.' ' Madam,' said he, ' thanks to your generosity I have earned one twice over ; but the fact is that my father is so loth to part with it that it would be no pleasure to me to take it.'

' Never mind,' she answered ; ' it's just as well to try and deserve it. As you must take back a lovely princess with you next time I will be on the look-out for one for you. In the meantime let us enjoy ourselves ; to-night I have ordered a battle between my cats and the river rats, on purpose to amuse you.' So this year slipped away even more pleasantly than the preceding ones. Sometimes the Prince could not help asking the White Cat how it was she could talk.

' Perhaps you are a fairy,' he said. ' Or has some enchanter changed you into a cat ? '

But she only gave him answers that told him nothing. Days go by so quickly when one is very happy that it is certain the Prince would never have thought of its being time to go back, when one evening as they sat together the White Cat said to him that if he wanted to take a lovely princess home with him the next day he must be prepared to do as she told him.

'Take this sword,' she said, 'and cut off my head!'

'I!' cried the Prince, 'I cut off your head! Blanchette darling, how could I do it?'

'I entreat you to do as I tell you, King's son,' she replied.

The tears came into the Prince's eyes as he begged her to ask him anything but that—to set him any task she pleased as a proof of his devotion, but to spare him the grief of killing his dear Pussy. But nothing he could say altered her determination, and at last he drew his sword, and desperately, with a trembling hand, cut off the little white head. But imagine his astonishment and delight when suddenly a lovely princess stood before him, and, while he was still speechless with amazement, the door opened and a goodly company of knights and ladies entered, each carrying a cat's skin!

They hastened with every sign of joy to the Princess, kissing her hand and congratulating her on being once more restored to her natural shape. She received them graciously, but after a few minutes begged that they would leave her alone with the Prince, to whom she said :

'You see, Prince, that you were right in supposing me to be no ordinary cat. My father reigned over six kingdoms. The Queen, my mother, whom he loved dearly, had a passion for travelling and exploring, and when I was only a few weeks old she obtained his permission to visit a certain mountain of which she had heard many marvellous tales, and set out, taking with her a number of her attendants. On the way they had to pass near an old castle belonging to the fairies. Nobody had ever been into it, but it was reported to be full of the most wonderful things, and my mother remembered to have heard that the fairies had in their garden such fruits as were to be seen and tasted nowhere else. She began to wish to try them for herself, and turned her steps in the direction of the garden. On arriving at the door, which blazed with gold and jewels, she ordered her servants to knock loudly, but it was useless ; it seemed as if all the inhabitants of the castle must be asleep or dead. Now the more difficult it became to obtain the fruit, the more the Queen was determined that have it she would. So she ordered that they should bring ladders, and get over the wall into the garden ; but though the wall did not look very high, and they tied the ladders together to make them very long, it was quite impossible to get to the top.

'The Queen was in despair, but as night was coming on she ordered that they should encamp just where they were, and went to bed herself, feeling quite ill, she was so disappointed. In the middle of the night she was suddenly awakened, and saw to her surprise a tiny, ugly old woman seated by her bedside, who said to her :

' " I must say that we consider it somewhat troublesome of your Majesty to insist upon tasting our fruit ; but, to save you any annoyance, my sisters and I will consent to give you as much as you can carry away, on one condition—that is, that you shall give us your little daughter to bring up as our own."

' " Ah ! my dear madam," cried the Queen, " is there nothing else that you will take for the fruit ? I will give you my kingdoms willingly."

' " No," replied the old fairy, " we will have nothing but your little daughter. She shall be as happy as the day is long, and we will give her everything that is worth having in fairy-land, but you must not see her again until she is married."

' " Though it is a hard condition," said the Queen, " I consent, for I shall certainly die if I do not taste the fruit, and so I should lose my little daughter either way."

' So the old fairy led her into the castle, and, though it was still the middle of the night, the Queen could see plainly that it was far more beautiful than she had been told, ' which you can easily believe, Prince,' said the White Cat, ' when I tell you that it was this castle that we are now in. " Will you gather the fruit yourself, Queen ? " said the old fairy, " or shall I call it to come to you ? "

' " I beg you to let me see it come when it is called," cried the Queen; " that will be something quite new." The old fairy whistled twice, then she cried :

' " Apricots, peaches, nectarines, cherries, plums, pears, melons, grapes, apples, oranges, lemons, gooseberries, strawberries, raspberries, come ! "

' And in an instant they came tumbling in, one over another, and yet they were neither dusty nor spoilt, and the Queen found them quite as good as she had fancied them. You see they grew upon fairy trees.

' The old fairy gave her golden baskets in which to take the fruit away, and it was as much as four hundred mules could carry. Then she reminded the Queen of her agreement, and led her back to the camp, and next morning she went back to her kingdom; but before she had gone very far she began to repent of her bargain, and when the King came out to meet her she looked so sad that he guessed that something had happened, and asked what was the matter. At first the Queen was afraid to tell him, but when, as soon as they reached the palace, five frightful little dwarfs were sent by the fairies to fetch me, she was obliged to confess what she had promised. The King was very angry, and had the Queen and myself shut up in a great tower and safely guarded, and drove the little dwarfs out of his kingdom; but the fairies sent a great dragon who ate up all the people he met, and whose breath burnt up everything as he passed through the country; and at last, after trying in vain to rid himself of the monster, the King, to save his subjects, was obliged to consent that I should be given up to the fairies. This time they came themselves to fetch me, in a chariot of pearl drawn by sea-horses, followed by the dragon, who was led with chains of diamonds. My cradle was placed between the old fairies, who loaded me with caresses, and away we whirled through the air to a tower which they had built on purpose for me. There I grew up surrounded with everything that was beautiful and rare, and learning everything that is ever taught to a princess, but without any companions but a parrot and a little dog, who could both talk; and receiving every day a visit from one of the old fairies, who came mounted upon the dragon. One day, however, as I sat at my window I saw a handsome young prince, who seemed to have been hunting in the forest which surrounded my prison, and who was

standing and looking up at me. When he saw that I observed him he saluted me with great deference. You can imagine that I was delighted to have some one new to talk to, and in spite of the height of my window our conversation was prolonged till night fell, then my prince reluctantly bade me farewell. But after that he came again many times, and at last I consented to marry him, but the question was how I was to escape from my tower. The fairies always supplied me with flax for my spinning, and by great diligence I made enough cord for a ladder that would reach to the foot of the tower; but, alas! just as my prince was helping me to descend it, the crossest and ugliest of the old fairies flew in. Before he had time to defend himself my unhappy lover was swallowed up by the dragon. As for me, the fairies, furious at having their plans defeated, for they intended me to marry the king of the dwarfs and I utterly refused, changed me into a white cat. When they brought me here I found all the lords and ladies of my father's court awaiting me under the same enchantment, while the people of lesser rank had been made invisible, all but their hands.

'As they laid me under the enchantment the fairies told me all my history, for until then I had quite believed that I was their child, and warned me that my only chance of regaining my natural form was to win the love of a prince who resembled in every way my unfortunate lover.'

'And you have won it, lovely Princess,' interrupted the Prince.

'You are indeed wonderfully like him,' resumed the Princess— 'in voice, in features, and everything; and if you really love me all my troubles will be at an end.'

'And mine too,' cried the Prince, throwing himself at her feet, 'if you will consent to marry me.'

'I love you already better than anyone in the world,' she said; 'but now it is time to go back to your father, and we shall hear what he says about it.'

So the Prince gave her his hand and led her out, and they mounted the chariot together; it was even more splendid than before, and so was the whole company. Even the horses' shoes were of rubies with diamond nails, and I suppose that is the first time such a thing was ever seen.

As the Princess was as kind and clever as she was beautiful, you may imagine what a delightful journey the Prince found it, for everything the Princess said seemed to him quite charming.

When they came near the castle where the brothers were to meet, the Princess got into a chair carried by four of the guards; it was hewn out of one splendid crystal, and had silken curtains, which she drew round her that she might not be seen.

The Prince saw his brothers walking upon the terrace, each with a lovely princess, and they came to meet him, asking if he had also found a wife. He said that he had found something much rarer—a little white cat! At which they laughed very much, and asked him if he was afraid of being eaten up by mice in the palace. And then they set out together for the town. Each prince and princess rode in a splendid carriage; the horses were decked with

THE PRINCE'S BRIDE.

plumes of feathers, and glittered with gold. After them came the youngest prince, and last of all the crystal chair, at which everybody looked with admiration and curiosity. When the courtiers saw them coming they hastened to tell the King.

' Are the ladies beautiful ? ' he asked anxiously.

And when they answered that nobody had ever before seen such lovely princesses he seemed quite annoyed.

However, he received them graciously, but found it impossible to choose between them.

Then turning to his youngest son he said :

' Have you come back alone, after all ? '

' Your Majesty,' replied the Prince, ' will find in that crystal chair a little white cat, which has such soft paws, and mews so prettily, that I am sure you will be charmed with it.'

The King smiled, and went to draw back the curtains himself, but at a touch from the Princess the crystal shivered into a thousand splinters, and there she stood in all her beauty; her fair hair floated over her shoulders and was crowned with flowers, and her softly falling robe was of the purest white. She saluted the King gracefully, while a murmur of admiration rose from all around.

' Sire,' she said, ' I am not come to deprive you of the throne you fill so worthily. I have already six kingdoms, permit me to bestow one upon you, and upon each of your sons. I ask nothing but your friendship, and your consent to my marriage with your youngest son; we shall still .have three kingdoms left for ourselves.'

The King and all the courtiers could not conceal their joy and astonishment, and the marriage of the three Princes was celebrated at once. The festivities lasted several months, and then each king and queen departed to their own kingdom and lived happily ever after.[1]

[1] *La Chatte blanche.* Par Madame la Comtesse d'Aulnoy.

THE WATER-LILY. THE GOLD-SPINNERS

ONCE upon a time, in a large forest, there lived an old woman and three maidens. They were all three beautiful, but the youngest was the fairest. Their hut was quite hidden by trees, and none saw their beauty but the sun by day, the moon by night, and the eyes of the stars. The old woman kept the girls hard at work, from morning till night, spinning gold flax into yarn, and when one distaff was empty another was given them, so they had no rest. The thread had to be fine and even, and when done was locked up in a secret chamber by the old woman, who twice or thrice every summer went a journey. Before she went she gave out work for each day of her absence, and always returned in the night, so that the girls never saw what she brought back with her, neither would she tell them whence the gold flax came, nor what it was to be used for.

Now, when the time came round for the old woman to set out on one of these journeys, she gave each maiden work for six days, with the usual warning: 'Children, don't let your eyes wander, and on no account speak to a man, for, if you do, your thread will lose its brightness, and misfortunes of all kinds will follow.' They laughed at this oft-repeated caution, saying to each other: 'How can our gold thread lose its brightness, and have we any chance of speaking to a man?'

On the third day after the old woman's departure a young prince, hunting in the forest, got separated from his companions, and completely lost. Weary of seeking his way, he flung himself down under a tree, leaving his horse to browse at will, and fell asleep.

The sun had set when he awoke and began once more to try and find his way out of the forest. At last he perceived a narrow foot-path, which he eagerly followed and found that it led him to a small hut. The maidens, who were sitting at the door of their hut

for coolness, saw him approaching, and the two elder were much
alarmed, for they remembered the old woman's warning; but the
youngest said : 'Never before have I seen anyone like him; let me
have one look.' They entreated her to come in, but, seeing that
she would not, left her, and the Prince, coming up, courteously
greeted the maiden, and told her he had lost his way in the forest
and was both hungry and weary. She set food before him, and was
so delighted with his conversation that she forgot the old woman's
caution, and lingered for hours. In the meantime the Prince's
companions sought him far and wide, but to no purpose, so they
sent two messengers to tell the sad news to the King, who immediately ordered a regiment of cavalry and one of infantry to go and
look for him.

After three days' search, they found the hut. The Prince was
still sitting by the door and had been so happy in the maiden's
company that the time had seemed like a single hour. Before
leaving he promised to return and fetch her to his father's court,
where he would make her his bride. When he had gone, she sat
down to her wheel to make up for lost time, but was dismayed
to find that her thread had lost all its brightness. Her heart
beat fast and she wept bitterly, for she remembered the old
woman's warning and knew not what misfortune might now befall
her.

The old woman returned in the night and knew by the tarnished
thread what had happened in her absence. She was furiously angry
and told the maiden that she had brought down misery both on

herself and on the Prince. The maiden could not rest for thinking of this. At last she could bear it no longer, and resolved to seek help from the Prince.

As a child she had learnt to understand the speech of birds, and this was now of great use to her, for, seeing a raven pluming itself on a pine bough, she cried softly to it : ' Dear bird, cleverest of all birds, as well as swiftest of wing, wilt thou help me ? ' ' How can I help thee ? ' asked the raven. She answered : ' Fly away, until thou comest to a splendid town, where stands a king's palace ; seek out the king's son and tell him that a great misfortune has befallen me.' Then she told the raven how her thread had lost its brightness, how terribly angry the old woman was, and how she feared some great disaster. The raven promised faithfully to do her bidding, and, spreading its wings, flew away. The maiden now went home and worked hard all day at winding up the yarn her elder sisters had spun, for the old woman would let her spin no longer. Towards evening she heard the raven's ' craa, craa ' from the pine tree and eagerly hastened thither to hear the answer.

By great good fortune the raven had found a wind wizard's son in the palace garden, who understood the speech of birds, and to him he had entrusted the message. When the Prince heard it, he was very sorrowful, and took counsel with his friends how to free the maiden. Then he said to the wind wizard's son : ' Beg the raven to fly quickly back to the maiden and tell her to be ready on the ninth night, for then will I come and fetch her away.' The wind wizard's son did this, and the raven flew so swiftly that it reached the hut that same evening. The maiden thanked the bird heartily and went home, telling no one what she had heard.

As the ninth night drew near she became very unhappy, for she feared lest some terrible mischance should arise and ruin all. On the night she crept quietly out of the house and waited trembling at some little distance from the hut. Presently she heard the muffled tramp of horses, and soon the armed troop appeared, led by the Prince, who had prudently marked all the trees beforehand, in order to know the way. When he saw the maiden he sprang from his horse, lifted her into the saddle, and then, mounting behind, rode homewards. The moon shone so brightly that they had no difficulty in seeing the marked trees.

By-and-by the coming dawn loosened the tongues of all the birds, and, had the Prince only known what they were saying, or the maiden been listening, they might have been spared much sorrow, but they were thinking only of each other, and when they came out of the forest the sun was high in the heavens.

Next morning, when the youngest girl did not come to her work, the old woman asked where she was. The sisters pretended not to know, but the old woman easily guessed what had happened, and, as she was in reality a wicked witch, determined to punish the fugitives. Accordingly, she collected nine different kinds of enchanters' nightshade, added some salt, which she first bewitched, and, doing all up in a cloth into the shape of a fluffy ball, sent it after them on the wings of the wind, saying :

> Whirlwind!--mother of the wind !
> Lend thy aid 'gainst her who sinned!
> Carry with thee this magic ball.
> Cast her from his arms for ever,
> Bury her in the rippling river.

At midday the Prince and his men came to a deep river, spanned by so narrow a bridge that only one rider could cross at a time. The horse on which the Prince and the maiden were riding had just reached the middle when the magic ball flew by. The horse in its fright suddenly reared, and before anyone could stop it flung the maiden into the swift current below. The Prince tried to jump in after her, but his men held him back, and in spite of his struggles led him home, where for six weeks he shut himself up in a secret chamber, and would neither eat nor drink, so great was his grief, At last he became so ill his life was despaired of, and in great alarm the King caused all the wizards of his country to be summoned. But none could cure him. At last the wind wizard's son said to the King : ' Send for the old wizard from Finland, he knows more than all the wizards of your kingdom put together.' A messenger was at once sent to Finland, and a week later the old wizard himself arrived on the wings of the wind. ' Honoured King,' said the wizard, ' the wind has blown this illness upon your son, and a magic ball has snatched away his beloved. This it is which makes him grieve so constantly. Let the wind blow upon him that it may blow away his sorrow.' Then the King made his son go out into the wind, and he gradually recovered and told his father all. ' Forget the maiden,' said the King, ' and take another bride ; ' but the Prince said he could never love another.

A year afterwards he came suddenly upon the bridge where his beloved had met her death. As he recalled the misfortune he wept bitterly, and would have given all he possessed to have her once more alive. In the midst of his grief he thought he heard a voice singing, and looked round, but could see no one. Then he heard the voice again, and it said:

> Alas ! bewitched and all forsaken,
> 'Tis I must lie for ever here !
> My beloved no thought has taken
> To free his bride, that was so dear.

He was greatly astonished, sprang from his horse, and looked every-where to see if no one were hidden under the bridge; but no one was there. Then he noticed a yellow water-lily floating on the surface of the water, half hidden by its broad leaves ; but flowers do not sing, and in great surprise he waited, hoping to hear more. Then again the voice sang:

> Alas ! bewitched and all forsaken,
> 'Tis I must lie for ever here !
> My beloved no thought has taken
> To free his bride, that was so dear.

The Prince suddenly remembered the gold-spinners, and said to himself: ' If I ride thither, who knows but that they could explain this to me ? ' He at once rode to the hut, and found the two maidens at the fountain. He told them what had befallen their sister the year before, and how he had twice heard a strange song, but yet could see no singer. They said that the yellow water-lily could be none other than their sister, who was not dead, but trans-formed by the magic ball. Before he went to bed, the eldest made a cake of magic herbs, which she gave him to eat. In the night he dreamt that he was living in the forest and could understand all that the birds said to each other. Next morning he told this to the maidens, and they said that the charmed cake had caused it, and advised him to listen well to the birds, and see what they could tell him, and when he had recovered his bride they begged him to return and deliver them from their wretched bondage.

Having promised this, he joyfully returned home, and as he was riding through the forest he could perfectly understand all that the birds said. He heard a thrush say to a magpie : ' How stupid men are ! they cannot understand the simplest thing. It is now quite a year since the maiden was transformed into a water-lily, and, though she sings so sadly that anyone going over the bridge must hear her, yet no one comes to her aid. Her former bridegroom

THE GOLD-SPINNERS.

rode over it a few days ago and heard her singing, but was no wiser than the rest.'

'And he is to blame for all her misfortunes,' added the magpie. 'If he heeds only the words of men she will remain a flower for ever. She were soon delivered were the matter only laid before the old wizard of Finland.'

After hearing this, the Prince wondered how he could get a message conveyed to Finland. He heard one swallow say to another : 'Come, let us fly to Finland : we can build better nests there.'

'Stop, kind friends !' cried the Prince. 'Will ye do something for me ?' The birds consented, and he said : 'Take a thousand greetings from me to the wizard of Finland, and ask him how I may restore a maiden transformed into a flower to her own form.'

The swallows flew away, and the Prince rode on to the bridge. There he waited, hoping to hear the song. But he heard nothing but the rushing of the water and the moaning of the wind, and, disappointed, rode home.

Shortly after, he was sitting in the garden, thinking that the swallows must have forgotten his message, when he saw an eagle flying above him. The bird gradually descended until it perched on a tree close to the Prince and said : 'The wizard of Finland greets thee and bids me say that thou mayst free the maiden thus : Go to the river and smear thyself all over with mud; then say: "From a man into a crab," and thou wilt become a crab. Plunge boldly into the water, swim as close as thou canst to the water-lily's roots, and loosen them from the mud and reeds. This done, fasten thy claws into the roots and rise with them to the surface. Let the water flow all over the flower, and drift with the current until thou comest to a mountain ash tree on the left bank. There is near it a large stone. Stop there and say : " From a crab into a man, from a water-lily into a maiden," and ye will both be restored to your own forms.'

Full of doubt and fear, the Prince let some time pass before he was bold enough to attempt to rescue the maiden. Then a crow said to him : 'Why dost thou hesitate ? The old wizard has not told thee wrong, neither have the birds deceived thee; hasten and dry the maiden's tears.'

'Nothing worse than death can befall me,' thought the Prince, 'and death is better than endless sorrow.' So he mounted his horse and went to the bridge. Again he heard the water-lily's lament, and, hesitating no longer, smeared himself all over with mud, and,

saying : ' From a man into a crab,' plunged into the river. For one
moment the water hissed in his ears, and then all was silent. He
swam up to the plant and began to loosen its roots, but so firmly
were they fixed in the mud and reeds that this took him a long
time. He then grasped them and rose to the surface, letting the
water flow over the flower. The current carried them down the
stream, but nowhere could he see the mountain ash. At last he
saw it, and close by the large stone. Here he stopped and said :
' From a crab into a man, from a water-lily into a maiden,' and to
his delight found himself once more a prince, and the maiden was
by his side. She was ten times more beautiful than before, and
wore a magnificent pale yellow robe, sparkling with jewels. She

thanked him for having freed her from the cruel witch's power,
and willingly consented to marry him.

But when they came to the bridge where he had left his horse
it was nowhere to be seen, for, though the Prince thought he had
been a crab only a few hours, he had in reality been under the
water for more than ten days. While they were wondering how
they should reach his father's court, they saw a splendid coach
driven by six gaily caparisoned horses coming along the bank. In
this they drove to the palace. The King and Queen were at church,
weeping for their son, whom they had long mourned for dead.
Great was their delight and astonishment when the Prince entered,
leading the beautiful maiden by the hand. The wedding was at

once celebrated, and there was feasting and merry-making throughout the kingdom for six weeks.

Some time afterwards the Prince and his bride were sitting in the garden, when a crow said to them: 'Ungrateful creatures! Have ye forgotten the two poor maidens who helped ye in your distress? Must they spin gold flax for ever? Have no pity on the old witch. The three maidens are princesses, whom she stole away when they were children together, with all the silver utensils, which she turned into gold flax. Poison were her fittest punishment.'

The Prince was ashamed of having forgotten his promise and set out at once, and by great good fortune reached the hut when the old woman was away. The maidens had dreamt that he was coming, and were ready to go with him, but first they made a cake in which they put poison, and left it on a table where the old woman was likely to see it when she returned. She *did* see it, and thought it looked so tempting that she greedily ate it up and at once died.

In the secret chamber were found fifty waggon-loads of gold flax, and as much more was discovered buried. The hut was razed to the ground, and the Prince and his bride and her two sisters lived happily ever after.

THE TERRIBLE HEAD

ONCE upon a time there was a king whose only child was a girl. Now the King had been very anxious to have a son, or at least a grandson, to come after him, but he was told by a prophet whom he consulted that his own daughter's son should kill him. This news terrified him so much that he determined never to let his daughter be married, for he thought it was better to have no grandson at all than to be killed by his grandson. He therefore called his workmen together, and bade them dig a deep round hole in the earth, and then he had a prison of brass built in the hole, and then, when it was finished, he locked up his daughter. No man ever saw her, and she never saw even the fields and the sea, but only the sky and the sun, for there was a wide open window in the roof of the house of brass. So the Princess would sit looking up at the sky, and watching the clouds float across, and wondering whether she should ever get out of her prison. Now one day it seemed to her that the sky opened above her, and a great shower of shining gold fell through the window in the roof, and lay glittering in her room. Not very long after, the princess had a baby, a little boy, but when the King her father heard of it he was very angry and afraid, for now the child was born that should be his death. Yet, cowardly as he was, he had not quite the heart to kill the Princess and her baby outright, but he had them put in a huge brass-bound chest and thrust out to sea, that they might either be drowned or starved, or perhaps come to a country where they would be out of his way.

So the Princess and the baby floated and drifted in the chest on the sea all day and all night, but the baby was not afraid of the waves nor of the wind, for he did not know that they could hurt him, and he slept quite soundly. And the Princess sang a song over him, and this was her song:

Child, my child, how sound you sleep!
Though your mother's care is deep,

You can lie with heart at rest
In the narrow brass-bound chest;
In the starless night and drear
You can sleep, and never hear
Billows breaking, and the cry
Of the night-wind wandering by;
In soft purple mantle sleeping
　　With your little face on mine,
Hearing not your mother weeping
　　And the breaking of the brine.

Well, the daylight came at last, and the great chest was driven by the waves against the shore of an island. There the brass-bound chest lay, with the Princess and her baby in it, till a man of that country came past, and saw it, and dragged it on to the beach, and when he had broken it open, behold! there was a beautiful lady and a little boy. So he took them home, and was very kind to them, and brought up the boy till he was a young man. Now when the boy had come to his full strength the King of that country fell in love with his mother, and wanted to marry her, but he knew that she would never part from her boy. So he thought of a plan to get rid of the boy, and this was his plan. A great queen of a country not far off was going to be married, and this king said that all his subjects must bring him wedding presents to give her. And he made a feast to which he invited them all, and they all brought their presents; some brought gold cups, and some brought necklaces of gold and amber, and some brought beautiful horses; but the boy had nothing, though he was the son of a princess, for his mother had nothing to give him. Then the rest of the company began to laugh at him, and the King said: 'If you have nothing else to give, at least you might go and fetch the Terrible Head.'

The boy was proud, and spoke without thinking:

'Then I swear that I *will* bring the Terrible Head, if it may be brought by a living man. But of what head you speak I know not.'

Then they told him that somewhere, a long way off, there dwelt three dreadful sisters, monstrous ogrish women, with golden wings and claws of brass, and with serpents growing on their heads instead of hair. Now these women were so awful to look on that whoever saw them was turned at once into stone. And two of them could not be put to death, but the youngest, whose face was very beautiful, could be killed, and it was *her* head that the boy had promised to bring. You may imagine it was no easy adventure.

When he heard all this he was perhaps sorry that he had sworn to bring the Terrible Head, but he was determined to keep his oath. So he went out from the feast, where they all sat drinking and making merry, and he walked alone beside the sea in the dusk of the evening, at the place where the great chest, with himself and his mother in it, had been cast ashore.

There he went and sat down on a rock, looking towards the sea, and wondering how he should begin to fulfil his vow. Then he felt some one touch him on the shoulder; and he turned, and saw a young man like a king's son, having with him a tall and beautiful lady, whose blue eyes shone like stars. They were taller than mortal men, and the young man had a staff in his hand with golden wings on it, and two golden serpents twisted round it, and he had wings on his cap and on his shoes. He spoke to the boy, and asked him why he was so unhappy; and the boy told him how he had sworn to bring the Terrible Head, and knew not how to begin to set about the adventure.

Then the beautiful lady also spoke, and said that 'it was a foolish oath and a hasty, but it might be kept if a brave man had sworn it.' Then the boy answered that he was not afraid, if only he knew the way.

Then the lady said that to kill the dreadful woman with the golden wings and the brass claws, and to cut off her head, he needed three things: first, a Cap of Darkness, which would make him invisible when he wore it; next, a Sword of Sharpness, which would cleave iron at one blow; and last, the Shoes of Swiftness, with which he might fly in the air.

The boy answered that he knew not where such things were to be procured, and that, wanting them, he could only try and fail. Then the young man, taking off his own shoes, said: 'First, you shall use these shoes till you have taken the Terrible Head, and then you must give them back to me. And with these shoes you will fly as fleet as a bird, or a thought, over the land or over the waves of the sea, wherever the shoes know the way. But there are ways which they do not know, roads beyond the borders of the world. And these roads have you to travel. Now first you must go to the Three Grey Sisters, who live far off in the north, and are so very old that they have only one eye and one tooth among the three. You must creep up close to them, and as one of them passes the eye to the other you must seize it, and refuse to give it up till they have told you the way to the Three Fairies of the Garden, and *they* will give you the Cap of Darkness and the Sword of Sharpness, and show you how to wing beyond this world to the land of the Terrible Head.'

Then the beautiful lady said: 'Go forth at once, and do not return to say good-bye to your mother, for these things must be done quickly, and the Shoes of Swiftness themselves will carry you to the land of the Three Grey Sisters—for they know the measure of that way.'

So the boy thanked her, and he fastened on the Shoes of Swiftness, and turned to say good-bye to the young man and the lady. But, behold! they had vanished, he knew not how or where! Then he leaped in the air to try the Shoes of Swiftness, and they carried him more swiftly than the wind, over the warm blue sea, over the happy lands of the south, over the northern peoples who drank mare's milk and lived in great waggons, wandering after their flocks. Across the wide rivers, where the wild fowl rose and fled before him, and over the plains and the cold North Sea he went, over the fields of snow and the hills of ice, to a place where the world ends, and all water is frozen, and there are no men, nor beasts, nor any green grass. There in a blue cave of the ice he found the Three Grey Sisters, the oldest of living things. Their

hair was as white as the snow, and their flesh of an icy blue, and they mumbled and nodded in a kind of dream, and their frozen breath hung round them like a cloud. Now the opening of the cave in the ice was narrow, and it was not easy to pass in without touching one of the Grey Sisters. But, floating on the Shoes of Swiftness, the boy just managed to steal in, and waited till one of the sisters said to another, who had their one eye :

'Sister, what do you see? do you see old times coming back?'

'No, sister.'

'Then give *me* the eye, for perhaps I can see farther than you.'

Then the first sister passed the eye to the second, but as the second groped for it the boy caught it cleverly out of her hand.

' Where is the eye, sister ? ' said the second grey woman.

' You have taken it yourself, sister,' said the first grey woman.

' Have you lost the eye, sister ? have you lost the eye ? ' said the third grey woman ; ' shall we *never* find it again, and see old times coming back ? '

Then the boy slipped from behind them out of the cold cave into the air, and he laughed aloud.

When the grey women heard that laugh they began to weep, for now they knew that a stranger had robbed them, and that they could not help themselves, and their tears froze as they fell from the hollows where no eyes were, and rattled on the icy ground of the cave. Then they began to implore the boy to give them their eye back again, and he could not help being sorry for them, they were so pitiful. But he said he would never give them the eye till they told him the way to the Fairies of the Garden.

Then they wrung their hands miserably, for they guessed why he had come, and how he was going to try to win the Terrible Head. Now the Dreadful Women were akin to the Three Grey Sisters, and it was hard for them to tell the boy the way. But at last they told him to keep always south, and with the land on his left and the sea on his right, till he reached the Island of the Fairies of the Garden. Then he gave them back the eye, and they began to look out once more for the old times coming back again. But the boy flew south between sea and land, keeping the land always on his left hand, till he saw a beautiful island crowned with flowering trees. There he alighted, and there he found the Three Fairies of the Garden. They were like three very beautiful young women, dressed one in green, one in white, and one in red, and they were dancing and singing round an apple tree with apples of gold, and this was their song :

THE SONG OF THE WESTERN FAIRIES.

Round and round the apples of gold,
  Round and round dance we ;
Thus do we dance from the days of old
  About the enchanted tree ;
Round, and round, and round we go,
While the spring is green, or the stream shall flow,
  Or the wind shall stir the sea !

There is none may taste of the golden fruit
　　Till the golden new times come;
Many a tree shall spring from shoot,
Many a blossom be withered at root,
　　　Many a song be dumb;
Broken and still shall be many a lute
　　Or ever the new times come!

Round and round the tree of gold,
　　Round and round dance we,
So doth the great world spin from of old,
Summer and winter, and fire and cold,
Song that is sung, and tale that is told,
Even as we dance, that fold and unfold
　　Round the stem of the fairy tree!

These grave dancing fairies were very unlike the Grey Women, and they were glad to see the boy, and treated him kindly. Then they asked him why he had come; and he told them how he was sent to find the Sword of Sharpness and the Cap of Darkness. And the fairies gave him these, and a wallet, and a shield, and belted the sword, which had a diamond blade, round his waist, and the cap they set on his head, and told him that now even they could not see him though they were fairies. Then he took it off, and they each kissed him and wished him good fortune, and then they began again their eternal dance round the golden tree, for it is their business to guard it till the new times come, or till the world's ending. So the boy put the cap on his head, and hung the wallet round his waist, and the shining shield on his shoulders, and flew beyond the great river that lies coiled like a serpent round the whole world. And by the banks of that river, there he found the three Terrible Women all asleep beneath a poplar tree, and the dead poplar leaves lay all about them. Their golden wings were folded and their brass claws were crossed, and two of them slept with their hideous heads beneath their wings like birds, and the serpents in their hair writhed out from under the feathers of gold. But the youngest slept between her two sisters, and she lay on her back, with her beautiful sad face turned to the sky; and though she slept her eyes were wide open. If the boy had seen her he would have been changed into stone by the terror and the pity of it, she was so awful; but he had thought of a plan for killing her without looking on her face. As soon as he caught sight of the three from far off he took his shining shield from his shoulders, and held it up like a mirror, so that he saw the Dreadful Women reflected in it, and did not see the Terrible Head itself. Then he came nearer and nearer, till he reckoned that he was within a sword's stroke of the youngest, and he guessed where he should strike a back blow behind him. Then he drew the Sword of Sharpness and struck once, and the Terrible Head was cut from the shoulders of the creature, and the blood leaped out and struck him like a blow. But he thrust the Terrible Head into his wallet, and flew away without looking behind. Then the two Dreadful Sisters who were left wakened, and rose in the air like great birds; and though they could not see him because of his Cap of Darkness, they flew after him up the wind, following by the scent through the clouds, like hounds hunting in a wood. They came so close that he could hear the clatter of their golden wings, and their shrieks to each other: '*Here, here,*'

' *No, there ; this way he went*,' as they chased him.   But the Shoes
of Swiftness flew too fast for them, and at last their cries and the
rattle of their wings died away as he crossed the great river that
runs round the world.

Now when the horrible creatures were far in the distance, and
the boy found himself on the right side of the river, he flew straight
eastward, trying to seek his own country.   But as he looked down
from the air he saw a very strange sight—a beautiful girl chained to
a stake at the high-water mark of the sea.   The girl was so frightened or so tired that she was only prevented from falling by the
iron chain about her waist, and there she hung, as if she were dead.
The boy was very sorry for her, and flew down and stood beside her.
When he spoke she raised her head and looked round, but his voice
only seemed to frighten her.   Then he remembered that he was wearing the Cap of Darkness, and that she could only hear him, not see him.
So he took it off, and there he stood before her, the handsomest young
man she had ever seen in all her life, with short curly yellow hair,
and blue eyes, and a laughing face.   And he thought her the most
beautiful girl in the world.   So first with one blow of the Sword of
Sharpness he cut the iron chain that bound her, and then he asked
her what she did here, and why men treated her so cruelly.   And
she told him that she was the daughter of the King of that country,
and that she was tied there to be eaten by a monstrous beast out of
the sea; for the beast came and devoured a girl every day.   Now
the lot had fallen on her; and as she was just saying this a long
fierce head of a cruel sea creature rose out of the waves and
snapped at the girl.   But the beast had been too greedy and too
hurried, so he missed his aim the first time.   Before he could rise
and bite again the boy had whipped the Terrible Head out of his
wallet and held it up.   And when the sea beast leaped out once
more its eyes fell on the head, and instantly it was turned into
a stone.   And the stone beast is there on the sea-coast to this
day.

Then the boy and the girl went to the palace of the King, her
father, where everyone was weeping for her death, and they could
hardly believe their eyes when they saw her come back well.   And
the King and Queen made much of the boy, and could not contain
themselves for delight when they found he wanted to marry their
daughter.   So the two were married with the most splendid rejoicings, and when they had passed some time at court they went

home in a ship to the boy's own country. For he could not carry his bride through the air, so he took the Shoes of Swiftness, and the Cap of Darkness, and the Sword of Sharpness up to a lonely place in the hills. There he left them, and there they were found by the man and woman who had met him at home beside the sea, and had helped him to start on his journey.

When this had been done the boy and his bride set forth for home, and landed at the harbour of his native land. But whom should he meet in the very street of the town but his own mother, flying for her life from the wicked King, who now wished to kill her because he found that she would never marry him! For if she had liked the King ill before, she liked him far worse now that he had caused her son to disappear so suddenly. She did not know, of course, where the boy had gone, but thought the King had slain him secretly. So now she was running for her very life, and the wicked King was following her with a sword in his hand. Then, behold! she ran into her son's very arms, but he had only time to kiss her and step in front of her, when the King struck at him with his sword. The boy caught the blow on his shield, and cried to the King:

'I swore to bring you the Terrible Head, and see how I keep my oath!'

Then he drew forth the head from his wallet, and when the king's eyes fell on it, instantly he was turned into stone, just as he stood there with his sword lifted!

Now all the people rejoiced, because the wicked King should rule them no longer. And they asked the boy to be their king, but he said no, he must take his mother home to her father's house. So the people chose for king the man who had been kind to his mother when first she was cast on the island in the great chest.

Presently the boy and his mother and his wife set sail for his mother's own country, from which she had been driven so unkindly. But on the way they stayed at the court of a king, and it happened that he was holding games, and giving prizes to the best runners, boxers, and quoit-throwers. Then the boy would try his strength with the rest, but he threw the quoit so far that it went beyond what had ever been thrown before, and fell in the crowd, striking a man so that he died. Now this man was no other than the father of the boy's mother, who had fled away from his own kingdom for

fear his grandson should find him and kill him after all.   Thus he
was destroyed by his own cowardice and by chance, and thus the
prophecy was fulfilled.   But the boy and his wife and his mother
went back to the kingdom that was theirs, and lived long and
happily after all their troubles.

THE STORY OF PRETTY GOLDILOCKS

ONCE upon a time there was a princess who was the prettiest creature in the world. And because she was so beautiful, and because her hair was like the finest gold, and waved and rippled nearly to the ground, she was called Pretty Goldilocks. She always wore a crown of flowers, and her dresses were embroidered with diamonds and pearls, and everybody who saw her fell in love with her.

Now one of her neighbours was a young king who was not married. He was very rich and handsome, and when he heard all that was said about Pretty Goldilocks, though he had never seen her, he fell so deeply in love with her that he could neither eat nor drink. So he resolved to send an ambassador to ask her in marriage. He had a splendid carriage made for his ambassador, and gave him more than a hundred horses and a hundred servants, and told him to be sure to bring the Princess back with him. After he had started nothing else was talked of at Court, and the King felt so sure that the Princess would consent that he set his people to work at pretty dresses and splendid furniture, that they might be ready by the time she came. Meanwhile, the ambassador arrived at the Princess's palace and delivered his little message, but whether she happened to be cross that day, or whether the compliment did not please her, is not known. She only answered that she was very much obliged to the King, but she had no wish to be married. The ambassador set off sadly on his homeward way, bringing all the King's presents back with him, for the Princess was too well brought up to accept the pearls and diamonds when she would not accept the King, so she had only kept twenty-five English pins that he might not be vexed.

When the ambassador reached the city, where the King was waiting impatiently, everybody was very much annoyed with him for not bringing the Princess, and the King cried like a baby, and nobody could console him. Now there was at the Court a young man, who was more clever and handsome than anyone else. He

was called Charming, and everyone loved him, excepting a few
envious people who were angry at his being the King's favourite
and knowing all the State secrets. He happened one day to be with
some people who were speaking of the ambassador's return and
saying that his going to the Princess had not done much good, when
Charming said rashly :

'If the King had sent me to the Princess Goldilocks I am sure
she would have come back with me.'

His enemies at once went to the King and said :

'You will hardly believe, sire, what Charming has the audacity
to say—that if *he* had been sent to the Princess Goldilocks she
would certainly have come back with him. He seems to think that
he is so much handsomer than you that the Princess would have
fallen in love with him and followed him willingly.' The King was
very angry when he heard this.

'Ha, ha!' said he; 'does he laugh at my unhappiness, and
think himself more fascinating than I am ? Go, and let him be
shut up in my great tower to die of hunger.'

So the King's guards went to fetch Charming, who had thought
no more of his rash speech, and carried him off to prison with great
cruelty. The poor prisoner had only a little straw for his bed, and
but for a little stream of water which flowed through the tower he
would have died of thirst.

One day when he was in despair he said to himself ·

'How can I have offended the King ? I am his most faithful
subject, and have done nothing against him.'

The King chanced to be passing the tower and recognised the
voice of his former favourite. He stopped to listen in spite of
Charming's enemies, who tried to persuade him to have nothing
more to do with the traitor. But the King said :

'Be quiet, I wish to hear what he says.'

And then he opened the tower door and called to Charming, who
came very sadly and kissed the King's hand, saying :

'What have I done, sire, to deserve this cruel treatment ? '

'You mocked me and my ambassador,' said the King, 'and you
said that if I had sent you for the Princess Goldilocks you would
certainly have brought her back.'

'It is quite true, sire,' replied Charming; 'I should have drawn
such a picture of you, and represented your good qualities in such a
way, that I am certain the Princess would have found you irresist-
ible. But I cannot see what there is in that to make you angry.'

The King could not see any cause for anger either when the matter was presented to him in this light, and he began to frown very fiercely at the courtiers who had so misrepresented his favourite.

So he took Charming back to the palace with him, and after seeing that he had a very good supper he said to him:

'You know that I love Pretty Goldilocks as much as ever, her refusal has not made any difference to me; but I don't know how to make her change her mind: I really should like to send you, to see if you can persuade her to marry me.'

Charming replied that he was perfectly willing to go, and would set out the very next day.

'But you must wait till I can get a grand escort for you,' said the King. But Charming said that he only wanted a good horse to ride, and the King, who was delighted at his being ready to start so promptly, gave him letters to the Princess, and bade him good speed. It was on a Monday morning that he set out all alone upon his errand, thinking of nothing but how he could persuade the Princess Goldilocks to marry the King. He had a writing-book in his pocket, and whenever any happy thought struck him he dismounted from his horse and sat down under the trees to put it into the harangue which he was preparing for the Princess, before he forgot it.

One day when he had started at the very earliest dawn, and was riding over a great meadow, he suddenly had a capital idea, and, springing from his horse, he sat down under a willow tree which

grew by a little river.   When he had written it down he was looking round him, pleased to find himself in such a pretty place, when
all at once he saw a great golden carp lying gasping and exhausted
upon the grass.   In leaping after little flies she had thrown herself
high upon the bank, where she had lain till she was nearly dead.
Charming had pity upon her, and, though he couldn't help thinking
that she would have been very nice for dinner, he picked her up
gently and put her back into the water.   As soon as Dame Carp
felt the refreshing coolness of the water she sank down joyfully to
the bottom of the river, then, swimming up to the bank quite boldly,
she said:

'I thank you, Charming, for the kindness you have done me.
You have saved my life; one day I will repay you.'   So saying,
she sank down into the water again, leaving Charming greatly
astonished at her politeness.

Another day, as he journeyed on, he saw a raven in great distress.   The poor bird was closely pursued by an eagle, which would
soon have eaten it up, had not Charming quickly fitted an arrow to
his bow and shot the eagle dead.   The raven perched upon a tree
very joyfully.

'Charming,' said he, 'it was very generous of you to rescue a
poor raven; I am not ungrateful, some day I will repay you.'

Charming thought it was very nice of the raven to say so, and
went on his way.

Before the sun rose he found himself in a thick wood where it
was too dark for him to see his path, and here he heard an owl
crying as if it were in despair.

'Hark!' said he, 'that must be an owl in great trouble, I
am sure it has got into a snare;' and he began to hunt about, and
presently found a great net which some bird-catchers had spread
the night before.

'What a pity it is that men do nothing but torment and persecute
poor creatures which never do them any harm!' said he, and he took
out his knife and cut the cords of the net, and the owl flitted away
into the darkness, but then turning, with one flicker of her wings,
she came back to Charming and said:

'It does not need many words to tell you how great a service
you have done me.   I was caught; in a few minutes the fowlers
would have been here—without your help I should have been killed.
I am grateful, and one day I will repay you.'

These three adventures were the only ones of any consequence that befell Charming upon his journey, and he made all the haste he could to reach the palace of the Princess Goldilocks.

When he arrived he thought everything he saw delightful and magnificent. Diamonds were as plentiful as pebbles, and the gold and silver, the beautiful dresses, the sweetmeats and pretty things that were everywhere quite amazed him ; he thought to himself : ' If the Princess consents to leave all this, and come with me to marry the King, he may think himself lucky ! '

Then he dressed himself carefully in rich brocade, with scarlet and white plumes, and threw a splendid embroidered scarf over his shoulder, and, looking as gay and as graceful as possible, he presented himself at the door of the palace, carrying in his arm a tiny pretty dog which he had bought on the way. The guards saluted him respectfully, and a messenger was sent to the Princess to announce the arrival of Charming as ambassador of her neighbour the King.

' Charming,' said the Princess, ' the name promises well ; I have no doubt that he is good-looking and fascinates everybody.'

' Indeed he does, madam,' said all her maids of honour in one breath. ' We saw him from the window of the garret where we were spinning flax, and we could do nothing but look at him as long as he was in sight.'

' Well to be sure ! ' said the Princess, ' that's how you amuse yourselves, is it ? Looking at strangers out of the window ! Be quick and give me my blue satin embroidered dress, and comb out my golden hair. Let somebody make me fresh garlands of flowers, and give me my high-heeled shoes and my fan, and tell them to sweep my great hall and my throne, for I want everyone to say I am really " Pretty Goldilocks." '

You can imagine how all her maids scurried this way and that to make the Princess ready, and how in their haste they knocked their heads together and hindered each other, till she thought they would never have done. However, at last they led her into the gallery of mirrors that she might assure herself that nothing was lacking in her appearance, and then she mounted her throne of gold, ebony, and ivory, while her ladies took their guitars and began to sing softly. Then Charming was led in, and was so struck with astonishment and admiration that at first not a word could he say. But presently he took courage and delivered his harangue, bravely ending by begging the Princess to spare him the disappointment of going back without her.

'Sir Charming,' answered she, 'all the reasons you have given me are very good ones, and I assure you that I should have more pleasure in obliging you than anyone else, but you must know that a month ago as I was walking by the river with my ladies I took off my glove, and as I did so a ring that I was wearing slipped off my finger and rolled into the water. As I valued it more than my kingdom, you may imagine how vexed I was at losing it, and I vowed never to listen to any proposal of marriage unless the ambassador first brought me back my ring. So now you know what is expected of you, for if you talked for fifteen days and fifteen nights you could not make me change my mind.'

Charming was very much surprised by this answer, but he bowed low to the Princess, and begged her to accept the embroidered scarf and the tiny dog he had brought with him. But she answered that she did not want any presents, and that he was to remember what she had just told him. When he got back to his lodging he went to bed without eating any supper, and his little dog, who was called Frisk, couldn't eat any either, but came and lay down close to him. All night long Charming sighed and lamented.

'How am I to find a ring that fell into the river a month ago?' said he. 'It is useless to try; the Princess must have told me to do it on purpose, knowing it was impossible.' And then he sighed again.

Frisk heard him and said :

' My dear master, don't despair ; the luck may change, you are too good not to be happy. Let us go down to the river as soon as it is light.'

But Charming only gave him two little pats and said nothing, and very soon he fell asleep.

At the first glimmer of dawn Frisk began to jump about, and when he had waked Charming they went out together, first into the garden, and then down to the river's brink, where they wandered up and down. Charming was thinking sadly of having to go back unsuccessful when he heard someone calling : ' Charming, Charming !' He looked all about him and thought he must be dreaming, as he could not see anybody. Then he walked on and the voice called again : ' Charming, Charming !'

' Who calls me ?' said he. Frisk, who was very small and could look closely into the water, cried out : ' I see a golden carp coming.' And sure enough there was the great carp, who said to Charming :

' You saved my life in the meadow by the willow tree, and I promised that I would repay you. Take this, it is Princess Goldilock's ring.' Charming took the ring out of Dame Carp's mouth, thanking her a thousand times, and he and tiny Frisk went straight to the palace, where someone told the Princess that he was asking to see her.

' Ah ! poor fellow,' said she, ' he must have come to say goodbye, finding it impossible to do as I asked.'

So in came Charming, who presented her with the ring and said :

' Madam, I have done your bidding. Will it please you to marry my master ?' When the Princess saw her ring brought back to her unhurt she was so astonished that she thought she must be dreaming.

' Truly, Charming,' said she, ' you must be the favourite of some fairy, or you could never have found it.'

' Madam,' answered he, ' I was helped by nothing but my desire to obey your wishes.'

' Since you are so kind,' said she, ' perhaps you will do me another service, for till it is done I will never be married. There is a prince not far from here whose name is Galifron, who once wanted to marry me, but when I refused he uttered the most terrible threats against me, and vowed that he would lay waste my country. But what could I do? I could not marry a frightful giant as tall as a tower, who eats up people as a monkey eats chestnuts, and who talks so loud that anybody who has to listen to him becomes quite deaf. Nevertheless, he does not cease to persecute me and to kill my subjects. So before I can listen to your proposal you must kill him and bring me his head.'

Charming was rather dismayed at this command, but he answered:

'Very well, Princess, I will fight this Galifron; I believe that he will kill me, but at any rate I shall die in your defence.'

Then the Princess was frightened and said everything she could think of to prevent Charming from fighting the giant, but it was of no use, and he went out to arm himself suitably, and then, taking little Frisk with him, he mounted his horse and set out for Galifron's country. Everyone he met told him what a terrible giant Galifron was, and that nobody dared go near him; and the more he heard the more frightened he grew. Frisk tried to encourage him by saying:

'While you are fighting the giant, dear master, I will go and bite his heels, and when he stoops down to look at me you can kill him.'

Charming praised his little dog's plan, but knew that his help would not do much good.

At last he drew near the giant's castle, and saw to his horror that every path that led to it was strewn with bones. Before long he saw Galifron coming. His head was higher than the tallest trees, and he sang in a terrible voice:

> 'Bring out your little boys and girls,
> Pray do not stay to do their curls,
> For I shall eat so very many,
> I shall not know if they have any.'

Thereupon Charming sang out as loud as he could to the same tune:

> 'Come out and meet the valiant Charming,
> Who finds you not at all alarming;
> Although he is not very tall,
> He's big enough to make you fall.'

The rhymes were not very correct, but you see he had made them up so quickly that it is a miracle that they were not worse; especially as he was horribly frightened all the time. When Galifron heard these words he looked all about him, and saw Charming standing, sword in hand; this put the giant into a terrible rage, and he aimed a blow at Charming with his huge iron club, which would certainly have killed him if it had reached him, but at that instant a raven perched upon the giant's head, and, pecking with its strong beak and beating with its great wings, so confused and blinded him that all his blows fell harmlessly upon the air, and Charming, rushing in, gave him several strokes with his sharp sword so that he fell to the ground. Whereupon Charming cut off his head before he knew anything about it, and the raven from a tree close by croaked out:

'You see I have not forgotten the good turn you did me in killing the eagle. To-day I think I have fulfilled my promise of repaying you.'

'Indeed, I owe you more gratitude than you ever owed me,' replied Charming.

And then he mounted his horse and rode off with Galifron's head.

When he reached the city the people ran after him in crowds, crying:

'Behold the brave Charming, who has killed the giant!' And their shouts reached the Princess's ear, but she dared not ask what was happening, for fear she should hear that Charming had been killed. But very soon he arrived at the palace with the giant's head, of which she was still terrified, though it could no longer do her any harm.

'Princess,' said Charming, 'I have killed your enemy; I hope you will now consent to marry the King my master.'

'Oh dear! no,' said the Princess, 'not until you have brought me some water from the Gloomy Cavern.

'Not far from here there is a deep cave, the entrance to which is guarded by two dragons with fiery eyes, who will not allow anyone to pass them. When you get into the cavern you will find an immense hole, which you must go down, and it is full of toads and snakes; at the bottom of this hole there is another little cave, in which rises the Fountain of Health and Beauty. It is some of this water that I really must have: everything it touches becomes wonderful. The beautiful things will always remain beautiful, and the ugly things become lovely. If one is young one never grows old, and if one is old one becomes young. You see, Charming, I could not leave my kingdom without taking some of it with me.'

' Princess,' said he, ' you at least can never need this water, but I am an unhappy ambassador, whose death you desire. Where you send me I will go, though I know I shall never return.'

And, as the Princess Goldilocks showed no sign of relenting, he started with his little dog for the Gloomy Cavern. Everyone he met on the way said:

' What a pity that a handsome young man should throw away his life so carelessly! He is going to the cavern alone, though if he had a hundred men with him he could not succeed. Why does the Princess ask impossibilities ? '

Charming said nothing, but he was very sad. When he was near the top of a hill he dismounted to let his horse graze, while Frisk amused himself by chasing flies. Charming knew he could not be far from the Gloomy Cavern, and on looking about him he saw a black hideous rock from which came a thick smoke, followed in a moment by one of the dragons with fire blazing from his mouth and eyes. His body was yellow and green, and his claws scarlet, and his tail was so long that it lay in a hundred coils. Frisk was so terrified at the sight of it that he did not know where to hide. Charming, quite determined to get the water or die, now drew his sword, and, taking the crystal flask which Pretty Goldilocks had given him to fill, said to Frisk :

' I feel sure that I shall never come back from this expedition ; when I am dead, go to the Princess and tell her that her errand has cost me my life. Then find the King my master, and relate all my adventures to him.'

As he spoke he heard a voice calling : ' Charming, Charming ! '

' Who calls me ?' said he ; then he saw an owl sitting in a hollow tree, who said to him :

'You saved my life when I was caught in the net, now I can repay you. Trust me with the flask, for I know all the ways of the Gloomy Cavern, and can fill it from the Fountain of Beauty.' Charming was only too glad to give her the flask, and she flitted into the cavern quite unnoticed by the dragon, and after some time returned with the flask, filled to the very brim with sparkling water. Charming thanked her with all his heart, and joyfully hastened back to the town.

He went straight to the palace and gave the flask to the Princess, who had no further objection to make. So she thanked

Charming, and ordered that preparations should be made for her departure, and they soon set out together. The Princess found Charming such an agreeable companion that she sometimes said to him:

'Why didn't we stay where we were? I could have made you king, and we should have been so happy!'

But Charming only answered:

'I could not have done anything that would have vexed my

master so much, even for a kingdom, or to please you, though I think you are as beautiful as the sun.'

At last they reached the King's great city, and he came out to meet the Princess, bringing magnificent presents, and the marriage was celebrated with great rejoicings. But Goldilocks was so fond of Charming that she could not be happy unless he was near her, and she was always singing his praises.

'If it hadn't been for Charming,' she said to the King, 'I should never have come here; you ought to be very much obliged to him, for he did the most impossible things and got me water from the Fountain of Beauty, so I can never grow old, and shall get prettier every year.'

Then Charming's enemies said to the King:

'It is a wonder that you are not jealous, the Queen thinks there is nobody in the world like Charming. As if anybody you had sent could not have done just as much!'

'It is quite true, now I come to think of it,' said the King. 'Let him be chained hand and foot, and thrown into the tower.'

So they took Charming, and as a reward for having served the King so faithfully he was shut up in the tower, where he only saw the gaoler, who brought him a piece of black bread and a pitcher of water every day.

However, little Frisk came to console him, and told him all the news.

When Pretty Goldilocks heard what had happened she threw herself at the King's feet and begged him to set Charming free, but the more she cried the more angry he was, and at last she saw that it was useless to say any more; but it made her very sad. Then the King took it in his head that perhaps he was not handsome enough to please the Princess Goldilocks, and he thought he would bathe his face with the water from the Fountain of Beauty, which was in the flask on a shelf in the Princess's room, where she had placed it that she might see it often. Now it happened that one of the Princess's ladies in chasing a spider had knocked the flask off the shelf and broken it, and every drop of the water had been spilt. Not knowing what to do, she had hastily swept away the pieces of crystal, and then remembered that in the King's room she had seen a flask of exactly the same shape, also filled with sparkling water. So, without saying a word, she fetched it and stood it upon the Queen's shelf.

Now the water in this flask was what was used in the kingdom

for getting rid of troublesome people. Instead of having their
heads cut off in the usual way, their faces were bathed with the
water, and they instantly fell asleep and never woke up any more.
So, when the King, thinking to improve his beauty, took the flask
and sprinkled the water upon his face, *he* fell asleep, and nobody
could wake him.

Little Frisk was the first to hear the news, and he ran to tell
Charming, who sent him to beg the Princess not to forget the poor
prisoner. All the palace was in confusion on account of the King's
death, but tiny Frisk made his way through the crowd to the
Princess's side, and said:

'Madam, do not forget poor Charming!'

Then she remembered all he had done for her, and without
saying a word to anyone went straight to the tower, and with her
own hands took off Charming's chains. Then, putting a golden
crown upon his head, and the royal mantle upon his shoulders, she
said:

'Come, faithful Charming, I make you king, and will take you
for my husband.'

Charming, once more free and happy, fell at her feet and
thanked her for her gracious words.

Everybody was delighted that he should be king, and the
wedding, which took place at once, was the prettiest that can be
imagined, and Prince Charming and Princess Goldilocks lived
happily ever after.[1]

[1] Madame d'Aulnoy.

THE HISTORY OF WHITTINGTON

DICK WHITTINGTON was a very little boy when his father and mother died; so little indeed, that he never knew them, nor the place where he was born. He strolled about the country as ragged as a colt, till he met with a waggoner who was going to London, and who gave him leave to walk all the way by the side of his waggon without paying anything for his passage. This pleased little Whittington very much, as he wanted to see London sadly, for he had heard that the streets were paved with gold, and he was willing to get a bushel of it; but how great was his disappointment, poor boy! when he saw the streets covered with dirt instead of gold, and found himself in a strange place, without a friend, without food, and without money.

Though the waggoner was so charitable as to let him walk up by the side of the waggon for nothing, he took care not to know him when he came to town, and the poor boy was, in a little time, so cold and so hungry that he wished himself in a good kitchen and by a warm fire in the country.

In this distress he asked charity of several people, and one of them bid him ' Go to work for an idle rogue.' ' That I will,' says Whittington, ' with all my heart; I will work for you if you will let me.'

The man, who thought this savoured of wit and impertinence (though the poor lad intended only to show his readiness to work), gave him a blow with a stick which broke his head so that the blood ran down. In this situation, and fainting for want of food, he laid himself down at the door of one Mr. Fitzwarren, a merchant, where the cook saw him, and, being an ill-natured hussey, ordered him to go about his business or she would scald him. At this time Mr. Fitzwarren came from the Exchange, and began also to scold at the poor boy, bidding him to go to work.

Whittington answered that he should be glad to work if anybody would employ him, and that he should be able if he could get some victuals to eat, for he had had nothing for three days, and he was a poor country boy, and knew nobody, and nobody would employ him.

He then endeavoured to get up, but he was so very weak that he fell down again, which excited so much compassion in the merchant that he ordered the servants to take him in and give him some meat and drink, and let him help the cook to do any dirty work that she had to set him about. People are too apt to reproach those who beg with being idle, but give themselves no concern to put them in the way of getting business to do, or considering whether they are able to do it, which is not charity.

But we return to Whittington, who would have lived happy in this worthy family had he not been bumped about by the cross cook, who must be always roasting or basting, and when the spit was idle employed her hands upon poor Whittington! At last Miss Alice, his master's daughter, was informed of it, and then she took compassion on the poor boy, and made the servants treat him kindly.

Besides the crossness of the cook, Whittington had another difficulty to get over before he could be happy. He had, by order of his master, a flock-bed placed for him in a garret, where there was a number of rats and mice that often ran over the poor boy's nose and disturbed him in his sleep. After some time, however, a gentleman who came to his master's house gave Whittington a penny for brushing his shoes. This he put into his pocket, being determined to lay it out to the best advantage; and the next day, seeing a woman in the street with a cat under her arm, he ran up to know the price of it. The woman (as the cat was a good mouser) asked a deal of money for it, but on Whittington's telling her he had but a penny in the world, and that he wanted a cat sadly, she let him have it.

This cat Whittington concealed in the garret, for fear she should be beat about by his mortal enemy the cook, and here she soon killed or frightened away the rats and mice, so that the poor boy could now sleep as sound as a top.

Soon after this the merchant, who had a ship ready to sail, called for his servants, as his custom was, in order that each of them might venture something to try their luck; and whatever they sent was to pay neither freight nor custom, for he thought justly that God Almighty would bless him the more for his readiness to let the poor partake of his fortune.

All the servants appeared but poor Whittington, who, having neither money nor goods, could not think of sending anything to try his luck; but his good friend Miss Alice, thinking his poverty kept him away, ordered him to be called.

She then offered to lay down something for him, but the merchant told his daughter that would not do, it must be something of his own. Upon which poor Whittington said he had nothing but a cat which he bought for a penny that was given him. ' Fetch thy cat, boy,' said the merchant, ' and send her.' Whittington brought

poor puss and delivered her to the captain, with tears in his eyes,
for he said he should now be disturbed by the rats and mice as
much as ever. All the company laughed at the adventure but Miss
Alice, who pitied the poor boy, and gave him something to buy
another cat.

While puss was beating the billows at sea, poor Whittington
was severely beaten at home by his tyrannical mistress the cook,
who used him so cruelly, and made such game of him for sending
his cat to sea, that at last the poor boy determined to run away
from his place, and, having packed up the few things he had, he
set out very early in the morning on All-Hallows day. He
travelled as far as Holloway, and there sat down on a stone to
consider what course he should take; but while he was thus
ruminating, Bow bells, of which there were only six, began to
ring; and he thought their sounds addressed him in this manner:

'Turn again, Whittington,
Thrice Lord Mayor of London.'

'Lord Mayor of London!' said he to himself; 'what would not
one endure to be Lord Mayor of London, and ride in such a fine
coach? Well, I'll go back again, and bear all the pummelling and
ill-usage of Cicely rather than miss the opportunity of being Lord
Mayor!' So home he went, and happily got into the house and
about his business before Mrs. Cicely made her appearance.

We must now follow Miss Puss to the coast of Africa. How
perilous are voyages at sea, how uncertain the winds and the
waves, and how many accidents attend a naval life!

The ship which had the cat on board was long beaten at sea,
and at last, by contrary winds, driven on a part of the coast of
Barbary which was inhabited by Moors unknown to the English.
These people received our countrymen with civility, and therefore
the captain, in order to trade with them, showed them the patterns
of the goods he had on board, and sent some of them to the King of
the country, who was so well pleased that he sent for the captain
and the factor to his palace, which was about a mile from the sea.
Here they were placed, according to the custom of the country,
on rich carpets, flowered with gold and silver; and the King and
Queen being seated at the upper end of the room, dinner was
brought in, which consisted of many dishes; but no sooner were
the dishes put down but an amazing number of rats and mice
came from all quarters, and devoured all the meat in an instant.

The factor, in surprise, turned round to the nobles and asked if these vermin were not offensive. 'Oh! yes,' said they, 'very offensive; and the King would give half his treasure to be freed of them, for they not only destroy his dinner, as you see, but they assault him in his chamber, and even in bed, so that he is obliged to be watched while he is sleeping, for fear of them.'

The factor jumped for joy; he remembered poor Whittington and his cat, and told the King he had a creature on board the ship that would despatch all these vermin immediately. The King's heart heaved so high at the joy which this news gave him that his turban dropped off his head. 'Bring this creature to me,' said he; 'vermin are dreadful in a court, and if she will perform what you say I will load your ship with gold and jewels in exchange for her.' The factor, who knew his business, took this opportunity to set forth the merits of Miss Puss. He told his Majesty that it would be inconvenient to part with her, as, when she was gone, the rats and mice might destroy the goods in the ship—but to oblige his Majesty he would fetch her. 'Run, run,' said the Queen; 'I am impatient to see the dear creature.'

Away flew the factor, while another dinner was providing, and returned with the cat just as the rats and mice were devouring that also. He immediately put down Miss Puss, who killed a great number of them.

The King rejoiced greatly to see his old enemies destroyed by so small a creature, and the Queen was highly pleased, and desired the cat might be brought near that she might look at her. Upon which the factor called ' Pussy, pussy, pussy!' and she came to him. He then presented her to the Queen, who started back, and was afraid to touch a creature who had made such a havoc among the rats and mice ; however, when the factor stroked the cat and called ' Pussy, pussy!' the Queen also touched her and cried ' Putty, putty!' for she had not learned English.

He then put her down on the Queen's lap, where she, purring, played with her Majesty's hand, and then sang herself to sleep.

The King having seen the exploits of Miss Puss, and being informed that her kittens would stock the whole country, bargained with the captain and factor for the whole ship's cargo, and then gave them ten times as much for the cat as all the rest amounted to. On which, taking leave of their Majesties and other great personages at court, they sailed with a fair wind for England, whither we must now attend them.

The morn had scarcely dawned when Mr. Fitzwarren arose to count over the cash and settle the business for that day. He had just entered the counting-house, and seated himself at the desk, when somebody came, tap, tap, at the door. 'Who's there?' said Mr. Fitzwarren. 'A friend,' answered the other. 'What friend can come at this unseasonable time?' 'A real friend is never unseasonable,' answered the other. 'I come to bring you good news of your ship *Unicorn.*' The merchant bustled up in such a hurry that he forgot his gout; instantly opened the door, and

who should be seen waiting but the captain and factor, with a cabinet of jewels, and a bill of lading, for which the merchant lifted up his eyes and thanked heaven for sending him such a prosperous voyage. Then they told him the adventures of the cat, and showed him the cabinet of jewels which they had brought for Mr. Whittington. Upon which he cried out with great earnestness, but not in the most poetical manner:

'Go, send him in, and tell him of his fame,
And call him Mr. Whittington by name.'

It is not our business to animadvert upon these lines; we are not critics, but historians. It is sufficient for us that they are the words of Mr. Fitzwarren; and though it is beside our purpose, and perhaps not in our power to prove him a good poet, we shall soon convince the reader that he was a good man, which was a much better character; for when some who were present told him that this treasure was too much for such a poor boy as Whittington, he said; 'God forbid that I should deprive him of a penny; it is his own, and he shall have it to a farthing.' He then ordered Mr. Whittington in, who was at this time cleaning the kitchen and would have excused himself from going into the counting-house, saying the room was swept and his shoes were dirty and full of hob-nails. The merchant, however, made him come in, and ordered a chair to be set for him. Upon which, thinking they intended to make sport of him, as had been too often the case in the kitchen, he besought his master not to mock a poor simple fellow who intended them no harm, but let him go about his business. The merchant, taking him by the hand, said: 'Indeed, Mr. Whittington, I am in earnest with you, and sent for you to congratulate you on your great success. Your cat has procured you more money than I am worth in the world, and may you long enjoy it and be happy!'

At length, being shown the treasure, and convinced by them that all of it belonged to him, he fell upon his knees and thanked the Almighty for his providential care of such a poor and miserable creature. He then laid all the treasure at his master's feet, who refused to take any part of it, but told him he heartily rejoiced at his prosperity, and hoped the wealth he had acquired would be a comfort to him, and would make him happy. He then applied to his mistress, and to his good friend Miss Alice, who refused to take any part of the money, but told him she heartily rejoiced at his good success, and wished him all imaginable felicity. He then gratified the captain, factor, and the ship's crew for the care they had taken of his cargo. He likewise distributed presents to all the servants in the house, not forgetting even his old enemy the cook, though she little deserved it.

After this Mr. Fitzwarren advised Mr. Whittington to send for the necessary people and dress himself like a gentleman, and made him the offer of his house to live in till he could provide himself with a better.

Now it came to pass when Mr. Whittington's face was washed,

his hair curled, and he dressed in a rich suit of clothes, that he turned out a genteel young fellow; and, as wealth contributes much to give a man confidence, he in a little time dropped that sheepish behaviour which was principally occasioned by a depression of spirits, and soon grew a sprightly and good companion, insomuch that Miss Alice, who had formerly pitied him, now fell in love with him.

When her father perceived they had this good liking for each other he proposed a match between them, to which both parties cheerfully consented, and the Lord Mayor, Court of Aldermen, Sheriffs, the Company of Stationers, the Royal Academy of Arts, and a number of eminent merchants attended the ceremony, and were elegantly treated at an entertainment made for that purpose.

History further relates that they lived very happy, had several children, and died at a good old age. Mr. Whittington served Sheriff of London and was three times Lord Mayor. In the last year of his mayoralty he entertained King Henry V. and his Queen, after his conquest of France, upon which occasion the King, in consideration of Whittington's merit, said: 'Never had prince such a subject;' which being told to Whittington at the table, he replied: 'Never had subject such a king.' His Majesty, out of respect to his good character, conferred the honour of knighthood on him soon after.

Sir Richard many years before his death constantly fed a great number of poor citizens, built a church and a college to it, with a yearly allowance for poor scholars, and near it erected a hospital.

He also built Newgate for criminals, and gave liberally to St. Bartholomew's Hospital and other public charities.

THE WONDERFUL SHEEP

ONCE upon a time—in the days when the fairies lived—there was a king who had three daughters, who were all young, and clever, and beautiful; but the youngest of the three, who was called Miranda, was the prettiest and the most beloved.

The King, her father, gave her more dresses and jewels in a month than he gave the others in a year; but she was so generous that she shared everything with her sisters, and they were all as happy and as fond of one another as they could be.

Now, the King had some quarrelsome neighbours, who, tired of leaving him in peace, began to make war upon him so fiercely that he feared he would be altogether beaten if he did not make an effort to defend himself. So he collected a great army and set off to fight them, leaving the Princesses with their governess in a castle where news of the war was brought every day—sometimes that the King had taken a town, or won a battle, and, at last, that he had altogether overcome his enemies and chased them out of his kingdom, and was coming back to the castle as quickly as possible, to see his dear little Miranda whom he loved so much.

The three Princesses put on dresses of satin, which they had had made on purpose for this great occasion, one green, one blue, and the third white; their jewels were the same colours. The eldest wore emeralds, the second turquoises, and the youngest diamonds, and thus adorned they went to meet the King, singing verses which they had composed about his victories.

When he saw them all so beautiful and so gay he embraced them tenderly, but gave Miranda more kisses than either of the others.

Presently a splendid banquet was served, and the King and his daughters sat down to it, and as he always thought that there was some special meaning in everything, he said to the eldest:

'Tell me why you have chosen a green dress.'

'Sire,' she answered, 'having heard of your victories I thought
that green would signify my joy and the hope of your speedy
return.'

'That is a very good answer,' said the King; 'and you, my
daughter,' he continued, 'why did you take a blue dress?'

'Sire,' said the Princess, 'to show that we constantly hoped
for your success, and that the sight of you is as welcome to me as
the sky with its most beautiful stars.'

'Why,' said the King, 'your wise answers astonish me; and
you, Miranda. What made you dress yourself all in white?'

'Because, sire,' she answered, 'white suits me better than anything else.'

'What!' said the King angrily, 'was that all you thought of,
vain child?'

'I thought you would be pleased with me,' said the Princess;
'that was all.'

The King, who loved her, was satisfied with this, and even
pretended to be pleased that she had not told him all her reasons at
first.

'And now,' said he, 'as I have supped well, and it is not time
yet to go to bed, tell me what you dreamed last night.'

The eldest said she had dreamed that he brought her a dress,
and the precious stones and gold embroidery on it were brighter
than the sun.

The dream of the second was that the King had brought her a spinning wheel and a distaff, that she might spin him some shirts.

But the youngest said: 'I dreamed that my second sister was to be married, and on her wedding-day, you, father, held a golden ewer and said: ' 'Come, Miranda, and I will hold the water that you may dip your hands in it.' '

The King was very angry indeed when he heard this dream, and frowned horribly; indeed, he made such an ugly face that everyone knew how angry he was, and he got up and went off to bed in a great hurry; but he could not forget his daughter's dream. 'Does the proud girl wish to make me her slave?' he said to himself. 'I am not surprised at her choosing to dress herself in white satin without a thought of me. She does not think me worthy of her consideration! But I will soon put an end to her pretensions!'

He rose in a fury, and although it was not yet daylight, he sent for the Captain of his Bodyguard, and said to him:

'You have heard the Princess Miranda's dream? I consider that it means strange things against me, therefore I order you to take her away into the forest and kill her, and, that I may be sure it is done, you must bring me her heart and her tongue. If you attempt to deceive me you shall be put to death!'

The Captain of the Guard was very much astonished when he heard this barbarous order, but he did not dare to contradict the King for fear of making him still more angry, or causing him to send someone else, so he answered that he would fetch the Princess and do as the King had said. When he went to her room they would hardly let him in, it was still so early, but he said that the King had sent for Miranda, and she got up quickly and came out; a little black girl called Patypata held up her train, and her pet monkey and her little dog ran after her. The monkey was called Grabugeon, and the little dog Tintin.

The Captain of the Guard begged Miranda to come down into the garden where the King was enjoying the fresh air, and when they got there, he pretended to search for him, but as he was not to be found, he said:

'No doubt his Majesty has strolled into the forest,' and he opened the little door that led to it and they went through.

By this time the daylight had begun to appear, and the Princess, looking at her conductor, saw that he had tears in his eyes and seemed too sad to speak.

'What is the matter?' she said in the kindest way. 'You seem very sorrowful.'

'Alas! Princess,' he answered, 'who would not be sorrowful who was ordered to do such a terrible thing as I am? The King has commanded me to kill you here, and carry your heart and your tongue to him, and if I disobey I shall lose my life.'

The poor Princess was terrified, she grew very pale and began to cry softly.

Looking up at the Captain of the Guard with her beautiful eyes, she said gently:

'Will you really have the heart to kill me? I have never done

you any harm, and have always spoken well of you to the King. If I had deserved my father's anger I would suffer without a murmur, but, alas! he is unjust to complain of me, when I have always treated him with love and respect.'

'Fear nothing, Princess,' said the Captain of the Guard. 'I would far rather die myself than hurt you; but even if I am killed you will not be safe: we must find some way of making the King believe that you are dead.'

'What can we do?' said Miranda; 'unless you take him my heart and my tongue he will never believe you.

The Princess and the Captain of the Guard were talking so earnestly that they did not think of Patypata, but she had overheard all they said, and now came and threw herself at Miranda's feet.

' Madam,' she said, ' I offer you my life; let me be killed, I shall be only too happy to die for such a kind mistress.'

' Why, Patypata,' cried the Princess, kissing her, ' that would never do ; your life is as precious to me as my own, especially after such a proof of your affection as you have just given me.'

' You are right, Princess,' said Grabugeon, coming forward, ' to love such a faithful slave as Patypata ; she is of more use to you than I am, I offer you my tongue and my heart most willingly, especially as I wish to make a great name for myself in Goblin Land.'

' No, no, my little Grabugeon,' replied Miranda ; ' I cannot bear the thought of taking your life.'

' Such a good little dog as I am,' cried Tintin, ' could not think of letting either of you die for his mistress. If anyone is to die for her it must be me.'

And then began a great dispute between Patypata, Grabugeon, and Tintin, and they came to high words, until at last Grabugeon, who was quicker than the others, ran up to the very top of the nearest tree, and let herself fall, head first, to the ground, and there she lay—quite dead !

The Princess was very sorry, but as Grabugeon was really dead, she allowed the Captain of the Guard to take her tongue; but, alas! it was such a little one—not bigger than the Princess's thumb, that they decided sorrowfully that it was no use at all : the King would not have been taken in by it for a moment !

' Alas ! my little monkey,' cried the Princess, ' I have lost you, and yet I am no better off than I was before.'

' The honour of saving your life is to be mine,' interrupted Patypata, and, before they could prevent her, she had picked up a knife and cut her head off in an instant.

But when the Captain of the Guard would have taken her tongue it turned out to be quite black, so that would not have deceived the King either.

' Am I not unlucky ? ' cried the poor Princess ; ' I lose everything I love, and am none the better for it.'

' If you had accepted my offer,' said Tintin, ' you would only have had me to regret, and I should have had all your gratitude.'

Miranda kissed her little dog, crying so bitterly, that at last she could bear it no longer, and turned away into the forest. When she looked back the Captain of the Guard was gone, and she was alone, except for Patypata, Grabugeon, and Tintin, who lay upon the ground. She could not leave the place until she had buried them in a pretty little mossy grave at the foot of a tree, and she wrote their names upon the bark of the tree, and how they had all died to save her life. And then she began to think where she could go for safety—for this forest was so close to her father's castle that she might be seen and recognised by the first passer-by, and, beside that, it was full of lions and wolves, who would have snapped up a princess just as soon as a stray chicken. So she began to walk as fast as she could, but the forest was so large and the sun was so hot that she nearly died of heat and terror and fatigue ; look which way she would there seemed to be no end to the forest, and she was so frightened that she fancied every minute that she heard the King running after her to kill her. You may imagine how miserable she was, and how she cried as she went on, not knowing which path to follow, and with the thorny bushes scratching her dreadfully and tearing her pretty frock to pieces.

At last she heard the bleating of a sheep, and said to herself:

' No doubt there are shepherds here with their flocks ; they will show me the way to some village where I can live disguised as a peasant girl. Alas ! it is not always kings and princes who are the happiest people in the world. Who could have believed that I should ever be obliged to run away and hide because the King, for no reason at all, wishes to kill me ? '

So saying she advanced towards the place where she heard the bleating, but what was her surprise when, in a lovely little glade quite surrounded by trees, she saw a large sheep ; its wool was as white as snow, and its horns shone like gold ; it had a garland of flowers round its neck, and strings of great pearls about its legs, and a collar of diamonds ; it lay upon a bank of orange-flowers, under a canopy of cloth of gold which protected it from the heat of the sun. Nearly a hundred other sheep were scattered about, not eating the grass, but some drinking coffee, lemonade, or sherbet, others eating ices, strawberries and cream, or sweetmeats, while others, again, were playing games. Many of them wore golden collars with jewels, flowers, and ribbons.

Miranda stopped short in amazement at this unexpected sight, and was looking in all directions for the shepherd of this surprising flock, when the beautiful sheep came bounding towards her.

'Approach, lovely Princess,' he cried; 'have no fear of such gentle and peaceable animals as we are.'

'What a marvel!' cried the Princess, starting back a little. 'Here is a sheep who can talk.'

'Your monkey and your dog could talk, madam,' said he; 'are you more astonished at us than at them?'

'A fairy gave them the power to speak,' replied Miranda. 'So I was used to them.'

'Perhaps the same thing has happened to us,' he said, smiling sheepishly. 'But, Princess, what can have led you here?'

'A thousand misfortunes, Sir Sheep,' she answered. 'I am the unhappiest princess in the world, and I am seeking a shelter against my father's anger.'

'Come with me, madam,' said the Sheep; 'I offer you a hiding-place which you only will know of, and where you will be mistress of everything you see.'

'I really cannot follow you,' said Miranda, 'for I am too tired to walk another step.'

The Sheep with the golden horns ordered that his chariot should be fetched, and a moment after appeared six goats, harnessed to a pumpkin, which was so big that two people could quite well sit in it, and was all lined with cushions of velvet and down. The Princess stepped into it, much amused at such a new kind of carriage, the King of the Sheep took his place beside her, and the goats ran away with them at full speed, and only stopped when they reached a cavern, the entrance to which was blocked by a great stone. This the King touched with his foot, and immediately it fell down, and he invited the Princess to enter without fear. Now, if she had not been so alarmed by everything that had happened, nothing could have induced her to go into this frightful cave, but she was so afraid of what might be behind her that she would have thrown herself even down a well at this moment. So, without hesitation, she followed the Sheep, who went before her, down, down, down, until she thought they must come out at the other side of the world—indeed, she was not sure that he wasn't leading her into Fairyland. At last she saw before her a great plain, quite covered with all sorts of flowers, the scent of which seemed to her nicer than anything she had ever smelt before; a broad river of orange-flower water flowed round it, and fountains of wine of every kind ran in all directions and made the prettiest little cascades and brooks. The plain was covered with the strangest trees, there were whole avenues where partridges, ready roasted, hung from every branch, or, if you preferred pheasants, quails, turkeys, or rabbits, you had only to turn to the right hand or to the left and you were sure to find them. In places the air was darkened by showers of lobster-patties, white puddings, sausages, tarts, and all sorts of sweetmeats, or with pieces of gold and silver, diamonds and pearls. This unusual kind of rain, and the pleasantness of the whole place, would, no doubt, have attracted numbers of people to it, if the King of the Sheep had been of a more sociable disposition, but from all accounts it is evident that he was as grave as a judge.

As it was quite the nicest time of the year when Miranda arrived in this delightful land the only palace she saw was a long row of orange trees, jasmines, honeysuckles, and musk-roses, and their interlacing branches made the prettiest rooms possible, which were hung with gold and silver gauze, and had great mirrors and candlesticks, and most beautiful pictures. The wonderful Sheep begged that the Princess would consider herself queen over all that she saw, and assured her that, though for some years he had been very sad and in great trouble, she had it in her power to make him forget all his grief.

'You are so kind and generous, noble Sheep,' said the Princess, 'that I cannot thank you enough, but I must confess that all I see here seems to me so extraordinary that I don't know what to think of it.'

As she spoke a band of lovely fairies came up and offered her amber baskets full of fruit, but when she held out her hands to them they glided away, and she could feel nothing when she tried to touch them.

'Oh!' she cried, 'what can they be? Whom am I with?' and she began to cry.

At this instant the King of the Sheep came back to her, and was so distracted to find her in tears that he could have torn his wool.

'What is the matter, lovely Princess?' he cried. 'Has anyone failed to treat you with due respect?'

'Oh! no,' said Miranda; 'only I am not used to living with sprites and with sheep that talk, and everything here frightens me. It was very kind of you to bring me to this place, but I shall be even more grateful to you if you will take me up into the world again.'

'Do not be afraid,' said the wonderful Sheep; 'I entreat you to have patience, and listen to the story of my misfortunes. I was once a king, and my kingdom was the most splendid in the world. My subjects loved me, my neighbours envied and feared me. I was respected by everyone, and it was said that no king ever deserved it more.

'I was very fond of hunting, and one day, while chasing a stag, I left my attendants far behind; suddenly I saw the animal leap into a pool of water, and I rashly urged my horse to follow it, but before we had gone many steps I felt an extraordinary heat, instead of the coolness of the water; the pond dried up, a great gulf opened before me, out of which flames of fire shot up, and I fell helplessly to the bottom of a precipice.

'I gave myself up for lost, but presently a voice said: "Ungrateful Prince, even this fire is hardly enough to warm your cold heart!"

'"Who complains of my coldness in this dismal place?" I cried.

'"An unhappy being who loves you hopelessly," replied the voice, and at the same moment the flames began to flicker and cease to burn, and I saw a fairy, whom I had known as long as I could remember, and whose ugliness had always horrified me. She was leaning upon the arm of a most beautiful young girl, who wore chains of gold on her wrists and was evidently her slave.

'"Why, Ragotte," I said, for that was the fairy's name, "what is the meaning of all this? Is it by your orders that I am here?"

'"And whose fault is it," she answered, "that you have never understood me until now? Must a powerful fairy like myself condescend to explain her doings to you who are no better than an ant by comparison, though you think yourself a great king?"

'"Call me what you like," I said impatiently; "but what is it that you want—my crown, or my cities, or my treasures?"

'"Treasures!" said the fairy, disdainfully. "If I chose I could make any one of my scullions richer and more powerful than you. I do not want your treasures, but," she added softly, "if you will give me your heart—if you will marry me—I will add twenty kingdoms to the one you have already; you shall have a hundred castles full of gold and five hundred full of silver, and, in short, anything you like to ask me for."

'"Madam Ragotte," said I, "when one is at the bottom of a pit where one has fully expected to be roasted alive, it is impossible to think of asking such a charming person as you are to marry one! I beg that you will set me at liberty, and then I shall hope to answer you fittingly."

'"Ah!" said she, "if you loved me really you would not care

where you were—a cave, a wood, a fox-hole, a desert, would please you equally well. Do not think that you can deceive me; you fancy you are going to escape, but I assure you that you are going to stay here, and the first thing I shall give you to do will be to keep my sheep—they are very good company and speak quite as well as you do.''

' As she spoke she advanced, and led me to this plain where we now stand, and showed me her flock, but I paid little attention to it, or to her ; to tell the truth I was so lost in admiration of her beautiful slave that I forgot everything else, and the cruel Ragotte, perceiving this, turned upon her so furious and terrible a look that she fell lifeless to the ground.

' At this dreadful sight I drew my sword and rushed at Ragotte, and should certainly have cut off her head had she not by her magic arts chained me to the spot on which I stood ; all my efforts to move were useless, and at last, when I threw myself down on the ground in despair, she said to me, with a scornful smile :

' '' I intend to make you feel my power. It seems that you are a lion at present, I mean you to be a sheep.''

' So saying, she touched me with her wand, and I became what you see. I did not lose the power of speech, or of feeling the misery of my present state.

' '' For five years,'' she said, '' you shall be a sheep, and lord of this pleasant land, while I, no longer able to see your face, which I loved so much, shall be better able to hate you as you deserve to be hated.''

' She disappeared as she finished speaking, and if I had not been too unhappy to care about anything I should have been glad that she was gone.

' The talking sheep received me as their king, and told me that they, too, were unfortunate princes who had, in different ways, offended the revengeful fairy, and had been added to her flock for a certain number of years ; some more, some less. From time to time, indeed, one regains his own proper form and goes back again to his place in the upper world; but the other beings whom you saw are the rivals or the enemies of Ragotte, whom she has imprisoned for a hundred years or so ; though even they will go back at last. The young slave of whom I told you is one of these ; I have seen her often, and it has been a great pleasure to me. She never speaks to me, and if I went nearer to her I know I should find her only a shadow, which would be very annoying. However,

I noticed that one of my companions in misfortune was also very attentive to this little sprite, and I found out that he had been her lover, whom the cruel Ragotte had taken away from her long before; since then I have cared for, and thought of, nothing but how I might regain my freedom. I have often been into the forest; that is where I have seen you, lovely Princess, sometimes driving your chariot, which you did with all the grace and skill in the world; sometimes riding to the chase on so spirited a horse that it seemed as if no one but yourself could have managed it, and sometimes running races on the plain with the Princesses of your Court—running so lightly that it was you always who won the prize. Oh! Princess, I have loved you so long, and yet how dare I tell you of my love! what hope can there be for an unhappy sheep like myself?'

Miranda was so surprised and confused by all that she had heard that she hardly knew what answer to give to the King of the Sheep, but she managed to make some kind of little speech, which certainly did not forbid him to hope, and said that she should not be afraid of the shadows now she knew that they would some day come to life again. 'Alas!' she continued, 'if my poor Patypata, my dear Grabugeon, and pretty little Tintin, who all died for my sake, were equally well off, I should have nothing left to wish for here!'

Prisoner though he was, the King of the Sheep had still some powers and privileges.

'Go,' said he to his Master of the Horse, 'go and seek the shadows of the little black girl, the monkey, and the dog: they will amuse our Princess.'

And an instant afterwards Miranda saw them coming towards her, and their presence gave her the greatest pleasure, though they did not come near enough for her to touch them.

The King of the Sheep was so kind and amusing, and loved Miranda so dearly, that at last she began to love him too. Such a handsome sheep, who was so polite and considerate, could hardly fail to please, especially if one knew that he was really a king, and that his strange imprisonment would soon come to an end. So the Princess's days passed very gaily while she waited for the happy time to come. The King of the Sheep, with the help of all the flock, got up balls, concerts, and hunting parties, and even the shadows joined in all the fun, and came, making believe to be their own real selves.

One evening, when the couriers arrived (for the King sent most carefully for news — and they always brought the very best kinds), it was announced that the sister of the Princess Miranda was going to be married to a great prince, and that nothing could be more splendid than all the preparations for the wedding.

'Ah!' cried the young Princess, 'how unlucky I am to miss the sight of so many pretty things! Here am I prisoned under the earth, with no company but sheep and shadows, while my sister is to be adorned like a queen and surrounded by all who love and admire her, and everyone but myself can go to wish her joy!'

'Why do you complain, Princess?' said the King of the Sheep. 'Did I say that you were not to go to the wedding? Set out as soon as you please; only promise me that you will come back, for I love you too much to be able to live without you.'

Miranda was very grateful to him, and promised faithfully that nothing in the world should keep her from coming back. The King caused an escort suitable to her rank to be got ready for her, and she dressed herself splendidly, not forgetting anything that could make her more beautiful. Her chariot was of mother-of-pearl, drawn by six dun-coloured griffins just brought from the other side of the world, and she was attended by a number of guards in splendid uniforms, who were all at least eight feet high and had come from far and near to ride in the Princess's train.

Miranda reached her father's palace just as the wedding ceremony began, and everyone, as soon as she came in, was struck with surprise at her beauty and the splendour of her jewels. She heard exclamations of admiration on all sides; and the King her father looked at her so attentively that she was afraid he must recognise her; but he was so sure that she was dead that the idea never occurred to him.

However, the fear of not getting away made her leave before the marriage was over. She went out hastily, leaving behind her a little coral casket set with emeralds. On it was written in diamond letters: 'Jewels for the Bride,' and when they opened it, which they did as soon as it was found, there seemed to be no end to the pretty things it contained. The King, who had hoped to join the unknown Princess and find out who she was, was dreadfully disappointed when she disappeared so suddenly, and gave orders that if she ever came again the doors were to be shut that she might not get away so easily. Short as Miranda's absence had been it had seemed like a hundred years to the King of the Sheep. He was waiting for her by a fountain in the thickest part of the forest, and the ground was strewn with splendid presents which he had prepared for her to show his joy and gratitude at her coming back.

As soon as she was in sight he rushed to meet her, leaping and bounding like a real sheep. He caressed her tenderly, throwing himself at her feet and kissing her hands, and told her how uneasy he had been in her absence, and how impatient for her return, with an eloquence which charmed her.

After some time came the news that the King's second daughter was going to be married. When Miranda heard it she begged the King of the Sheep to allow her to go and see the wedding as before. This request made him feel very sad, as if some misfortune must surely come of it, but his love for the Princess being stronger than anything else he did not like to refuse her.

'You wish to leave me, Princess,' said he; 'it is my unhappy fate—you are not to blame. I consent to your going, but, believe me, I can give you no stronger proof of my love than by so doing.'

The Princess assured him that she would only stay a very short time, as she had done before, and begged him not to be uneasy, as she would be quite as much grieved if anything detained her as he could possibly be.

So, with the same escort, she set out, and reached the palace as the marriage ceremony began. Everybody was delighted to see her; she was so pretty that they thought she must be some fairy princess, and the Princes who were there could not take their eyes off her.

The King was more glad than anyone else that she had come again, and gave orders that the doors should all be shut and bolted that very minute. When the wedding was all but over the Princess got up quickly, hoping to slip away unnoticed among the crowd, but to her great dismay she found every door fastened.

She felt more at ease when the King came up to her, and with the greatest respect begged her not to run away so soon, but at least to honour him by staying for the splendid feast which was prepared for the Princes and Princesses. He led her into a magnificent hall, where all the Court was assembled, and himself taking up the golden bowl full of water, he offered it to her that she might dip her pretty fingers into it.

At this the Princess could no longer contain herself; throwing herself at the King's feet, she cried out:

' My dream has come true after all—you have offered me water to wash my hands on my sister's wedding-day, and it has not vexed you to do it.'

The King recognised her at once—indeed, he had already thought several times how much like his poor little Miranda she was.

' Oh! my dear daughter,' he cried, kissing her, ' can you ever forget my cruelty? I ordered you to be put to death because I thought your dream portended the loss of my crown. And so it did,' he added, ' for now your sisters are both married and have kingdoms of their own—and mine shall be for you.' So saying he put his crown on the Princess's head and cried:

' Long live Queen Miranda!'

All the Court cried: ' Long live Queen Miranda!' after him, and the young Queen's two sisters came running up, and threw their arms round her neck, and kissed her a thousand times, and then there was such a laughing and crying, talking and kissing, all at once, and Miranda thanked her father, and began to ask after everyone—particularly the Captain of the Guard, to whom she owed so much; but, to her great sorrow, she heard that he was dead. Presently they sat down to the banquet, and the King asked Miranda to tell them all that had happened to her since the terrible morning when he had sent the Captain of the Guard to fetch her. This she did with so much spirit that all the guests listened with breathless interest. But while she was thus enjoying herself with the King and her sisters, the King of the Sheep was waiting impatiently for the time of her return, and when it came and went, and no Princess appeared, his anxiety became so great that he could bear it no longer.

'She is not coming back any more,' he cried. 'My miserable sheep's face displeases her, and without Miranda what is left to me, wretched creature that I am! Oh! cruel Ragotte; my punishment is complete.'

For a long time he bewailed his sad fate like this, and then, seeing that it was growing dark, and that still there was no sign of the Princess, he set out as fast as he could in the direction of the town. When he reached the palace he asked for Miranda, but by this time everyone had heard the story of her adventures, and did not want her to go back again to the King of the Sheep, so they refused sternly to let him see her. In vain he begged and prayed

them to let him in; though his entreaties might have melted hearts of stone they did not move the guards of the palace, and at last, quite broken-hearted, he fell dead at their feet.

In the meantime the King, who had not the least idea of the sad thing that was happening outside the gate of his palace, proposed to Miranda that she should be driven in her chariot all round the town, which was to be illuminated with thousands and thousands of torches, placed in windows and balconies, and in all the grand squares. But what a sight met her eyes at the very entrance of the palace! There lay her dear, kind Sheep, silent and motionless, upon the pavement!

She threw herself out of the chariot and ran to him, crying bitterly, for she realised that her broken promise had cost him his life, and for a long, long time she was so unhappy that they thought she would have died too.

So you see that even a princess is not always happy—especially if she forgets to keep her word ; and the greatest misfortunes often happen to people just as they think they have obtained their heart's desires ! [1]

[1] Madame d'Aulnoy.

LITTLE THUMB

THERE was, once upon a time, a man and his wife, fagot-makers by trade, who had seven children, all boys. The eldest was but ten years old, and the youngest only seven.

They were very poor, and their seven children incommoded them greatly, because not one of them was able to earn his bread. That which gave them yet more uneasiness was that the youngest was of a very puny constitution, and scarce ever spake a word, which made them take that for stupidity which was a sign of good sense. He was very little, and when born no bigger than one's thumb, which made him be called *Little Thumb*.

The poor child bore the blame of whatsoever was done amiss in the house, and, guilty or not, was always in the wrong; he was, notwithstanding, more cunning and had a far greater share of wisdom than all his brothers put together; and, if he spake little, he heard and thought the more.

There happened now to come a very bad year, and the famine was so great that these poor people resolved to rid themselves of their children. One evening, when they were all in bed and the fagot-maker was sitting with his wife at the fire, he said to her, with his heart ready to burst with grief:

'Thou seest plainly that we are not able to keep our children, and I cannot see them starve to death before my face; I am resolved to lose them in the wood to-morrow, which may very easily be done; for, while they are busy in tying up the fagots, we may run away, and leave them, without their taking any notice.'

'Ah!' cried out his wife; 'and canst thou thyself have the heart to take thy children out along with thee on purpose to lose them?'

In vain did her husband represent to her their extreme poverty: she would not consent to it; she was indeed poor, but she was their mother. However, having considered what a grief it would

be to her to see them perish with hunger, she at last consented, and went to bed all in tears.

Little Thumb heard every word that had been spoken; for observing, as he lay in his bed, that they were talking very busily, he got up softly, and hid himself under his father's stool, that he might hear what they said without being seen. He went to bed again, but did not sleep a wink all the rest of the night, thinking on what he had to do. He got up early in the morning, and went to the river-side, where he filled his pockets full of small white pebbles, and then returned home.

They all went abroad, but Little Thumb never told his brothers one syllable of what he knew. They went into a very thick forest, where they could not see one another at ten paces distance. The fagot-maker began to cut wood, and the children to gather up the sticks to make faggots. Their father and mother, seeing them busy at their work, got away from them insensibly, and ran away from them all at once, along a by-way through the winding bushes.

When the children saw they were left alone, they began to cry as loud as they could. Little Thumb let them cry on, knowing very well how to get home again, for, as he came, he took care to drop all along the way the little white pebbles he had in his pockets. Then he said to them:

'Be not afraid, brothers: father and mother have left us here, but I will lead you home again, only follow me.'

They did so, and he brought them home by the very same way they came into the forest. They dared not go in, but sat themselves down at the door, listening to what their father and mother were talking.

The very moment the fagot-maker and his wife were got home the lord of the manor sent them ten crowns, which he had owed them a long while, and which they never expected. This gave them new life, for the poor people were almost famished. The fagot-maker sent his wife immediately to the butcher's. As it was a long while since they had eaten a bit, she bought thrice as much meat as would sup two people. When they had eaten, the woman said:

'Alas! where are now our poor children? they would make a good feast of what we have left here; but it was you, William, who had a mind to lose them: I told you we should repent of it. What are they now doing in the forest? Alas! dear God, the wolves have perhaps already eaten them up: thou art very inhuman thus to have lost thy children.'

The fagot-maker grew at last quite out of patience, for she repeated it above twenty times, that they should repent of it, and that she was in the right of it for so saying. He threatened to beat

her if she did not hold her tongue. It was not that the fagot-maker was not, perhaps, more vexed than his wife, but that she teased him, and that he was of the humour of a great many others, who love wives who speak well, but think those very importunate who are continually doing so. She was half-drowned in tears, crying out:

'Alas! where are now my children, my poor children?'

She spake this so very loud that the children, who were at the gate, began to cry out all together:

'Here we are! Here we are!'

She ran immediately to open the door, and said, hugging them:

'I am glad to see you, my dear children; you are very hungry and weary; and my poor Peter, thou art horribly bemired; come in and let me clean thee.'

Now, you must know that Peter was her eldest son, whom she loved above all the rest, because he was somewhat *carroty*, as she herself was. They sat down to supper, and ate with such a good appetite as pleased both father and mother, whom they acquainted how frightened they were in the forest, speaking almost always all together. The good folks were extremely glad to see their children once more at home, and this joy continued while the ten crowns lasted; but, when the money was all gone, they fell again into their former uneasiness, and resolved to lose them again; and, that they might be the surer of doing it, to carry them to a much greater distance than before.

They could not talk of this so secretly but they were over-heard by Little Thumb, who made account to get out of this difficulty as well as the former; but, though he got up very betimes in the morning to go and pick up some little pebbles, he was disappointed, for he found the house-door double-locked, and was at a stand what to do. When their father had given each of them a piece of bread for their breakfast, he fancied he might make use of this instead of the pebbles, by throwing it in little bits all along the way they should pass; and so he put it in his pocket.

Their father and mother brought them into the thickest and most obscure part of the forest, when, stealing away into a by-path, they there left them. Little Thumb was not very uneasy at it, for he thought he could easily find the way again by means of his bread, which he had scattered all along as he came; but he was very much surprised when he could not find so much as one crumb: the birds had come and had eaten it up, every bit. They were now in great affliction, for the farther they went the more they were out of their way, and were more and more bewildered in the forest.

Night now came on, and there arose a terrible high wind, which made them dreadfully afraid. They fancied they heard on every side of them the howling of wolves coming to eat them up. They scarce dared to speak or turn their heads. After this, it rained very hard, which wetted them to the skin; their feet slipped at every step they took, and they fell into the mire, whence they got up in a very dirty pickle; their hands were quite benumbed.

Little Thumb climbed up to the top of a tree, to see if he could discover anything; and having turned his head about on every side, he saw at last a glimmering light, like that of a candle, but a long way from the forest. He came down, and, when upon the ground, he could see it no more, which grieved him sadly. However, having walked for some time with his brothers towards that side on which he had seen the light, he perceived it again as he came out of the wood.

They came at last to the house where this candle was, not without an abundance of fear : for very often they lost sight of it, which happened every time they came into a bottom. They knocked at the door, and a good woman came and opened it ; she asked them what they would have.

Little Thumb told her they were poor children who had been lost in the forest, and desired to lodge there for God's sake

The woman, seeing them so very pretty, began to weep, and said to them :

'Alas ! poor babies ; whither are ye come ? Do ye know that this house belongs to a cruel ogre who eats up little children ? '

' Ah ! dear madam,' answered Little Thumb (who trembled every joint of him, as well as his brothers), ' what shall we do ? To be sure the wolves of the forest will devour us to-night if you refuse us to lie here ; and so we would rather the gentleman should eat us ; and perhaps he may take pity upon us, especially if you please to beg it of him.'

The Ogre's wife, who believed she could conceal them from her husband till morning, let them come in, and brought them to warm themselves at a very good fire ; for there was a whole sheep upon the spit, roasting for the Ogre's supper.

As they began to be a little warm they heard three or four great raps at the door ; this was the Ogre, who was come home. Upon this she hid them under the bed and went to open the door. The Ogre presently asked if supper was ready and the wine drawn, and then sat himself down to table. The sheep was as yet all raw and bloody ; but he liked it the better for that. He sniffed about to the right and left, saying :

' I smell fresh meat.'

' What you smell so,' said his wife, ' must be the calf which I have just now killed and flayed.'

' I smell fresh meat, I tell thee once more,' replied the Ogre, looking crossly at his wife ; ' and there is something here which I do not understand.'

As he spoke these words he got up from the table and went directly to the bed.

'Ah, ah!' said he; 'I see then how thou wouldst cheat me,
thou cursed woman; I know not why I do not eat thee up too,
but it is well for thee that thou art a tough old carrion. Here is
good game, which comes very luckily to entertain three ogres of
my acquaintance who are to pay me a visit in a day or two.'

With that he dragged them out from under the bed, one by

C.P.J.H.

one. The poor children fell upon their knees, and begged his
pardon; but they had to do with one of the most cruel ogres in
the world, who, far from having any pity on them, had already
devoured them with his eyes, and told his wife they would be
delicate eating when tossed up with good savoury sauce. He then
took a great knife, and, coming up to these poor children, whetted
it upon a great whet-stone which he held in his left hand. He

had already taken hold of one of them when his wife said to him :

'What need you do it now? Is it not time enough to-morrow?'

'Hold your prating,' said the Ogre; 'they will eat the tenderer.'

'But you have so much meat already,' replied his wife, 'you have no occasion; here are a calf, two sheep, and half a hog.'

'That is true,' said the Ogre; 'give them their belly full that they may not fall away, and put them to bed.'

The good woman was over-joyed at this, and gave them a good supper; but they were so much afraid they could not eat a bit. As for the Ogre, he sat down again to drink, being highly pleased that he had got wherewithal to treat his friends. He drank a dozen glasses more than ordinary, which got up into his head and obliged him to go to bed.

The Ogre had seven daughters, all little children, and these young ogresses had all of them very fine complexions, because they used to eat fresh meat like their father; but they had little grey eyes, quite round, hooked noses, and very long sharp teeth, standing at a good distance from each other. They were not as yet over and above mischievous, but they promised very fair for it, for they had already bitten little children, that they might suck their blood.

They had been put to bed early, with every one a crown of gold upon her head. There was in the same chamber a bed of the like bigness, and it was into this bed the Ogre's wife put the seven little boys, after which she went to bed to her husband.

Little Thumb, who had observed that the Ogre's daughters had crowns of gold upon their heads, and was afraid lest the Ogre should repent his not killing them, got up about midnight, and, taking his brothers' bonnets and his own, went very softly and put them upon the heads of the seven little ogresses, after having taken off their crowns of gold, which he put upon his own head and his brothers', that the Ogre might take them for his daughters, and his daughters for the little boys whom he wanted to kill.

All this succeeded according to his desire; for, the Ogre waking about midnight, and sorry that he deferred to do that till morning which he might have done over-night, threw himself hastily out of bed, and, taking his great knife,

'Let us see,' said he, 'how our little rogues do, and not make two jobs of the matter.'

He then went up, groping all the way, into his daughters'

chamber, and, coming to the bed where the little boys lay, and who were every soul of them fast asleep, except Little Thumb, who was terribly afraid when he found the Ogre fumbling about his head, as he had done about his brothers', the Ogre, feeling the golden crowns, said :

'I should have made a fine piece of work of it, truly; I find I drank too much last night.'

Then he went to the bed where the girls lay ; and, having found the boys' little bonnets,

'Ah!' said he, 'my merry lads, are you there?   Let us work as we ought.'

And saying these words, without more ado, he cut the throats of all his seven daughters.

Well pleased with what he had done, he went to bed again to his wife.   So soon as Little Thumb heard the Ogre snore, he waked his brothers, and bade them put on their clothes presently and follow him.   They stole down softly into the garden, and got over the wall.   They kept running about all night, and trembled all the while, without knowing which way they went.

The Ogre, when he awoke, said to his wife : ' Go upstairs and dress those young rascals who came here last night.'

The Ogress was very much surprised at this goodness of her husband, not dreaming after what manner she should dress them ; but, thinking that he had ordered her to go and put on their clothes, she went up, and was strangely astonished when she perceived her seven daughters killed, and weltering in their blood.

She fainted away, for this is the first expedient almost all women find in such cases.   The Ogre, fearing his wife would be too long in doing what he had ordered, went up himself to help her.   He was no less amazed than his wife at this frightful spectacle.

'Ah! what have I done?' cried he.   'The wretches shall pay for it, and that instantly.'

He threw a pitcher of water upon his wife's face, and, having brought her to herself,

'Give me quickly,' cried he, 'my boots of seven leagues, that I may go and catch them.'

He went out, and, having run over a vast deal of ground, both on this side and that, he came at last into the very road where the poor children were, and not above a hundred paces from their father's house.   They espied the Ogre, who went at one step from

mountain to mountain, and over rivers as easily as the narrowest
kennels. Little Thumb, seeing a hollow rock near the place where
they were, made his brothers hide themselves in it, and crowded
into it himself, minding always what would become of the Ogre.

The Ogre, who found himself much tired with his long and
fruitless journey (for these boots of seven leagues greatly fatigued
the wearer), had a great mind to rest himself, and, by chance, went
to sit down upon the rock where the little boys had hid themselves.
As it was impossible he could be more weary than he was, he fell
asleep, and, after reposing himself some time, began to snore so

frightfully that the poor children were no less afraid of him than
when he held up his great knife and was going to cut their throats.
Little Thumb was not so much frightened as his brothers, and told
them that they should run away immediately towards home while
the Ogre was asleep so soundly, and that they should not be in
any pain about him. They took his advice, and got home presently.
Little Thumb came up to the Ogre, pulled off his boots gently
and put them on his own legs. The boots were very long and
large, but as they were fairies, they had the gift of becoming big
and little, according to the legs of those who wore them; so that
they fitted his feet and legs as well as if they had been made on

purpose for him. He went immediately to the Ogre's house, where he saw his wife crying bitterly for the loss of her murdered daughters.

'Your husband,' said Little Thumb, 'is in very great danger, being taken by a gang of thieves, who have sworn to kill him if he does not give them all his gold and silver. The very moment they held their daggers at his throat he perceived me, and desired me to come and tell you the condition he is in, and that you should give me whatsoever he has of value, without retaining any one thing: for otherwise they will kill him without mercy; and, as his case is very pressing, he desired me to make use (you see I have them on) of his boots, that I might make the more haste and to show you that I do not impose upon you.'

The good woman, being sadly frightened, gave him all she had: for this Ogre was a very good husband, though he used to eat up little children. Little Thumb, having thus got all the Ogre's money, came home to his father's house, where he was received with abundance of joy.

There are many people who do not agree in this circumstance, and pretend that Little Thumb never robbed the Ogre at all, and that he only thought he might very justly, and with a safe conscience, take off his boots of seven leagues, because he made no other use of them but to run after little children. These folks affirm that they are very well assured of this, and the more as having drunk and eaten often at the fagot-maker's house. They aver that when Little Thumb had taken off the Ogre's boots he went to Court, where he was informed that they were very much in pain about a certain army, which was two hundred leagues off, and the success of a battle. He went, say they, to the King, and told him that, if he desired it, he would bring him news from the army before night.

The King promised him a great sum of money upon that condition. Little Thumb was as good as his word, and returned that very same night with the news; and, this first expedition causing him to be known, he got whatever he pleased, for the King paid him very well for carrying his orders to the army. After having for some time carried on the business of a messenger, and gained thereby great wealth, he went home to his father, where it was impossible to express the joy they were all in at his return. He made the whole family very easy, bought places for his father and brothers, and, by that means, settled them very handsomely in the world, and, in the meantime, made his court to perfection.[1]

[1] Charles Perrault.

THE FORTY THIEVES

IN a town in Persia there dwelt two brothers, one named Cassim, the other Ali Baba. Cassim was married to a rich wife and lived in plenty, while Ali Baba had to maintain his wife and children by cutting wood in a neighbouring forest and selling it in the town. One day, when Ali Baba was in the forest, he saw a troop of men on horseback, coming towards him in a cloud of dust. He was afraid they were robbers, and climbed into a tree for safety. When they came up to him and dismounted, he counted forty of them. They unbridled their horses and tied them to trees. The finest man among them, whom Ali Baba took to be their captain, went a little way among some bushes, and said: 'Open, Sesame!' [1] so plainly that Ali Baba heard him. A door opened in the rocks, and having made the troop go in, he followed them, and the door shut again of itself. They stayed some time inside, and Ali Baba, fearing they might come out and catch him, was forced to sit patiently in the tree. At last the door opened again, and the Forty Thieves came out. As the Captain went in last he came out first, and made them all pass by him; he then closed the door, saying: 'Shut, Sesame!' Every man bridled his horse and mounted, the Captain put himself at their head, and they returned as they came.

Then Ali Baba climbed down and went to the door concealed among the bushes, and said: 'Open, Sesame!' and it flew open. Ali Baba, who expected a dull, dismal place, was greatly surprised to find it large and well lighted, and hollowed by the hand of man in the form of a vault, which received the light from an opening in the ceiling. He saw rich bales of merchandise—silk, stuff-brocades all piled together, and gold and silver in heaps, and money in leather purses. He went in and the door shut behind him. He did not look at the silver, but brought out as many bags of gold as he thought his asses, which were browsing outside, could carry, loaded

---

[1] Sesame is a kind of grain.

"OPEN, SESAME!"

them with the bags, and hid it all with fagots. Using the words:
' Shut, Sesame ! ' he closed the door and went home.

Then he drove his asses into the yard, shut the gates, carried
the money bags to his wife, and emptied them out before her. He
bade her keep the secret, and he would go and bury the gold. ' Let
me first measure it,' said his wife. ' I will go borrow a measure of
someone, while you dig the hole.' So she ran to the wife of Cassim
and borrowed a measure. Knowing Ali Baba's poverty, the sister
was curious to find out what sort of grain his wife wished to measure,
and artfully put some suet at the bottom of the measure. Ali Baba's
wife went home and set the measure on the heap of gold, and filled
it and emptied it often, to her great content. She then carried it
back to her sister, without noticing that a piece of gold was sticking to it, which Cassim's wife perceived directly her back was
turned. She grew very curious, and said to Cassim when he came
home : ' Cassim, your brother is richer than you. He does not count
his money, he measures it.' He begged her to explain this riddle,
which she did by showing him the piece of money and telling him
where she found it. Then Cassim grew so envious that he could not
sleep, and went to his brother in the morning before sunrise. ' Ali
Baba,' he said, showing him the gold piece, ' you pretend to be poor
and yet you measure gold.' By this Ali Baba perceived that through
his wife's folly Cassim and his wife knew their secret, so he confessed
all and offered Cassim a share. ' That I expect,' said Cassim ; ' but
I must know where to find the treasure, otherwise I will discover all,
and you will lose all.' Ali Baba, more out of kindness than fear,
told him of the cave, and the very words to use. Cassim left Ali Baba,
meaning to be beforehand with him and get the treasure for himself.
He rose early next morning, and set out with ten mules loaded with
great chests. He soon found the place, and the door in the rock. He
said : ' Open, Sesame ! ' and the door opened and shut behind him.
He could have feasted his eyes all day on the treasures, but he now
hastened to gather together as much of it as possible ; but when he
was ready to go he could not remember what to say for thinking of
his great riches. Instead of ' Sesame,' he said : ' Open, Barley ! ' and
the door remained fast. He named several different sorts of grain,
all but the right one, and the door still stuck fast. He was so
frightened at the danger he was in that he had as much forgotten
the word as if he had never heard it.

About noon the robbers returned to their cave, and saw Cassims'
mules roving about with great chests on their backs. This gave them

the alarm : they drew their sabres, and went to the door, which opened on their Captain's saying : ' Open, Sesame ! ' Cassim, who had heard the trampling of their horses' feet, resolved to sell his life dearly, so when the door opened he leaped out and threw the Captain down.   In vain, however, for the robbers with their sabres soon killed him.   On entering the cave they saw all the bags laid ready, and could not imagine how anyone had got in without know-ing their secret.   They cut Cassim's body into four quarters, and nailed them up inside the cave, in order to frighten anyone who should venture in, and went away in search of more treasure.

As night drew on Cassim's wife grew very uneasy, and ran to her brother-in-law, and told him where her husband had gone.   Ali Baba did his best to comfort her, and set out to the forest in search of Cassim.   The first thing he saw on entering the cave was his dead brother.   Full of horror, he put the body on one of his asses, and bags of gold on the other two, and, covering all with some fagots, returned home.   He drove the two asses laden with gold into his own yard, and led the other to Cassim's house.   The door was opened by the slave Morgiana, whom he knew to be both brave and cunning. Unloading the ass, he said to her : ' This is the body of your master, who has been murdered, but whom we must bury as though he had died in his bed.   I will speak with you again, but now tell your mistress I am come.'   The wife of Cassim, on learning the fate of her husband, broke out into cries and tears, but Ali Baba offered to take her to live with him and his wife if she would promise to keep his counsel and leave everything to Morgiana ; whereupon she agreed, and dried her eyes.

Morgiana, meanwhile, sought an apothecary and asked him for some lozenges.   ' My poor master,' she said, ' can neither eat nor speak, and no one knows what his distemper is.'   She carried home the lozenges and returned next day weeping, and asked for an essence only given to those just about to die.   Thus, in the evening, no one was surprised to hear the wretched shrieks and cries of Cassim's wife and Morgiana, telling everyone that Cassim was dead.   The day after Morgiana went to an old cobbler near the gates of the town who opened his stall early, put a piece of gold in his hand, and bade him follow her with his needle and thread.   Having bound his eyes with a handkerchief, she took him to the room where the body lay, pulled off the bandage, and bade him sew the quarters together, after which she covered his eyes again and led him home.   Then they buried Cassim, and Morgiana his slave

followed him to the grave, weeping and tearing her hair, while
Cassim's wife stayed at home uttering lamentable cries.   Next day
she went to live with Ali Baba, who gave Cassim's shop to his eldest
son.

The Forty Thieves, on their return to the cave, were much
astonished to find Cassim's body gone and some of their money-
bags.   'We are certainly discovered,' said the Captain, ' and shall

be undone if we cannot find out who it is that knows our secret.
Two men must have known it ; we have killed one, we must now find
the other. To this end one of you who is bold and artful must go into
the city dressed as a traveller, and discover whom we have killed,
and whether men talk of the strange manner of his death.   If the
messenger fails he must lose his life, lest we be betrayed.' One of the
thieves started up and offered to do this, and after the rest had highly

commended him for his bravery he disguised himself, and happened to enter the town at daybreak, just by Baba Mustapha's stall. The thief bade him good-day, saying : 'Honest man, how can you possibly see to stitch at your age ? ' 'Old as I am,' replied the cobbler, 'I have very good eyes, and you will believe me when I tell you that I sewed a dead body together in a place where I had less light than I have now.' The robber was over-joyed at his good fortune, and, giving him a piece of gold, desired to be shown the house where he stitched up the dead body. At first Mustapha refused, saying that he had been blindfolded ; but when the robber gave him another piece of gold he began to think he might remember the turnings if blindfolded as before. This means succeeded ; the robber partly led him, and was partly guided by him, right in front of Cassim's house, the door of which the robber marked with a piece of chalk. Then, well pleased, he bade farewell to Baba Mustapha and returned to the forest. By-and-by Morgiana, going out, saw the mark the robber had made, quickly guessed that some mischief was brewing, and fetching a piece of chalk marked two or three doors on each side, without saying anything to her master or mistress.

The thief, meantime, told his comrades of his discovery. The Captain thanked him, and bade him show him the house he had marked. But when they came to it they saw that five or six of the houses were chalked in the same manner. The guide was so confounded that he knew not what answer to make, and when they returned he was at once beheaded for having failed. Another robber was despatched, and, having won over Baba Mustapha, marked the house in red chalk ; but Morgiana being again too clever for them, the second messenger was put to death also. The Captain now resolved to go himself, but, wiser than the others, he did not mark the house, but looked at it so closely that he could not fail to remember it. He returned, and ordered his men to go into the neighbouring villages and buy nineteen mules, and thirty-eight leather jars, all empty, except one which was full of oil. The Captain put one of his men, fully armed, into each, rubbing the outside of the jars with oil from the full vessel. Then the nineteen mules were loaded with thirty-seven robbers in jars, and the jar of oil, and reached the town by dusk. The Captain stopped his mules in front of Ali Baba's house, and said to Ali Baba, who was sitting outside for coolness : 'I have brought some oil from a dis-tance to sell at to-morrow's market, but it is now so late that I know not where to pass the night, unless you will do me the favour to take me in.' Though Ali Baba had seen the Captain of the robbers in the forest, he did not recognise him in the disguise of an oil merchant. He bade him welcome, opened his gates for the mules to enter, and went to Morgiana to bid her prepare a bed and supper for his guest. He brought the stranger into his hall, and after they had supped went again to speak to Morgiana in the kitchen, while the Captain went into the yard under pretence of seeing after his mules, but really to tell his men what to do. Beginning at the first jar and ending at the last, he said to each man: 'As soon as I throw some stones from the window of the chamber where I lie, cut the jars open with your knives and come out, and I will be with you in a trice.' He returned to the house, and Morgiana led him to his chamber. She then told Abdallah, her fellow-slave, to set on the pot to make some broth for her master, who had gone to bed. Meanwhile her lamp went out, and she had no more oil in the house. 'Do not be uneasy,' said Abdallah; 'go into the yard and take some out of one of those jars.' Morgiana thanked him for his advice, took the oil pot, and went into the yard. When she came to the first jar the robber inside said softly: 'Is it time?'

Any other slave but Morgiana, on finding a man in the jar instead of the oil she wanted, would have screamed and made a noise; but she, knowing the danger her master was in, bethought herself of a plan, and answered quietly: 'Not yet, but presently.' She went to all the jars, giving the same answer, till she came to the jar of oil. She now saw that her master, thinking to entertain an oil merchant, had let thirty-eight robbers into his house. She filled her oil pot, went back to the kitchen, and, having lit her lamp, went again to the oil jar and filled a large kettle full of oil. When it boiled she went and poured enough oil into every jar to stifle and kill the robber inside. When this brave deed was done she went back to the kitchen, put out the fire and the lamp, and waited to see what would happen.

In a quarter of an hour the Captain of the robbers awoke, got up, and opened the window. As all seemed quiet he threw down some little pebbles which hit the jars. He listened, and as none of his men seemed to stir he grew uneasy, and went down into the yard. On going to the first jar and saying: 'Are you asleep?' he smelt the hot boiled oil, and knew at once that his plot to murder Ali Baba and his household had been discovered. He found all the

gang were dead, and, missing the oil out of the last jar, became
aware of the manner of their death. He then forced the lock of a
door leading into a garden, and climbing over several walls made

his escape. Morgiana
heard and saw all this,
and, rejoicing at her success, went to bed and fell
asleep.

At daybreak Ali Baba
arose, and, seeing the oil
jars there still, asked why
the merchant had not
gone with his mules. Mor-
giana bade him look in
the first jar and see if
there was any oil. See-
ing a man, he started back
in terror. ' Have no fear,'
said Morgiana; ' the man
cannot harm you: he is
dead.' Ali Baba, when
he had recovered some-
what from his astonish-
ment, asked what had be-
come of the merchant.
' Merchant!' said she,
' he is no more a mer-
chant than I am!' and
she told him the whole story, assuring him that it was a plot of the
robbers of the forest, of whom only three were left, and that the
white and red chalk marks had something to do with it. Ali Baba
at once gave Morgiana her freedom, saying that he owed her his
life. They then buried the bodies in Ali Baba's garden, while the
mules were sold in the market by his slaves.

The Captain returned to his lonely cave, which seemed frightful
to him without his lost companions, and firmly resolved to avenge
them by killing Ali Baba. He dressed himself carefully, and went
into the town, where he took lodgings in an inn. In the course of
a great many journeys to the forest he carried away many rich
stuffs and much fine linen, and set up a shop opposite that of Ali
Baba's son. He called himself Cogia Hassan, and as he was both

civil and well dressed he soon made friends with Ali Baba's son, and through him with Ali Baba, whom he was continually asking to sup with him. Ali Baba, wishing to return his kindness, invited him into his house and received him smiling, thanking him for his kindness to his son. When the merchant was about to take his leave Ali Baba stopped him, saying: ' Where are you going, sir, in such haste ? Will you not stay and sup with me ? ' The merchant refused, saying that he had a reason ; and, on Ali Baba's asking him what that was, he replied : ' It is, sir, that I can eat no victuals that have any salt in them.' ' If that is all,' said Ali Baba, ' let me tell you that there shall be no salt in either the meat or the bread that we eat to-night.' He went to give this order to Morgiana, who was much surprised. ' Who is this man,' she said, ' who eats no salt with his meat ? ' ' He is an honest man, Morgiana,' returned her master ; ' therefore do as I bid you.' But she could not withstand a desire to see this strange man, so she helped Abdallah to carry up the dishes, and saw in a moment that Cogia Hassan was the robber Captain , and carried a dagger under his garment. ' I am not surprised,' she said to herself, ' that this wicked man, who intends to kill my master, will eat no salt with him ; but I will hinder his plans.'

She sent up the supper by Abdallah, while she made ready for one of the boldest acts that could be thought on. When the dessert had been served, Cogia Hassan was left alone with Ali Baba and his son, whom he thought to make drunk and then to murder them. Morgiana, meanwhile, put on a head-dress like a dancing-girl's, and clasped a girdle round her waist, from which hung a dagger with a silver hilt, and said to Abdallah : ' Take your tabor, and let us go and divert our master and his guest.' Abdallah took his tabor and played before Morgiana until they came to the door, where Abdallah stopped playing and Morgiana made a low courtesy. ' Come in, Morgiana,' said Ali Baba, ' and let Cogia Hassan see what you can do ;' and, turning to Cogia Hassan, he said : ' She's my slave and my housekeeper.' Cogia Hassan was by no means pleased, for he feared that his chance of killing Ali Baba was gone for the present ; but he pretended great eagerness to see Morgiana, and Abdallah began to play and Morgiana to dance. After she had performed several dances she drew her dagger and made passes with it, sometimes pointing it at her own breast. sometimes at her master's, as if it were part of the dance. Suddenly, out of breath, she snatched the tabor from Abdallah with her left hand. and, holding the dagger in her right, held out the tabor to her master. Ali Baba and his son put a piece of gold into it, and Cogia Hassan, seeing that she was coming to him, pulled out his purse to make her a present, but while he was putting his hand into it Morgiana plunged the dagger into his heart.

'Unhappy girl!' cried Ali Baba and his son, 'what have you done to ruin us?' 'It was to preserve you, master, not to ruin you,' answered Morgiana. 'See here,' opening the false merchant's garment and showing the dagger; 'see what an enemy you have entertained! Remember, he would eat no salt with you, and what more would you have? Look at him! he is both the false oil merchant and the Captain of the Forty Thieves.'

Ali Baba was so grateful to Morgiana for thus saving his life that he offered her to his son in marriage, who readily consented, and a few days after the wedding was celebrated with great splendour. At the end of a year Ali Baba, hearing nothing of the two remaining robbers, judged they were dead, and set out to the cave. The door opened on his saying: 'Open, Sesame!' He went in, and saw that nobody had been there since the Captain left it. He brought away as much gold as he could carry, and returned to town. He told his son the secret of the cave, which his son handed down in his turn, so the children and grandchildren of Ali Baba were rich to the end of their lives.[1]

[1] *Arabian Nights.*

HANSEL AND GRETTEL

ONCE upon a time there dwelt on the outskirts of a large forest a poor woodcutter with his wife and two children; the boy was called Hansel and the girl Grettel. He had always little enough to live on, and once, when there was a great famine in the land, he couldn't even provide them with daily bread. One night, as he was tossing about in bed, full of cares and worry, he sighed and said to his wife: ' What's to become of us ? how are we to support our poor children, now that we have nothing more for ourselves ? ' ' I'll tell you what, husband,' answered the woman; ' early to-morrow morning we'll take the children out into the thickest part of the wood; there we shall light a fire for them and give them each a piece of bread; then we'll go on to our work and leave them alone. They won't be able to find their way home, and we shall thus be rid of them.' ' No, wife,' said her husband, ' that I won't do; how could I find it in my heart to leave my children alone in the wood ? the wild beasts would soon come and tear them to pieces.' ' Oh! you fool,' said she, ' then we must all four die of hunger, and you may just as well go and plane the boards for our coffins;' and she left him no peace till he consented. ' But I can't help feeling sorry for the poor children,' added the husband.

The children, too, had not been able to sleep for hunger, and had heard what their step-mother had said to their father. Grettel wept bitterly and spoke to Hansel: ' Now it's all up with us.' ' No, no, Grettel,' said Hansel, ' don't fret yourself; I'll be able to find a way of escape, no fear.' And when the old people had fallen asleep he got up, slipped on his little coat, opened the back door and stole out. The moon was shining clearly, and the white pebbles which lay in front of the house glittered like bits of silver. Hansel bent down and filled his pocket with as many of them as he could cram in. Then he went back and said to Grettel: ' Be comforted, my dear little sister, and go to sleep: God will not desert us;' and he lay down in bed again.

At daybreak, even before the sun was up, the woman came and woke the two children: ' Get up, you lie-abeds, we're all going to the forest to fetch wood.' She gave them each a bit of bread and spoke: 'There's something for your luncheon, but don't you eat it up before, for it's all you'll get.' Grettel took the bread under her apron, as Hansel had the stones in his pocket. Then they all set out together on the way to the forest. After they had walked for a little, Hansel stood still and looked back at the house, and this manœuvre he repeated again and again. His father observed him, and spake: ' Hansel, what are you gazing at there, and why do you always remain behind? Take care, and don't lose your footing.' ' Oh! father,' said Hansel, ' I am looking back at my white kitten, which is sitting on the roof, waving me a farewell.' The woman exclaimed: ' What a donkey you are! that isn't your kitten, that's the morning sun shining on the chimney.' But Hansel had not looked back at his kitten, but had always dropped one of the white pebbles out of his pocket on to the path.

When they had reached the middle of the forest the father said: ' Now, children, go and fetch a lot of wood, and I'll light a fire that you mayn't feel cold.' Hansel and Grettel heaped up brushwood till they had made a pile nearly the size of a small hill. The brushwood was set fire to, and when the flames leaped high the woman said: ' Now lie down at the fire, children, and rest yourselves: we are going into the forest to cut down wood; when we've finished we'll come back and fetch you.' Hansel and Grettel sat down beside the fire, and at midday ate their little bits of bread. They heard the strokes of the axe, so they thought their father was quite near. But it was no axe they heard, but a bough he had tied on to a dead tree, and that was blown about by the wind. And when they had sat for a long time their eyes closed with fatigue, and they fell fast asleep. When they awoke at last it was pitch-dark. Grettel began to cry, and said: ' How are we ever to get out of the wood?' But Hansel comforted her. ' Wait a bit,' he said, ' till the moon is up, and then we'll find our way sure enough.' And when the full moon had risen he took his sister by the hand and followed the pebbles, which shone like new threepenny bits, and showed them the path. They walked all through the night, and at daybreak reached their father's house again. They knocked at the door, and when the woman opened it she exclaimed: ' You naughty children, what a time you've slept in the wood! we thought you were never going to come back.' But the father rejoiced, for his conscience had reproached him for leaving his children behind by themselves.

Not long afterwards there was again great dearth in the land, and the children heard their mother address their father thus in bed one night : ' Everything is eaten up once more ; we have only half a loaf in the house, and when that's done it's all up with us. The children must be got rid of ; we'll lead them deeper into the wood this time, so that they won't be able to find their way out again. There is no other way of saving ourselves.' The man's heart smote him heavily, and he thought : ' Surely it would be better to share the last bite with one's children ! ' But his wife wouldn't listen to his arguments, and did nothing but scold and reproach him. If a man yields once he's done for, and so, because he had given in the first time, he was forced to do so the second.

But the children were awake, and had heard the conversation. When the old people were asleep Hansel got up, and wanted to go out and pick up pebbles again, as he had done the first time ; but the woman had barred the door, and Hansel couldn't get out. But he consoled his little sister, and said : ' Don't cry, Grettel, and sleep peacefully, for God is sure to help us.'

At early dawn the woman came and made the children get up. They received their bit of bread, but it was even smaller than the time before. On the way to the wood Hansel crumbled it in his pocket, and every few minutes he stood still and dropped a crumb on the ground. ' Hansel, what are you stopping and looking about you for ? ' said the father. ' I'm looking back at my little pigeon, which is sitting on the roof waving me a farewell,' answered

Hansel. 'Fool!' said the wife; 'that isn't your pigeon, it's the morning sun glittering on the chimney.' But Hansel gradually threw all his crumbs on to the path. The woman led the children still deeper into the forest, farther than they had ever been in their lives before. Then a big fire was lit again, and the mother said : 'Just sit down there, children, and if you're tired you can sleep a bit; we're going into the forest to cut down wood, and in the evening when we're finished we'll come back to fetch you.' At midday Grettel divided her bread with Hansel, for he had strewed his all along their path. Then they fell asleep, and evening passed away, but nobody came to the poor children. They didn't awake till it was pitch-dark, and Hansel comforted his sister, saying : 'Only wait, Grettel, till the moon rises, then we shall see the bread-crumbs I scattered along the path; they will show us the way back to the house.' When the moon appeared they got up, but they found no crumbs, for the thousands of birds that fly about the woods and fields had picked them all up. 'Never mind,' said Hansel to Grettel; 'you'll see we'll still find a way out;' but all the same they did not. They wandered about the whole night, and the next day, from morning till evening, but they could not find a path out of the wood. They were very hungry, too, for they had nothing to eat but a few berries they found growing on the ground. And at last they were so tired that their legs refused to carry them any longer, so they lay down under a tree and fell fast asleep.

On the third morning after they had left their father's house they set about their wandering again, but only got deeper and deeper into the wood, and now they felt that if help did not come to them soon they must perish. At midday they saw a beautiful little snow-white bird sitting on a branch, which sang so sweetly that they stopped still and listened to it. And when its song was finished it flapped its wings and flew on in front of them. They followed it and came to a little house, on the roof of which it perched; and when they came quite near they saw that the cottage was made of bread and roofed with cakes, while the window was made of transparent sugar. 'Now we'll set to,' said Hansel, 'and have a regular blow-out.[1] I'll eat a bit of the roof, and you, Grettel, can eat some of the window, which you'll find a sweet morsel.' Hansel stretched up his hand and broke off a little bit of the roof to see what it was like, and Grettel went to the casement and began to nibble at it. Thereupon a shrill voice called out from the room inside :

[1] 'He was a vulgar boy !'

'Nibble, nibble, little mouse,
Who's nibbling my house?'

The children answered:

' 'Tis Heaven's own child,
The tempest wild,'

and went on eating, without putting themselves about. Hansel,
who thoroughly appreciated the roof, tore down a big bit of it, while
Grettel pushed out a whole round window-pane, and sat down the

better to enjoy it. Suddenly the door opened, and an ancient dame
leaning on a staff hobbled out. Hansel and Grettel were so terrified
that they let what they had in their hands fall. But the old woman
shook her head and said: 'Oh, ho! you dear children, who led you
here? Just come in and stay with me, no ill shall befall you.' She
took them both by the hand and led them into the house, and laid
a most sumptuous dinner before them—milk and sugared pancakes,
with apples and nuts. After they had finished, two beautiful little

white beds were prepared for them, and when Hansel and Grettel lay down in them they felt as if they had got into heaven.

The old woman had appeared to be most friendly, but she was really an old witch who had waylaid the children, and had only built the little bread house in order to lure them in. When anyone came into her power she killed, cooked, and ate him, and held a regular feast-day for the occasion. Now witches have red eyes, and cannot see far, but, like beasts, they have a keen sense of smell, and know when human beings pass by. When Hansel and Grettel fell into her hands she laughed maliciously, and said jeeringly : ' I've got them now ; they shan't escape me.' Early in the morning, before the children were awake, she rose up, and when she saw them both sleeping so peacefully, with their round rosy cheeks, she muttered to herself : ' That'll be a dainty bite.' Then she seized Hansel with her bony hand and carried him into a little stable, and barred the door on him ; he might scream as much as he liked, it did him no good. Then she went to Grettel, shook her till she awoke, and cried : ' Get up, you lazy-bones, fetch water and cook something for your brother. When he's fat I'll eat him up.' Grettel began to cry bitterly, ut it was of no use : she had to do what the wicked witch bade her.

So the best food was cooked for poor Hansel, but Grettel got nothing but crab-shells. Every morning the old woman hobbled out to the stable and cried : ' Hansel, put out your finger, that I may feel if you are getting fat.' But Hansel always stretched out a bone, and the old dame, whose eyes were dim, couldn't see it, and thinking always it was Hansel's finger, wondered why he fattened so slowly. When four weeks passed and Hansel still remained thin, she lost patience and determined to wait no longer. ' Hi ! Grettel,' she called to the girl, ' be quick and get some water. Hansel may be fat or thin, I'm going to kill him to-morrow and cook him.' Oh ! how the poor little sister sobbed as she carried the water, and how the tears rolled down her cheeks ! ' Kind heaven help us now ! ' she cried ; ' if only the wild beasts in the wood had eaten us, then at least we should have died together.' ' Just hold your peace,' said the old hag ; ' it won't help you.'

Early in the morning Grettel had to go out and hang up the kettle full of water, and light the fire. ' First we'll bake,' said the old dame ; ' I've heated the oven already and kneaded the dough ' She pushed Grettel out to the oven, from which fiery flames were already issuing. ' Creep in,' said the witch, ' and see if it's properly heated, so that we can shove in the bread.' For when she had got Grettel in she meant to close the oven and let the girl bake, that she might eat her up too. But Grettel perceived her intention, and spoke: 'I don't know how I'm to do it; how do I get in?' 'You silly goose!' said the hag, 'the opening is big enough; see, I could get in myself;' and she crawled towards it, and poked her head into the oven. Then Grettel gave her a shove that sent her right in, shut the iron door, and drew the bolt. Gracious! how she yelled! it was quite horrible; but Grettel fled, and the wretched old woman was left to perish miserably.

Grettel flew straight to Hansel, opened the little stable-door, and cried: 'Hansel, we are free; the old witch is dead.' Then Hansel sprang like a bird out of a cage when the door is opened. How they rejoiced, and fell on each other's necks, and jumped for joy, and kissed one another! And as they had no longer any cause for fear, they went into the old hag's house, and there they found, in every corner of the room, boxes with pearls and precious stones. 'These are even better than pebbles,' said Hansel, and crammed his pockets full of them; and Grettel said: 'I too will bring something home;' and she filled her apron full. 'But now,' said Hansel, 'let's go and get well away from the witches' wood.' When they had wandered about for some hours they came to a big lake. 'We can't get over,' said Hansel; 'I see no bridge of any sort or kind.' 'Yes, and there's no ferry-boat either,' answered Grettel; 'but look, there swims a white duck; if I ask her she'll help us over;' and she called out:

> 'Here are two children, mournful very,
> Seeing neither bridge nor ferry;
> Take us upon your white back,
> And row us over, quack, quack!'

The duck swam towards them, and Hansel got on her back and bade his little sister sit beside him. 'No,' answered Grettel, 'we should be too heavy a load for the duck: she shall carry us across separately.' The good bird did this, and when they were landed safely on the other side, and had gone on for a while, the wood became more and more familiar to them, and at length they saw their father's house in the distance. Then they set off to run, and bounding into the room fell on their father's neck. The man had not passed a happy hour since he left them in the wood, but the woman had died. Grettel shook out her apron so that the pearls and precious stones rolled about the room, and Hansel threw down one handful after the other out of his pocket. Thus all their troubles were ended, and they all lived happily ever afterwards.

My story is done. See! there runs a little mouse; anyone who catches it may make himself a large fur cap out of it.[1]

[1] Grimm.

SNOW-WHITE AND ROSE-RED

A POOR widow once lived in a little cottage with a garden in front of it, in which grew two rose trees, one bearing white roses and the other red. She had two children, who were just like the two rose trees; one was called Snow-white and the other Rose-red, and they were the sweetest and best children in the world, always diligent and always cheerful; but Snow-white was quieter and more gentle than Rose-red. Rose-red loved to run about the fields and meadows, and to pick flowers and catch butterflies; but Snow-white sat at home with her mother and helped her in the household, or read aloud to her when there was no work to do. The two children loved each other so dearly that they always walked about hand-in-hand whenever they went out together, and when Snow-white said: 'We will never desert each other,' Rose-red answered: 'No, not as long as we live;' and the mother added: 'Whatever one gets she shall share with the other.' They often roamed about in the woods gathering berries and no beast offered to hurt them; on the contrary, they came up to them in the most confiding manner; the little hare would eat a cabbage leaf from their hands, the deer grazed beside them, the stag would bound past them merrily, and the birds remained on the branches and sang to them with all their might. No evil ever befell them; if they tarried late in the wood and night overtook them, they lay down together on the moss and slept till morning, and their mother knew they were quite safe, and never felt anxious about them. Once, when they had slept the night in the wood and had been wakened by the morning sun, they perceived a beautiful child in a shining white robe sitting close to their resting-place. The figure got up, looked at them kindly, but said nothing, and vanished into the wood. And when they looked round about them they became aware that they had slept quite close to a precipice, over which they would certainly have fallen had they gone on a few steps further in the darkness. And when they told their mother of their adventure, she said what they had seen must have been the angel that guards good children.

Snow-white and Rose-red kept their mother's cottage so beautifully clean and neat that it was a pleasure to go into it. In summer Rose-red looked after the house, and every morning before her mother awoke she placed a bunch of flowers before the bed, from each tree a rose. In winter Snow-white lit the fire and put on the kettle, which was made of brass, but so beautifully polished that it shone like gold. In the evening when the snowflakes fell their mother said: 'Snow-white, go and close the shutters;' and they drew round the fire, while the mother put on her spectacles and read aloud from a big book and the two girls listened and sat and span. Beside them on the ground lay a little lamb, and behind them perched a little white dove with its head tucked under its wings.

One evening as they sat thus cosily together someone knocked at the door as though he desired admittance. The mother said: 'Rose-red, open the door quickly; it must be some traveller seeking shelter.' Rose-red hastened to unbar the door, and thought she saw a poor man standing in the darkness outside; but it was no such thing, only a bear, who poked his thick black head through the door. Rose-red screamed aloud and sprang back in terror, the lamb began to bleat, the dove flapped its wings, and Snow-white ran and hid behind her mother's bed. But the bear began to speak, and said: 'Don't be afraid: I won't hurt you. I am half frozen, and only wish to warm myself a little.' 'My poor bear,' said the mother, 'lie down by the fire, only take care you don't burn your fur.' Then she called out: 'Snow-white and Rose-red, come out; the bear will do you no harm: he is a good, honest creature.' So they both came out of their hiding-places, and gradually the lamb and dove drew near too, and they all forgot their fear. The bear asked the children to beat the snow a little out of his fur, and they fetched a brush and scrubbed him till he was dry. Then the beast stretched himself in front of the fire, and growled quite happily and comfortably. The children soon grew quite at their ease with him, and led their helpless guest a fearful life. They tugged his fur with their hands, put their small feet on his back, and rolled him about here and there, or took a hazel wand and beat him with it; and if he growled they only laughed. The bear submitted to everything with the best possible good-nature, only when they went too far he cried: 'Oh! children, spare my life!

Snow-white and Rose-red,
Don't beat your lover dead.'

When it was time to retire for the night, and the others went to bed,
the mother said to the bear: 'You can lie there on the hearth, in
heaven's name; it will be shelter for you from the cold and wet.'
As soon as day dawned the children let him out, and he trotted over
the snow into the wood.   From this time on the bear came every
evening at the same hour, and lay down by the hearth and let the
children play what pranks they liked with him; and they got so
accustomed to him that the door was never shut till their black
friend had made his appearance.

When spring came, and all outside was green, the bear said one
morning to Snow-white: 'Now I must go away, and not return
again the whole summer.' 'Where are you going to, dear bear?'
asked Snow-white. 'I must go to the wood and protect my treasure
from the wicked dwarfs. In winter, when the earth is frozen hard,
they are obliged to remain underground, for they can't work their
way through; but now, when the sun has thawed and warmed the
ground, they break through and come up above to spy the land and
steal what they can : what once falls into their hands and into their
caves is not easily brought back to light.' Snow-white was quite
sad over their friend's departure, and when she unbarred the door
for him, the bear, stepping out, caught a piece of his fur in the door-

knocker, and Snow-white thought she caught sight of glittering gold beneath it, but she couldn't be certain of it; and the bear ran hastily away, and soon disappeared behind the trees.

A short time after this the mother sent the children into the wood to collect fagots. They came in their wanderings upon a big tree which lay felled on the ground, and on the trunk among the long grass they noticed something jumping up and down, but what it was they couldn't distinguish. When they approached nearer they perceived a dwarf with a wizened face and a beard a yard

long. The end of the beard was jammed into a cleft of the tree, and the little man sprang about like a dog on a chain, and didn't seem to know what he was to do. He glared at the girls with his fiery red eyes, and screamed out: 'What are you standing there for? can't you come and help me?' 'What were you doing, little man?' asked Rose-red. 'You stupid, inquisitive goose!' replied the dwarf; 'I wanted to split the tree, in order to get little chips of wood for our kitchen fire; those thick logs that serve to make fires for coarse, greedy people like yourselves quite burn up all the little food we need. I had successfully driven in the wedge, and all was going well, but the cursed wood was so slippery that it suddenly sprang out, and the tree closed up so rapidly that I had no time to take my beautiful white beard out, so here I am stuck fast, and I can't get away; and you silly, smooth-faced, milk-and-water girls just stand and laugh! Ugh! what wretches you are!'

The children did all in their power, but they couldn't get the beard out; it was wedged in far too firmly. 'I will run and fetch somebody,' said Rose-red. 'Crazy blockheads!' snapped the dwarf; 'what's the good of calling anyone else? you're already two too many for me. Does nothing better occur to you than that?' 'Don't be so impatient,' said Snow-white, 'I'll see you get help;' and taking her scissors out of her pocket she cut the end off his beard. As soon as the dwarf felt himself free he seized a bag full of gold which was hidden among the roots of the tree, lifted it up, and muttered aloud: 'Curse these rude wretches, cutting off a piece of my splendid beard!' With these words he swung the bag over his back, and disappeared without as much as looking at the children again.

Shortly after this Snow-white and Rose-red went out to get a dish of fish. As they approached the stream they saw something which looked like an enormous grasshopper, springing towards the water as if it were going to jump in. They ran forward and recognised their old friend the dwarf. 'Where are you going to?' asked Rose-red; 'you're surely not going to jump into the water?' 'I'm not such a fool,' screamed the dwarf. 'Don't you see that cursed fish is trying to drag me in?' The little man had been sitting on the bank fishing, when unfortunately the wind had entangled his beard in the line; and when immediately afterwards a big fish bit, the feeble little creature had no strength to pull it out; the fish had the upper fin, and dragged the dwarf towards him. He clung on with all his might to every rush and blade of grass, but it didn't help him much; he had to follow every movement of the fish, and was in great danger of being drawn into the water. The girls came up just at the right moment, held him firm, and did all they could to disentangle his beard from the line; but in vain, beard and line were in a hopeless muddle. Nothing remained but to produce the scissors and cut the beard, by which a small part of it was sacrificed.

When the dwarf perceived what they were about he yelled to them: 'Do you call that manners, you toadstools! to disfigure a fellow's face? it wasn't enough that you shortened my beard before, but you must now needs cut off the best bit of it. I can't appear like this before my own people. I wish you'd been at Jericho first.' Then he fetched a sack of pearls that lay among the rushes, and without saying another word he dragged it away and disappeared behind a stone.

It happened that soon after this the mother sent the two girls to the town to buy needles, thread, laces, and ribbons. Their road led over a heath where huge boulders of rock lay scattered here and there. While trudging along they saw a big bird hovering in the air, circling slowly above them, but always descending lower, till at last it settled on a rock not far from them. Immediately afterwards they heard a sharp, piercing cry. They ran forward, and saw with horror that the eagle had pounced on their old friend the dwarf, and was about to carry him off. The tender-hearted children seized a hold of the little man, and struggled so long with the bird that at last he let go his prey. When the dwarf had recovered from the first shock he screamed in his screeching voice : ' Couldn't you have treated me more carefully ? you have torn my thin little coat all to shreds, useless, awkward hussies that you are ! ' Then he took a bag of precious stones and vanished under the rocks into his cave. The girls were accustomed to his ingratitude, and went on their way and did their business in town. On their way home, as they were again passing the heath, they surprised the dwarf pouring out his precious stones on an open space, for he had thought no one would pass by at so late an hour. The evening sun shone on the glittering stones, and they glanced and gleamed so beautifully that the children stood still and gazed on them. ' What are you standing there gaping for ? ' screamed the dwarf, and his ashen-grey face became scarlet with rage. He was about to go off with these angry words when a sudden growl was heard, and a black bear trotted out of the wood. The dwarf jumped up in a great fright, but he hadn't time to reach his place of retreat, for the bear was already close to him. Then he cried in terror : ' Dear Mr. Bear, spare me ! I'll give you all my treasure. Look at those beautiful precious stones lying there. Spare my life ! what pleasure would you get from a poor feeble little fellow like me ? You won't feel me between your teeth. There, lay hold of these two wicked girls, they will be a tender morsel for you, as fat as young quails ; eat them up, for heaven's sake.' But the bear, paying no attention to his words, gave the evil little creature one blow with his paw, and he never moved again.

The girls had run away, but the bear called after them : ' Snow-

white and Rose-red, don't be afraid; wait, and I'll come with you.'
Then they recognised his voice and stood still, and when the bear
was quite close to them his skin suddenly fell off, and a beautiful
man stood beside them, all dressed in gold. 'I am a king's son,' he
said, 'and have been doomed by that unholy little dwarf, who had
stolen my treasure, to roam about the woods as a wild bear till his

death should set me free. Now he has got his well-merited punishment.'

Snow-white married him, and Rose-red his brother, and they
divided the great treasure the dwarf had collected in nis cave between them. The old mother lived for many years peacefully with
her children ; and she carried the two rose trees with her, and they
stood in front of her window, and every year they bore the finest
red and white roses.[1]

[1] Grimm.

THE GOOSE-GIRL

ONCE upon a time an old queen, whose husband had been dead for many years, had a beautiful daughter. When she grew up she was betrothed to a prince who lived a great way off. Now, when the time drew near for her to be married and to depart into a foreign kingdom, her old mother gave her much costly baggage, and many ornaments, gold and silver, trinkets and knicknacks, and, in fact, everything that belonged to a royal trousseau, for she loved her daughter very dearly. She gave her a waiting-maid also, who was to ride with her and hand her over to the bridegroom, and she provided each of them with a horse for the journey. Now the Princess's horse was called Falada, and could speak.

When the hour for departure drew near the old mother went to her bedroom, and taking a small knife she cut her fingers till they bled; then she held a white rag under them, and letting three drops of blood fall into it, she gave it to her daughter, and said : ' Dear child, take great care of this rag : it may be of use to you on the journey.'

So they took a sad farewell of each other, and the Princess stuck the rag in front of her dress, mounted her horse, and set forth on the journey to her bridegroom's kingdom. After they had ridden for about an hour the Princess began to feel very thirsty, and said to her waiting-maid : ' Pray get down and fetch me some water in my golden cup out of yonder stream : I would like a drink.' ' If you're thirsty,' said the maid, ' dismount yourself, and lie down by the water and drink; I don't mean to be your servant any longer.' The Princess was so thirsty that she got down, bent over the stream, and drank, for she wasn't allowed to drink out of the golden goblet. As she drank she murmured : ' Oh ! heaven, what am I to do ? ' and the three drops of blood replied :

> ' If your mother only knew,
> Her heart would surely break in two.'

But the Princess was meek, and said nothing about her maid's rude behaviour, and quietly mounted her horse again. They rode on their way for several miles, but the day was hot, and the sun's

rays smote fiercely on them, so that the Princess was soon overcome by thirst again. And as they passed a brook she called once more to her waiting-maid : ' Pray get down and give me a drink from my golden cup,' for she had long ago forgotten her maid's rude words.

But the waiting-maid replied, more haughtily even than before:
'If you want a drink, you can dismount and get it; I don't mean
to be your servant.' Then the Princess was compelled by her
thirst to get down, and bending over the flowing water she cried
and said: 'Oh! heaven, what am I to do?' and the three drops of
blood replied:

> 'If your mother only knew,
> Her heart would surely break in two.'

And as she drank thus, and leant right over the water, the rag containing the three drops of blood fell from her bosom and floated
down the stream, and she in her anxiety never even noticed her
loss. But the waiting-maid had observed it with delight, as she
knew it gave her power over the bride, for in losing the drops of
blood the Princess had become weak and powerless. When she
wished to get on her horse Falada again, the waiting-maid called
out: 'I mean to ride Falada: you must mount my beast;' and this
too she had to submit to. Then the waiting-maid commanded her
harshly to take off her royal robes, and to put on her common ones,
and finally she made her swear by heaven not to say a word about
the matter when they reached the palace; and if she hadn't taken
this oath she would have been killed on the spot. But Falada
observed everything, and laid it all to heart.

The waiting-maid now mounted Falada, and the real bride the
worse horse, and so they continued their journey till at length
they arrived at the palace yard. There was great rejoicing over the
arrival, and the Prince sprang forward to meet them, and taking
the waiting-maid for his bride, he lifted her down from her horse
and led her upstairs to the royal chamber. In the meantime the
real Princess was left standing below in the courtyard. The old
King, who was looking out of his window, beheld her in this plight,
and it struck him how sweet and gentle, even beautiful, she
looked. He went at once to the royal chamber, and asked the
bride who it was she had brought with her and had left thus standing in the court below. 'Oh!' replied the bride, 'I brought her with
me to keep me company on the journey; give the girl something
to do, that she mayn't be idle.' But the old King had no work for
her, and couldn't think of anything; so he said, 'I've a small boy
who looks after the geese, she'd better help him.' The youth's name
was Curdken, and the real bride was made to assist him in herding
geese.

Soon after this the false bride said to the Prince: 'Dearest hus-band, I pray you grant me a favour.' He answered: 'That I will.'
' Then let the slaughterer cut off the head of the horse I rode here upon, because it behaved very badly on the journey.' But the truth was she was afraid lest the horse should speak and tell how she had treated the Princess. She carried her point, and the faithful Falada was doomed to die. When the news came to the ears of the real Princess she went to the slaughterer, and secretly promised him a piece of gold if he would do something for her. There was in the town a large dark gate, through which she had to pass night and morning with the geese; would he ' kindly hang up Falada's head there, that she might see it once again ? ' The slaughterer said he would do as she desired, chopped off the head, and nailed it firmly over the gateway.

Early next morning, as she and Curdken were driving their flock through the gate, she said as she passed under:

> ' Oh ! Falada, 'tis you hang there ; '

and the head replied :

> ' 'Tis you ; pass under, Princess fair :
> If your mother only knew,
> Her heart would surely break in two.'

Then she left the tower and drove the geese into a field. And when they had reached the common where the geese fed she sat down and unloosed her hair, which was of pure gold. Curdken loved to see it glitter in the sun, and wanted much to pull some hair out. Then she spoke :

> ' Wind, wind, gently sway,
> Blow Curdken's hat away ;
> Let him chase o'er field and wold
> Till my locks of ruddy gold,
> Now astray and hanging down,
> Be combed and plaited in a crown.'

Then a gust of wind blew Curdken's hat away, and he had to chase it over hill and dale. When he returned from the pursuit she had finished her combing and curling, and his chance of getting any hair was gone. Curdken was very angry, and wouldn't speak to her. So they herded the geese till evening and then went home.

The next morning, as they passed under the gate, the girl said :

> ' Oh ! Falada, 'tis you hang there ; '

and the head replied:

> ' 'Tis you; pass under, Princess fair
> If your mother only knew,
> Her heart would surely break in two.

H. J. Ford

Then she went on her way till she came to the common, where she
sat down and began to comb out her hair ; then Curdken ran up to
her and wanted to grasp some of the hair from her head, but she
called out hastily :

> ' Wind, wind, gently sway,
> Blow Curdken's hat away ;
> Let him chase o'er field and wold
> Till my locks of ruddy gold,
> Now astray and hanging down,
> Be combed and plaited in a crown.'

Then a puff of wind came and blew Curdken's hat far away, so
that he had to run after it ; and when he returned she had long
finished putting up her golden locks, and he couldn't get any hair ;
so they watched the geese till it was dark.

But that evening when they got home Curdken went to the old
King, and said : ' I refuse to herd geese any longer with that girl.'
' For what reason ? ' asked the old King. ' Because she does nothing
but annoy me all day long,' replied Curdken ; and he proceeded to
relate all her iniquities, and said : ' Every morning as we drive the
flock through the dark gate she says to a horse's head that hangs
on the wall :

> ' " Oh ! Falada, 'tis you hang there ; "

and the head replies :

> ' " 'Tis you ; pass under, Princess fair :
> If your mother only knew,
> Her heart would surely break in two." '

And Curdken went on to tell what passed on the common where
the geese fed, and how he had always to chase his hat.

The old King bade him go and drive forth his flock as usual
next day ; and when morning came he himself took up his position
behind the dark gate, and heard how the goose-girl greeted Falada.
Then he followed her through the field, and hid himself behind a
bush on the common. He soon saw with his own eyes how the
goose-boy and the goose-girl looked after the geese, and how after a
time the maiden sat down and loosed her hair, that glittered like
gold, and repeated :

> ' Wind, wind, gently sway,
> Blow Curdken's hat away ;
> Let him chase o'er field and wold
> Till my locks of ruddy gold,

        Now astray and hanging down,
        Be combed and plaited in a crown.'

Then a gust of wind came and blew Curdken's hat away, so that he
had to fly over hill and dale after it, and the girl in the meantime
quietly combed and plaited her hair : all this the old King observed,
and returned to the palace without any one having noticed him. In
the evening when the goose-girl came home he called her aside,
and asked her why she behaved as she did. 'I mayn't tell you
why; how dare I confide my woes to anyone? for I swore not to by
heaven, otherwise I should have lost my life.'   The old King begged

her to tell him all, and left her no peace, but he could get nothing
out of her. At last he said : ' Well, if you won't tell me, confide your
trouble to the iron stove there ; ' and he went away. Then she crept
to the stove, and began to sob and cry and to pour out her poor
little heart, and said : ' Here I sit, deserted by all the world, I who
am a king's daughter, and a false waiting-maid has forced me to
take off my own clothes, and has taken my place with my bridegroom, while I have to fulfil the lowly office of goose-girl.

      ' If my mother only knew,
       Her heart would surely break in two.'

But the old King stood outside at the stove chimney, and listened to her words. Then he entered the room again, and bidding her leave the stove, he ordered royal apparel to be put on her, in which she looked amazingly lovely. Then he summoned his son, and revealed to him that he had got the false bride, who was nothing but a waiting-maid, while the real one, in the guise of the ex-goose-girl, was standing at his side. The young King rejoiced from his heart when he saw her beauty and learnt how good she was, and a great banquet was prepared, to which everyone was bidden. The bridegroom sat at the head of the table, the Princess on one side of him and the waiting-maid on the other; but she was so dazzled that she did not recognise the Princess in her glittering garments. Now when they had eaten and drunk, and were merry, the old King asked the waiting-maid to solve a knotty point for him. 'What,' said he, 'should be done to a certain person who has deceived everyone?' and he proceeded to relate the whole story, ending up with, 'Now what sentence should be passed?' Then the false bride answered: 'She deserves to be put stark naked into a barrel lined with sharp nails, which should be dragged by two white horses up and down the street till she is dead.'

'You are the person,' said the King, 'and you have passed sentence on yourself; and even so it shall be done to you.' And when the sentence had been carried out the young King was married to his real bride, and both reigned over the kingdom in peace and happiness.[1]

[1] Grimm.

TOADS AND DIAMONDS

THERE was once upon a time a widow who had two daughters. The eldest was so much like her in the face and humour that whoever looked upon the daughter saw the mother. They were both so disagreeable and so proud that there was no living with them.

The youngest, who was the very picture of her father for courtesy and sweetness of temper, was withal one of the most beautiful girls ever seen. As people naturally love their own likeness, this mother even doted on her eldest daughter, and at the same time had a horrible aversion for the youngest—she made her eat in the kitchen and work continually.

Among other things, this poor child was forced twice a day to draw water above a mile and a-half off the house, and bring home a pitcher full of it. One day, as she was at this fountain, there came to her a poor woman, who begged of her to let her drink.

'Oh! ay, with all my neart, Goody, said this pretty little girl; and rinsing immediately the pitcher, she took up some water from the clearest place of the fountain, and gave it to her, holding up the pitcher all the while, that she might drink the easier.

The good woman having drunk, said to her:

'You are so very pretty, my dear, so good and so mannerly, that I cannot help giving you a gift.' For this was a fairy, who had taken the form of a poor country-woman, to see how far the civility and good manners of this pretty girl would go. 'I will give you for gift,' continued the Fairy, 'that, at every word you speak, there shall come out of your mouth either a flower or a jewel.'

When this pretty girl came home her mother scolded at her for staying so long at the fountain.

'I beg your pardon, mamma,' said the poor girl, 'for not making more haste.'

And in speaking these words there came out of her mouth two roses, two pearls, and two diamonds.

'What is it I see there?' said her mother, quite astonished. 'I think I see pearls and diamonds come out of the girl's mouth! How happens this, child?'

This was the first time she ever called her child.

The poor creature told her frankly all the matter, not without dropping out infinite numbers of diamonds.

'In good faith,' cried the mother, 'I must send my child thither. Come hither, Fanny; look what comes out of thy sister's mouth

when she speaks. Wouldst not thou be glad, my dear, to have the same gift given to thee? Thou hast nothing else to do but go and draw water out of the fountain, and when a certain poor woman asks you to let her drink, to give it her very civilly.'

'It would be a very fine sight indeed,' said this ill-bred minx, 'to see me go draw water.'

'You shall go, hussey!' said the mother; 'and this minute.'

So away she went, but grumbling all the way, taking with her the best silver tankard in the house.

She was no sooner at the fountain than she saw coming out of the wood a lady most gloriously dressed, who came up to her, and asked to drink. This was, you must know, the very fairy who appeared to her sister, but had now taken the air and dress of a princess, to see how far this girl's rudeness would go.

'Am I come hither,' said the proud, saucy slut, 'to serve you with water, pray? I suppose the silver tankard was brought

purely for your ladyship, was it? However, you may drink out of it, if you have a fancy.'

'You are not over and above mannerly,' answered the Fairy, without putting herself in a passion. 'Well, then, since you have so little breeding, and are so disobliging, I give you for gift that at every word you speak there shall come out of your mouth a snake or a toad.'

So soon as her mother saw her coming she cried out:

'Well, daughter?'

'Well, mother?' answered the pert hussey, throwing out of her mouth two vipers and two toads.

'Oh! mercy,' cried the mother; 'what is it I see? Oh! it is that wretch her sister who has occasioned all this; but she shall pay for it'; and immediately she ran to beat her. The poor child fled away from her, and went to hide herself in the forest, not far from thence.

The King's son, then on his return from hunting, met her, and seeing her so very pretty, asked her what she did there alone and why she cried.

'Alas! sir, my mamma has turned me out of doors.'

The King's son, who saw five or six pearls and as many diamonds come out of her mouth, desired her to tell him how that happened. She hereupon told him the whole story; and so the King's son fell in love with her, and, considering with himself that such a gift was worth more than any marriage portion, conducted her to the palace of the King his father, and there married her.

As for her sister, she made herself so much hated that her own mother turned her off; and the miserable wretch, having wandered about a good while without finding anybody to take her in, went to a corner of the wood, and there died.[1]

[1] Charles Perrault.

PRINCE DARLING

ONCE upon a time there lived a king who was so just and kind that his subjects called him 'the Good King.' It happened one day, when he was out hunting, that a little white rabbit, which his dogs were chasing, sprang into his arms for shelter. The King stroked it gently, and said to it:

'Well, bunny, as you have come to me for protection I will see that nobody hurts you.'

And he took it home to his palace and had it put in a pretty little house, with all sorts of nice things to eat.

That night, when he was alone in his room, a beautiful lady suddenly appeared before him; her long dress was as white as snow, and she had a crown of white roses upon her head. The good King was very much surprised to see her, for he knew his door had been tightly shut, and he could not think how she had got in. But she said to him:

'I am the Fairy Truth. I was passing through the wood when you were out hunting, and I wished to find out if you were really good, as everybody said you were, so I took the shape of a little rabbit and came to your arms for shelter, for I know that those who are merciful to animals will be still kinder to their fellow-men. If you had refused to help me I should have been certain that you were wicked. I thank you for the kindness you have shown me, which has made me your friend for ever. You have only to ask me for anything you want and I promise that I will give it to you.'

'Madam,' said the good King, 'since you are a fairy, you no doubt know all my wishes. I have but one son, whom I love very dearly, that is why he is called Prince Darling. If you are really good enough to wish to do me a favour, I beg that you will become his friend.'

'With all my heart,' answered the Fairy. 'I can make your

son the handsomest prince in the world, or the richest, or the
most powerful; choose whichever you like for him.'

'I do not ask either of these things for my son,' replied the
good King; 'but if you will make him the best of princes, I shall
indeed be grateful to you. What good would it do him to be rich,
or handsome, or to possess all the kingdoms of the world if he were
wicked? You know well he would still be unhappy. Only a good
man can be really contented.'

'You are quite right,' answered the Fairy; 'but it is not in my
power to make Prince Darling a good man unless he will help me;
he must himself try hard to become good; I can only promise to
give him good advice, to scold him for his faults, and to punish
him if he will not correct
and punish himself.'

The good King was
quite satisfied with this
promise; and very soon
afterwards he died.

Prince Darling was
very sorry, for he loved
his father with all his
heart, and he would will-
ingly have given all his
kingdoms and all his treasures of gold and silver if
they could have kept the
good King with him. Two
days afterwards, when
the Prince had gone to
bed, the Fairy suddenly
appeared to him and said:

'I promised your
father that I would be
your friend, and to keep
my word I have come to
bring you a present.' At the same time she put a little gold ring
upon his finger.

'Take great care of this ring,' she said: 'it is more precious than
diamonds; every time you do a bad deed it will prick your finger,
but if, in spite of its pricking, you go on in your own evil way, you
will lose my friendship, and I shall become your enemy.'

So saying, the Fairy disappeared, leaving Prince Darling very much astonished.

For some time he behaved so well that the ring never pricked him, and that made him so contented that his subjects called him Prince Darling the Happy.

One day, however, he went out hunting, but could get no sport, which put him in a very bad temper; it seemed to him as he rode along that his ring was pressing into his finger, but as it did not prick him he did not heed it. When he got home and went to his own room, his little dog Bibi ran to meet him, jumping round him with pleasure. 'Get away!' said the Prince, quite gruffly. 'I don't want you, you are in the way.'

The poor little dog, who didn't understand this at all, pulled at his coat to make him at least look at her, and this made Prince Darling so cross that he gave her quite a hard kick.

Instantly his ring pricked him sharply, as if it had been a pin. He was very much surprised, and sat down in a corner of his room feeling quite ashamed of himself.

'I believe the Fairy is laughing at me,' he thought. 'Surely I can have done no great wrong in just kicking a tiresome animal! What is the good of my being ruler of a great kingdom if I am not even allowed to beat my own dog?'

'I am not making fun of you,' said a voice, answering Prince Darling's thoughts. 'You have committed three faults. First of all, you were out of temper because you could not have what you wanted, and you thought all men and animals were only made to do your pleasure; then you were really angry, which is very naughty indeed; and lastly, you were cruel to a poor little animal who did not in the least deserve to be ill-treated.

'I know you are far above a little dog, but if it were right and allowable that great people should ill-treat all who are beneath them, I might at this moment beat you, or kill you, for a fairy is greater than a man. The advantage of possessing a great empire is not to be able to do the evil that one desires, but to do all the good that one possibly can.'

The Prince saw how naughty he had been, and promised to try and do better in future, but he did not keep his word. The fact was that he had been brought up by a foolish nurse, who had spoilt him when he was little. If he wanted anything he only had to cry and fret and stamp his feet and she would give him whatever he asked for, which had made him self-willed; also she had told him from morning to night that he would one day be a king, and that kings were very happy, because everyone was bound to obey and respect them, and no one could prevent them from doing just as they liked.

When the Prince grew old enough to understand, he soon learnt that there could be nothing worse than to be proud, obstinate, and conceited, and he had really tried to cure himself of these defects, but by that time his faults had become habits; and a bad habit is very hard to get rid of. Not that he was naturally of a bad disposition; he was truly sorry when he had been naughty, and said:

'I am very unhappy to have to struggle against my anger and pride every day; if I had been punished for them when I was little they would not be such a trouble to me now.'

His ring pricked him very often, and sometimes he left off what he was doing at once; but at other times he would not attend to it. Strangely enough, it gave him only a slight prick for a trifling fault, but when he was really naughty it made his finger actually bleed. At last he got tired of being constantly reminded, and wanted to be able to do as he liked, so he threw his ring aside, and thought himself the happiest of men to have got rid of its teasing pricks. He gave himself up to doing every foolish thing that occurred to him, until he became quite wicked and nobody could like him any longer.

One day, when the Prince was walking about, he saw a young girl, who was so very pretty that he made up his mind at once that he would marry her. Her name was Celia, and she was as good as she was beautiful.

Prince Darling fancied that Celia would think herself only too happy if he offered to make her a great queen, but she said fearlessly:

'Sire, I am only a shepherdess, and a poor girl, but, nevertheless, I will not marry you.'

'Do you dislike me?' asked the Prince, who was very much vexed at this answer.

'No, my Prince,' replied Celia; 'I cannot help thinking you very handsome; but what good would riches be to me, and all the grand dresses and splendid carriages that you would give me, if the bad deeds which I should see you do every day made me hate and despise you?'

The Prince was very angry at this speech, and commanded his

officers to make Celia a prisoner and carry her off to his palace. All day long the remembrance of what she had said annoyed him, but as he loved her he could not make up his mind to have her punished.

One of the Prince's favourite companions was his foster-brother, whom he trusted entirely; but he was not at all a good man, and gave Prince Darling very bad advice, and encouraged him in all his evil ways. When he saw the Prince so downcast he asked what was the matter, and when he explained that he could not bear Celia's bad opinion of him, and was resolved to be a better man in order to please her, this evil adviser said to him:

'You are very kind to trouble yourself about this little girl; if I were you I would soon make her obey me. Remember that you are a king, and that it would be laughable to see you trying to please a shepherdess, who ought to be only too glad to be one of your slaves. Keep her in prison, and feed her on bread and water for a little while, and then, if she still says she will not marry you, have her head cut off, to teach other people that you mean to be obeyed. Why, if you cannot make a girl like that do as you wish, your subjects will soon forget that they are only put into the world for our pleasure.'

'But,' said Prince Darling, 'would it not be a shame if I had an innocent girl put to death? For Celia really has done nothing to deserve punishment.'

'If people will not do as you tell them they ought to suffer for it,' answered his foster-brother; 'but even if it were unjust, you had better be accused of that by your subjects than that they should find out that they may insult and thwart you as often as they please.'

In saying this he was touching a weak point in his brother's character; for the Prince's fear of losing any of his power made him at once abandon his first idea of trying to be good, and resolve to try and frighten the shepherdess into consenting to marry him.

His foster-brother, who wanted him to keep this resolution, invited three young courtiers, as wicked as himself, to sup with the Prince, and they persuaded him to drink a great deal of wine, and continued to excite his anger against Celia by telling him that she had laughed at his love for her; until at last, in quite a furious rage, he rushed off to find her, declaring that if she still refused to marry him she should be sold as a slave the very next day.

But when he reached the room in which Celia had been locked

up, he was greatly surprised to find that she was not in it, though he had had the key in his own pocket all the time. His anger was terrible, and he vowed vengeance against whoever had helped her to escape. His bad friends, when they heard him, resolved to turn his wrath upon an old nobleman who had formerly been his tutor; and who still dared sometimes to tell the Prince of his faults, for he loved him as if he had been his own son. At first Prince Darling had thanked him, but after a time he grew impatient and thought it must be just mere love of fault-finding that made his old tutor blame him when everyone else was praising and flattering him. So he ordered him to retire from his Court, though he still, from time to time, spoke of him as a worthy man whom he respected, even if he no longer loved him. His unworthy friends feared that he might some day take it into his head to recall his old tutor, so they thought they now had a good opportunity of getting him banished for ever.

They reported to the Prince that Suliman, for that was the tutor's name, had boasted of having helped Celia to escape, and they bribed three men to say that Suliman himself had told them about it. The Prince, in great anger, sent his foster-brother with a number of soldiers to bring his tutor before him, in chains, like a criminal. After giving this order he went to his own room, but he had scarcely got into it when there was a clap of thunder which made the ground shake, and the Fairy Truth appeared suddenly before him.

'I promised your father,' said she sternly, 'to give you good advice, and to punish you if you refused to follow it. You have despised my counsel, and have gone your own evil way until you are only outwardly a man; really you are a monster—the horror of everyone who knows you. It is time that I should fulfil my promise, and begin your punishment. I condemn you to resemble the animals whose ways you have imitated. You have made yourself like the lion by your anger, and like the wolf by your greediness. Like a snake, you have ungratefully turned upon one who was a second father to you; your churlishness has made you like a bull. Therefore, in your new form, take the appearance of all these animals.'

The Fairy had scarcely finished speaking when Prince Darling saw to his horror that her words were fulfilled. He had a lion's head, a bull's horns, a wolf's feet, and a snake's body. At the same instant he found himself in a great forest, beside a clear lake, in which he could see plainly the horrible creature he had become, and a voice said to him :

'Look carefully at the state to which your wickedness has brought you ; believe me, your soul is a thousand times more hideous than your body.'

Prince Darling recognised the voice of the Fairy Truth, and turned in a fury to catch her and eat her up if he possibly could ; but he saw no one, and the same voice went on :

'I laugh at your powerlessness and anger, and I intend to punish your pride by letting you fall into the hands of your own subjects.'

The Prince began to think that the best thing he could do would be to get as far away from the lake as he could, then at least he would not be continually reminded of his terrible ugliness. So he ran towards the wood, but before he had gone many yards he fell into a deep pit which had been made to trap bears, and the hunters, who were hiding in a tree, leapt down, and secured him with several chains, and led him into the chief city of his own kingdom.

On the way, instead of recognising that his own faults had brought this punishment upon him, he accused the Fairy of being the cause of all his misfortunes, and bit and tore at his chains furiously.

As they approached the town he saw that some great rejoicing was being held, and when the hunters asked what had happened they were told that the Prince, whose only pleasure it was to torment his people, had been found in his room, killed by a thunder-bolt (for that was what was supposed to have become of him). Four of his courtiers, those who had encouraged him in his wicked doings, had tried to seize the kingdom and divide it between them, but the people, who knew it was their bad counsels which had so changed the Prince, had cut off their heads, and had offered the crown to Suliman, whom the Prince had left in prison. This noble lord had just been crowned, and the deliverance of the kingdom was the cause of the rejoicing. 'For,' they said, 'he is a good and just man, and we shall once more enjoy peace and prosperity.'

Prince Darling roared with anger when he heard this ; but it was still worse for him when he reached the great square before his own palace. He saw Suliman seated upon a magnificent throne, and all the people crowded round, wishing him a long life that he might undo all the mischief done by his predecessor.

Presently Suliman made a sign with his hand that the people should be silent, and said : 'I have accepted the crown you have offered me, but only that I may keep it for Prince Darling, who is not dead as you suppose; the Fairy has assured me that there is still hope that you may some day see him again, good and virtuous as he was when he first came to the throne. Alas!' he continued, 'he was led away by flatterers. I knew his heart, and am certain that if it had not been for the bad influence of those who surrounded him he would have been a good king and a father to his people. We may hate his faults, but let us pity him and hope for his restoration. As for me, I would die gladly if that could bring back our Prince to reign justly and worthily once more.'

These words went to Prince Darling's heart; he realised the true affection and faithfulness of his old tutor, and for the first time reproached himself for all his evil deeds; at the same instant he felt all his anger melting away, and he began quietly to think over his past life, and to admit that his punishment was not more than he had deserved. He lett off tearing at the iron bars of the cage in which he was shut up, and became as gentle as a lamb.

The hunters who had caught him took him to a great menagerie, where he was chained up among all the other wild beasts, and he determined to show his sorrow for his past bad behaviour by being gentle and obedient to the man who had to take care of him. Unfortunately, this man was very rough and unkind, and though the poor monster was quite quiet, he often beat him without rhyme or reason when he happened to be in a bad temper. One day when this keeper was asleep a tiger broke its chain, and flew at him to eat him up. Prince Darling, who saw what was going on, at first felt quite pleased to think that he should be delivered from his persecutor, but soon he thought better of it and wished that he were free.

'I would return good for evil,' he said to himself, 'and save the unhappy man's life.' He had hardly wished this when his iron cage flew open, and he rushed to the side of the keeper, who was awake and was defending himself against the tiger. When he saw the monster had got out he gave himself up for lost, but his fear was soon changed into joy, for the kind monster threw itself upon the tiger and very soon killed it, and then came and crouched at the feet of the man it had saved.

Overcome with gratitude the keeper stooped to caress the strange creature which had done him such a great service; but suddenly a voice said in his ear:

'A good action should never go unrewarded,' and at the same

instant the monster disappeared, and he saw at his feet only a pretty little dog!

Prince Darling, delighted by the change, frisked about the keeper, showing his joy in every way he could, and the man, taking him up in his arms, carried him to the King, to whom he told the whole story.

The Queen said she would like to have this wonderful little dog, and the Prince would have been very happy in his new home if he could have forgotten that he was a man and a king. The Queen petted and took care of him, but she was so afraid that he would get too fat that she consulted the court-physician, who said that he was to be fed only upon bread, and was not to have much even of that. So poor Prince Darling was terribly hungry all day long, but he was very patient about it.

One day, when they gave him his little loaf for breakfast, he thought he would like to eat it out in the garden; so he took it up in his mouth and trotted away towards a brook that he knew of a long way from the palace. But he was surprised to find that the brook was gone, and where it had been stood a great house that seemed to be built of gold and precious stones. Numbers of people splendidly dressed were going into it, and sounds of music and dancing and feasting could be heard from the windows.

But what seemed very strange was that those people who came out of the house were pale and thin, and their clothes were torn, and hanging in rags about them. Some fell down dead as they came out, before they had time to get away—others crawled farther with great difficulty, while others again lay on the ground, fainting with hunger, and begged a morsel of bread from those who were going into the house, but they would not so much as look at the poor creatures.

Prince Darling went up to a young girl who was trying to eat a few blades of grass—she was so hungry. Touched with compassion, he said to himself:

' I am very hungry, but I shall not die of starvation before I get my dinner; if I give my breakfast to this poor creature perhaps I may save her life.'

So he laid his piece of bread in the girl's hand, and saw her eat it up eagerly.

She soon seemed to be quite well again, and the Prince, delighted to have been able to help her, was thinking of going home to the palace, when he heard a great outcry, and turning round saw

Celia, who was being carried against her will into the great house.

For the first time the Prince regretted that he was no longer the monster, then he would have been able to rescue Celia—now he could only bark feebly at the people who were carrying her off, and try to follow them, but they chased and kicked him away.

He determined not to quit the place till he knew what had become of Celia, and blamed himself for what had befallen her.

'Alas!' he said to himself, 'I am furious with the people who are carrying Celia off, but isn't that exactly what I did myself, and if I had not been prevented did I not intend to be still more cruel to her?'

Here he was interrupted by a noise above his head—someone was opening a window, and he saw with delight that it was Celia herself, who came forward and threw out a plate of most delicious-looking food, then the window was shut again, and Prince Darling, who had not had anything to eat all day, thought he might as well

take the opportunity of getting something. He ran forward to
begin, but the young girl to whom he had given his bread gave a
cry of terror and took him up in her arms, saying:

'Don't touch it, my poor little dog—that house is the palace of
pleasure, and everything that comes out of it is poisoned!'

At the same moment a voice said:

'You see a good action always brings its reward,' and the

Prince found himself changed into a beautiful white dove. He
remembered that white was the favourite colour of the Fairy Truth,
and began to hope that he might at last win back her favour. But
just now his first care was for Celia, and rising into the air he flew
round and round the house, until he saw an open window; but he
searched through every room in vain. No trace of Celia was to be
seen, and the Prince, in despair, determined to search through the
world till he found her. He flew on and on for several days, till

he came to a great desert, where he saw a cavern—and to his delight there sat Celia, sharing the simple breakfast of an old hermit.

Over-joyed to have found her, Prince Darling perched upon her shoulder, trying to express by his caresses how glad he was to see her again, and Celia, surprised and delighted by the tameness of this pretty white dove, stroked it softly, and said, though she never thought of its understanding her :

' I accept the gift that you make me of yourself—and I will love you always.'

' Take care what you are saying, Celia,' said the old hermit ; ' are you prepared to keep that promise ? '

' Indeed I hope so, my sweet shepherdess,' cried the Prince, who was at that moment restored to his natural shape. ' You promised to love me always ; tell me that you really mean what you said, or I shall have to ask the Fairy to give me back the form of the dove which pleased you so much.'

' You need not be afraid that she will change her mind,' said the Fairy, throwing off the hermit's robe in which she had been disguised, and appearing before them.

' Celia has loved you ever since she first saw you, only she would not tell you while you were so obstinate and naughty. Now you have repented and mean to be good you deserve to be happy, and so she may love you as much as she likes.'

Celia and Prince Darling threw themselves at the Fairy's feet, and the Prince was never tired of thanking her for her kindness. Celia was delighted to hear how sorry he was for all his past follies and misdeeds, and promised to love him as long as she lived.

' Rise, my children,' said the Fairy, ' and I will transport you to the palace, and Prince Darling shall have back again the crown he forfeited by his bad behaviour.'

While she was speaking they found themselves in Suliman's hall, and his delight was great at seeing his dear master once more. He gave up the throne joyfully to the Prince, and remained always the most faithful of his subjects.

Celia and Prince Darling reigned for many years, but he was so determined to govern worthily and to do his duty that his ring, which he took to wearing again, never once pricked him severely.[1]

[1] *Cabinet des Fées.*

BLUE BEARD

THERE was a man who had fine houses, both in town and country, a deal of silver and gold plate, embroidered furniture, and coaches gilded all over with gold. But this man was so unlucky as to have a blue beard, which made him so frightfully ugly that all the women and girls ran away from him.

One of his neighbours, a lady of quality, had two daughters who were perfect beauties. He desired of her one of them in marriage, leaving to her choice which of the two she would bestow on him. They would neither of them have him, and sent him backwards and forwards from one another, not being able to bear the thoughts of marrying a man who had a blue beard, and what besides gave them disgust and aversion was his having already been married to several wives, and nobody ever knew what became of them.

Blue Beard, to engage their affection, took them, with the lady their mother and three or four ladies of their acquaintance, with other young people of the neighbourhood, to one of his country seats, where they stayed a whole week.

There was nothing then to be seen but parties of pleasure, hunting, fishing, dancing, mirth, and feasting. Nobody went to bed, but all passed the night in rallying and joking with each other. In short, every thing succeeded so well that the youngest daughter began to think the master of the house not to have a beard so very blue, and that he was a mighty civil gentleman.

As soon as they returned home, the marriage was concluded. About a month afterwards, Blue Beard told his wife that he was obliged to take a country journey for six weeks at least, about affairs of very great consequence, desiring her to divert herself in his absence, to send for her friends and acquaintances, to carry them into the country, if she pleased, and to make good cheer wherever she was.

'Here,' said he, 'are the keys of the two great wardrobes,

wherein I have my best furniture ; these are of my silver and gold plate, which is not every day in use ; these open my strong boxes, which hold my money, both gold and silver ; these my caskets of jewels ; and this is the master-key to all my apartments. But for this little one here, it is the key of the closet at the end of the great gallery on the ground floor. Open them all ; go into all and every one of them, except that little closet, which I forbid you, and forbid it in such a manner that, if you happen to open it, there's nothing but what you may expect from my just anger and resentment.'

She promised to observe, very exactly, whatever he had ordered ; when he, after having embraced her, got into his coach and proceeded on his journey.

Her neighbours and good friends did not stay to be sent for by the new married lady, so great was their impatience to see all the rich furniture of her house, not daring to come while her husband was there, because of his blue beard, which frightened them. They ran through all the rooms, closets, and wardrobes, which were all so fine and rich that they seemed to surpass one another.

After that they went up into the two great rooms, where were the best and richest furniture ; they could not sufficiently admire the number and beauty of the tapestry, beds, couches, cabinets, stands, tables, and looking-glasses, in which you might see yourself from head to foot ; some of them were framed with glass, others with silver, plain and gilded, the finest and most magnificent ever were seen.

They ceased not to extol and envy the happiness of their friend, who in the meantime in no way diverted herself in looking upon all these rich things, because of the impatience she had to go and open the closet on the ground floor. She was so much pressed by her curiosity that, without considering that it was very uncivil to leave her company, she went down a little back staircase, and with such excessive haste that she had twice or thrice like to have broken her neck.

Being come to the closet-door, she made a stop for some time, thinking upon her husband's orders, and considering what unhappiness might attend her if she was disobedient ; but the temptation was so strong she could not overcome it. She then took the little key, and opened it, trembling, but could not at first see anything plainly, because the windows were shut. After some moments she began to perceive that the floor was all covered over with clotted blood, on which lay the bodies of several dead women, ranged against the walls. (These were all the wives whom Blue Beard had married and murdered, one after another.) She thought she should have died for fear, and the key, which she pulled out of the lock, fell out of her hand.

After having somewhat recovered her surprise, she took up the

key, locked the door, and went upstairs into her chamber to recover herself; but she could not, so much was she frightened. Having observed that the key of the closet was stained with blood, she tried two or three times to wipe it off, but the blood would not come out; in vain did she wash it, and even rub it with soap and sand, the blood still remained, for the key was magical and she could never make it quite clean; when the blood was gone off from one side, it came again on the other.

Blue Beard returned from his journey the same evening, and said he had received letters upon the road, informing him that the affair he went about was ended to his advantage. His wife did all she could to convince him she was extremely glad of his speedy return.

Next morning he asked her for the keys, which she gave him, but with such a trembling hand that he easily guessed what had happened.

'What!' said he, 'is not the key of my closet among the rest?'

'I must certainly,' said she, 'have left it above upon the table.'

'Fail not,' said Blue Beard, 'to bring it me presently.'

After several goings backwards and forwards she was forced to bring him the key. Blue Beard, having very attentively considered it, said to his wife,

'How comes this blood upon the key?'

'I do not know,' cried the poor woman, paler than death.

'You do not know!' replied Blue Beard. 'I very well know. You were resolved to go into the closet, were you not? Mighty well, madam; you shall go in, and take your place among the ladies you saw there.'

Upon this she threw herself at her husband's feet, and begged his pardon with all the signs of a true repentance, vowing that she would never more be disobedient. She would have melted a rock, so beautiful and sorrowful was she; but Blue Beard had a heart harder than any rock!

'You must die, madam,' said he, 'and that presently.'

'Since I must die,' answered she (looking upon him with her eyes all bathed in tears), 'give me some little time to say my prayers.'

'I give you,' replied Blue Beard, 'half a quarter of an hour, but not one moment more.'

When she was alone she called out to her sister, and said to her:

'Sister Anne' (for that was her name), 'go up, I beg you, upon the top of the tower, and look if my brothers are not coming; they promised me that they would come to-day, and if you see them, give them a sign to make haste.'

Her sister Anne went up upon the top of the tower, and the poor afflicted wife cried out from time to time:

'Anne, sister Anne, do you see anyone coming?'

And sister Anne said:

'I see nothing but the sun, which makes a dust, and the grass, which looks green.'

In the meanwhile Blue Beard, holding a great sabre in his hand, cried out as loud as he could bawl to his wife:

'Come down instantly, or I shall come up to you.'

'One moment longer, if you please,' said his wife; and then she cried out very softly, 'Anne, sister Anne, dost thou see anybody coming?'

And sister Anne answered:

'I see nothing but the sun, which makes a dust, and the grass, which is green.'

'Come down quickly,' cried Blue Beard, 'or I will come up to you.'

'I am coming,' answered his wife; and then she cried, 'Anne, sister Anne, dost thou not see anyone coming?'

'I see,' replied sister Anne, 'a great dust, which comes on this side here.'

'Are they my brothers?'

'Alas! no, my dear sister, I see a flock of sheep.'

'Will you not come down?' cried Blue Beard.

'One moment longer,' said his wife, and then she cried out: 'Anne, sister Anne, dost thou see nobody coming?'

'I see,' said she, 'two horsemen, but they are yet a great way off.'

'God be praised,' replied the poor wife joyfully: 'they are my brothers; I will make them a sign, as well as I can, for them to make haste.'

Then Blue Beard bawled out so loud that he made the whole

house tremble. The distressed wife came down, and threw herself at his feet, all in tears, with her hair about her shoulders.

'This signifies nothing,' says Blue Beard; 'you must die'; then, taking hold of her hair with one hand, and lifting up the sword with the other, he was going to take off her head. The poor lady, turning about to him, and looking at him with dying eyes, desired him to afford her one little moment to recollect herself.

'No, no,' said he, 'recommend thyself to God,' and was just ready to strike . . .

At this very instant there was such a loud knocking at the gate that Blue Beard made a sudden stop. The gate was opened, and presently entered two horsemen, who, drawing their swords, ran directly to Blue Beard. He knew them to be his wife's brothers, one a dragoon, the other a musketeer; so that he ran away immediately to save himself; but the two brothers pursued so close that they overtook him before he could get to the steps of the porch, when they ran their swords through his body and left him dead. The poor wife was almost as dead as her husband, and had not strength enough to rise and welcome her brothers.

Blue Beard had no heirs, and so his wife became mistress of all his estate. She made use of one part of it to marry her sister Anne to a young gentleman who had loved her a long while; another part to buy captains' commissions for her brothers, and the rest to marry herself to a very worthy gentleman, who made her forget the ill time she had passed with Blue Beard.[1]

[1] Charles Perrault.

TRUSTY JOHN

ONCE upon a time there was an old king who was so ill that he thought to himself, 'I am most likely on my death-bed.' Then he said, 'Send Trusty John to me.' Now Trusty John was his favourite servant, and was so called because all his life he had served him so

faithfully. When he approached the bed the King spake to him. 'Most trusty John, I feel my end is drawing near, and I could face it without a care were it not for my son. He is still too young to decide everything for himself, and unless you promise me to instruct him in all he should know, and to be to him as a father, I shall not close my eyes in peace.' Then Trusty John answered : ' I will never desert him, and will serve him faithfully, even though it should cost me my life.' Then the old King said : ' Now I die comforted and in peace ; ' and then he went on : ' After my death you must show him the whole castle, all the rooms and apartments and vaults, and all the treasures that lie in them ; but you must not show him the last room in the long passage, where the picture of the Princess of the Golden Roof is hidden. When he beholds that picture he will fall violently in love with it and go off into a dead faint, and for her sake he will encounter many dangers ; you must guard him from this.' And when Trusty John had again given the King his hand upon it the old man became silent, laid his head on the pillow, and died.

When the old King had been carried to his grave, Trusty John told the young King what he had promised his father on his death-bed, and added : ' And I shall assuredly keep my word, and shall be faithful to you as I have been to him, even though it should cost me my life.'

Now when the time of mourning was over, Trusty John said to him : ' It is time you should see your inheritance. I will show you your ancestral castle.' So he took him over everything, and let him see all the riches and splendid apartments, only the one room where the picture was he did not open. But the picture was placed so that if the door opened you gazed straight upon it, and it was so beautifully painted that you imagined it lived and moved, and that it was the most lovable and beautiful thing in the whole world. But the young King noticed that Trusty John always missed over one door, and said : ' Why do you never open this one for me ? ' ' There is something inside that would appal you,' he answered. But the King replied : ' I have seen the whole castle, and shall find out what is in there ; ' and with these words he approached the door and wanted to force it open. But Trusty John held him back, and said : ' I promised your father before his death that you shouldn't see what that room contains. It might bring both you and me to great grief.' ' Ah ! no,' answered the young King ; ' if I don't get in, it will be my certain destruction ; I should have no peace night or day till I had seen what was in the room with my own eyes. Now I don't budge from the spot till you have opened the door.'

Then Trusty John saw there was no way out of it, so with a heavy heart and many sighs he took the key from the big bunch. When he had opened the door he stepped in first, and thought to cover

the likeness so that the King might not perceive it ; but it was hopeless : the King stood on tiptoe and looked over his shoulder. And
when he saw the picture of the maid, so beautiful and glittering
with gold and precious stones, he fell swooning to the ground.
Trusty John lifted him up, carried him to bed, and thought sorrowfully : ' The curse has come upon us ; gracious heaven ! what will be
the end of it all ? ' Then he poured wine down his throat till he
came to himself again. The first words he spoke were : ' Oh ! who
is the original of the beautiful picture ? ' ' She is the Princess of
the Golden Roof,' answered Trusty John. Then the King continued :
' My love for her is so great that if all the leaves on the trees had
tongues they could not express it ; my very life depends on my
winning her. You are my most trusty John : you must stand by
me.'

The faithful servant pondered long how they were to set about
the matter, for it was said to be difficult even to get into the presence
of the Princess. At length he hit upon a plan, and spoke to the
King. ' All the things she has about her—tables, chairs, dishes,
goblets, bowls, and all her household furniture—are made of gold.
You have in your treasure five tons of gold ; let the goldsmiths of
your kingdom manufacture them into all manner of vases and
vessels, into all sorts of birds and game and wonderful beasts ; that
will please her. We shall go to her with them and try our luck.' The
King summoned all his goldsmiths, and they had to work hard day
and night, till at length the most magnificent things were completed.
When a ship had been laden with them the faithful John disguised
himself as a merchant, and the King had to do the same, so that
they should be quite unrecognisable. And so they crossed the seas
and journeyed till they reached the town where the Princess of
the Golden Roof dwelt.

Trusty John made the King remain behind on the ship and
await his return. ' Perhaps,' he said, ' I may bring the Princess
back with me, so see that everything is in order : let the gold ornaments be arranged and the whole ship decorated.' Then he took
a few of the gold things in his apron, went ashore, and proceeded
straight to the palace. When he came to the courtyard he found
a beautiful maiden standing at the well, drawing water with two
golden pails. And as she was about to carry away the glittering
water she turned round and saw the stranger, and asked him who
he was. Then he replied : ' I am a merchant ;' and opening his
apron, he let her peep in. ' Oh ! my,' she cried ; ' what beautiful gold

wares!' she set down her pails, and examined one thing after the
other. Then she said: 'The Princess must see this, she has such a
fancy for gold things that she will buy up all you have got.' She
took him by the hand and let him into the palace, for she was the
lady's-maid.

When the Princess had seen the wares she was quite enchanted,
and said: 'They are all so beautifully made that I shall buy everything you have.' But Trusty John said: 'I am only the servant of
a rich merchant, what I have here is nothing compared to what my
master has on his ship; his merchandise is more artistic and costly
than anything that has ever been made in gold before.' She desired
to have everything brought up to her, but he said: 'There is such a
quantity of things that it would take many days to bring them up,
and they would take up so many rooms that you would have no
space for them in your house.' Thus her desire and curiosity were
excited to such an extent
that at last she said: 'Take
me to your ship; I shall
go there myself and view
your master's treasures.'

Then Trusty John was
quite delighted, and
brought her to the ship;
and the King, when he
beheld her, saw that she
was even more beautiful
than her picture, and
thought every moment
that his heart would burst.
She stepped on to the
ship, and the King led
her inside. But Trusty
John remained behind
with the steersman, and
ordered the ship to push
off. 'Spread all sail, that
we may fly on the ocean like a bird in the air.' Meanwhile the
King showed the Princess inside all his gold wares, every single bit
of it—dishes, goblets, bowls, the birds and game, and all the wonderful beasts. Many hours passed thus, and she was so happy that she
did not notice that the ship was sailing away. After she had seen

the last thing she thanked the merchant and prepared to go home ;
but when she came to the ship's side she saw that they were on the
high seas, far from land, and that the ship was speeding on its way
under full canvas. 'Oh!' she cried in terror, 'I am deceived,
carried away and betrayed into the power of a merchant ; I would
rather have died !' But the King seized her hand and spake : 'I
am no merchant, but a king of as high birth as yourself; and it was
my great love for you that made me carry you off by stratagem.
The first time I saw your likeness I fell to the ground in a swoon.'
When the Princess of the Golden Roof heard this she was comforted, and her heart went out to him, so that she willingly consented to become his wife.

Now it happened one day, while they were sailing on the high
seas, that Trusty John, sitting on the fore part of the ship, fiddling
away to himself, observed three ravens in the air flying towards
him. He ceased playing, and listened to what they were saying,
for he understood their language. The one croaked: 'Ah, ha! so
he's bringing the Princess of the Golden Roof home.' 'Yes,'
answered the second, 'but he's not got her yet.' 'Yes, he has,'
spake the third, 'for she's sitting beside him on the ship.' Then
number one began again and cried : 'That'll not help him ! When
they reach the land a chestnut horse will dash forward to greet
them : the King will wish to mount it, and if he does it will gallop
away with him, and disappear into the air, and he will never see
his bride again.' 'Is there no escape for him ?' asked number two.
'Oh! yes, if someone else mounts quickly and shoots the horse
dead with the pistol that is sticking in the holster, then the young
King is saved. But who's to know that ? and anyone who knows it
and tells him will be turned into stone from his feet to his knees.'
Then spake number two : 'I know more than that : even if the
horse is slain, the young King will still not keep his bride : when
they enter the palace together they will find a ready-made wedding
shirt in a cupboard, which looks as though it were woven of gold
and silver, but is really made of nothing but sulphur and tar :
when the King puts it on it will burn him to his marrow and bones.'
Number three asked : 'Is there no way of escape, then ?' 'Oh!
yes,' answered number two : 'if someone seizes the shirt with
gloved hands and throws it into the fire, and lets it burn, then the
young King is saved. But what's the good ? anyone knowing this
and telling it will have half his body turned into stone, from his
knees to his heart.' Then number three spake : 'I know yet

more : though the bridal shirt too be burnt, the King hasn't even then secured his bride : when the dance is held after the wedding, and the young Queen is dancing, she will suddenly grow deadly white, and drop down like one dead, and unless some one lifts her up and draws three drops of blood from her right side, and spits them out again, she will die. But if anyone who knows this betrays it, he will be turned into stone from the crown of his head to the soles of his feet.' When the ravens had thus conversed they fled onwards, but Trusty John had taken it all in, and was sad and depressed from that time forward ; for if he were silent to his master concerning what he had heard, he would involve him in misfortune ; but if he took him into his confidence, then he himself would forfeit his life. At last he said : ' I will stand by my master, though it should be my ruin.'

Now when they drew near the land it came to pass just as the ravens had predicted, and a splendid chestnut horse bounded forward. ' Capital ! ' said the King ; ' this animal shall carry me to my palace,' and was about to mount, but Trusty John was too sharp for him, and, springing up quickly, seized the pistol out of the holster, and shot the horse dead. Then the other servants of the King, who at no time looked favourably on Trusty John, cried out : ' What a sin to kill the beautiful beast that was to bear the King to his palace ! ' But the King spake : ' Silence ! let him alone ; he is ever my most trusty John. Who knows for what good end he may have done this thing ? ' So they went on their way and entered the palace, and there in the hall stood a cupboard in which lay the ready-made bridal shirt, looking for all the world as though it were made of gold and silver. The young King went towards it and was about to take hold of it, but Trusty John, pushing him aside, seized it with his gloved hands, threw it hastily into the fire, and let it burn. The other servants commenced grumbling again, and said : ' See, he's actually burning the King's bridal shirt.' But the young King spoke : ' Who knows for what good purpose he does it ? Let him alone, he is my most trusty John.' Then the wedding was celebrated, the dance began, and the bride joined in, but Trusty John watched her countenance carefully. Of a sudden she grew deadly white, and fell to the ground as if she were dead. He at once sprang hastily towards her, lifted her up, and bore her to a room, where he laid her down, and kneeling beside her he drew three drops of blood from her right side, and spat them out. She soon breathed again and came to herself ; but the young King had watched the proceeding,

and not knowing why Trusty John had acted as he did, he flew into
a passion, and cried : 'Throw him into prison.'   On the following
morning sentence was passed on Trusty John, and he was condemned to be hanged.   As he stood on the gallows he said : 'Every
one doomed to death has the right to speak once before he dies; am
I to have this privilege ? ' ' Yes,' said the King, ' it shall be granted
to you.'   So Trusty John spoke : ' I am unjustly condemned, for
I have always been faithful to you ; ' and he proceeded to relate
how he had heard the ravens' conversation on the sea, and how he

had to do all he did in order to save his master.   Then the King
cried : ' Oh ! my most trusty John, pardon ! pardon ! Take him
down.' But as he uttered the last word Trusty John had fallen lifeless to the ground, and was a stone.

     The King and Queen were in despair, and the King spake : 'Ah !
how ill have I rewarded such great fidelity ! ' and made them lift up
the stone image and place it in his bedroom near his bed. As
often as he looked at it he wept and said : 'Oh ! if I could only
restore you to life, my most trusty John ! '   After a time the Queen

gave birth to twins, two small sons, who throve and grew, and were a constant joy to her. One day when the Queen was at church, and the two children sat and played with their father, he gazed again full of grief on the stone statue, and sighing, wailed: 'Oh! if I could only restore you to life, my most trusty John!' Suddenly the stone began to speak, and said: 'Yes, you can restore me to life again if you are prepared to sacrifice what you hold most dear.' And the King cried out: 'All I have in the world will I give up for your sake.' The stone continued: 'If you cut off with your own hand the heads of your two children, and smear me with their blood, I shall come back to life.' The King was aghast when he heard that he had himself to put his children to death; but when he thought of Trusty John's fidelity, and how he had even died for him, he drew his sword, and with his own hand cut the heads off his children. And when he had smeared the stone with their blood, life came back, and Trusty John stood once more safe and sound before him. He spake to the King: 'Your loyalty shall be rewarded, and taking up the heads of the children, he placed them on their bodies, smeared the wounds with their blood, and in a minute they were all right again and jumping about as if nothing had happened. Then the King was full of joy, and when he saw the Queen coming, he hid Trusty John and the two children in a big cupboard. As she entered he said to her: 'Did you pray in church?' 'Yes,' she answered; 'but my thoughts dwelt constantly on Trusty John, and of what he has suffered for us.' Then he spake: 'Dear wife, we can restore him to life, but the price asked is our two little sons; we must sacrifice them.' The Queen grew white and her heart sank, but she replied: 'We owe it to him on account of his great fidelity.' Then he rejoiced that she was of the same mind as he had been, and going forward he opened the cupboard, and fetched the two children and Trusty John out, saying: 'God be praised! Trusty John is free once more, and we have our two small sons again.' Then he related to her all that had passed, and they lived together happily ever afterwards.[1]

[1] Grimm.

THE BRAVE LITTLE TAILOR

ONE summer's day a little tailor sat on his table by the window in the best of spirits, and sewed for dear life. As he was sitting thus a peasant woman came down the street, calling out: ' Good jam to sell, good jam to sell.' This sounded sweetly in the tailor's ears ; he put his frail little head out of the window, and shouted: ' Up here, my good woman, and you'll find a willing customer.' The woman climbed up the three flights of stairs with her heavy basket to the tailor's room, and he made her spread out all the pots in a row before him. He examined them all, lifted them up and smelt them, and said at last : ' This jam seems good, weigh me four ounces of it, my good woman ; and even if it's a quarter of a pound I won't stick at it.' The woman, who had hoped to find a good market, gave him what he wanted, but went away grumbling wrathfully. ' Now heaven shall bless this jam for my use,' cried the little tailor, ' and it shall sustain and strengthen me.' He fetched some bread out of a cupboard, cut a round off the loaf, and spread the jam on it. ' That won't taste amiss,' he said ; ' but I'll finish that waistcoat first before I take a bite.' He placed the bread beside him, went on sewing, and out of the lightness of his heart kept on making his stitches bigger and bigger. In the meantime the smell of the sweet jam rose to the ceiling, where heaps of flies were sitting, and attracted them to such an extent that they swarmed on to it in masses. ' Ha ! who invited you ? ' said the tailor, and chased the unwelcome guests away. But the flies, who didn't understand English, refused to let themselves be warned off, and returned again in even greater numbers. At last the little tailor, losing all patience, reached out of his chimney corner for a duster, and exclaiming : ' Wait, and I'll give it to you,' he beat them mercilessly with it. When he left off he counted the slain, and no fewer than seven lay dead before him with outstretched legs. ' What a desperate fellow I am ! ' said he, and was filled with admiration at his

own courage. 'The whole town must know about this;' and in great
haste the little tailor cut out a girdle, hemmed it, and embroidered
on it in big letters, 'Seven at a blow.' 'What did I say, the town?
no, the whole world shall hear of it,' he said; and his heart beat
for joy as a lamb wags his tail.

The tailor strapped the girdle round his waist and set out into
the wide world, for he considered his workroom too small a field
for his prowess. Before he set forth he looked round about him,
to see if there was anything in the house he could take with him
on his journey; but he found nothing except an old cheese, which
he took possession of. In front of the house he observed a bird

that had been caught in some bushes, and this he put into his wallet beside the cheese. Then he went on his way merrily, and being light and agile he never felt tired. His way led up a hill, on the top of which sat a powerful giant, who was calmly surveying the landscape. The little tailor went up to him, and greeting him cheerfully said : ' Good-day, friend ; there you sit at your ease viewing the whole wide world. I'm just on my way there. What do you say to accompanying me ? ' The giant looked contemptuously at the tailor, and said : ' What a poor wretched little creature you are ! ' ' That's a good joke,' answered the little tailor, and unbuttoning his coat he showed the giant the girdle. ' There now, you can read what sort of a fellow I am.' The giant read : ' Seven at a blow ; ' and thinking they were human beings the tailor had slain, he conceived a certain respect for the little man. But first he thought he'd test him, so taking up a stone in his hand, he squeezed it till some drops of water ran out. ' Now you do the same,' said the giant, ' if you really wish to be thought strong.' ' Is that all ? ' said the little tailor ; ' that's child's play to me,' so he dived into his wallet, brought out the cheese, and pressed it till the whey ran out. ' My squeeze was in sooth better than yours,' said he. The giant didn't know what to say, for he couldn't have believed it of the little fellow. To prove him again, the giant lifted a stone and threw it so high that the eye could hardly follow it. ' Now, my little pigmy, let me see you do that.' ' Well thrown,' said the tailor ; ' but, after all, your stone fell to the ground ; I'll throw one that won't come down at all.' He dived into his wallet again, and grasping the bird in his hand, he threw it up into the air. The bird, enchanted to be free, soared up into the sky, and flew away never to return. ' Well, what do you think of that little piece of business, friend ? ' asked the tailor. ' You can certainly throw,' said the giant ; ' but now let's see if you can carry a proper weight.' With these words he led the tailor to a huge oak tree which had been felled to the ground, and said : ' If you are strong enough, help me to carry the tree out of the wood.' ' Most certainly,' said the little tailor : ' just you take the trunk on your shoulder ; I'll bear the top and branches, which is certainly the heaviest part.' The giant laid the trunk on his shoulder, but the tailor sat t his ease among the branches ; and the giant, who couldn't see what was going on behind him, had to carry the whole tree, and the little tailor into the bargain. There he sat behind in the best of spirits, lustily whistling a tune, as if carrying the tree were mere sport.

The giant, after dragging the heavy weight for some time, could get on no further, and shouted out : ' Hi ! I must let the tree fall.' The tailor sprang nimbly down, seized the tree with both hands as if he had carried it the whole way, and said to the giant : ' Fancy a big lout like you not being able to carry a tree ! '

They continued to go on their way together, and as they passed by a cherry tree the giant grasped the top of it, where the ripest fruit hung, gave the branches into the tailor's hand, and bade him eat. But the little tailor was far too weak to hold the tree down, and when the giant let go the tree swung back into the air, bearing the little tailor with it. When he had fallen to the ground again without hurting himself, the giant said : ' What ! do you mean to tell me you haven't the strength to hold down a feeble twig ? ' ' It wasn't strength that was wanting,' replied the tailor; ' do you think that would have been anything for a man who has killed seven at a blow ? I jumped over the tree because the hunstmen are shooting among the branches near us. Do you do the like if you dare.' The giant made an attempt, but couldn't get over the tree, and stuck fast in the branches, so that here too the little tailor had the better of him.

' Well, you're a fine fellow, after all,' said the giant; ' come and spend the night with us in our cave.' The little tailor willingly consented to do this, and following his friend they went on till they reached a cave where several other giants were sitting round a fire, each holding a roast sheep in his hand, of which he was eating. The little tailor looked about him, and thought : ' Yes, there's certainly more room to turn round in here than in my workshop.' The giant showed him a bed, and bade him lie down and have a good sleep. But the bed was too big for the little tailor, so he didn't get into it, but crept away into the corner. At midnight, when the giant thought the little tailor was fast asleep, he rose up, and taking his big iron walking-stick, he broke the bed in two with a blow, and thought he had made an end of the little grasshopper. At early dawn the giants went off to the wood, and quite forgot about the little tailor, till all of a sudden they met him trudging along in the most cheerful manner. The giants were terrified at the apparition, and, fearful lest he should slay them, they all took to their heels as fast as they could.

The little tailor continued to follow his nose, and after he had wandered about for a long time he came to the courtyard of a royal palace, and feeling tired he lay down on the grass and fell asleep.

While he lay there the people came, and looking him all over read on his girdle : ' Seven at a blow.' ' Oh ! ' they said, ' what can this great hero of a hundred fights want in our peaceful land ? He must indeed be a mighty man of valour.' They went and told the King about him, and said what a weighty and useful man he'd be in time of war, and that it would be well to secure him at any price. This counsel pleased the King, and he sent one of his courtiers down to the little tailor, to offer him, when he awoke, a commission in their army. The messenger remained standing by the sleeper, and waited till he stretched his limbs and opened his eyes, when he tendered his proposal. ' That's the very thing I came here for,' he answered ; ' I am quite ready to enter the King's service.' So he was received with all honour, and given a special house of his own to live in.

But the other officers resented the success of the little tailor, and wished him a thousand miles away. ' What's to come of it all ? ' they asked each other ; ' if we quarrel with him, he'll let out at us, and at every blow seven will fall. There'll soon be an end of us.' So they resolved to go in a body to the King, and all to send in their papers. ' We are not made,' they said, ' to hold out against a man who kills seven at a blow.' The King was grieved at the thought of los-ing all his faithful servants for the sake of one man, and he wished heartily that he had never set eyes on him, or that he could get rid of him. But he didn't dare to send him away, for he feared he might kill him along with his people, and place himself on the throne. He pondered long and deeply over the matter, and finally came to a conclusion. He sent to the tailor and told him that, see-ing what a great and warlike hero he was, he was about to make him an offer. In a certain wood of his kingdom there dwelt two giants who did much harm ; by the way they robbed, murdered, burnt, and plundered everything about them ; ' no one could ap-proach them without endangering his life. But if he could over-come and kill these two giants he should have his only daughter for a wife, and half his kingdom into the bargain ; he might have a hundred horsemen, too, to back him up.' ' That's the very thing for a man like me,' thought the little tailor ; ' one doesn't get the offer of a beautiful princess and half a kingdom every day.' ' Done with you,' he answered ; ' I'll soon put an end to the giants. But I haven't the smallest need of your hundred horsemen ; a fellow who can slay seven men at a blow need not be afraid of two.'

The little tailor set out, and the hundred horsemen followed

him. When he came to the outskirts of the wood he said to his
followers : ' You wait here, I'll manage the giants by myself ; ' and he
went on into the wood, casting his sharp little eyes right and left
about him.   After a while he spied the two giants lying asleep
under a tree, and snoring till the very boughs bent with the breeze.
The little tailor lost no time in filling his wallet with stones, and
then climbed up the tree under which they lay.   When he got to

about the middle of it he slipped along a branch till he sat just
above the sleepers, when he threw down one stone after the other
on the nearest giant.   The giant felt nothing for a long time, but
at last he woke up, and pinching his companion said : ' What did
you strike me for ? '   ' I didn't strike you,' said the other ' you
must be dreaming.'   They both lay down to sleep again, and the
tailor threw down a stone on the second giant, who sprang up and
cried : ' What's that for ?   Why did you throw something at me ? '

'I didn't throw anything,' growled the first one. They wrangled on for a time, till, as both were tired, they made up the matter and fell asleep again. The little tailor began his game once more, and flung the largest stone he could find in his wallet with all his force, and hit the first giant on the chest. 'This is too much of a good thing!' he yelled, and springing up like a madman, he knocked his companion against the tree till he trembled. He gave, however, as good as he got, and they became so enraged that they tore up trees and beat each other with them, till they both fell dead at once on the ground. Then the little tailor jumped down. 'It's a mercy,' he said, 'that they didn't root up the tree on which I was perched, or I should have had to jump like a squirrel on to another, which, nimble though I am, would have been no easy job.' He drew his sword and gave each of the giants a very fine thrust or two on the breast, and then went to the horsemen and said : 'The deed is done, I've put an end to the two of them; but I assure you it has been no easy matter, for they even tore up trees in their struggle to defend themselves; but all that's of no use against one who slays seven men at a blow.' 'Weren't you wounded?' asked the horsemen. 'No fear,' answered the tailor ; 'they haven't touched a hair of my head.' But the horsemen wouldn't believe him till they rode into the wood and found the giants weltering in their blood, and the trees lying around, torn up by the roots.

The little tailor now demanded the promised reward from the King, but he repented his promise, and pondered once more how he could rid himself of the hero. 'Before you obtain the hand of my daughter and half my kingdom,' he said to him, 'you must do another deed of valour. A unicorn is running about loose in the wood, and doing much mischief; you must first catch it.' 'I'm even less afraid of one unicorn than of two giants; seven at a blow, that's my motto.' He took a piece of cord and an axe with him, went out to the wood, and again told the men who had been sent with him to remain outside. He hadn't to search long, for the unicorn soon passed by, and, on perceiving the tailor, dashed straight at him as though it were going to spike him on the spot. 'Gently, gently,' said he, 'not so fast, my friend ;' and standing still he waited till the beast was quite near, when he sprang lightly behind a tree ; the unicorn ran with all its force against the tree, and rammed its horn so firmly into the trunk that it had no strength left to pull it out again, and was thus successfully captured. 'Now I've caught my bird,' said the tailor, and he came out from behind the tree, placed the cord round its neck first, then struck the horn out of the tree with his axe, and when everything was in order led the beast before the King.

Still the King didn't want to give him the promised reward, and made a third demand. The tailor was to catch a wild boar for him that did a great deal of harm in the wood; and he might have the huntsmen to help him. 'Willingly,' said the tailor; 'that's mere child's play.' But he didn't take the huntsmen into the wood with him, and they were well enough pleased to remain behind, for the wild boar had often received them in a manner which did not make them desire its further acquaintance. As soon as the boar perceived the tailor it ran at him with foaming mouth and gleaming teeth, and tried to knock him down; but our alert little friend ran into a chapel that stood near, and got out of the window again with a jump. The boar pursued him into the church, but the tailor skipped round to the door, and closed it securely. So the raging beast was caught, for it was far too heavy and unwieldy to spring out of the window. The little tailor summoned the huntsmen together, that they might see the prisoner with their own eyes. Then the hero betook himself to the King, who was obliged now, whether he liked it or not, to keep his promise, and hand him over his daughter and half his kingdom. Had he known that no hero-warrior, but only a little tailor stood before him, it would have gone even more to his heart. So the wedding was celebrated with much splendour and little joy, and the tailor became a king.

After a time the Queen heard her husband saying one night in his sleep: 'My lad, make that waistcoat and patch these trousers, or I'll box your ears.' Thus she learnt in what rank the young gentleman had been born, and next day she poured forth her woes to her father, and begged him to help her to get rid of a husband who was nothing more nor less than a tailor. The King comforted her, and said: 'Leave your bedroom door open to-night, my servants shall stand outside, and when your husband is fast asleep they shall enter, bind him fast, and carry him on to a ship, which shall sail away out into the wide ocean.' The Queen was well satisfied with the idea, but the armour-bearer, who had overheard everything, being much attached to his young master, went straight to him and revealed the whole plot. 'I'll soon put a stop to the business,' said the tailor. That night he and his wife went to bed at the usual time; and when she thought he had fallen asleep she got up, opened the door, and then lay down again. The little tailor, who had only pretended to be asleep, began to call out in a clear voice: 'My lad, make that waistcoat and patch those trousers, or I'll box your ears. I have killed seven at a blow, slain two giants, led a unicorn captive, and caught a wild boar, then why should I be afraid of those men standing outside my door?' The men, when they heard the tailor saying these words, were so terrified that they fled as if pursued by a wild army, and didn't dare go near him again. So the little tailor was and remained a king all the days of his life.

A VOYAGE TO LILLIPUT

CHAPTER I.

MY father had a small estate in Nottinghamshire, and I was the third of four sons. He sent me to Cambridge at fourteen years old, and after studying there three years I was bound apprentice to Mr. Bates, a famous surgeon in London. There, as my father now and then sent me small sums of money, I spent them in learning navigation, and other arts useful to those who travel, as I always believed it would be some time or other my fortune to do.

Three years after my leaving him my good master, Mr. Bates, recommended me as ship's surgeon to the 'Swallow,' on which I voyaged three years. When I came back I settled in London, and, having taken part of a small house, I married Miss Mary Burton, daughter of Mr. Edmund Burton, hosier.

But my good master Bates died two years after; and as I had few friends my business began to fail, and I determined to go again to sea. After several voyages I accepted an offer from Captain W. Prichard, master of the 'Antelope,' who was making a voyage to the South Sea. We set sail from Bristol, May 4, 1699; and our voyage at first was very prosperous.

But in our passage to the East Indies we were driven by a violent storm to the north-west of Van Diemen's Land. Twelve of our crew died from hard labour and bad food, and the rest were in a very weak condition. On the 5th of November, the weather being very hazy, the seamen spied a rock within 120 yards of the ship; but the wind was so strong that we were driven straight upon it, and immediately split. Six of the crew, of whom I was one, letting down the boat, got clear of the ship, and we rowed about three leagues, till we could work no longer. We therefore trusted ourselves to the mercy of the waves; and in about half an hour the boat was upset by a sudden squall. What became of my companions in the boat, or those who escaped on the rock or were left in the vessel, I cannot tell; but I conclude they were all lost. For my part, I swam as fortune directed me, and was pushed forward by wind and tide; but when I was able to struggle no longer I found myself within my depth. By this time the storm was much abated. I reached the shore at last, about eight o'clock in the evening, and advanced nearly half a mile inland, but could not discover any sign of inhabitants. I was extremely tired, and with the heat of the weather I found myself much inclined to sleep. I lay down on the grass, which was very short and soft, and slept sounder than ever I did in my life for about nine hours. When I woke, it was just daylight. I attempted to rise, but could not; for as I happened to be lying on my back, I found my arms and legs were fastened on each side to the ground; and my hair, which was long and thick, tied down in the same manner. I could only look upwards. The sun began to grow hot, and the light hurt my eyes. I heard a confused noise about me, but could see nothing except the sky. In a little time I felt something alive moving on my left leg, which, advancing gently over my breast, came almost up to my chin, when, bending my eyes downward, I perceived it to be a human creature, not six inches high, with a bow and arrow in his hands, and a quiver at his back. In the meantime I felt at least forty more following the first. I was in the utmost astonishment, and roared so loud that they all ran back in a fright; and some of them were hurt with the falls they got by leaping from my sides upon the ground. However, they soon returned, and one of them, who ventured so far as to get a full sight of my face, lifted up his hands in admiration. I lay all this while in great uneasiness; but at length, struggling to get loose, I succeeded in breaking the strings that fastened my left arm to the ground; and at the same time, with a violent pull that gave me extreme pain, I a little loosened the strings that tied down my hair, so that I was just able to turn my head about two inches. But the creatures ran off a second time before I could seize them, whereupon there was a great shout, and in an instant I felt above a hundred arrows discharged on my left hand, which pricked me like so many needles. Moreover, they shot another flight into the air, of which some fell on my face, which I immediately covered with my left hand. When this shower of arrows was over I groaned with grief and pain, and then, striving again to get loose, they discharged another flight of arrows larger than the first, and some of them tried to stab me with their spears; but by good luck

I had on a leather jacket, which they could not pierce. By this time I thought it most prudent to lie still till night, when, my left hand being already loose, I could easily free myself; and as for the inhabitants, I thought I might be a match for the greatest army they could bring against me if they were all of the same size with him I saw. When the people observed that I was quiet they discharged no more arrows, but by the noise I heard I knew that their number was increased; and about four yards from me, for more than an hour, there was a knocking, like people at work. Then, turning my head that way as well as the pegs and strings would let me, I saw a stage set up, about a foot and a half from the ground, with two or three ladders to mount it. From this, one of them, who seemed to be a person of quality, made me a long

speech, of which I could not understand a word, though I could tell from his manner that he sometimes threatened me, and sometimes spoke with pity and kindness. I answered in few words, but in the most submissive manner; and, being almost famished with hunger, I could not help showing my impatience by putting my finger frequently to my mouth, to signify that I wanted food. He understood me very well, and, descending from the stage, commanded that several ladders should be set against my sides, on which more than a hundred of the inhabitants mounted, and walked towards my mouth with baskets full of food, which had been sent by the King's orders when he first received tidings of me. There were legs and shoulders like mutton, but smaller than the wings of a lark. I ate them two or three at a mouthful, and took three loaves at a time. They supplied me as fast as they could, with a thousand marks of wonder at my appetite. I then made a sign that I wanted something to drink. They guessed that a small quantity would not suffice me, and, being a most ingenious people, they slung up one of their largest hogsheads, then rolled it towards my hand, and beat out the top. I drank it off at a draught, which I might well do, for it did not hold half a pint. They brought me a second hogshead, which I drank, and made signs for more; but they had none to give me. However, I could not wonder enough at the daring of these tiny mortals, who ventured to mount and walk upon my body, while one of my hands was free, without trembling at the very sight of so huge a creature as I must have seemed to them. After some time there appeared before me a person of high rank from his Imperial Majesty. His Excellency, having mounted my right leg, advanced to my face, with about a dozen of his retinue, and spoke about ten minutes, often pointing forwards, which, as I afterwards found, was towards the capital city, about half a mile distant, whither it was commanded by his Majesty that I should be conveyed. I made a sign with my hand that was loose, putting it to the other (but over his Excellency's head, for fear of hurting him or his train), to show that I desired my liberty. He seemed to understand me well enough, for he shook his head, though he made other signs to let me know that I should have meat and drink enough, and very good treatment. Then I once more thought of attempting to escape; but when I felt the smart of their arrows on my face and hands, which were all in blisters, and observed likewise that the number of my enemies increased, I gave tokens to let them know that they might do with me what they pleased. Then they daubed my face and hands with a sweet-smelling ointment, which in a few minutes removed all the smart of the arrows. The relief from pain and hunger made me drowsy, and presently I fell asleep. I slept about eight hours, as I was told afterwards; and it was no wonder, for the physicians, by the Emperor's order, had mingled a sleeping draught in the hogsheads of wine.

It seems that, when I was discovered sleeping on the ground after my landing, the Emperor had early notice of it, and determined that I should be tied in the manner I have related (which was done in the night, while I slept), that plenty of meat and drink should be sent me, and a machine prepared to carry me to the capital city. Five hundred carpenters and engineers were immediately set to work to prepare the engine. It was a frame of wood, raised three inches from the ground, about seven feet long and four wide, moving upon twenty-two wheels. But the difficulty was to place me on it. Eighty poles were erected for this purpose, and very strong cords fastened to bandages which the workmen had tied round my neck, hands, body, and legs. Nine hundred of the strongest men were employed to draw up these cords by pulleys fastened on the poles, and in less than three hours I was raised and slung into the engine, and there tied fast. Fifteen hundred of the Emperor's largest horses, each about four inches and a half high, were then employed to draw me towards the capital. But while all this was done I still lay in a deep sleep, and I did not wake till four hours after we began our journey.

The Emperor and all his Court came out to meet us when we reached the capital ; but his great officials would not suffer his Majesty to risk his person by mounting on my body. Where the carriage stopped there stood an ancient temple, supposed to be the largest in the whole kingdom, and here it was determined that I should lodge. Near the great gate, through which I could easily creep, they fixed ninety-one chains, like those which hang to a lady's watch, which were locked to my left leg with thirty-six padlocks ; and when the workmen found it was impossible for me to break loose, they cut all the strings that bound me. Then I rose up, feeling as melancholy as ever I did in my life. But the noise and astonishment of the people on seeing me rise and walk were inexpressible. The chains that held my left leg were about two yards long, and gave me not only freedom to walk backwards and forwards in a semicircle, but to creep in and lie at full length inside the temple.

CHAPTER II.

The Emperor, advancing towards me from among his courtiers, all most magnificently clad, surveyed me with great admiration, but kept beyond the length of my chain. He was taller by about the breadth of my nail than any of his Court, which alone was enough to strike awe into the beholders, and graceful and majestic. The better to behold him, I lay down on my side, so that my face was level with his, and he stood three yards off. However, I have had him since many times in my hand, and therefore cannot be deceived. His dress was very simple ; but he wore a light helmet of gold, adorned with jewels and a plume. He held his sword drawn in his hand, to defend himself if I should break loose; it was almost three inches long, and the hilt was of gold, enriched with diamonds. His voice was shrill, but very clear. His Imperial Majesty spoke often to me, and I answered; but neither of us could understand a word.

After about two hours the Court retired, and I was left with a strong guard to keep away the crowd, some of whom had the impudence to shoot their arrows at me as I sat by the door of my house. But the colonel ordered six of them to be seized and delivered bound into my hands. I put five of them into my coat pocket; and as to the sixth, I made a face as if I would eat him alive. The poor man screamed terribly, and the colonel and his officers were much distressed, especially when they saw me take out my penknife. But I soon set them at ease, for, cutting the strings he was bound with, I put him gently on the ground, and away he ran. I treated the rest in the same manner, taking them one by one out of my pocket; and I saw that both the soldiers and people were highly delighted at this mark of my kindness.

Towards night I got with some difficulty into my house, where I lay on the ground, as I had to do for a fortnight, till a bed was prepared for me out of six hundred beds of the ordinary measure.

Six hundred servants were appointed me, and three hundred tailors made me a suit of clothes. Moreover, six of his Majesty's

greatest scholars were employed to teach me their language, so that soon I was able to converse after a fashion with the Emperor, who often honoured me with his visits. The first words I learned were to desire that he would please to give me my liberty, which I every day repeated on my knees; but he answered that this must be a work of time, and that first I must swear a peace with him and his kingdom. He told me also that by the laws of the nation I must be searched by two of his officers, and that as this could not be done without my help, he trusted them in my hands, and whatever they took from me should be returned when I left the country. I took up the two officers, and put them into my coat pockets. These gentlemen, having pen, ink, and paper about them, made an exact list of everything they saw, which I afterwards translated into English, and which ran as follows :

' In the right coat pocket of the great *Man-Mountain* we found only one great piece of coarse cloth, large enough to cover the carpet of your Majesty's chief room of state. In the left pocket we saw a huge silver chest, with a silver cover, which we could not lift. We desired that it should be opened, and one of us stepping into it found himself up to the mid-leg in a sort of dust, some of which flying into our faces sent us both into a fit of sneezing. In his right waistcoat pocket we found a number of white thin substances, folded one over another, about the size of three men, tied with a strong cable, and marked with black figures, which we humbly conceive to be writings. In the left there was a sort of engine, from the back of which extended twenty long poles, with which, we conjecture, the *Man-Mountain* combs his head. In the smaller pocket on the right side were several round flat pieces of white and red metal, of different sizes. Some of the white, which appeared to be silver, were so large and heavy that my comrade and I could hardly lift them. From another pocket hung a huge silver chain, with a wonderful kind of engine fastened to it, a globe half silver and half of some transparent metal; for on the transparent side we saw certain strange figures, and thought we could touch them till we found our fingers stopped by the shining substance. This engine made an incessant noise, like a water-mill, and we conjecture it is either some unknown animal, or the god he worships, but probably the latter, for he told us that he seldom did anything without consulting it.

' This is a list of what we found about the body of the *Man-Mountain*, who treated us with great civility.'

I had one private pocket which escaped their search, containing a pair of spectacles and a small spy-glass, which, being of no consequence to the Emperor, I did not think myself bound in honour to discover.

CHAPTER III.

My gentleness and good behaviour gained so far on the Emperor and his Court, and, indeed, on the people in general, that I began to have hopes of getting my liberty in a short time. The natives came by degrees to be less fearful of danger from me. I would sometimes lie down and let five or six of them dance on my hand ; and at last the boys and girls ventured to come and play at hide-and-seek in my hair.

The horses of the army and of the royal stables were no longer shy, having been daily led before me; and one of the Emperor's huntsmen, on a large courser, took my foot, shoe and all, which was indeed a prodigious leap. I amused the Emperor one day in a very extraordinary manner. I took nine sticks, and fixed them firmly in the ground in a square. Then I took four other sticks, and tied them parallel at each corner, about two feet from the ground. I

fastened my handkerchief to the nine sticks that stood erect, and extended it on all sides till it was as tight as the top of a drum; and I desired the Emperor to let a troop of his best horse, twenty-four in number, come and exercise upon this plain. His Majesty approved of the proposal, and I took them up one by one, with the proper officers to exercise them. As soon as they got into order they divided into two parties, discharged blunt arrows, drew their swords, fled and pursued, and, in short, showed the best military discipline I ever beheld. The parallel sticks secured them and their horses from falling off the stage, and the Emperor was so much delighted that he ordered this entertainment to be repeated several days, and persuaded the Empress herself to let me hold her in her chair within two yards of the stage, whence she could view the whole performance. Fortunately no accident happened, only once a fiery horse, pawing with his hoof, struck a hole in my handkerchief, and overthrew his rider and himself. But I immediately relieved them both, and covering the hole with one hand, I set down the troop with the other as I had taken them up. The horse that fell was strained in the shoulder, but the rider was not hurt, and I repaired my handkerchief as well as I could. However, I would not trust to the strength of it any more in such dangerous enterprises.

I had sent so many petitions for my liberty that his Majesty at length mentioned the matter in a full council, where it was opposed by none except Skyresh Bolgolam, admiral of the realm, who was pleased without any provocation to be my mortal enemy. However, he agreed at length, though he succeeded in himself drawing up the conditions on which I should be set free. After they were read I was requested to swear to perform them in the method prescribed by their laws, which was to hold my right foot in my left hand, and to place the middle finger of my right hand on the crown of my head, and my thumb on the top of my right ear. But I have made a translation of the conditions, which I here offer to the public.

'*Golbaste Momarem Evlame Gurdile Shefin Mully Ully Gue*, Most Mighty Emperor of Lilliput, delight and terror of the universe, whose dominions extend to the ends of the globe, monarch of all monarchs, taller than the sons of men, whose feet press down to the centre, and whose head strikes against the sun, at whose nod the princes of the earth shake their knees, pleasant as the spring, comfortable as the summer, fruitful as autumn, dreadful as winter: His Most Sublime Majesty proposeth to the *Man-Mountain*, lately arrived at our celestial dominions, the following articles, which by a solemn oath he shall be obliged to perform:

'First. The *Man-Mountain* shall not depart from our dominions without our licence under the great seal.

'Second. He shall not presume to come into our metropolis without our express order, at which time the inhabitants shall have two hours' warning to keep within doors.

'Third. The said *Man-Mountain* shall confine his walks to our principal high roads, and not offer to walk or lie down in a meadow or field of corn.

'Fourth. As he walks the said roads he shall take the utmost care not to trample upon the bodies of any of our loving subjects, their horses or carriages, nor take any of our subjects into his hands without their own consent.

'Fifth. If an express requires extraordinary speed the *Man-Mountain* shall be obliged to carry in his pocket the messenger and horse a six days' journey, and return the said messenger (if so required) safe to our imperial presence.

'Sixth. He shall be our ally against our enemies in the island of Blefuscu, and do his utmost to destroy their fleet, which is now preparing to invade us.

'Lastly. Upon his solemn oath to observe all the above articles, the said *Man-Mountain* shall have a daily allowance of meat and drink sufficient for the support of 1,724 of our subjects, with free access to our royal person, and other marks of our favour.—Given at our palace at Belfaborac, the twelfth day of the ninety-first moon of our reign.'

I swore to these articles with great cheerfulness, whereupon my chains were immediately unlocked, and I was at full liberty.

One morning, about a fortnight after I had obtained my freedom, Reldresal, the Emperor's secretary for private affairs, came to my house, attended only by one servant. He ordered his coach to wait at a distance, and desired that I would give him an hour's audience. I offered to lie down that he might the more conveniently reach my ear; but he chose rather to let me hold him in my hand during our conversation. He began with compliments on my liberty, but he added that, save for the present state of things at Court, perhaps I might not have obtained it so soon. 'For,' he said, 'however flourishing we may seem to foreigners, we are in danger of an invasion from the island of Blefuscu, which is the other great empire of the universe, almost as large and as powerful as this of his Majesty. For as to what we have heard you say, that there are other kingdoms in the world, inhabited by human creatures as large as yourself, our philosphers are very doubtful, and rather conjecture that you dropped from the moon, or one of the stars, because a hundred mortals of your size would soon destroy all the fruit and cattle of his Majesty's dominions. Besides, our histories of six thousand moons make no mention of any other regions than the two mighty empires of Lilliput and Blefuscu, which, as I was going to tell you,

are engaged in a most obstinate war, which began in the following manner :—It is allowed on all hands that the primitive way of
breaking eggs was upon the larger end ; but his present Majesty's
grandfather, while he was a boy, going to eat an egg, and breaking
it according to the ancient practice, happened to cut one of his fingers. Whereupon the Emperor, his father, made a law command-
ing all his subjects to break the smaller end of their eggs. The
people so highly resented this law that there have been six rebel-
lions raised on that account, wherein one emperor lost his life, and
another his crown. It is calculated that eleven hundred persons have at different times suffered death rather than break their
eggs at the smaller end. But these rebels, the Bigendians, have
found so much encouragement at the Emperor of Blefuscu's
Court, to which they always fled for refuge, that a bloody war, as I
said, has been carried on between the two empires for six-and-
thirty moons; and now the Blefuscudians have equipped a large
fleet, and are preparing to descend upon us. Therefore his Imperial Majesty, placing great confidence in your valour and strength,
has commanded me to set the case before you.'

I desired the secretary to present my humble duty to the
Emperor, and to let him know that I was ready, at the risk of my
life, to defend him against all invaders.

CHAPTER IV.

It was not long before I communicated to his Majesty the plan I
formed for seizing the enemy's whole fleet. The Empire of Blefuscu
is an island parted from Lilliput only by a channel eight hundred
yards wide. I consulted the most experienced seamen on the depth
of the channel, and they told me that in the middle, at high water,
it was seventy *glumgluffs* (about six feet of European measure).
I walked towards the coast, where, lying down behind a hillock, I
took out my spy-glass, and viewed the enemy's fleet at anchor—
about fifty men-of-war, and other vessels. I then came back to my
house and gave orders for a great quantity of the strongest cables
and bars of iron. The cable was about as thick as packthread, and
the bars of the length and size of a knitting-needle. I trebled the
cable to make it stronger, and for the same reason twisted three of
the iron bars together, bending the ends into a hook. Having thus
fixed fifty hooks to as many cables, I went back to the coast, and

taking off my coat, shoes, and stockings, walked into the sea in my leather jacket about half an hour before high water. I waded with what haste I could, swimming in the middle about thirty yards, till I felt ground, and thus arrived at the fleet in less than half an hour. The enemy were so frightened when they saw me that they leaped out of their ships and swam ashore, where there could not be fewer than thirty thousand. Then, fastening a hook to the hole at the prow of each ship, I tied all the cords together at the end. Meanwhile the enemy discharged several thousand arrows, many of which stuck in my hands and face. My greatest fear was for my eyes, which I should have lost if I had not suddenly thought of the pair of spectacles which had escaped the Emperor's searchers. These I took out and fastened upon my nose, and thus armed went on with my work in spite of the arrows, many of which struck against the glasses of my spectacles, but without any other effect than slightly disturbing them. Then, taking the knot in my hand, I began to pull; but not a ship would stir, for they were too fast held by their anchors. Thus the boldest part of my enterprise remained. Letting go the cord, I resolutely cut with my knife the cables that fastened the anchors, receiving more than two hundred shots in my face and hands. Then I took up again the knotted end of the cables to which my hooks were tied, and with great ease drew fifty of the enemy's largest men-of-war after me.

When the Blefuscudians saw the fleet moving in order, and me pulling at the end, they set up a scream of grief and despair that it is impossible to describe. When I had got out of danger I stopped awhile to pick out the arrows that stuck in my hands and face, and rubbed on some of the same ointment that was given me at my arrival. I then took off my spectacles, and after waiting about an hour, till the tide was a little fallen, I waded on to the royal port of Lilliput.

The Emperor and his whole Court stood on the shore awaiting me. They saw the ships move forward in a large half-moon, but could not discern me, who, in the middle of the channel, was under water up to my neck. The Emperor concluded that I was drowned, and that the enemy's fleet was approaching in a hostile manner. But he was soon set at ease, for, the channel growing shallower every step I made, I came in a short time within hearing, and holding up the end of the cable by which the fleet was fastened, I cried in a loud voice : ' Long live the most puissant Emperor of Lilliput ! ' The Prince received me at my landing with all possible joy, and made me a *Nardal* on the spot, which is the highest title of honour among them.

His Majesty desired that I would take some opportunity to bring

all the rest of his enemy's ships into his ports, and seemed to think of nothing less than conquering the whole Empire of Blefuscu, and becoming the sole monarch of the world. But I plainly protested that I would never be the means of bringing a free and brave people into slavery; and though the wisest of the Ministers were of my opinion, my open refusal was so opposed to his Majesty's ambition that he could never forgive me. And from this time a plot began between himself and those of his Ministers who were my enemies, that nearly ended in my utter destruction.

About three weeks after this exploit there arrived an embassy from Blefuscu, with humble offers of peace, which was soon concluded, on terms very advantageous to our Emperor. There were six ambassadors, with a train of about five hundred persons, all very magnificent. Having been privately told that I had befriended them, they made me a visit, and paying me many compliments on my valour and generosity, invited me to their kingdom in the Emperor their master's name. I asked them to present my most humble respects to the Emperor their master, whose royal person I resolved to attend before I returned to my own country. Accordingly, the next time I had the honour to see our Emperor I desired his general permission to visit the Blefuscudian monarch. This he granted me, but in a very cold manner, of which I afterwards learned the reason.

When I was just preparing to pay my respects to the Emperor of Blefuscu, a distinguished person at Court, to whom I had once done a great service, came to my house very privately at night, and without sending his name desired admission. I put his lordship into my coat pocket, and, giving orders to a trusty servant to admit no one, I fastened the door, placed my visitor on the table, and sat down by it. His lordship's face was full of trouble; and he asked me to hear him with patience, in a matter that highly concerned my honour and my life.

'You are aware,' he said, 'that Skyresh Bolgolam has been your mortal enemy ever since your arrival, and his hatred is increased since your great success against Blefuscu, by which his glory as admiral is obscured. This lord and others have accused you of treason, and several councils have been called in the most private manner on your account. Out of gratitude for your favours I procured information of the whole proceedings, venturing my head for your service, and this was the charge against you:

'First, that you, having brought the imperial fleet of Blefuscu into the royal port, were commanded by his Majesty to seize all the other ships, and to put to death all the Bigendian exiles, and also all the people of the empire who would not immediately consent to break their eggs at the smaller end. And that, like a false traitor to his Most Serene Majesty, you excused yourself from the service on pretence of unwillingness to force the consciences and destroy the liberties and lives of an innocent people.

'Again, when ambassadors arrived from the Court of Blefuscu, like a false traitor, you aided and entertained them, though you knew them to be servants of a prince lately in open war against his Imperial Majesty.

'Moreover, you are now preparing, contrary to the duty of a faithful subject, to voyage to the Court of Blefuscu.

'In the debate on this charge,' my friend continued, 'his Majesty often urged the services you had done him, while the admiral and treasurer insisted that you should be put to a shameful death. But Reldresal, secretary for private affairs, who has always proved himself your friend, suggested that if his Majesty would please to spare your life and only give orders to put out both your eyes, justice might in some measure be satisfied. At this Bolgolam rose up in fury, wondering how the secretary dared desire to preserve the life of a traitor ; and the treasurer, pointing out the expense of keeping you, also urged your death. But his Majesty was graciously pleased to say that since the council thought the loss of your eyes too easy a punishment, some other might afterwards be inflicted. And the secretary, humbly desiring to be heard again, said that as to expense your allowance might be gradually lessened, so that, for want of sufficient food you should grow weak and faint, and die in a few months, when his Majesty's subjects might cut your flesh from your bones and bury it, leaving the skeleton for the admiration of posterity.

'Thus, through the great friendship of the secretary, the affair was arranged. It was commanded that the plan of starving you by degrees should be kept a secret ; but the sentence of putting out your eyes was entered on the books. In three days your friend the secretary will come to your house and read the accusation before you, and point out the great mercy of his Majesty, that only con- demns you to the loss of your eyes—which, he does not doubt, you will submit to humbly and gratefully. Twenty of his Majesty's surgeons will attend, to see the operation well performed, by dis- charging very sharp-pointed arrows into the balls of your eyes as you lie on the ground.

'I leave you,' said my friend, 'to consider what measures you will take ; and, to escape suspicion, I must immediately return, as secretly as I came.'

His lordship did so ; and I remained alone, in great perplexity. At first I was bent on resistance; for while I had liberty I could easily with stones pelt the metropolis to pieces; but I soon rejected that idea with horror, remembering the oath I had made to the Emperor, and the favours I had received from him. At last, having his Majesty's leave to pay my respects to the Emperor of Blefuscu, I resolved to take this opportunity. Before the three days had passed I wrote a letter to my friend the secretary telling him of my resolution; and, without waiting for an answer, went to the coast, and entering the channel, between wading and swimming reached the port of Blefuscu, where the people, who had long expected me, led me to the capital.

His Majesty, with the royal family and great officers of the Court, came out to receive me, and they entertained me in a manner suited to the generosity of so great a prince. I did not, however, mention my disgrace with the Emperor of Lilliput, since I did not suppose that prince would disclose the secret while I was out of his power. But in this, it soon appeared, I was deceived.

CHAPTER V.

THREE days after my arrival, walking out of curiosity to the northeast coast of the island, I observed at some distance in the sea something that looked like a boat overturned. I pulled off my shoes and stockings, and wading two or three hundred yards, I plainly saw it to be a real boat, which I supposed might by some tempest have been driven from a ship. I returned immediately to the city for help, and after a huge amount of labour I managed to get my boat to the royal port of Blefuscu, where a great crowd of people appeared, full of wonder at the sight of so prodigious a vessel. I told the Emperor that my good fortune had thrown this boat in my way to carry me to some place whence I might return to my native country, and begged his orders for materials to fit it up, and leave to depart—which, after many kindly speeches, he was pleased to grant.

Meanwhile the Emperor of Lilliput, uneasy at my long absence (but never imagining that I had the least notice of his designs) sent a person of rank to inform the Emperor of Blefuscu of my disgrace; this messenger had orders to represent the great mercy of his master, who was content to punish me with the loss of my eyes, and who expected that his brother of Blefuscu would have me sent back to Lilliput, bound hand and foot, to be punished as a traitor. The Emperor of Blefuscu answered with many civil excuses. He said that as for sending me bound, his brother knew it was impossible. Moreover, though I had taken away his fleet he was grateful to me for many good offices I had done him in making the peace. But that both their Majesties would soon be made easy; for I had found a prodigious vessel on the shore, able to carry me on the sea, which he had given orders to fit up; and he hoped in a few weeks both empires would be free from me.

With this answer the messenger returned to Lilliput; and I

(though the monarch of Blefuscu secretly offered me his gracious protection if I would continue in his service) hastened my departure, resolving never more to put confidence in princes.

In about a month I was ready to take leave. The Emperor of Blefuscu, with the Empress and the royal family, came out of the palace; and I lay down on my face to kiss their hands, which they graciously gave me. His Majesty presented me with fifty purses of sprugs (their greatest gold coin) and his picture at full length, which I put immediately into one of my gloves, to keep it from being hurt. Many other ceremonies took place at my departure.

I stored the boat with meat and drink, and took six cows and two bulls alive, with as many ewes and rams, intending to carry them into my own country; and to feed them on board, I had a good bundle of hay and a bag of corn. I would gladly have taken a dozen of the natives; but this was a thing the Emperor would by no means permit, and besides a diligent search into my pockets, his Majesty pledged my honour not to carry away any of his subjects, though with their own consent and desire.

Having thus prepared all things as well as I was able, I set sail. When I had made twenty-four leagues, by my reckoning, from the island of Blefuscu, I saw a sail steering to the north-east. I hailed her, but could get no answer; yet I found I gained upon her, for the wind slackened; and in half an hour she spied me, and discharged a gun. I came up with her between five and six in the evening, Sept. 26, 1701; but my heart leaped within me to see her English colours. I put my cows and sheep into my coat pockets, and got on board with all my little cargo. The captain received me with kindness, and asked me to tell him what place I came from last; but at my answer he thought I was raving. However, I took my black cattle and sheep out of my pocket, which, after great astonishment, clearly convinced him.

We arrived in England on the 13th of April, 1702. I stayed two months with my wife and family; but my eager desire to see foreign countries would suffer me to remain no longer. However, while in England I made great profit by showing my cattle to persons of quality and others; and before I began my second voyage I sold them for 600*l*. I left 1,500*l*. with my wife, and fixed her in a good house; then, taking leave of her and my boy and girl, with tears on both sides, I sailed on board the ' Adventure.' [1]

[1] Swift.

THE PRINCESS ON THE GLASS HILL

ONCE upon a time there was a man who had a meadow which lay on the side of a mountain, and in the meadow there was a barn in which he stored hay. But there had not been much hay in the barn for the last two years, for every St. John's eve, when the grass was in the height of its vigour, it was all eaten clean up, just as if a whole flock of sheep had gnawed it down to the ground during the night. This happened once, and it happened twice, but then the man got tired of losing his crop, and said to his sons—he had three of them, and the third was called Cinderlad—that one of them must go and sleep in the barn on St. John's night, for it was absurd to let the grass be eaten up again, blade and stalk, as it had been the last two years, and the one who went to watch must keep a sharp look-out, the man said.

The eldest was quite willing to go to the meadow; he would watch the grass, he said, and he would do it so well that neither man, nor beast, nor even the devil himself should have any of it. So when evening came he went to the barn, and lay down to sleep, but when night was drawing near there was such a rumbling and such an earthquake that the walls and roof shook again, and the lad jumped up and took to his heels as fast as he could, and never even looked back, and the barn remained empty that year just as it had been for the last two.

Next St. John's eve the man again said that he could not go on in this way, losing all the grass in the outlying field year after year, and that one of his sons must just go there and watch it, and watch well too. So the next oldest son was willing to show what he could do. He went to the barn and lay down to sleep, as his brother had done; but when night was drawing near there was a great rumbling, and then an earthquake, which was even worse than that on the former St. John's night, and when the youth heard it he was terrified, and went off, running as if for a wager.

The year after, it was Cinderlad's turn, but when he made ready to go the others laughed at him, and mocked him. 'Well, you are just the right one to watch the hay, you who have never learnt anything but how to sit among the ashes and bake yourself!' said they. Cinderlad, however, did not trouble himself about what they said, but when evening drew near rambled away to the outlying field. When he got there he went into the barn and lay down, but in about an hour's time the rumbling and creaking began, and it was frightful to hear it. 'Well, if it gets no worse than that, I can manage to stand it,' thought Cinderlad. In a little time the creaking began

again, and the earth quaked so that all the hay flew about the boy. 'Oh! if it gets no worse than that I can manage to stand it,' thought Cinderlad. But then came a third rumbling, and a third earthquake, so violent that the boy thought the walls and roof had fallen down, but when that was over everything suddenly grew as still as death around him. 'I am pretty sure that it will come again,' thought Cinderlad; but no, it did not. Everything was quiet, and everything stayed quiet, and when he had lain still a short time he heard something that sounded as if a horse were standing chewing just outside the barn door. He stole away to the door, which was ajar, to see what was there, and a horse was standing eating. It was so big, and fat, and fine a horse that Cinderlad had never seen one like it before, and a saddle and bridle lay upon it, and a complete suit of armour for a knight, and everything was of copper, and so bright that it shone again. 'Ha, ha! it is thou who eatest up our hay then,' thought the boy; 'but I will stop that.' So he made haste, and took out his steel for striking fire, and threw it over the horse, and then it had no power to stir from the spot, and became so tame that the boy could do what he liked with it. So he mounted it and rode away to a place which no one knew of but himself, and there he tied it up. When he went home again his brothers laughed and asked how he had got on.

'You didn't lie long in the barn, if even you have been so far as the field!' said they.

'I lay in the barn till the sun rose, but I saw nothing and heard nothing, not I,' said the boy. 'God knows what there was to make you two so frightened.'

'Well, we shall soon see whether you have watched the meadow or not,' answered the brothers, but when they got there the grass was all standing just as long and as thick as it had been the night before.

The next St. John's eve it was the same thing once again: neither of the two brothers dared to go to the outlying field to watch the crop, but Cinderlad went, and everything happened exactly the same as on the previous St. John's eve : first there was a rumbling and an earthquake, and then there was another, and then a third; but all three earthquakes were much, very much more violent than they had been the year before. Then everything became still as death again, and the boy heard something chewing outside the barn door, so he stole as softly as he could to the door, which was slightly ajar, and again there was a horse standing close by the wall of the house, eating and chewing, and it was far larger and fatter than the first horse, and it had a saddle on its back, and a bridle was on it too, and a full suit of armour for a knight, all of bright silver, and as beautiful as anyone could wish to see. 'Ho, ho!' thought the boy, 'is it thou who eatest up our hay in the night? but I will put a stop to that.' So he took out his steel for striking fire, and threw it over the horse's mane, and the beast stood there as quiet as a lamb. Then the boy rode this horse, too, away to the place where he kept the other, and then went home again.

'I suppose you will tell us that you have watched well again this time,' said the brothers.

'Well, so I have,' said Cinderlad. So they went there again, and there the grass was, standing as high and as thick as it had been before, but that did not make them any kinder to Cinderlad.

When the third St. John's night came neither of the two elder brothers dared to lie in the outlying barn to watch the grass, for they had been so heartily frightened the night that they had slept there that they could not get over it, but Cinderlad dared to go, and everything happened just the same as on the two former nights. There were three earthquakes, each worse than the other, and the last flung the boy from one wall of the barn to the other, but then everything suddenly became still as death. When he had lain quietly a short time, he heard something chewing outside the barn door; then he once more stole to the door, which was slightly ajar, and behold, a horse was standing just outside it, which was much larger and fatter than the two others he had caught. 'Ho, ho! it is thou, then, who art eating up our hay this time,' thought the boy; 'but I will put a stop to that.' So he pulled out his steel for striking fire, and threw it over the horse, and it stood as still as if it had been nailed to the field, and the boy could do just what he liked with it. Then he mounted it and rode away to the place where he had the two others, and then he went home again. Then the two brothers mocked him just as they had done before, and told him that they could see that he must have watched the grass very carefully that night, for he looked just as if he were walking in his sleep; but Cinderlad did not trouble himself about that, but just bade them go to the field and see. They did go, and this time too the grass was standing, looking as fine and as thick as ever.

The King of the country in which Cinderlad's father dwelt had a daughter whom he would give to no one who could not ride up to the top of the glass hill, for there was a high, high hill of glass, slippery as ice, and it was close to the King's palace. Upon the very top of this the King's daughter was to sit with three gold apples in her lap, and the man who could ride up and take the three golden apples should marry her, and have half the kingdom. The King had this proclaimed in every church in the whole kingdom, and in many other kingdoms too. The Princess was very beautiful, and all who saw her fell violently in love with her, even in spite of themselves. So it is needless to say that all the princes and knights were eager to win her, and half the kingdom besides, and that for this cause they came riding thither from the very end of the world, dressed so splendidly that their raiments gleamed in the sunshine, and riding on horses which seemed to dance as they went, and there was not one of these princes who did not think that he was sure to win the Princess.

When the day appointed by the King had come, there was such a host of knights and princes under the glass hill that they seemed to swarm, and everyone who could walk or even creep was there too, to see who won the King's daughter. Cinderlad's two brothers were there too, but they would not hear of letting him go with them, for he was so dirty and black with sleeping and grubbing among the ashes that they said everyone would laugh at them if they were seen in the company of such an oaf.

' Well, then, I will go all alone by myself,' said Cinderlad.

When the two brothers got to the glass hill, all the princes and knights were trying to ride up it, and their horses were in a foam ; but it was all in vain, for no sooner did the horses set foot upon the hill than down they slipped, and there was not one which could get even so much as a couple of yards up. Nor was that strange, for the hill was as smooth as glass window-pane, and as steep as the side of a house. But they were all eager to win the King's daughter and half the kingdom, so they rode and they slipped, and thus it went on. At length all the horses were so tired that they could do no more, and so hot that the foam dropped from them and the riders were forced to give up the attempt. The King was just thinking that he would cause it to be proclaimed that the riding should begin afresh on the following day, when perhaps it might go better, when suddenly a knight came riding up on so fine a horse that no one had ever seen the like of it before, and the knight had armour of copper, and his bridle was of copper too, and all his ac-coutrements were so bright that they shone again. The other knights all called out to him that he might just as well spare him-self the trouble of trying to ride up the glass hill, for it was of no use to try ; but he did not heed them, and rode straight off to it, and went up as if it were nothing at all. Thus he rode for a long way—it may have been a third part of the way up—but when he had got so far he turned his horse round and rode down again. But the Princess thought that she had never yet seen so handsome a knight, and while he was riding up she was sitting thinking : ' Oh ! how I hope he may be able to come up to the top ! ' And when she saw that he was turning his horse back she threw one of the golden apples down after him, and it rolled into his shoe. But when he had come down from off the hill he rode away, and that so fast that no one knew what had become of him.

So all the princes and knights were bidden to present themselves before the King that night, so that he who had ridden so far up the glass hill might show the golden apple which the King's daughter had thrown down. But no one had anything to show. One knight presented himself after the other, and none could show the apple.

At night, too, Cinderlad's brothers came home again and had a long story to tell about the riding up the glass hill. At first, they said, there was not one who was able to get even so much as one step up, but then came a knight who had armour of copper, and a bridle of copper, and his armour and trappings were so bright that they shone to a great distance, and it was something like a sight to see him riding. He rode one-third of the way up the glass hill, and he could easily have ridden the whole of it if he had liked; but he had turned back, for he had made up his mind that that was enough for once. 'Oh! I should have liked to see him too, that I should,' said Cinderlad, who was as usual sitting by the chimney among the cinders. 'You indeed!' said the brothers, 'you look as if you were fit to be among such great lords, nasty beast that you are to sit there!'

Next day the brothers were for setting out again, and this time too Cinderlad begged them to let him go with them and see who rode; but no, they said he was not fit to do that, for he was much too ugly and dirty. 'Well, well, then I will go all alone by myself,' said Cinderlad. So the brothers went to the glass hill, and all the princes and knights began to ride again, and this time they had taken care to rough the shoes of their horses; but that did not help them: they rode and they slipped as they had done the day before, and not one of them could even get so far as a yard up the hill. When they had tired out their horses, so that they could do no more, they again had to stop altogether. But just as the King was thinking that it would be well to proclaim that the riding should take place next day for the last time, so that they might have one more chance, he suddenly bethought himself that it would be well to wait a little longer to see if the knight in copper armour would come on this day too. But nothing was to be seen of him. Just as they were still looking for him, however, came a knight riding on a steed that was much, much finer than that which the knight in copper armour had ridden, and this knight had silver armour and a silver saddle and bridle, and all were so bright that they

shone and glistened when he was a long way off. Again the other
knights called to him, and said that he might just as well give up
the attempt to ride up the glass hill, for it was useless to try ; but
the knight paid no heed to that, but rode straight away to the glass
hill, and went still farther up than the knight in copper armour
had gone ; but when he had ridden two-thirds of the way up he

turned his horse round, and rode down again. The Princess liked
this knight still better than she had liked the other, and sat longing
that he might be able to get up above, and when she saw him turning back she threw the second apple after him, and it rolled into
his shoe, and as soon as he had got down the glass hill he rode
away so fast that no one could see what had become of him.

In the evening, when everyone was to appear before the King and Princess, in order that he who had the golden apple might show it, one knight went in after the other, but none of them had a golden apple to show.

At night the two brothers went home as they had done the night before, and told how things had gone, and how everyone had ridden, but no one had been able to get up the hill. 'But last of all,' they said, ' came one in silver armour, and he had a silver bridle on his horse, and a silver saddle, and oh, but he could ride! He took his horse two-thirds of the way up the hill, but then he turned back. He was a fine fellow,' said the brothers, ' and the Princess threw the second golden apple to him ! '

' Oh, how I should have liked to see him too ! ' said Cinderlad.

' Oh, indeed ! He was a little brighter than the ashes that you sit grubbing among, you dirty black creature ! ' said the brothers.

On the third day everything went just as on the former days. Cinderlad wanted to go with them to look at the riding, but the two brothers would not have him in their company, and when they got to the glass hill there was no one who could ride even so far as a yard up it, and everyone waited for the knight in silver armour, but he was neither to be seen nor heard of. At last, after a long time, came a knight riding upon a horse that was such a fine one, its equal had never yet been seen. The knight had golden armour, and the horse a golden saddle and bridle, and these were all so bright that they shone and dazzled everyone, even while the knight was still at a great distance. The other princes and knights were not able even to call to tell him how useless it was to try to ascend the hill, so amazed were they at the sight of his magnificence. He rode straight away to the glass hill, and galloped up it as if it were no hill at all, so that the Princess had not even time to wish that he might get up the whole way. As soon as he had ridden to the top, he took the third golden apple from the lap of the Princess, and then turned his horse about and rode down again, and vanished from their sight before anyone was able to say a word to him.

When the two brothers came home again at night, they had much to tell of how the riding had gone off that day, and at last they told about the knight in the golden armour too. 'He was a fine fellow, that was ! Such another splendid knight is not to be found on earth ! ' said the brothers.

' Oh, how I should have liked to see him too ! ' said Cinderlad.

' Well, he shone nearly as brightly as the coal-heaps that thou art always lying raking amongst, dirty black creature that thou art!' said the brothers.

Next day all the knights and princes were to appear before the King and the Princess—it had been too late for them to do it the night before—in order that he who had the golden apple might produce it. They all went in turn, first princes, and then knights, but none of them had a golden apple.

'But somebody must have it,' said the King, 'for with our own eyes we all saw a man ride up and take it. So he commanded that everyone in the kingdom should come to the palace, and see if he could show the apple. And one after the other they all came, but no one had the golden apple, and after a long, long time Cinderlad's two brothers came likewise. They were the last of all, so the King inquired of them if there was no one else in the kingdom left to come.

' Oh ! yes, we have a brother,' said the two, ' but he never got the golden apple ! He never left the cinder-heap on any of the three days.'

' Never mind that,' said the King ; ' as everyone else has come to the palace, let him come too.'

So Cinderlad was forced to go to the King's palace.

' Hast thou the golden apple ? ' asked the King.

' Yes, here is the first, and here is the second, and here is the third, too,' said Cinderlad, and he took all the three apples out of his pocket, and with that threw off his sooty rags, and appeared there before them in his bright golden armour, which gleamed as he stood.

' Thou shalt have my daughter, and the half of my kingdom, and thou hast well earned both ! ' said the King. So there was a wedding, and Cinderlad got the King's daughter, and everyone made merry at the wedding, for all of them could make merry, though they could not ride up the glass hill, and if they have not left off their merry-making they must be at it still.[1]

[1] Asbjornsen and Möe.

THE STORY OF PRINCE AHMED AND THE
FAIRY PARIBANOU

THERE was a sultan, who had three sons and a niece. The eldest of the Princes was called Houssain, the second Ali, the youngest Ahmed, and the Princess, his niece, Nouronnihar.

The Princess Nouronnihar was the daughter of the younger brother of the Sultan, who died, and left the Princess very young. The Sultan took upon himself the care of his daughter's education, and brought her up in his palace with the three Princes, proposing to marry her when she arrived at a proper age, and to contract an alliance with some neighbouring prince by that means. But when he perceived that the three Princes his sons loved her passionately, he thought more seriously on that affair. He was very much concerned; the difficulty he foresaw was to make them agree, and that the two youngest should consent to yield her up to their elder brother. As he found them positively obstinate, he sent for them all together, and said to them : ' Children, since for your good and quiet I have not been able to persuade you no longer to aspire to the Princess, your cousin, I think it would not be amiss if every one travelled separately into different countries, so that you might not meet each other. And, as you know I am very curious, and delight in everything that's singular, I promise my niece in marriage to him that shall bring me the most extraordinary rarity; and for the purchase of the rarity you shall go in search after, and the expense of travelling, I will give you every one a sum of money.'

As the three Princes were always submissive and obedient to the Sultan's will, and each flattered himself fortune might prove favourable to him, they all consented to it. The Sultan paid them the money he promised them ; and that very day they gave orders for the preparations for their travels, and took their leaves of the Sultan, that they might be the more ready to go the next morning. Accordingly they all set out at the same gate of the city, each dressed like a merchant, attended by an officer of confidence dressed like a slave, and all well mounted and equipped. They went the first day's journey together, and lay all at an inn, where the road was divided into three different tracts. At night, when they were at supper together, they all agreed to travel for a year, and to meet at that inn; and that the first that came should wait for the rest; that, as they had all three taken their leaves together of the Sultan, they might all return together. The next morning by break of day, after they had embraced and wished each other good success, they mounted their horses and took each a different road.

Prince Houssain, the eldest brother, arrived at Bisnagar, the capital of the kingdom of that name, and the residence of its king. He went and lodged at a khan appointed for foreign merchants; and, having learnt that there were four principal divisions where merchants of all sorts sold their commodities, and kept shops, and in the midst of which stood the castle, or rather the King's palace, he went to one of these divisions the next day.

Prince Houssain could not view this division without admiration. It was large, and divided into several streets, all vaulted and shaded from the sun, and yet very light too. The shops were all of a size, and all that dealt in the same sort of goods lived in one street; as also the handicrafts-men, who kept their shops in the smaller streets.

The multitude of shops, stocked with all sorts of merchandises, as the finest linens from several parts of India, some painted in the most lively colours, and representing beasts, trees, and flowers; silks and brocades from Persia, China, and other places, porcelain both from Japan and China, and tapestries, surprised him so much that he knew not how to believe his own eyes; but when he came to the goldsmiths and jewellers he was in a kind of ecstacy to behold such prodigious quantities of wrought gold and silver, and was dazzled by the lustre of the pearls, diamonds, rubies, emeralds, and other jewels exposed to sale.

Another thing Prince Houssain particularly admired was the great number of rose-sellers who crowded the streets; for the Indians are so great lovers of that flower that not one will stir without a nosegay in his hand or a garland on his head; and the merchants keep them in pots in their shops, that the air is perfectly perfumed.

After Prince Houssain had run through that division, street by street, his thoughts fully employed on the riches he had seen, he was very much tired, which a merchant perceiving civilly invited him to sit down in his shop, and he accepted; but had not been sat down long before he saw a crier pass by with a piece of tapestry on his arm, about six feet square, and cried at thirty purses. The Prince called to the crier, and asked to see the tapestry, which seemed to him to be valued at an exorbitant price, not only for the size of it, but the meanness of the stuff; when he had examined it well, he told the crier that he could not comprehend how so

small a piece of tapestry, and of so indifferent appearance, could be set at so high a price.

The crier, who took him for a merchant replied: 'If this price seems so extravagant to you, your amazement will be greater when I tell you I have orders to raise it to forty purses, and not to part with it under.' 'Certainly,' answered Prince Houssain, 'it must have something very extraordinary in it, which I know nothing of.' 'You have guessed it, sir,' replied the crier, 'and will own it when you come to know that whoever sits on this piece of tapestry may be transported in an instant wherever he desires to be, without being stopped by any obstacle.'

At this discourse of the crier the Prince of the Indies, considering that the principal motive of his travel was to carry the Sultan, his father, home some singular rarity, thought that he could not meet with any which could give him more satisfaction. ' If the tapestry,' said he to the crier, ' has the virtue you assign it, I shall not think forty purses too much, but shall make you a present besides.' ' Sir,' replied the crier, 'I have told you the truth; and it is an easy matter to convince you of it, as soon as you have made the bargain for forty purses, on condition I show you the experiment. But, as I suppose you have not so much about you, and to receive them I must go with you to your khan, where you lodge, with the leave of the master of the shop, we will go into the back shop, and I will spread the tapestry; and when we have both sat down, and you have formed the wish to be transported into your apartment of the khan, if we are not transported thither it shall be no bargain, and you shall be at your liberty. As to your present, though I am paid for my trouble by the seller, I shall receive it as a favour, and be very much obliged to you, and thankful.'

On the credit of the crier, the Prince accepted the conditions, and concluded the bargain; and, having got the master's leave, they went into his back shop; they both sat down on it, and as soon as the Prince formed his wish to be transported into his apartment at the khan he presently found himself and the crier there; and, as he wanted not a more sufficient proof of the virtue of the tapestry, he counted the crier out forty purses of gold, and gave him twenty pieces for himself.

In this manner Prince Houssain became the possessor of the tapestry, and was overjoyed that at his arrival at Bisnagar he had found so rare a piece, which he never disputed would gain him the hand of Nouronnihar. In short, he looked upon it as an impossible thing for the Princes his younger brothers to meet with anything to be compared with it. It was in his power, by sitting on his tapestry, to be at the place of meeting that very day; but, as he was obliged to stay there for his brothers, as they had agreed, and as he was curious to see the King of Bisnagar and his Court, and to inform himself of the strength, laws, customs, and religion of the kingdom, he chose to make a longer abode there, and to spend some months in satisfying his curiosity.

Prince Houssain might have made a longer abode in the kingdom and Court of Bisnagar, but he was so eager to be nearer the Princess that, spreading the tapestry, he and the officer he had brought with him sat down, and as soon as he had formed his wish were transported to the inn at which he and his brothers were to meet, and where he passed for a merchant till they came.

Prince Ali, Prince Houssain's second brother, who designed to travel into Persia, took the road, having three days after he parted with his brothers joined a caravan, and after four days' travel arrived at Schiraz, which was the capital of the kingdom of Persia. Here he passed for a jeweller.

The next morning Prince Ali, who travelled only for his pleasure, and had brought nothing but just necessaries along with him, after he had dressed himself, took a walk into that part of the town which they at Schiraz called the bezestein.

Among all the criers who passed backwards and forwards with several sorts of goods, offering to sell them, he was not a little surprised to see one who held an ivory telescope in his hand of about a foot in length and the thickness of a man's thumb, and cried it at thirty purses. At first he thought the crier mad, and to inform himself went to a shop, and said to the merchant, who stood at the door: ' Pray, sir, is not that man ' (pointing to the crier who cried the ivory perspective glass at thirty purses) ' mad ? If he is not, I am very much deceived.' ' Indeed, sir,' answered the merchant, ' he was in his right senses yesterday; and I can assure you he is one of the ablest criers we have, and the most employed of any when anything valuable is to be sold. And if he cries the ivory perspective glass at thirty purses it must be worth as much or more, on some account or other. He will come by presently, and we will call him, and you shall be satisfied ; in the meantime sit down on my sofa, and rest yourself.'

Prince Ali accepted the merchant's obliging offer, and presently afterwards the crier passed by. The merchant called him by his name, and, pointing to the Prince, said to him : ' Tell that gentleman, who asked me if you were in your right senses, what you mean by crying that ivory perspective glass, which seems not to be worth much, at thirty purses. I should be very much amazed myself if I did not know you.' The crier, addressing himself to Prince Ali, said : ' Sir, you are not the only person that takes me for a madman on the account of this perspective glass. You shall judge yourself whether I am or no, when I have told you its property : and I hope you will value it at as high a price as those I have showed it to already, who had as bad an opinion of me as you.

' First, sir,' pursued the crier, presenting the ivory pipe to the

Prince, ' observe that this pipe is furnished with a glass at both ends ; and consider that by looking through one of them you see whatever object you wish to behold.' ' I am,' said the Prince, ' ready to make you all imaginable reparation for the scandal I have thrown on you if you will make the truth of what you advance appear,' and as he had the ivory pipe in his hand, after he had looked at the two glasses he said : ' Show me at which of these ends I must look that I may be satisfied.' The crier presently showed him, and he looked through, wishing at the same time to see the Sultan his father, whom he

immediately beheld in perfect health, set on his throne, in the midst of his council. Afterwards, as there was nothing in the world so dear to him, after the Sultan, as the Princess Nouronnihar, he wished to see her ; and saw her at her toilet laughing, and in a pleasant humour, with her women about her.

Prince Ali wanted no other proof to be persuaded that this perspective glass was the most valuable thing in the world, and believed that if he should neglect to purchase it he should never meet again with such another rarity. He therefore took the crier with him to the khan where he lodged, and told him out the money, and received the perspective glass.

Prince Ali was over-joyed at his bargain, and persuaded himself that, as his brothers would not be able to meet with anything so rare and admirable, the Princess Nouronnihar would be the recompense of his fatigue and trouble; that he thought of nothing but visiting the Court of Persia incognito, and seeing whatever was curious in Schiraz and thereabouts, till the caravan with which he came returned back to the Indies. As soon as the caravan was ready to set out, the Prince joined them, and arrived happily without any accident or trouble, otherwise than the length of the journey and fatigue of travelling, at the place of rendezvous, where he found Prince Houssain, and both waited for Prince Ahmed.

Prince Ahmed, who took the road of Samarcand, the next day after his arrival there went, as his brothers had done, into the bezestein, where he had not walked long but heard a crier, who had an artificial apple in his hand, cry it at five and thirty purses; upon which he stopped the crier, and said to him: ' Let me see that apple, and tell me what virtue and extraordinary properties it has, to be valued at so high a rate.' ' Sir,' said the crier, giving it into his hand, ' if you look at the outside of this apple, it is very worthless, but if you consider its properties, virtues, and the great use and benefit it is of to mankind, you will say it is no price for it, and that he who possesses it is master of a great treasure. In short, it cures all sick persons of the most mortal diseases; and if the patient is dying it will recover him immediately and restore him to perfect health; and this is done after the easiest manner in the world, which is by the patient's smelling the apple.'

' If I may believe you,' replied Prince Ahmed, ' the virtues of this apple are wonderful, and it is invaluable ; but what ground have I, for all you tell me, to be persuaded of the truth of this matter ? ' ' Sir,' replied the crier, ' the thing is known and averred by the whole city of Samarcand; but, without going any farther, ask all these merchants you see here, and hear what they say. You will find several of them will tell you they had not been alive this day if they had not made use of this excellent remedy. And, that you may the better comprehend what it is, I must tell you it is the fruit of the study and experiments of a celebrated philosopher of this city, who applied himself all his lifetime to the study and knowledge of the virtues of plants and minerals, and at last attained to this composition, by which he performed such surprising cures in this town as will never be forgot, but died suddenly himself, before he could apply his sovereign remedy, and left his wife and a great many young children behind him, in very indifferent circumstances, who, to support her family and provide for her children, is resolved to sell it.'

While the crier informed Prince Ahmed of the virtues of the artificial apple, a great many persons came about them and confirmed what he said; and one among the rest said he had a friend

dangerously ill, whose life was despaired of: and that was a favourable opportunity to show Prince Ahmed the experiment. Upon which Prince Ahmed told the crier he would give him forty purses if he cured the sick person.

The crier, who had orders to sell it at that price, said to Prince Ahmed: 'Come, sir, let us go and make the experiment, and the apple shall be yours; and I can assure you that it will always have the desired effect.' In short, the experiment succeeded, and the Prince, after he had counted out to the crier forty purses, and he had delivered the apple to him, waited patiently for the first caravan that should return to the Indies, and arrived in perfect health at the inn where the Princes Houssain and Ali waited for him.

When the princes met they showed each other their treasures, and immediately saw through the glass that the Princess was dying. They then sat down on the carpet, wished themselves with her, and were there in a moment.

Prince Ahmed no sooner perceived himself in Nouronnihar's chamber than he rose off the tapestry, as did also the other two Princes, and went to the bedside, and put the apple under her nose; some moments after the Princess opened her eyes, and turned her head from one side to another, looking at the persons who stood about her; and then rose up in the bed, and asked to be dressed, just as if she had waked out of a sound sleep. Her women having presently informed her, in a manner that showed their joy, that she was obliged to the three Princes for the sudden recovery of her health, and particularly to Prince Ahmed, she immediately expressed her joy to see them, and thanked them all together, and afterwards Prince Ahmed in particular.

While the Princess was dressing the Princes went to throw themselves at the Sultan their father's feet, and pay their respects to him. But when they came before him they found he had been informed of their arrival by the chief of the Princess's eunuchs, and by what means the Princess had been perfectly cured. The Sultan received and embraced them with the greatest joy, both for their return and the recovery of the Princess his niece, whom he loved as well as if she had been his own daughter, and who had been given over by the physicians. After the usual ceremonies and compliments the Princes presented each his rarity : Prince Houssain his tapestry, which he had taken care not to leave behind him in the Princess's chamber ; Prince Ali his ivory perspective glass, and Prince Ahmed his artificial apple : and after each had commended their present, when they put it into the Sultan's hands, they begged of him to pronounce their fate, and declare to which of them he would give the Princess Nouronnihar for a wife, according to his promise.

The Sultan of the Indies, having heard, without interrupting them, all that the Princes could represent further about their rarities, and being well informed of what had happened in relation to the Princess Nouronnihar's cure, remained some time silent, as if he were thinking on what answer he should make. At last he

broke silence, and said to them : ' I would declare for one of you
children with a great deal of pleasure if I could do it with justice :
but consider whether I can do it or no. 'Tis true, Prince Ahmed,
the Princess my niece is obliged to your artificial apple for her cure ;
but I must ask you whether or no you could have been so service-
able to her if you had not known by Prince Ali's perspective glass
the danger she was in, and if Prince Houssain's tapestry had not
brought you so soon. Your perspective glass, Prince Ali, informed
you and your brothers that you were like to lose the Princess your
cousin, and there you must own a great obligation.

' You must also grant that that knowledge would have been of
no service without the artificial apple and the tapestry. And lastly,
Prince Houssain, the Princess would be very ungrateful if she
should not show her acknowledgment of the service of your tapestry,
which was so necessary a means towards her cure. But consider,
it would have been of little use if you had not been acquainted with
the Princess's illness by Prince Ali's glass, and Prince Ahmed had
not applied his artificial apple. Therefore, as neither tapestry, ivory
perspective glass, nor artificial apple have the least preference one
before the other, but, on the contrary, there's a perfect equality, I
cannot grant the Princess to any one of you ; and the only fruit you
have reaped from your travels is the glory of having equally con-
tributed to restore her health.

' If all this be true,' added the Sultan, ' you see that I must have
recourse to other means to determine certainly in the choice I ought
to make among you ; and that, as there is time enough between this
and night, I'll do it to-day. Go and get each of you a bow and
arrow, and repair to the great plain, where they exercise horses.
I'll soon come to you ; and declare I will give the Princess Nouronnihar to him that shoots the farthest.'

The three Princes had nothing to say against the decision of the
Sultan. When they were out of his presence they each provided
themselves with a bow and arrow, which they delivered to one of
their officers, and went to the plain appointed, followed by a great
concourse of people.

The Sultan did not make them wait long for him, and as soon as
he arrived Prince Houssain, as the eldest, took his bow and arrow
and shot first ; Prince Ali shot next, and much beyond him ; and
Prince Ahmed last of all, but it so happened that nobody could see
where his arrow fell ; and, nothwithstanding all the diligence that
was used by himself and everybody else, it was not to be found far

or near. And though it was believed that he shot the farthest, and that he therefore deserved the Princess Nouronnihar, it was, however, necessary that his arrow should be found to make the matter more evident and certain ; and, notwithstanding his remonstrance, the Sultan judged in favour of Prince Ali, and gave orders for preparations to be made for the wedding, which was celebrated a few days after with great magnificence.

Prince Houssain would not honour the feast with his presence. In short, his grief was so violent and insupportable that he left the

Court, and renounced all right of succession to the crown, to turn hermit.

Prince Ahmed, too, did not come to Prince Ali's and the Princess Nouronnihar's wedding, any more than his brother Houssain, but did not renounce the world as he had done. But, as he could not imagine what had become of his arrow, he stole away from his attendants and resolved to search after it, that he might not have anything to reproach himself with. With this intent he went to the place where the Princes Houssain and Ali's were gathered up, and, going straight forwards from there, looking carefully on both sides of him, he went so far that at last he began to think his labour was all in vain; but yet could not help going forwards, till he came to some steep craggy rocks, which were bounds to his journey, and were situated in a barren country, about four leagues distant from where he set out.

II.

WHEN Prince Ahmed came pretty nigh to these rocks he perceived an arrow, which he gathered up, looked earnestly at, and was in the greatest astonishment to find it was the same he shot away. ' Certainly,' said he to himself, ' neither I nor any man living could shoot an arrow so far,' and, finding it laid flat, not sticking into the ground, he judged that it rebounded against the rock. ' There must be some mystery in this,' said he to himself again, ' and it may be advantageous to me. Perhaps fortune, to make me amends for depriving me of what I thought the greatest happiness, may have reserved a greater blessing for my comfort.'

As these rocks were full of caves and some of those caves were deep, the Prince entered into one, and, looking about, cast his eyes on an iron door, which seemed to have no lock, but he feared it was fastened. However, thrusting against it, it opened, and discovered an easy descent, but no steps, which he walked down with his arrow in his hand. At first he thought he was going into a dark, obscure place, but presently a quite different light succeeded that which he came out of, and, entering into a large, spacious place, at about fifty or sixty paces distant, he perceived a magnificent palace, which he had not then time enough to look at. At the same time a lady of majestic port and air advanced as far as the porch, attended by a large troop of ladies, so finely dressed and beautiful that it was difficult to distinguish which was the mistress.

As soon as Prince Ahmed perceived the lady, he made all imaginable haste to go and pay his respects; and the lady, on her part, seeing him coming, prevented him from addressing his discourse to her first, but said to him : ' Come nearer, Prince Ahmed, you are welcome.'

It was no small surprise to the Prince to hear himself named in a place he had never heard of, though so nigh to his father's capital, and he could not comprehend how he should be known to a lady who was a stranger to him. At last he returned the lady's compliment by throwing himself at her feet, and, rising up again, said to her : ' Madam, I return you a thousand thanks for the assurance you give me of a welcome to a place where I believed my imprudent curiosity had made me penetrate too far. But, madam, may I, without being guilty of ill manners, dare to ask you by what adventure you know me ? and how you, who live in the same neighbourhood with me, should be so great a stranger to me ? ' ' Prince,' said the lady, ' let us go into the hall, there I will gratify you in your request.'

After these words the lady led Prince Ahmed into the hall. Then she sat down on a sofa, and when the Prince by her entreaty had done the same she said : ' You are surprised, you say, that I should know you and not be known by you, but you will be no longer surprised when I inform you who I am. You are undoubtedly sensible that your religion teaches you to believe that the world is inhabited by genies as well as men. I am the daughter of one of the most powerful and distinguished genies, and my name is Paribanou. The only thing that I have to add is, that you seemed to me worthy of a more happy fate than that of possessing the Princess Nouronnihar ; and, that you might attain to it, I was present when you drew your arrow, and foresaw it would not go beyond Prince Houssain's. I took it in the air, and gave it the necessary motion to strike against the rocks near which you found it, and I tell you that it lies in your power to make use of the favourable opportunity which presents itself to make you happy.'

As the Fairy Paribanou pronounced these last words with a different tone, and looked, at the same time, tenderly upon Prince Ahmed, with a modest blush on her cheeks, it was no hard matter for the Prince to comprehend what happiness she meant. He presently considered that the Princess Nouronnihar could never be his, and that the Fairy Paribanou excelled her infinitely in beauty, agreeableness, wit, and, as much as he could conjecture by the magnificence of the palace, in immense riches. He blessed the moment that he thought of seeking after his arrow a second time, and, yielding to his love : ' Madam,' replied he, ' should I all my life have the happiness of being your slave, and the admirer of the many charms which ravish my soul, I should think myself the most blest of men. Pardon in me the boldness which inspires me to ask this favour, and don't refuse to admit me into your Court, a prince who is entirely devoted to you.'

' Prince,' answered the Fairy, ' will you not pledge your faith to

me, as well as I give mine to you?' 'Yes, madam,' replied the
Prince, in an ecstacy of joy; 'what can I do better, and with greater
pleasure? Yes, my sultaness, my queen, I'll give you my heart
without the least reserve.' 'Then,' answered the Fairy, 'you are
my husband, and I am your wife. But, as I suppose,' pursued
she, 'that you have eaten nothing to-day, a slight repast shall be
served up for you, while preparations are making for our wedding
feast at night, and then I will show you the apartments of my
palace, and you shall judge if this hall is not the meanest part
of it.'

Some of the Fairy's women, who came into the hall with them,
and guessed her intentions, went immediately out, and returned
presently with some excellent meats and wines.

When Prince Ahmed had ate and drunk as much as he cared
for, the Fairy Paribanou carried him through all the apartments,
where he saw diamonds, rubies, emeralds, and all sorts of fine jewels,
intermixed with pearls, agate, jasper, porphyry, and all sorts of the
most precious marbles. But, not to mention the richness of the
furniture, which was inestimable, there was such profuseness

throughout that the Prince, instead of ever having seen anything like it, owned that he could not have imagined that there was anything in the world that could come up to it. 'Prince,' said the Fairy, if you admire my palace so much, which, indeed, is very beautiful, what would you say to the palaces of the chief of our genies, which are much more beautiful, spacious, and magnificent? I could also charm you with my gardens, but we will let that alone till another time. Night draws near, and it will be time to go to supper.'

The next hall which the Fairy led the Prince into, and where the cloth was laid for the feast, was the last apartment the Prince had not seen, and not in the least inferior to the others. At his entrance into it he admired the infinite number of sconces of wax candles perfumed with amber, the multitude of which, instead of being confused, were placed with so just a symmetry as formed an agreeable and pleasant sight. A large side table was set out with all sorts of gold plate, so finely wrought that the workmanship was much more valuable than the weight of the gold. Several choruses of beautiful women richly dressed, and whose voices were ravishing, began a concert, accompanied with all sorts of the most harmonious instruments; and when they were set down at table the Fairy Paribanou took care to help Prince Ahmed with the most delicate meats, which she named as she invited him to eat of them, and which the Prince found to be so exquisitely nice that he commended them with exaggeration, and said that the entertainment far surpassed those of men. He found also the same excellence in the wines, which neither he nor the Fairy tasted of till the dessert was served up, which consisted of the choicest sweetmeats and fruits.

The wedding feast was continued the next day, or, rather, the days following the celebration were a continual feast.

At the end of six months Prince Ahmed, who always loved and honoured the Sultan his father, conceived a great desire to know how he was, and that desire could not be satisfied without his going to see; he told the Fairy of it, and desired she would give him leave.

'Prince,' said she, 'go when you please. But first, don't take it amiss that I give you some advice how you shall behave yourself where you are going. First, I don't think it proper for you to tell the Sultan your father of our marriage, nor of my quality, nor the place where you have been. Beg of him to be satisfied in knowing

you are happy, and desire no more; and let him know that the
sole end of your visit is to make him easy, and inform him of your
fate.'

She appointed twenty gentlemen, well mounted and equipped,
to attend him.   When all was ready Prince Ahmed took his leave
of the Fairy, embraced her, and renewed his promise to return soon.
Then his horse, which was most finely caparisoned, and was as
beautiful a creature as any in the Sultan of the Indies' stables, was

led to him, and he mounted him with an extraordinary grace; and,
after he had bid her a last adieu, set forward on his journey.

As it was not a great way to his father's capital, Prince Ahmed
soon arrived there.   The people, glad to see him again, received
him with acclamations of joy, and followed him in crowds to the
Sultan's apartment.   The Sultan received and embraced him with
great joy, complaining at the same time, with a fatherly tenderness,
of the affliction his long absence had been to him, which he said
was the more grievous for that, fortune having decided in favour of

Prince Ali his brother, he was afraid he might have committed some rash action.

The Prince told a story of his adventures without speaking of the Fairy, whom he said that he must not mention, and ended: 'The only favour I ask of your Majesty is to give me leave to come often and pay you my respects, and to know how you do.'

'Son,' answered the Sultan of the Indies, 'I cannot refuse you the leave you ask me; but I should much rather you would resolve to stay with me; at least tell me where I may send to you if you should fail to come, or when I may think your presence necessary.' 'Sir,' replied Prince Ahmed, 'what your Majesty asks of me is part of the mystery I spoke to your Majesty of. I beg of you to give me leave to remain silent on this head, for I shall come so frequently that I am afraid that I shall sooner be thought troublesome than be accused of negligence in my duty.'

The Sultan of the Indies pressed Prince Ahmed no more, but said to him: 'Son, I penetrate no farther into your secrets, but leave you at your liberty: but can tell you that you could not do me a greater pleasure than to come, and by your presence restore to me the joy I have not felt this long time, and that you shall always be welcome when you come, without interrupting your business or pleasure.'

Prince Ahmed stayed but three days at the Sultan his father's Court, and the fourth returned to the Fairy Paribanou, who did not expect him so soon.

A month after Prince Ahmed's return from paying a visit to his father, as the Fairy Paribanou had observed that the Prince, since the time that he gave her an account of his journey, his discourse with his father, and the leave he asked to go and see him often, had never talked of the Sultan, as if there had been no such person in the world, whereas before he was always speaking of him, she thought he forebore on her account; therefore she took an opportunity to say to him one day: 'Prince, tell me, have you forgot the Sultan your father? Don't you remember the promise you made to go and see him often? For my part, I have not forgot what you told me at your return, and so put you in mind of it, that you may not be long before you acquit yourself of your promise.'

So Prince Ahmed went the next morning with the same attendance as before, but much finer, and himself more magnificently mounted, equipped, and dressed, and was received by the Sultan with the same joy and satisfaction. For several months he constantly paid his visits, and always in a richer and finer equipage.

At last some viziers, the Sultan's favourites, who judged of Prince Ahmed's grandeur and power by the figure he cut, made the Sultan jealous of his son, saying it was to be feared he might inveigle himself into the people's favour and dethrone him.

The Sultan of the Indies was so far from thinking that Prince Ahmed could be capable of so pernicious a design as his favourites would make him believe that he said to them : ' You are mistaken ; my son loves me, and I am certain of his tenderness and fidelity, as I have given him no reason to be disgusted.'

But the favourites went on abusing Prince Ahmed till the Sultan said : ' Be it as it will, I don't believe my son Ahmed is so wicked as you would persuade me he is ; however, I am obliged to you for your good advice, and don't dispute but that it proceeds from your good intentions.'

The Sultan of the Indies said this that his favourites might not know the impressions their discourse had made on his mind : which had so alarmed him that he resolved to have Prince Ahmed watched unknown to his grand vizier. So he sent for a female magician, who was introduced by a back door into his apartment. 'Go immediately,' he said, 'and follow my son, and watch him so well as to find out where he retires, and bring me word.'

The magician left the Sultan, and, knowing the place where Prince Ahmed found his arrow, went immediately thither, and hid herself near the rocks, so that nobody could see her.

The next morning Prince Ahmed set out by daybreak, without taking leave either of the Sultan or any of his Court, according to custom. The magician, seeing him coming, followed him with her eyes, till on a sudden she lost sight of him and his attendants.

As the rocks were very steep and craggy, they were an insurmountable barrier, so that the magician judged that there were but two things for it : either that the Prince retired into some cavern, or an abode of genies or fairies. Thereupon she came out of the place where she was hid, and went directly to the hollow way, which she traced till she came to the farther end, looking carefully about on all sides ; but, notwithstanding all her diligence, could perceive no opening, not so much as the iron gate which Prince Ahmed discovered. which was to be seen and opened to none but men, and only to such whose presence was agreeable to the Fairy Paribanou.

The magician, who saw it was in vain for her to search any

farther, was obliged to be satisfied with the discovery she had made, and returned to give the Sultan an account.

The Sultan was very well pleased with the magician's conduct, and said to her: 'Do you as you think fit; I'll wait patiently the event of your promises;' and to encourage her made her a present of a diamond of great value.

As Prince Ahmed had obtained the Fairy Paribanou's leave to go to the Sultan of the Indies' Court once a month, he never failed, and the magician, knowing the time, went a day or two before to the foot of the rock where she lost sight of the Prince and his attendants, and waited there.

The next morning Prince Ahmed went out, as usual, at the iron gate, with the same attendants as before, and passed by the magician, whom he knew not to be such, and, seeing her lie with her head against the rock, and complaining as if she were in great pain, he pitied her, turned his horse about, and went to her, and asked her what was the matter with her, and what he could do to ease her.

The artful sorceress looked at the Prince in a pitiful manner, without ever lifting up her head, and answered in broken words and sighs, as if she could hardly fetch her breath, that she was going to the capital city, but on the way thither she was taken with so violent a fever that her strength failed her, and she was forced to lie down where he saw her, far from any habitation, and without any hopes of assistance.

'Good woman,' replied Prince Ahmed, 'you are not so far from help as you imagine. I am ready to assist you, and convey you where you will meet with a speedy cure; only get up, and let one of my people take you behind him.'

At these words the magician, who pretended sickness only to know where the Prince lived and what he did, refused not the charitable offer he made her, and that her actions might correspond with her words she made many pretended vain endeavours to get up. At the same time two of the Prince's attendants, alighting off their horses, helped her up, and set her behind another, and mounted their horses again, and followed the Prince, who turned back to the iron gate, which was opened by one of his retinue who rode before. And when he came into the outward court of the Fairy, without dismounting himself, he sent to tell her he wanted to speak with her.

The Fairy Paribanou came with all imaginable haste, not knowing what made Prince Ahmed return so soon; who, not giving her

time to ask him the reason, said : ' Princess, I desire you would have
compassion on this good woman,' pointing to the magician, who was
held up by two of his retinue. ' I found her in the condition you
see her in, and promised her the assistance she stands in need of,
and am persuaded that you, out of your own goodness, as well as
upon my entreaty, will not abandon her.'

The Fairy Paribanou, who had her eyes fixed upon the pretended
sick woman all the time that the Prince was talking to her, ordered
two of her women who followed her to take her from the two men

that held her, and carry her into an apartment of the palace, and
take as much care of her as herself.

Whilst the two women executed the Fairy's commands, she went
up to Prince Ahmed, and, whispering him in the ear, said : ' Prince,
this woman is not so sick as she pretends to be ; and I am very
much mistaken if she is not an impostor, who will be the cause of
a great trouble to you. But don't be concerned, let what will be
devised against you ; be persuaded that I will deliver you out of all
the snares that shall be laid for you. Go and pursue your journey.'

This discourse of the Fairy's did not in the least frighten Prince

Ahmed. ' My Princess,' said he, ' as I do not remember I ever did
or designed anybody an injury, I cannot believe anybody can have
a thought of doing me one, but if they have I shall not, nevertheless, forbear doing good whenever I have an opportunity.' Then
he went back to his father's palace.

In the meantime the two women carried the magician into a
very fine apartment, richly furnished. First they sat her down upon
a sofa, with her back supported with a cushion of gold brocade,
while they made a bed on the same sofa before her, the quilt of
which was finely embroidered with silk, the sheets of the finest
linen, and the coverlet cloth-of-gold. When they had put her into
bed (for the old sorceress pretended that her fever was so violent
she could not help herself in the least) one of the women went out,
and returned soon again with a china dish in her hand, full of a
certain liquor, which she presented to the magician, while the other
helped her to sit up. ' Drink this liquor,' said she ; ' it is the Water
of the Fountain of Lions, and a sovereign remedy against all fevers
whatsoever. You will find the effect of it in less than an hour's
time.'

The magician, to dissemble the better, took it after a great deal
of entreaty ; but at last she took the china dish, and, holding back
her head, swallowed down the liquor. When she was laid down
again the two women covered her up. ' Lie quiet,' said she who
brought her the china cup, ' and get a little sleep if you can. We'll
leave you, and hope to find you perfectly cured when we come
again an hour hence.'

The two women came again at the time they said they should,
and found the magician got up and dressed, and sitting upon the
sofa. ' O admirable potion !' she said : ' it has wrought its cure much
sooner than you told me it would, and I shall be able to prosecute
my journey.'

The two women, who were fairies as well as their mistress, after
they had told the magician how glad they were that she was cured
so soon, walked before her, and conducted her through several
apartments, all more noble than that wherein she lay, into a large
hall, the most richly and magnificently furnished of all the palace.

Paribanou was sat in this hall on a throne of massive gold,
enriched with diamonds, rubies, and pearls of an extraordinary size,
and attended on each hand by a great number of beautiful fairies,
all richly clothed. At the sight of so much majesty, the magician
was not only dazzled, but was so amazed that, after she had pro-

strated herself before the throne, she could not open her lips to
thank the Fairy as she proposed. However, Paribanou saved her
the trouble, and said to her : ' Good woman, I am glad I had an
opportunity to oblige you, and to see you are able to pursue your
journey. I won't detain you, but perhaps you may not be displeased
to see my palace ; follow my women, and they will show it you.'

Then the magician went back and related to the Sultan of the
Indies all that had happened, and how very rich Prince Ahmed
was since his marriage with the Fairy, richer than all the kings in
the world, and how there was danger that he should come and take
the throne from his father.

Though the Sultan of the Indies was very well persuaded that
Prince Ahmed's natural disposition was good, yet he could not help
being concerned at the discourse of the old sorceress, to whom, when
she was for taking her leave, he said : ' I thank thee for the pains
thou hast taken, and thy wholesome advice. I am so sensible of
the great importance it is to me that I shall deliberate upon it in
council.'

Now the favourites advised that the Prince should be killed, but the magician advised differently : ' Make him give you all kinds of wonderful things, by the Fairy's help, till she tires of him and sends him away. As, for example, every time your Majesty goes into the field, you are obliged to be at a great expense, not only in pavilions and tents for your army, but likewise in mules and camels to carry their baggage. Now, might not you engage him to use his interest with the Fairy to procure you a tent which might be carried in a man's hand, and which should be so large as to shelter your whole army against bad weather ? '

When the magician had finished her speech, the Sultan asked his favourites if they had anything better to propose; and, finding them all silent, determined to follow the magician's advice, as the most reasonable and most agreeable to his mild government.

Next day the Sultan did as the magician had advised him, and asked for the pavilion.

Prince Ahmed never expected that the Sultan his father would have asked such a thing, which at first appeared so difficult, not to say impossible. Though he knew not absolutely how great the power of genies and fairies was, he doubted whether it extended so far as to compass such a tent as his father desired. At last he replied : ' Though it is with the greatest reluctance imaginable, I will not fail to ask the favour of my wife your Majesty desires, but will not promise you to obtain it ; and if I should not have the honour to come again to pay you my respects that shall be the sign that I have not had success. But, beforehand, I desire you to forgive me, and consider that you yourself have reduced me to this extremity.'

' Son,' replied the Sultan of the Indies, ' I should be very sorry if what I ask of you should cause me the displeasure of never seeing you more. I find you don't know the power a husband has over a wife; and yours would show that her love to you was very indifferent if she, with the power she has of a fairy, should refuse you so trifling a request as this I desire you to ask of her for my sake.'

The Prince went back, and was very sad for fear of offending the Fairy. She kept pressing him to tell her what was the matter, and at last he said : ' Madam, you may have observed that hitherto I have been content with your love, and have never asked you any other favour. Consider then, I conjure you, that it is not I, but the Sultan my father, who indiscreetly, or at least I think so, begs of you a pavilion large enough to shelter him, his Court, and army from the violence of the weather, and which a man may carry in his hand. But remember it is the Sultan my father asks this favour.'

'Prince,' replied the Fairy, smiling, 'I am sorry that so small a matter should disturb you, and make you so uneasy as you appeared to me.'

Then the Fairy sent for her treasurer, to whom, when she came, she said: 'Nourgihan'—which was her name—'bring me the largest pavilion in my treasury.' Nourgihan returned presently with the pavilion, which she could not only hold in her hand, but in the palm of her hand when she shut her fingers, and presented it to her mistress, who gave it to Prince Ahmed to look at.

When Prince Ahmed saw the pavilion which the Fairy called the largest in her treasury, he fancied she had a mind to jest with him, and thereupon the marks of his surprise appeared presently in his countenance ; which Paribanou perceiving burst out a-laughing. 'What! Prince,' cried she, 'do you think I jest with you? You'll see presently that I am in earnest. Nourgihan,' said she to her treasurer, taking the tent out of Prince Ahmed's hands, 'go and set it up, that the Prince may judge whether it may be large enough for the Sultan his father.'

The treasurer went out immediately with it out of the palace, and carried it a great way off; and when she had set it up one end reached to the very palace: at which time the Prince, thinking it small, found it large enough to shelter two greater armies than that of the Sultan his father's, and then said to Paribanou: 'I ask my Princess a thousand pardons for my incredulity; after what I have seen I believe there is nothing impossible to you.' 'You see,' said the Fairy, 'that the pavilion is larger than what your father may have occasion for; for you must know that it has one property—that it is larger or smaller according to the army it is to cover.'

The treasurer took down the tent again, and brought it to the Prince, who took it, and, without staying any longer than till the next day, mounted his horse, and went with the same attendants to the Sultan his father.

The Sultan, who was persuaded that there could not be any such thing as such a tent as he asked for, was in a great surprise at the Prince's diligence. He took the tent, and after he had admired its smallness his amazement was so great that he could not recover himself. When the tent was set up in the great plain, which we have before mentioned, he found it large enough to shelter an army twice as large as he could bring into the field.

But the Sultan was not yet satisfied. 'Son,' said he, 'I have already expressed to you how much I am obliged to you for the present of the tent you have procured me: that I look upon it as the most valuable thing in all my treasury. But you must do one thing more for me, which will be every whit as agreeable to me   I am informed that the Fairy your spouse makes use of a certain water, called the Water of the Fountain of Lions, which cures all sorts of fevers, even the most dangerous, and, as I am perfectly well persuaded my health is dear to you, I don't doubt but you will ask her for a bottle of that water for me, and bring it me as a sovereign medicine, which I may make use of when I have occasion. Do me this other important piece of service, and thereby complete the duty of a good son towards a tender father.'

The Prince returned and told the Fairy what his father had said. 'There's a great deal of wickedness in this demand,' she answered, 'as you will understand by what I am going to tell you. The Fountain of Lions is situated in the middle of a court of a great castle, the entrance into which is guarded by four fierce lions, two of which sleep alternately, while the other two are awake. But don't let that frighten you; I'll give you means to pass by them without any danger.'

THE FOUNTAIN OF LIONS.

The Fairy Paribanou was at that time very hard at work, and, as she had several clews of thread by her, she took up one, and, presenting it to Prince Ahmed, said : ' First take this clew of thread. I'll tell you presently the use of it. In the second place, you must have two horses : one you must ride yourself, and the other you must lead, which must be loaded with a sheep cut into four quarters, that must be killed to-day. In the third place, you must be provided with a bottle, which I will give you, to bring the water in. Set out early to-morrow morning, and when you have passed the iron gate throw the clew of thread before you, which will roll till it comes to the gates of the castle. Follow it, and when it stops, as the gates will be open, you will see the four lions ; the two that are awake will, by their roaring, wake the other two, but don't be frightened, but throw each of them a quarter of mutton, and then clap spurs to your horse and ride to the fountain ; fill your bottle without alighting, and then return with the same expedition. The lions will be so busy eating they will let you pass by them.'

Prince Ahmed set out the next morning at the time appointed by the Fairy, and followed her directions punctually. When he arrived at the gates of the castle he distributed the quarters of mutton among the four lions, and, passing through the midst of them bravely, got to the fountain, filled his bottle, and returned back as safe and sound as he went. When he had gone a little distance from the castle gates he turned him about, and, perceiving two of the lions coming after him, he drew his sabre and prepared himself for defence. But as he went forwards he saw one of them turned out of the road at some distance, and showed by his head and tail that he did not come to do him any harm, but only to go before him, and that the other stayed behind to follow ; he put his sword up again in its scabbard. Guarded in this manner, he arrived at the capital of the Indies, but the lions never left him till they had conducted him to the gates of the Sultan's palace ; after which they returned the same way they came, though not without frightening all that saw them, for all they went in a very gentle manner and showed no fierceness.

A great many officers came to attend the Prince while he dismounted his horse, and afterwards conducted him into the Sultan's apartment, who was at that time surrounded with his favourites. He approached towards the throne, laid the bottle at the Sultan's feet, and kissed the rich tapestry which covered his footstool, and then said : ' I have brought you, sir, the healthful water which your

Majesty desired so much to keep among your other rarities in your treasury, but at the same time wish you such extraordinary health as never to have occasion to make use of it.'

After the Prince had made an end of his compliment the Sultan placed him on his right hand, and then said to him : ' Son, I am very much obliged to you for this valuable present, as also for the great danger you have exposed yourself to upon my account (which I have been informed of by a magician who knows the Fountain of Lions) ; but do me the pleasure,' continued he, ' to inform me by what address, or, rather, by what incredible power, you have been secured.'

' Sir,' replied Prince Ahmed, ' I have no share in the compliment your Majesty is pleased to make me ; all the honour is due to the Fairy my spouse, whose good advice I followed.' Then he informed the Sultan what those directions were, and by the relation of this his expedition let him know how well he had behaved himself. When he had done the Sultan, who showed outwardly all the demonstrations of great joy, but secretly became more jealous, retired into an inward apartment, where he sent for the magician.

The magician, at her arrival, saved the Sultan the trouble to tell her of the success of Prince Ahmed's journey, which she had heard of before she came, and therefore was prepared with an infallible means, as she pretended. This means she communicated to the Sultan, who declared it the next day to the Prince, in the midst of all his courtiers, in these words : ' Son,' said he, ' I have one thing more to ask of you, after which I shall expect nothing more from your obedience, nor your interest with your wife. This request is, to bring me a man not above a foot and a half high, and whose beard is thirty feet long, who carries a bar of iron upon his shoulders of five hundredweight, which he uses as a quarterstaff.'

Prince Ahmed, who did not believe that there was such a man in the world as his father described, would gladly have excused himself ; but the Sultan persisted in his demand, and told him the Fairy could do more incredible things.

The next day the Prince returned to his dear Paribanou, to whom he told his father's new demand, which, he said, he looked upon to be a thing more impossible than the two first ; ' for,' added he, ' I cannot imagine there can be such a man in the world ; without doubt, he has a mind to try whether or no I am so silly as to go about it, or he has a design on my ruin. In short, how can he suppose that I should lay hold on a man so well armed, though he is but little ? What arms can I make use of to reduce him to my will ? If there are any means, I beg you will tell them, and let me come off with honour this time.'

' Don't affright yourself, Prince,' replied the Fairy; ' you ran a risk in fetching the Water of the Fountain of Lions for your father, but there's no danger in finding out this man, who is my brother Schaibar, but is so far from being like me, though we both had the same father, that he is of so violent a nature that nothing can prevent his giving cruel marks of his resentment for a slight offence; yet, on the other hand, is so good as to oblige anyone in whatever they desire. He is made exactly as the Sultan your father has described him, and has no other arms than a bar of iron of five hundred pounds weight, without which he never stirs, and which makes him respected. I'll send for him, and you shall judge of the truth of what I tell you; but be sure to prepare yourself against being frightened at his extraordinary figure when you see him.' ' What ! my Queen,' replied Prince Ahmed, ' do you say Schaibar is your brother ? Let him be never so ugly or deformed I shall be so far from being frightened at the sight of him that, as our brother, I shall honour and love him.'

The Fairy ordered a gold chafing-dish to be set with a fire in it under the porch of her palace, with a box of the same metal, which was a present to her, out of which taking a perfume, and throwing it into the fire, there arose a thick cloud of smoke.

Some moments after the Fairy said to Prince Ahmed : ' See, there comes my brother.' The Prince immediately perceived Schaibar coming gravely with his heavy bar on his shoulder, his long beard, which he held up before him, and a pair of thick moustachios, which he tucked behind his ears and almost covered his face; his eyes were very small, and deep-set in his head, which was far from being of the smallest size, and on his head he wore a grenadier's cap : besides all this, he was very much hump-backed.

If Prince Ahmed had not known that Schaibar was Paribanou's brother, he would not have been able to have looked at him without fear, but, knowing first who he was, he stood by the Fairy without the least concern

Schaibar, as he came forwards, looked at the Prince earnestly enough to have chilled his blood in his veins, and asked Paribanou, when he first accosted her, who that man was. To which she replied : ' He is my husband, brother. His name is Ahmed ; he is son to the Sultan of the Indies. The reason why I did not invite you to my wedding was I was unwilling to divert you from an expedition you were engaged in, and from which I heard with pleasure you returned victorious, and so took the liberty now to call for you.'

At these words Schaibar, looking on Prince Ahmed favourably, said : 'Is there anything, sister, wherein I can serve him ? It is enough for me that he is your husband to engage me to do for him

whatever he desires.'   'The Sultan his father,' replied Paribanou, 'has a curiosity to see you, and I desire he may be your guide to the Sultan's Court.'   'He needs but lead me the way, I'll follow him.'   'Brother,' replied Paribanou, 'it is too late to go to-day, therefore stay till to-morrow morning ; and in the meantime I'll inform you of all that has passed between the Sultan of the Indies and Prince Ahmed since our marriage.'

The next morning, after Schaibar had been informed of the

affair, he and Prince Ahmed set out for the Sultan's Court. When they arrived at the gates of the capital the people no sooner saw Schaibar but they ran and hid themselves; and some shut up their shops and locked themselves up in their houses, while others flying communicated their fear to all they met, who stayed not to look behind them, but ran too; insomuch that Schaibar and Prince Ahmed, as they went along, found the streets all desolate till they came to the palace, where the porters, instead of keeping the gates, ran away too, so that the Prince and Schaibar advanced without any obstacle to the council-hall, where the Sultan was seated on his throne, and giving audience. Here likewise the ushers, at the approach of Schaibar, abandoned their posts, and gave them free admittance.

Schaibar went boldly and fiercely up to the throne, without waiting to be presented by Prince Ahmed, and accosted the Sultan of the Indies in these words: 'Thou hast asked for me,' said he; 'see, here I am: what wouldst thou have with me?'

The Sultan, instead of answering him, clapped his hands before his eyes, to avoid the sight of so terrible an object; at which uncivil and rude reception Schaibar was so much provoked, after he had given him the trouble to come so far, that he instantly lifted up his iron bar and killed him, before Prince Ahmed could intercede in his behalf. All that he could do was to prevent his killing the grand vizier, who sat not far from him, representing to him that he had always given the Sultan his father good advice. 'These are they, then,' said Schaibar, 'who gave him bad,' and as he pronounced these words he killed all the other viziers and flattering favourites of the Sultan who were Prince Ahmed's enemies. Every time he struck he killed some one or other, and none escaped but they who were not so frightened as to stand staring and gaping, and who saved themselves by flight.

When this terrible execution was over Schaibar came out of the council-hall into the midst of the courtyard with the iron bar upon his shoulder, and, looking hard at the grand vizier, who owed his life to Prince Ahmed, he said: 'I know here is a certain magician, who is a greater enemy of my brother-in-law's than all these base favourites I have chastised. Let the magician be brought to me presently.' The grand vizier immediately sent for her, and as soon as she was brought Schaibar said, at the time he fetched a stroke at her with his iron bar: 'Take the reward of thy pernicious counsel, and learn to feign sickness again.'

After this he said : ' This is not yet enough ; I will use the whole town after the same manner if they do not immediately acknowledge Prince Ahmed, my brother-in-law, for their Sultan and the Sultan of the Indies.'   Then all that were there present made the air echo again with the repeated acclamations of : ' Long life to Sultan Ahmed ' ; and immediately after he was proclaimed through the whole town. Schaibar made him be clothed in the royal vestments, installed him on the throne, and after he had caused all to swear

homage and fidelity to him went and fetched his sister Paribanou, whom he brought with all the pomp and grandeur imaginable, and made her to be owned Sultaness of the Indies.

As for Prince Ali and Princess Nouronnihar, as they had no hand in the conspiracy against Prince Ahmed, and knew nothing of any, Prince Ahmed assigned them a considerable province, with its capital, where they spent the rest of their lives. Afterwards he sent an officer to Prince Houssain to acquaint him with the change and make him an offer of which province he liked best ; but that

Prince thought himself so happy in his solitude that he bade the officer return the Sultan his brother thanks for the kindness he designed him, assuring him of his submission; and that the only favour he desired of him was to give him leave to live retired in the place he had made choice of for his retreat.[1]

---

[1] *Arabian Nights.*

THE HISTORY OF JACK THE GIANT-KILLER

IN the reign of the famous King Arthur there lived in Cornwall a lad named Jack, who was a boy of a bold temper, and took delight in hearing or reading of conjurers, giants, and fairies; and used to listen eagerly to the deeds of the knights of King Arthur's Round Table.

In those days there lived on St. Michael's Mount, off Cornwall, a huge giant, eighteen feet high and nine feet round; his fierce and savage looks were the terror of all who beheld him.

He dwelt in a gloomy cavern on the top of the mountain, and used to wade over to the mainland in search of prey; when he would throw half-a-dozen oxen upon his back, and tie three times as many sheep and hogs round his waist, and march back to his own abode.

The giant had done this for many years when Jack resolved to destroy him.

Jack took a horn, a shovel, a pickaxe, his armour, and a dark lantern, and one winter's evening he went to the mount. There he dug a pit twenty-two feet deep and twenty broad. He covered the top over so as to make it look like solid ground. He then blew such a tantivy that the giant awoke and came out of his den, crying out: 'You saucy villain! you shall pay for this. I'll broil you for my breakfast!'

He had just finished, when, taking one step further, he tumbled headlong into the pit, and Jack struck him a blow on the head with his pickaxe which killed him. Jack then returned home to cheer his friends with the news.

Another giant, called Blunderbore, vowed to be revenged on Jack if ever he should have him in his power. This giant kept an enchanted castle in the midst of a lonely wood; and some time after the death of Cormoran Jack was passing through a wood, and being weary sat down and went to sleep.

The giant, passing by and seeing Jack, carried him to his castle, where he locked him up in a large room, the floor of which was covered with the bodies, skulls, and bones of men and women.

Soon after the giant went to fetch his brother, who was likewise a giant, to take a meal off his flesh; and Jack saw with terror through the bars of his prison the two giants approaching.

Jack, perceiving in one corner of the room a strong cord, took courage, and making a slip-knot at each end, he threw them over their heads, and tied it to the window-bars; he then pulled till he

had choked them. When they were black in the face he slid down the rope and stabbed them to the heart.

Jack next took a great bunch of keys from the pocket of Blunderbore, and went into the castle again. He make a strict search through all the rooms, and in one of them found three ladies tied up by the hair of their heads, and almost starved to death. They told him that their husbands had been killed by the giants, who had then condemned them to be starved to death, because they would not eat the flesh of their own dead husbands.

'Ladies,' said Jack, 'I have put an end to the monster and his wicked brother; and I give you this castle and all the riches it contains, to make some amends for the dreadful pains you have felt.' He then very politely gave them the keys of the castle, and went further on his journey to Wales.

As Jack had but little money, he went on as fast as possible. At length he came to a handsome house. Jack knocked at the door, when there came forth a Welsh giant. Jack said he was a traveller who had lost his way, on which the giant made him welcome, and let him into a room where there there was a good bed to sleep in.

Jack took off his clothes quickly, but though he was weary he could not go to sleep. Soon after this he heard the giant walking backward and forward in the next room, and saying to himself:

'Though here you lodge with me this night,
You shall not see the morning light;
My club shall dash your brains out quite.'

'Say you so?' thought Jack. 'Are these your tricks upon travellers? But I hope to prove as cunning as you are.' Then, getting out of bed, he groped about the room, and at last found a large thick billet of wood. He laid it in his own place in the bed, and then hid himself in a dark corner of the room.

The giant, about midnight, entered the apartment, and with his bludgeon struck a many blows on the bed, in the very place where Jack had laid the log; and then he went back to his own room, thinking he had broken all Jack's bones.

Early in the morning Jack put a bold face upon the matter, and walked into the giant's room to thank him for his lodging. The giant started when he saw him, and began to stammer out: 'Oh! dear me; is it you? Pray how did you sleep last night? Did you hear or see anything in the dead of the night?'

'Nothing worth speaking of,' said Jack carelessly: 'a rat, I believe, gave me three or four slaps with its tail, and disturbed me a little; but I soon went to sleep again.'

The giant wondered more and more at this: yet he did not answer a word, but went to bring two great bowls of hasty-pudding for their breakfast. Jack wanted to make the giant believe that he could eat as much as himself, so he contrived to button a leathern bag inside his coat, and slip the hasty-pudding into this bag, while he seemed to put it into his mouth.

When breakfast was over he said to the giant: 'Now I will show you a fine trick. I can cure all wounds with a touch: I could cut off my head in one minute, and the next put it sound again on my shoulders. You shall see an example.' He then took hold of the knife, ripped up the leathern bag, and all the hasty-pudding tumbled out upon the floor.

'Ods splutter hur nails!' cried the Welsh giant, who was ashamed to be outdone by such a little fellow as Jack, 'hur can do that hurself;' so he snatched up the knife, plunged it into his own stomach, and in a moment dropped down dead.

Jack, having hitherto been successful in all his undertakings, resolved not to be idle in future; he therefore furnished himself with a horse, a cap of knowledge, a sword of sharpness, shoes of swiftness, and an invisible coat, the better to perform the wonderful enterprises that lay before him.

He travelled over high hills, and on the third day he came to a large and spacious forest through which his road lay. Scarcely had he entered the forest when he beheld a monstrous giant dragging along by the hair of their heads a handsome knight and his lady. Jack alighted from his horse, and tying him to an oak tree, put on his invisible coat, under which he carried his sword of sharpness.

When he came up to the giant he made several strokes at him, but could not reach his body, but wounded his thighs in several places; and at length putting both hands to his sword and aiming with all his might, he cut off both his legs. Then Jack, setting his foot upon his neck, plunged his sword into the giant's body, when the monster gave a groan and expired.

The knight and his lady thanked Jack for their deliverance, and invited him to their house, to receive a proper reward for his services. 'No,' said Jack, 'I cannot be easy till I find out this monster's habitation.' So taking the knight's directions, he mounted his horse, and soon after came in sight of another giant, who was sitting on a block of timber waiting for his brother's return.

Jack alighted from his horse, and, putting on his invisible coat, approached and aimed a blow at the giant's head, but missing his aim he only cut off his nose. On this the giant seized his club and laid about him most unmercifully.

'Nay,' said Jack, 'if this be the case I'd better dispatch you!' so jumping upon the block, he stabbed him in the back, when he dropped down dead.

Jack then proceeded on his journey, and travelled over hills and dales, till arriving at the foot of a high mountain he knocked at the door of a lonely house, when an old man let him in.

When Jack was seated the hermit thus addressed him: 'My son, on the top of this mountain is an enchanted castle, kept by the giant Galligantus and a vile magician. I lament the fate of a duke's daughter, whom they seized as she was walking in her father's garden, and brought hither transformed into a deer.'

Jack promised that in the morning, at the risk of his life, he

would break the enchantment; and after a sound sleep he rose early, put on his invisible coat, and got ready for the attempt.

When he had climbed to the top of the mountain he saw two fiery griffins; but he passed between them without the least fear of danger, for they could not see him because of his invisible coat. On the castle gate he found a golden trumpet, under which were written these lines:—

> Whoever can this trumpet blow
> Shall cause the giant's overthrow.

As soon as Jack had read this he seized the trumpet and blew a shrill blast, which made the gates fly open and the very castle itself tremble.

The giant and the conjurer now knew that their wicked course was at an end, and they stood biting their thumbs and shaking with fear. Jack, with his sword of sharpness, soon killed the giant, and the magician was then carried away by a whirlwind; and every knight and beautiful lady who had been changed into birds and beasts returned to their proper shapes. The castle vanished away like smoke, and the head of the giant Galligantus was then sent to King Arthur.

The knights and ladies rested that night at the old man's hermitage, and next day they set out for the Court. Jack then went up to the King, and gave his Majesty an account of all his fierce battles.

Jack's fame had now spread through the whole country, and at the King's desire the duke gave him his daughter in marriage, to the joy of all his kingdom. After this the King gave him a large estate, on which he and his lady lived the rest of their days in joy and contentment.[1]

[1] Old Chapbook.

THE BLACK BULL OF NORROWAY

And many a hunting song they sung,
    And song of game and glee;
Then tuned to plaintive strains their tongue,
    ' Of Scotland's luve and lee.'
To wilder measures next they turn
    ' The Black, Black Bull of Norroway!'
Sudden the tapers cease to burn,
    The minstrels cease to play.

                    ' *The Cout of Keeldar*,' by J. Leyden.

IN Norroway, langsyne, there lived a certain lady, and she had three dochters. The auldest o' them said to her mither: ' Mither, bake me a bannock, and roast me a collop, for I'm gaun awa' to seek my fortune.' Her mither did sae; and the dochter gaed awa' to an auld witch washerwife and telled her purpose. The auld wife bade her stay that day, and gang and look out o' her back door, and see what she could see. She saw nocht the first day. The second day she did the same, and saw nocht. On the third day she looked again, and saw a coach-and-six coming alang the road. She ran in and telled the auld wife what she saw. ' Aweel,' quo' the auld wife, ' yon's for you.' Sae they took her into the coach, and galloped aff.

The second dochter next says to her mither: ' Mither, bake me a bannock, and roast me a collop, for I'm gaun awa' to seek my fortune.' Her mither did sae; and awa' she gaed to the auld wife, as her sister had dune. On the third day she looked out o' the back door, and saw a coach-and-four coming alang the road. 'Aweel,' quo' the auld wife, ' yon's for you.' Sae they took her in, and aff they set.

The third dochter says to her mither : ' Mither, bake me a bannock, and roast me a collop, for I'm gaun awa' to seek my fortune.' Her mither did sae; and awa' she gaed to the auld witch-wife.

She bade her look out o' her back door, and see what she could see. She did sae; and when she came back said she saw nocht. The second day she did the same, and saw nocht. The third day she looked again, and on coming back said to the auld wife she saw nocht but a muckle Black Bull coming roaring alang the road. 'Aweel,' quo' the auld wife, 'yon's for you.' On hearing this she was next to distracted wi' grief and terror; but she was lifted up and set on his back, and awa' they went.

Aye they travelled, and on they travelled, till the lady grew faint wi' hunger. 'Eat out o' my right lug,' says the Black Bull, 'and drink out o' my left lug, and set by your leavings.' Sae she did as he said, and was wonderfully refreshed. And lang they gaed, and sair they rade, till they came in sight o' a very big and bonny castle. 'Yonder we maun be this night,' quo' the bull; 'for my auld brither lives yonder;' and presently they were at the place. They lifted her aff his back, and took her in, and sent him away to a park for the night. In the morning, when they brought the bull hame, they took the lady into a fine shining parlour, and gave her a beautiful apple, telling her no to break it till she was in the greatest strait ever mortal was in in the world, and that wad bring her out o't. Again she was lifted on the bull's back, and after she had ridden far, and farer than I can tell, they came in sight o' a far bonnier castle, and far farther awa' than the last. Says the bull till her: 'Yonder we maun be the night, for my second brither lives yonder;' and they were at the place directly. They lifted her down and took her in, and sent the bull to the field for the night. In the morning they took the lady into a fine and rich room, and gave her the finest pear she had ever seen, bidding her no to break it till she was in the greatest strait ever mortal could be in, and that wad get her out o't. Again she was lifted and set on his back, and awa' they went. And lang they gaed, and sair they rade, till they came in sight o' the far biggest castle, and far farthest aff, they had yet seen. 'We maun be yonder the night,' says the bull, 'for my young brither lives yonder;' and they were there directly. They lifted her down, took her in, and sent the bull to the field for the night. In the morning they took her into a room, the finest of a', and gied her a plum, telling her no to break it till she was in the greatest strait mortal could be in, and that wad get her out o't. Presently they brought hame the bull, set the lady on his back, and awa' they went.

And aye they gaed, and on they rade, till they came to a dark and ugsome glen, where they stopped, and the lady lighted down. Says the bull to her: 'Here ye maun stay till I gang and fight the deil. Ye maun seat yoursel' on that stane, and move neither hand nor fit till I come back, else I'll never find ye again. And if everything round about ye turns blue I hae beaten the deil; but should a' things turn red he'll hae conquered me.' She set hersel' down on the stane, and by-and-by a' round her turned blue. O'ercome wi' joy, she lifted the ae fit and crossed it owre the ither, sae glad was she that her companion was victorious. The bull returned and sought for but never could find her.

Lang she sat, and aye she grat, till she wearied. At last she rase and gaed awa', she kendna whaur till. On she wandered till she came to a great hill o' glass, that she tried a' she could to climb, but wasna able. Round the bottom o' the hill she gaed, sabbing and seeking a passage owre, till at last she came to a smith's house; and the smith promised, if she wad serve him seven years, he wad make her iron shoon, wherewi' she could climb owre the glassy hill. At seven years' end she got her iron shoon, clamb the glassy hill, and chanced to come to the auld washerwife's habitation. There she was telled of a gallant young knight that had given in some bluidy sarks to wash, and whaever washed thae sarks was to be his wife. The auld wife had washed till she was tired, and then she set to her dochter, and baith washed, and they washed, and they better washed, in hopes of getting the young knight; but a' they could do they couldna bring out a stain. At length they set the stranger damosel to wark; and whenever she began the stains came out pure and clean, but the auld wife made the knight believe it was her dochter had washed the sarks. So the knight and the eldest dochter were to be married, and the stranger damosel was distracted at the thought of it, for she was deeply in love wi' him. So she bethought her of her apple, and breaking it, found it filled with gold and precious jewellery, the richest she had ever seen. 'All these,' she said to the eldest dochter, ' I will give you, on condition that you put off your marriage for ae day, and allow me to go into his room alone at night.' So the lady consented; but meanwhile the auld wife had prepared a sleeping-drink, and given it to the knight, wha drank it, and never wakened till next morning. The lee-lang night the damosel sabbed and sang:

> ' Seven lang years I served for thee,
> The glassy hill I clamb for thee,
> The bluidy shirt I wrang for thee;
> And wilt thou no wauken and turn to me?'

Next day she kentna what to do for grief. She then brak the pear, and found it filled wi' jewellery far richer than the contents o' the apple. Wi' thae jewels she bargained for permission to be a second night in the young knight's chamber; but the auld wife gied him anither sleeping-drink, and he again sleepit till morning. A' night she kept sighing and singing as before:

> ' Seven lang years I served for thee,' &c.

Still he sleepit, and she nearly lost hope a'thegither. But that day when he was out at the hunting, somebody asked him what noise and moaning was yon they heard all last night in his bedchamber. He said he heardna ony noise. But they assured him there was sae; and he resolved to keep waking that night to try what he could hear. That being the third night, and the damosel being between hope and despair, she brak her plum, and it held far the richest jewellery of the three. She bargained as before; and the auld wife, as before, took in the sleeping-drink to the young knight's chamber;

but he telled her he couldna drink it that night without sweetening. And when she gaed awa' for some honey to sweeten it wi', he poured out the drink, and sae made the auld wife think he had drunk it. They a' went to bed again, and the damosel began, as before, singing :

> 'Seven lang years I served for thee,
> The glassy hill I clamb for thee,
> The bluidy shirt I wrang for thee ;
> And wilt thou no wauken and turn to me ? '

He heard, and turned to her. And she telled him a' that had befa'en her, and he telled her a' that had happened to him. And he caused the auld washerwife and her dochter to be burnt. And they were married, and he and she are living happy till this day, for aught I ken.[1]

---

[1] Chambers. *Popular Traditions of Scotland.*

THE RED ETIN

THERE were ance twa widows that lived on a small bit o' ground, which they rented from a farmer. Ane of them had twa sons, and the other had ane; and by-and-by it was time for the wife that had twa sons to send them away to seeke their fortune. So she told her eldest son ae day to take a can and bring her water from the well, that she might bake a cake for him; and however much or however little water he might bring, the cake would be

great or sma' accordingly; and that cake was to be a' that she could gie him when he went on his travels.

The lad gaed away wi' the can to the well, and filled it wi' water, and then came away hame again; but the can being broken the maist part o' the water had run out before he got back. So his cake was very sma'; yet sma' as it was, his mother asked if he was willing to take the half of it with her blessing, telling him that, if he chose rather to have the hale, he would only get it wi' her curse. The young man, thinking he might hae to travel a far way,

and not knowing when or how he might get other provisions, said
he would like to hae the hale cake, come of his mother's malison
what like; so she gave him the hale cake, and her malison alang
wi't. Then he took his brither aside, and gave him a knife to keep
till he should come back, desiring him to look at it every morning,
and as lang as it continued to be clear, then he might be sure that
the owner of it was well; but if it grew dim and rusty, then for
certain some ill had befallen him.

So the young man set out to seek his fortune. And he gaed
a' that day, and a' the next day; and on the third day, in the afternoon, he came up to where a shepherd was sitting with a flock o'
sheep. And he gaed up to the shepherd and asked him wha the
sheep belanged to; and the man answered:

> ' The Red Etin of Ireland
>   Ance lived in Bellygan,
> And stole King Malcolm's daughter,
>   The King of fair Scotland.
> He beats her, he binds her,
>   He lays her on a band;
> And every day he dings her
>   With a bright silver wand.
> Like Julian the Roman,
> He's one that fears no man.
> It's said there's ane predestinate
>   To be his mortal foe;
> But that man is yet unborn,
>   And lang may it be so.'

The young man then went on his journey; and he had not gone far
when he espied an old man with white locks herding a flock of
swine; and he gaed up to him and asked whose swine these were,
when the man answered:

> ' The Red Etin of Ireland '—
>   [*Repeat the verses above.*]

Then the young man gaed on a bit farther, and came to another
very old man herding goats; and when he asked whose goats they
were, the answer was:

> ' The Red Etin of Ireland '—
>   [*Repeat the verses again.*]

This old man also told him to beware o' the next beasts that he should meet, for they were of a very different kind from any he had yet seen.

So the young man went on, and by-and-by he saw a multitude of very dreadfu' beasts, ilk ane o' them wi' twa heads, and on every head four horns. And he was sore frightened, and ran away from them as fast as he could; and glad was he when he came to a castle that stood on a hillock, wi' the door standing wide to the wa'. And he gaed into the castle for shelter, and there he saw an auld wife sitting beside the kitchen fire. He asked the wife if he might stay there for the night, as he was tired wi' a lang journey; and the wife said he might, but it was not a good place for him to be in, as it belanged to the Red Etin, who was a very terrible beast, wi' three heads, that spared no living man he could get hold of. The young man would have gone away, but he was afraid of the beasts on the outside of the castle; so he beseeched the old woman to conceal him as well as she could, and not tell the Etin that he was there. He thought, if he could put over the night, he might get away in the morning without meeting wi' the beasts, and so escape. But he had not been long in his hidy-hole before the awful Etin came in; and nae sooner was he in than he was heard crying:

'Snouk but and snouk ben,
    I find the smell of an earthly man;
    Be he living, or be he dead,
        His heart this night shall kitchen ¹ my bread.'

The monster soon found the poor young man, and pulled him from his hole. And when he had got him out he told him that if he could answer him three questions his life should be spared. The first was: Whether Ireland or Scotland was first inhabited? The second was: Whether man was made for woman, or woman for man? The third was: Whether men or brutes were made first? The lad not being able to answer one of these questions, the Red Etin took a mace and knocked him on the head, and turned him into a pillar of stone.

On the morning after this happened the younger brither took out the knife to look at it, and he was grieved to find it a' brown wi' rust. He told his mother that the time was now come for him to go away upon his travels also; so she requested him to take the can to the well for water, that she might bake a cake for him. The

---

¹ 'Kitchen,' that is 'season.'

can being broken, he brought hame as little water as the other had done, and the cake was as little. She asked whether he would have the hale cake wi' her malison, or the half wi' her blessing; and, like his brither, he thought it best to have the hale cake, come o' the malison what might. So he gaed away; and everything happened to him that had happened to his brother!

The other widow and her son heard of a' that had happened frae a fairy, and the young man determined that he would also go upon his travels, and see if he could do anything to relieve his twa friends. So his mother gave him a can to go to the well and bring home water, that she might bake him a cake for his journey. And he gaed, and as he was bringing hame the water, a raven owre abune his head cried to him to look, and he would see that the water was running out. And he was a young man of sense, and seeing the water running out, he took some clay and patched up the holes, so that he brought home enough of water to bake a large cake. When his mother put it to him to take the half-cake wi' her blessing, he took it in preference to having the hale wi' her malison; and yet the half was bigger than what the other lads had got a'thegither.

So he gaed away on his journey; and after he had travelled a far way he met wi' an auld woman, that asked him if he would give her a bit of his bannock. And he said he would gladly do that, and so he gave her a piece of the bannock; and for that she gied him a magical wand, that she said might yet be of service to him if he took care to use it rightly. Then the auld woman, wha was a fairy, told him a great deal that would happen to him, and what he ought to do in a' circumstances; and after that she vanished in an instant out o' his sight. He gaed on a great way farther, and then he came up to the old man herding the sheep; and when he asked whose sheep these were, the answer was:

> ' The Red Etin of Ireland
>   Ance lived in Bellygan,
> And stole King Malcolm's daughter,
>   The King of fair Scotland.
> He beats her, he binds her,
>   He lays her on a band;
> And every day he dings her
>   With a bright silver wand.
> Like Julian the Roman,
> He's one that fears no man.

But now I fear his end is near,
    And destiny at hand;
And you're to be, I plainly see,
    The heir of all his land.'

[*Repeat the same inquiries to the man attending the swine
and the man attending the goats, with the same answer in
each case.*]

When he came to the place where the monstrous beasts were
standing, he did not stop nor run away, but went boldly through

amongst them. One came up roaring with open mouth to devour
him, when he struck it with his wand, and laid it in an instant
dead at his feet. He soon came to the Etin's castle, where he
knocked, and was admitted. The auld woman that sat by the fire
warned him of the terrible Etin, and what had been the fate of the
twa brithers; but he was not to be daunted. The monster soon
came in, saying:

'Snouk but and snouk ben,
I find the smell of an earthly man;
Be he living, or be he dead,
His heart shall be kitchen to my bread.'

He quickly espied the young man, and bade him come forth on the floor.   And then he put the three questions to him; but the young man had been told everything by the good fairy, so he was able to answer all the questions.   When the Etin found this he knew that his power was gone.   The young man then took up an axe and hewed off the monster's three heads.   He next asked the old woman to show him where the King's daughter lay; and the old woman took him upstairs and opened a great many doors, and out of every door came a beautiful lady who had been imprisoned there by the Etin; and ane o' the ladies was the King's daughter.   She also took him down into a low room, and there stood two stone pillars that he had only to touch wi' his wand, when his twa friends and neighbours started into life.   And the hale o' the prisoners were overjoyed at their deliverance, which they all acknowledged to be owing to the prudent young man.   Next day they a' set out for the King's Court, and a gallant company they made.   And the King married his daughter to the young man that had delivered her, and gave a noble's daughter to ilk ane o' the other young men; and so they a' lived happily a' the rest o' their days.[1]

[1] Chambers.   *Popular Traditions of Scotland.*